STORM

No.1 *Sunday Times* bestselling author and journalist Stephanie Merritt has worked as a critic and feature writer for a variety of newspapers and magazines, as well as radio and television. Writing as S. J. Parris, she is the fastest growing historical crime writer in the UK, with her series of thrillers set in Tudor England selling over a million copies. She currently writes for the *Observer* and the *Guardian*, and lives in Surrey with her son.

www.sjparris.com

🐦 @thestephmerritt

Also by Stephanie Merritt

While You Sleep

Writing as S. J. Parris

Heresy
Prophecy
Sacrilege
Treachery
Conspiracy
Execution
The Secret Dead (a novella)
The Academy of Secrets (a novella)
A Christmas Requiem (a novella)

STORM

STEPHANIE
MERRITT

HarperCollins*Publishers*

HarperCollins*Publishers* Ltd
1 London Bridge Street,
London SE1 9GF

www.harpercollins.co.uk

HarperCollins*Publishers*
1st Floor, Watermarque Building, Ringsend Road
Dublin 4, Ireland

First published by HarperCollins*Publishers* 2022
1

Typeset in Sabon LT Std by Palimpsest Book Production Ltd, Falkirk, Stirlingshire

Printed and Bound in the UK using 100% Renewable Electricity
at CPI Group (UK) Ltd

MIX
Paper from
responsible sources
FSC™ C007454

This book is produced from independently certified FSC™ paper to ensure
responsible forest management.

For more information visit: www.harpercollins.co.uk/green

Prologue

She wakes face down, tastes blood and dirt. Slowly, she registers sensations; her lips are numb, she can't feel her hands or feet, but her head is pounding fit to split her skull. A lone cry rips through the air like a warning; she jolts and blinks to see a large black bird eyeing her from a fallen log. Dry needles and leaves prick her cheek; overhead, the trees close in, the sky beyond a mosaic of white and grey. Daylight, then, though no clue as to what time. She rolls cautiously to one side, attempts to lever herself to her knees, but when she leans her weight on her left hand, pain slices up her arm and she curses as she slumps back. The bird flaps its wings, indignant, and hops a few feet further off. Jo squeezes her eyes tight and opens them again to clear her vision, sees a vertical cut running down the inside of her left wrist, blood dark and crusted against the tender skin. A memory almost finds her then; it dances for a moment, out of reach, and fades.

1

She runs her tongue around cracked lips and locates the cut and swelling where her teeth broke flesh as she fell. She has no idea where she is or how long she has been there. Pushing herself up with her good arm, she lurches to her feet; the bird skitters away, protesting. The light seems off-colour; queasy, she flails to catch the trunk of a tree as her legs threaten to collapse under her, and all at once she knows it, deep in her gut. Something terrible happened last night, but the hours before she woke are a void.

Jo leans against the tree, willing herself to recall. Images stutter and snag like an old home movie: she remembers running through the forest, branches tearing at her face, blood dripping down her arm. The clearing in the pines, the old leper chapel, white figures moving between the trees. The feeling of being watched. How much of it was real and how much the effect of the drugs, she can't work out. She thinks she remembers Storm's face in the firelight, all planes and hollows and stretching shadows. Flames glinting off a shard of glass.

Yes, the bottle; with sudden, awful clarity, Jo pictures her own fingers curled around it, the smooth fit of the neck in her palm, the broken edges catching the light as her arm swung back and arced through the air. A bitter taste rises in her throat; she bends and vomits on to the leaves at her feet. The trees spin around her. This is ancient forest, spreading for miles in all directions, she could wander for days and not be found. Her jacket is damp; it must have rained in the night. A quick pat of her pockets tells her that, by some miracle, she still has her phone, but when she draws it out, the battery is dead. Will the others have noticed she's missing?

She picks a direction and sets off, stumbling through the undergrowth and broken branches. If she keeps moving, there is a chance she will come across one of the old logging roads, if not the boundary fence to the chateau. Her vision glitches and she has to stop and spit bile. Whatever she smoked last night has wrecked her head, like nothing she has tried before. Did Storm give it to her on purpose? The cut on her wrist throbs, and she has a cloudy, uneasy sense that she did this to herself. Dread lodges heavy in the pit of her stomach.

She walks with no idea how long or how far. Sweat slicks her back and every few steps she is convulsed by shivers. The air is damp and the sky looks autumnal for the first time since they arrived three days ago. Only three, since Storm walked out of the dark and into their lives.

Jo passes mossy rocks and thin streams, the trails blurring into one another until she can't tell if she is retracing her steps. Without warning she emerges into the clearing and sees the jagged outline of the chapel on one side like a broken tooth. The light is cold here, last night's fire burned to ash, shards of glass strewn around the fallen masonry.

She stops short; in the shadows by the ruin, she sees two figures standing with their backs to her. Their heads are bent, eyes fixed on something at their feet, half-concealed inside the entrance. They are so intent on the object they are examining that they haven't heard her approach. She takes a step forward, and another, until she glimpses a shape on the ground, a flash of white through their legs. Her vision is still wavering; she struggles to focus as one of the men, catching a sound, turns to look at her and she sees, stark against the darkness in the doorway, the pale outstretched arm of a woman, fingers curled stiffly among the dead leaves.

PART ONE

1

October
Thursday

Golden autumn sun; a breeze scented with warm grass lifting her hair through the rolled-down window, and the sudden open vista as the taxi pulled under the stone arch of the gatehouse and rounded a curve in the drive that revealed a view of the chateau in full splendour, as beautiful as the first time Oliver had brought Jo here a decade earlier.

The main body of Chateau Henri dated from the fourteenth century, built in an L-shape around a manicured lawn with a spreading horse chestnut at its centre. Biscuit-coloured walls dripped with Virginia creeper beginning to turn fiery. The shorter branch of the L ended in a round turret with a conical roof like a hat, a watchtower that surveilled a drive flanked by box hedges, leading to the entrance and a single-track road. At the rear, beyond the outbuildings lovingly converted into a yoga studio and state-of-the-art gym, cultivated gardens gave way to wildflower meadows; further out still, hillsides of vines in geometric rows stretched away to a blue horizon. On the other side, a stream separated the formal grounds from a forest that marked the boundary between the chateau's land and the next village. Jo and Oliver had only been going out six months or so the first time he brought her here, and he was still showing off his friends and connections to impress her. The sight of the house brought back the giddiness of that weekend in a rush: the smell of wild garlic, birdsong, the quick dart of bats at twilight over the long outdoor table. She had hardly believed her luck, that she should have found someone like Oliver, that she was now part of his life, a life that included friends with houses like this. How innocent she had been.

Jo swung herself out of the car with a crunch and tilted her face, willing herself to appreciate the warmth of the sun, wishing she could swallow the knot of anxiety in her throat. This would be her first time here without her husband, and she couldn't predict how she would react on encountering the ghosts of their past selves around every corner. She was not sure, either, what was expected of her this weekend. When she had received the invitation from Cressida Connaught, 'an informal house party for our twenty-first, just the old gang', her initial instinct had been to find an excuse. 'The old gang' meant Oliver's three closest friends from university – Arlo, Max and Leo – and their partners. It had become clear to Jo, soon after she met Oliver, that his social life revolved almost exclusively around this group and so hers was expected to as well. She hadn't minded at first; her own friends from her teacher training course were scattered around the country, while Oliver's were based in London and saw each other all the time. Besides, his people were considerably more glamorous, and she had been beguiled by that at the beginning. But her status in the group had always felt uncertain, even when Oliver was alive, and it was all the more precarious now, as she sensed the others trying to work out what they owed her, for his sake, in terms of attention and inclusion.

For now she retained the sheen of tragic glamour that attached to young widowhood, but she knew it was beginning to wear thin. There was a limit to other people's indulgence of grief, and she was conscious that fifteen months was considered long enough to begin moving on, even as Jo still expected to find her husband standing in the kitchen in the mornings, espresso in hand, arguing with the radio. And yet, despite all these misgivings, here she was, because being around Oliver's friends, especially for Arlo and Cressida's wedding anniversary, was a way of feeling close to him.

The driver hoisted her case out of the trunk; she fumbled in her purse for notes and he made a shushing gesture, pursing his lips and tutting. Of course it was all taken care of, but she tried to press five euros into his hand for a tip; he declined politely, managing to imply that either the gesture or the amount was vulgar, and reversed out in a shower of gravel, leaving her to take in the house, glad and apprehensive at the same time.

She was interrupted by a shriek of laughter; two children with matching dark curls barrelled around the corner and slowed to a wary trot as they caught sight of her. She lifted her sunglasses and raised a hand; they offered a shy wave in return. Oscar and Grace Garrett, Leo and Nina's six-year-old twins; both absurdly, identically photogenic. They had once appeared in a Burberry Kids campaign, Jo recalled.

'Is Mummy inside?' she asked.

Grace shook her head and pointed across the lawn. 'They're all at the pool.'

'We're going to get our swimming stuff,' Oscar offered. 'Becca's coming with us.'

Jo picked up her case and set off around the edge of the lawn towards the open door that led to the main hallway, where she was met by a capable-looking, freckled young woman in her mid-twenties with hair pulled back in a bun, a blonde infant clamped to her hip.

'Hiya,' the girl said, in a Lancashire accent, ignoring the trail of juice that was dribbling down the front of her striped T-shirt from the child's sippy cup. 'Are you Jo? They're out at the pool. I'm Becca. The nanny,' she added, in case of doubt.

Jo smiled. 'Thanks. I think we've met at the Richmond house. Hey Clio.' She reached out to ruffle the baby's white downy hair, but Clio turned her face away to Becca's shoulder.

'She's in a filthy mood, but she won't let me put her down for a nap, will you, madam?' the nanny said, laughing. 'You should go on out, they've been waiting for you. Leave your case inside, someone will take it up.'

'Oh, I can do that,' Jo said quickly. 'Do you know what room I'm in?'

Becca shrugged. 'You'd better ask Cressida. She's in charge, as we all know.'

Was there the smallest hint of an eye-roll as she said that? The girl held Jo's gaze and grinned, as if daring her to complicity. Jo nodded and took her case to the door; she did not imagine that Cressida Connaught inspired warmth or loyalty in her staff, but she would not be drawn into criticism of her hostess, even in something as subtle as the exchange of knowing looks. That kind of thing tended to find its way back.

A path led from the horse chestnut lawn across a further grassy square bordered with flower beds, to a line of hedges that shielded the pool from the view of the house. She passed through the gap and down the stone steps, and the loveliness of it all took her breath away again. Sunlight scattered in bright patterns over blue water. Leo was swimming, his broad brown back and neon orange shorts cresting the surface with each determined breaststroke. It was Nina who saw her first, unfolding her long legs from her sun-lounger and rising to greet her, calling in her confident Californian accent: 'Jo's here, everybody!' Her glossy black hair was swept up in a loose twist; she wore a navy-blue one-shouldered swimsuit and a long, white floaty wrap, and her toenails were painted a perfect vivid violet that set off her olive skin. When they hugged, Jo caught a scent of vetiver, and felt suddenly conscious of how much she was sweating in a top and cardigan chosen hours earlier for a chilly October morning in London.

'Darling!' Cressida levered herself up on her elbows and lifted her sunglasses. Jo could not help noticing that the taut skin on her stomach was beginning to look a little leathery. 'How was the journey? Did the driver find you OK? Where's your stuff? Go and get your bikini, quick – you might get a dip in before the kids come down. Such a shame Hannah couldn't be here.'

Jo heard a hint of reproach in this. 'The state schools haven't broken up yet,' she said. 'They only get one week for half term.'

Cressida blinked. The workings of state schools were outside her frame of reference. 'Oh. She'd only have missed a day, surely? Is she with Oliver's parents?'

'She's with her friend Emily,' Jo said, and then, because Cressida appeared to require further justification, she added, 'they're taking her to Devon with them on Saturday, so the girls can go pony-trekking.'

'Well,' Cressida said, though she still looked put out, 'I suppose we can't compete with ponies.'

'Not in the eyes of a nine-year-old girl,' Jo said, forcing a smile.

Cressida shaped her mouth into a moue of sympathy. 'This last year must have been so hard for her. She and Oliver were so close. Still – nice for you to have some time to yourself.'

Jo was spared the trouble of answering because at that moment Oscar and Grace exploded through the gap in the hedge and hurled themselves into the water, creating a minor tsunami that smacked their father full in the face; he rose up, mock-angry, droplets streaming down his chest as he tucked one twin under each arm and pretended to dunk them while they screamed and giggled. Jo watched this with a small smile and looked away; seeing fathers with their children gave her a pang, though she couldn't tell if it was grief or resentment. Behind them, the nanny appeared, sturdy and pale in a green swimsuit, and descended placidly into the shallow end holding Clio in her inflatable ring. At least there was one other woman here who didn't look as if she'd stepped straight out of *Condé Nast Traveller*, Jo thought.

She glanced around the pool, taking them in. No sign of Arlo or Max yet, but at the far end of the grassy surround, in the shade of the box hedge, a tall, skinny youth sprawled on a lounger wearing a faded Pink Floyd T-shirt and black shorts, one arm and leg hanging off the side, his senses shut off by sunglasses and enormous headphones. Cressida followed her gaze and patted the bed next to her, grimacing in the boy's direction.

'Is Lucas lower sixth now?' Jo asked, lowering herself gingerly on to the lounger, feeling the heat of the sun through her jeans. 'I didn't know he was coming.'

'He's not bloody anything,' Cressida hissed through her teeth, glancing at him. 'Little shit's been kicked out of school.

Drugs,' she mouthed, leaning in. 'Maybe you should have a word with him, Jo.' She gave a mirthless laugh. 'We've tried to get him to see someone, but short of frogmarching him to therapy . . .' She shook her head. 'Arlo's livid, you can imagine.'

Jo nodded. 'You must be worried about him—'

Cressida gave her an odd look. 'With the school, I mean. You don't even want to know how much money we've thrown at them over the years, you'd think they'd have given him a second chance. But no – apparently they can't risk accusations of preferential treatment.' She snorted. 'They wouldn't have their new music block if it weren't for Arlo, how's that for *preferential treatment?*'

'It does seem harsh,' Jo said, careful to sound sympathetic. 'Find me a teenager in London who hasn't tried drugs at some point.'

'Oh, he wasn't *trying* them,' Cressida said, her voice rising. 'He's too smart for that. He was bloody dealing them to other people, including boys in the lower school. Thirteen-year-olds! The Head agreed not to involve the police as long as we took him out without a fuss. Arlo refused to let him go away with his friends, so we've had to bring him with us.'

'The spectre at the feast,' Lucas remarked, pulling off his headphones and making them both jump. He was staring at the sky behind his mirrored lenses. 'Sorry for ruining your anniversary, Mother. And as I have explained about a million times, no money changed hands, so it wasn't technically dealing.'

'I'm sure the police would have appreciated the distinction,' Cressida said acidly. 'I was just saying, perhaps you could talk to Jo while she's here. She does therapy for students, isn't that right, Jo – something along those lines?'

Lucas propped himself up and removed his glasses. 'I think that would be excruciating for both of us, Mother. You invited Jo here for a nice break, the last thing she wants is to shrink your reprobate child.' He seemed quite cheerful about the situation. Perhaps it was easy to be sanguine about wrecking your education when your parents could just buy you a place at some other, equally prestigious school that would be glad of a new music block.

'I'm not actually a therapist,' Jo said, though she was fairly sure Cressida knew this. 'I'm a welfare adviser. The students who come to me usually need help with hardship funds, visas, disability benefits, that kind of thing.'

'You see, Mother? Jo deals with people who have real problems,' he said, grinning at Jo. She couldn't help smiling back; she had always rather liked Lucas, despite the insouciance that was an unfortunate effect of his upbringing. He was a handsome boy, with Cressida's high cheekbones and blue eyes, and Arlo's square jaw and frank expression. For all his privilege, he came across as a friendly, open kid; while Jo may not have been a qualified shrink, it didn't take a doctorate to work out that, after fifteen years of being the only child of wealthy and indulgent parents, his nose might be somewhat out of joint since the unexpected arrival of a baby sister sixteen months ago. This acting out seemed entirely predictable.

'Oh, *real* people. Like your new friends, I suppose,' Cressida said. Then, to Jo: 'He's saying he doesn't want to do A levels. He's going to drop out and join an environmental protest. He wants to go and live in a van playing bongos with a bunch of crusties who shit in plastic bags.'

'Compostable bags, *please*. God, do you ever listen to yourself?' Lucas slammed to his feet and gathered up his phone and flip-flops. He pointed at the sun. 'We're all fucking burning to death. Do you think A levels are going to save the planet? I'm getting out there and doing something, while you're topping up your tan and Dad's flying to fucking San Francisco every fortnight as if it's business as usual. This is *politics*. You can't complain, it's in my blood.'

'Don't you dare! Your grandfather would turn in his grave if he could see you,' she yelled after him as he stomped away.

'Who's burning to death?' Grace asked, her small face crumpled in alarm as she perched on Leo's shoulders in the water.

'Lucas said *fucking*,' Oscar whispered, awed and delighted. 'Twice.'

'That doesn't mean you're allowed to,' Nina said automatically, without looking up from her magazine.

'God's sake.' Cressida's face was pinched and furious. 'I knew he'd ruin it. I said he should go to my brother's, but Arlo wanted him where we can keep an eye on him.' She shook her head. 'Sorry about that, Jo. Come and see your room and have a drink.' Cressida didn't touch alcohol, but she was always keen to push the contents of their expensive cellar on guests. She shaded her eyes with the edge of her hand and glanced up. 'Definitely not too early.'

2

'Sorry about Lukey,' Cressida said again, as they passed through the arched courtyard door into the shade of the entrance hall. Her sandals slapped purposefully across the flagstones. 'He's been an absolute nightmare since the summer. We let him go to a festival with his friends and he came back full of this protest business. He treats us like we're the antichrist.'

'He seems very passionate,' Jo said, weighing her words for potential offence, as she so often did with Cressida. 'I suppose it's good for him to have a social conscience.'

Cressida snorted. 'Social conscience, my arse. Is this your case?' She hoisted it easily with both hands and set off up the wide staircase. At five foot two, without a millimetre of spare flesh, Cressida reminded Jo of a tiny, perfect doll, a woman in miniature; beside her, Jo – who was six inches taller and a size 12 at most – always felt giant and ungainly. As she followed, she couldn't help noticing a dimpling of cellulite at the top of Cressida's thighs, and was not proud of how pleased this made her.

'All this man of the people stuff is pure antagonism, you

can see that,' Cressida continued, over her shoulder. 'He's kicking against the family name. We bought him a bloody Mini convertible for his seventeenth last month – Arlo suggested if he was so worried about the environment, we could take it back and replace it with an Oyster card, but he wasn't so keen on that idea, funnily enough. Seriously, though,' she added, as they reached the first landing and turned right, 'maybe you could try talking to him? You're used to dealing with teenage ups and downs all day, you must be better at it than us.' She gave a little, awkward laugh. 'We're completely out of our depth – he just won't communicate. He's threatening to go off with these dropouts and chain himself to an airport fence or God knows what. I think he *wants* to get arrested to make a point. Such a bloody *waste* – all his teachers say he could be Oxbridge material.' There was a slight waver in her voice, and Jo realised how much it must be costing her, to acknowledge the fissures in her perfect life.

Teenage ups and downs. Jo thought of the second-year psychology student who had come to see her the previous Tuesday because she had been forced out of her house-share after an administrative error meant her maintenance grant failed to arrive on time. The girl, who already worked two bar jobs to put herself through college, had found a room in a private rental not too far from the campus, where the landlord charged a very reasonable thirty pounds a week, as long as she made up the rest of the rent with sexual favours on demand. She had been so ashamed that she had lived with this arrangement for two months before she had found the courage to tell the student welfare service. Jo struggled to muster much sympathy for Lucas, who believed his biggest hurdles in life were the legacy of his famous grandfather and his father's obscene tech fortune.

'Well, they're different situations, the ones I deal with,' she managed. 'And I'm not a counsellor, as I say. I refer the students to trained specialists if there are addiction or mental health issues. But I'm sure I could recommend someone.'

Cressida set the case down outside a heavy oak door and leaned against the frame. 'Sorry, Jo, stupid of me – I had it in my head that you were some sort of shrink. I shouldn't have asked – you're on holiday. Forget I said anything – we'll try to ignore the horrible child. I've told him if he starts arguments at supper he won't be allowed to eat with us and he'll have to have his meals with the little children. Look, I've put you in Sauternes. Isn't it where you and Ollie stayed the first time? When you got pregnant with Hannah?'

'I'm the assistant head of student welfare,' Jo said, but she could see that Cressida was no longer listening. How could she remember which room they had stayed in ten years ago and not remember what Jo did for a living? Perhaps because they had never really regarded her as a person in her own right, separate from Oliver; or perhaps – and here a nasty suspicion prickled – because Oliver himself had led them to believe she was a qualified psychologist, as a way to enhance her status in their eyes. She even found herself wondering if that was why Cressida had invited her this weekend – so that she could deal with Lucas? No; she must stop second-guessing. It sounded as if the business with Lucas was recent and unexpected. Cressida's attention had already moved on; she was pointing out the new velvet curtains.

Jo made appreciative noises; she had no memory of the previous curtains, though she did remember Oliver tying her wrists to the supports of the four-poster bed, and the current of fear and guilty desire that used to surge through her in those days when he raised his hand to her. She caught sight of her reflection in the mottled antique mirror over the fire-place and thought how tired she looked. The ends of her hair, bunched up in a ponytail, remained a frayed blond, but it was months since she had bothered with highlights and the rest had grown back to mid-brown. The first time Oliver had taken her home to meet his parents she had overheard his mother approve her as a 'nice-looking girl, I suppose'; clearly a plus in Geraldine's view, implying that Jo was presentable in a modest way, without being anything so attention-seeking as gorgeous or beautiful. Still, Jo thought, tilting her head to let the sun gild her cheek, her skin was good for thirty-seven, pale but clear and unlined. Oliver had always told her he loved the colour of her eyes, an unusual shade of hazel that could appear green or gold depending on the light.

'. . . and we had the sofa reupholstered to match by this woman in Saint-Émilion, she's *amazing*, just a little cottage industry but she sources these incredible fabrics from all over, I'm using her for all the soft furnishings from now on . . .'

'Mm-hmm.' Jo wandered to the window. Sauternes was her favourite room, and not just because of the memories. Most of the others were painted in fashionably dark colours: slate grey, ink blue or oxblood, but in this one the designers had left one wall bare to show the texture of the original blond stone, and the rest were washed a pale oatmeal to complement the wooden beams of the ceiling and the crooked terracotta tiles. They had kept the furnishings simple: an antique wardrobe and dresser polished to a shine. Oliver had made her kneel on that Persian rug in front of the fireplace; at least, she assumed it was the same one. She had cried afterwards, in the roll-top bath, where he couldn't see.

'The flowers are beautiful, thank you,' she said, wrenching herself back to the present and indicating a silvered vase with three slender roses on the mantelpiece.

'Oh, Violette did those.' Cressida stared out of the window, one hand resting on the frame. 'He just speaks to us like we're shit on his shoe, Jo,' she said, her voice grown plaintive again. 'Everything we say, even if it's "good morning", he takes as the cue to start a fight. It's like he hates us. When I think of how much we've given him – so different from how I was raised. It's the ingratitude I can't bear.'

As far as Jo could remember, either Cressida's father or her grandfather was some sort of baronet. She wondered what deprivation looked like to Cressida. Only one pony each?

'It's normal for him to rebel,' she offered, aware that this was hardly insightful or helpful. 'Do you ever think he might be jealous of Clio?'

Cressida turned sharply at this, and Jo caught a flash of real anger. 'God, no! Why would he? He *adores* his sister. No – this is all about Arlo – and Hugh, of course. The young stag locking antlers with the old. I just hope he doesn't ruin the weekend for us. I want everything to be perfect.'

She looked suddenly fragile against the light, her shoulders so narrow and delicate under the straps of her bikini top.

'It's going to be lovely,' Jo said, reassuring. 'I can try having a word with Lucas, if he's willing.'

Cressida smiled, and Jo watched her compose herself, snap her bright expression back in place.

'Thanks, Jo. I knew we could count on you.' She patted Jo's arm. 'I'll let you unpack and get changed – oh, but first, come and see what we've done with the bathroom in our room.'

She hasn't asked once about Hannah, Jo thought, as

Cressida led her along the corridor and around the corner of the L. Pauillac was the largest room in the chateau, the master suite that Arlo and Cressida always kept for themselves when they stayed, with walls of peacock-blue, offset by cream leather armchairs, a large mirror in a silvered frame and a vast, vintage chandelier that spangled diamonds of sunlight from the tall windows. Cressida grabbed a yellow T-shirt dress from one of the chairs and pulled it over her head.

'Better cover up before I make my son vomit,' she said, with a forced breeziness. 'He told me this morning it was disgusting, letting it all hang out at my age. I'm forty-*one*, for God's sake. He's got schoolfriends with parents nearly two decades older.'

'Maybe that's the problem.'

'Well, exactly. Apparently some boy at school said I was a MILF and Lukey was so appalled he wants me to dress like the bloody Amish from now on. Come and see this amazing bathtub – Violette's husband found it randomly in a salvage yard near Toulouse, it's solid marble. We had to get the floor reinforced.'

She pushed open the door to the cavernous en suite, but Jo's eye had come to rest on a collection of photographs arranged on the deep windowsill. They were all pictures of Arlo and his friends from the wedding twenty-one years earlier, long before she knew them. She reached for one she recognised, in a dark frame; Oliver had kept a copy of it on the wall of his study. There was the groom, awkward in his morning suit, with his three best men in black tie, arms hooked around one another's necks, joshing together in front of a fountain on a lawn. How impossibly young they looked. She lifted the photo to the light for a closer look. Such an unlikely quartet, so different in their backgrounds, and yet

21

at university they had forged a bond that had made them inseparable for more than two decades.

In the centre, Arlo Connaught, with his floppy strawberry-blond fringe and serious stare into the camera: looks of Rupert Brooke, brain of Stephen Hawking, Oliver used to say. Child maths prodigy, computer genius, early-adopter web entrepreneur, forever battling to escape the shadow of his Conservative father, Hugh Connaught MP, who had had a brief stint in Thatcher's cabinet in the late Eighties before being discreetly shunted to the Lords when his party needed a modernising face-lift. Beside him, Oliver Lawless, squinting against the sun, brown curls falling in his eyes as he laughed at a long-forgotten joke. Oliver was solid Home Counties stock: solicitor father, headmistress mother; he had moved seamlessly from his independent boys' grammar school straight to his father's old Cambridge college and into a prestigious chambers, just as everyone had expected. The only thing Oliver had ever done to deviate from the path laid out for him at birth was to swap lucrative property law for human rights, which his father had been convinced was some sort of liberal 'phase' right up until Oliver's death at forty-two. On Arlo's right, Leo Garrett, the wild card, with his handsome chiselled face and knowing smile. Leo – raised on a Streatham estate by parents who ran a café – was the first in his family to apply to university, where he spent more hours putting together shows for the Edinburgh Fringe than he did in the library, but he had still managed to land a traineeship with the BBC when he graduated. And leaning on Leo's shoulder, awkward in his too-tight suit, Max Steadman, from Hampstead: father an academic, mother a trustee of a prestigious arts centre. Max, who had gone from the university paper to the politics desk of a national broadsheet and was now a respected columnist and a regular face

22

on current affairs programmes, but who – according to Oliver – could barely speak two words to a stranger when they had all found themselves living on the same staircase in freshers' week, and had relied on the others to engineer the loss of his virginity. Jo had asked Oliver more than once what had made the four of them so tight – none of them had even studied the same subject – but he always muttered something about college life and formative experiences, and how sometimes you just ended up tied to people, for better or worse. Whenever he said that, she assumed it was an oblique reference to their marriage.

Cressida stuck her head out of the bathroom, impatient to show the new tub, then saw what had distracted Jo.

'Weren't they handsome?' she said, her voice softening as she peered over Jo's shoulder. 'Well – not Max so much, he was a bit chubby, poor Max, but they did all scrub up nicely. I brought these from home – I was going to put a few out tomorrow so people could reminisce. Did you bring any?'

'Photos?' Jo looked at her.

'Yes. It was in the email. I thought it might be fun if everyone brought old pics of the gang so we could look back on the last twenty-one years. Don't worry if you haven't,' she said quickly, before Jo could make an excuse for not having read the email properly, 'I've got more than enough. Self-indulgent of me, but it was such a happy day.' She looked almost shy. 'God, we were so young. Whoever heard of having three best men? But he really couldn't have chosen between them.' There was a pause, and then she laid a hand on Jo's arm, gold bracelets softly clinking. 'We all miss him terribly, you know. Arlo almost didn't want to do this anniversary party. He said it wouldn't be the same without Ollie.'

Jo nodded mutely, but she could feel herself braced against Cressida's cool touch.

'Oliver would have wanted you to celebrate,' she said, as she was supposed to, but it sounded forced because her throat was closing up.

'That's what I told Arlo,' Cressida said, vindicated, then stopped at the sight of her face. 'Oh, Jo, I'm sorry – perhaps I shouldn't have brought the pictures. This must be so hard for you. Do you want a tissue?'

Jo shook her head. 'I'm fine, honestly.' She pinched the bridge of her nose between her finger and thumb and said, 'No Max yet, then?'

Cressida seemed relieved to change the subject. 'No! He texted to say he couldn't get away today, he's got to be in Parliament, but he's planning to come late tomorrow after the vote. And – did I tell you? – he's supposed to be bringing his new girlfriend.' Her eyes widened with the thrill of gossip.

'Oh.' Jo could not hide her surprise. 'How long's that been going on?' Of all Oliver's friends, Max was the only one she felt genuinely close to; she was oddly hurt that he hadn't confided in her about his new relationship.

'Not long, apparently, and I'm dying to know what the dirt is – he's been weirdly secretive about her, which is not like Max. Nina and I wonder if he got her from one of those Sugar Daddy websites. Can you imagine?' She gripped Jo's arm tighter.

'Max wouldn't go in for that, surely.'

'Oh, men will do the stupidest things for sex, Jo,' Cressida said, with an air of absolute certainty, as if handing down the wisdom of her foremothers. 'Between you and me, I wasn't at all happy about him bringing a complete stranger, but I could hardly say no, he's been so miserable since Fran left him. I hope she's not *actually* a hooker, though. Think how awkward that would be, having to make conversation.'

'I know a few students who are on those websites,' Jo

said, wondering if Cressida ever did listen to herself. 'They don't think of themselves as sex workers. They're just trying to get by.'

'Oh, *please*.' Cressida raised a perfectly arched eyebrow. 'You fuck a rich man in return for cash and expensive presents, what else do you call it?'

I don't know, Jo considered saying, glancing up at the chandelier, what have *you* called it all these years? Instead she reached forward and set the photograph carefully back on the windowsill. 'I might pop back to my room for an aspirin, actually,' she ventured. 'It's just . . . all the travelling.'

'God, of course, listen to me going on about baths – you haven't had a minute to yourself since you got here. Why don't you take some time to settle in, freshen up – come down for a glass of something cold and fizzy when you're ready. We're really so glad you could come, Jo, honestly,' she added as Jo reached the door, which had the effect of implying that there had been some doubt. 'We all admire you so much, how strong you're being for Hannah. How is she, by the way?'

Jo hesitated, before realising a real answer was not required. 'She's fine,' she said, smiling hard. No one had warned her, when Oliver died, about how much time she would have to spend reassuring other people that she and Hannah were coping, how it appeared to be her responsibility to make everyone else less uncomfortable about grief.

'Oh, good. Such a shame she couldn't miss a couple of days of school. Never mind – nice for you to have a bit of time for yourself, let your hair down, eh.' Cressida fixed her with a determined smile. 'We're going to have an amazing weekend.' It sounded almost like a threat. If anyone could make that come true by sheer force of will, Jo thought, it was Cressida.

3

Dinner was served outside in the courtyard. A long table had been laid with white linen, silverware and a blaze of candles in hurricane lamps. There were slim vases with creamy roses, silver ice buckets on stands at either end, and citronella burners placed at intervals on the ground to keep bugs away. It all looked magical, Jo conceded as she stepped into the cool evening air and found a champagne flute thrust into her hand by Violette, the housekeeper, who stood by the kitchen door with a tray of glasses and a face like a grudge. Jo noticed, glancing around with dismay, that she had misjudged the dress code, as usual. She had brought the jade-green fitted shift that was her failsafe smart wedding outfit, thinking it was the only thing she owned appropriate for evening dinners; it was a little tighter these days than she would have liked, but she had put on ten pounds since Oliver died, and felt acutely conscious of it in the dress that, she now saw, was too shiny and formal compared to the other women. Cressida was wearing a pair of white linen palazzo pants and a black silk sleeveless top with tiny pearl buttons; Nina was in a loose tiger-print shirt dress, her hair tied back with a green scarf. Leo wore a pink polo shirt and jeans, but Leo would look good in a bin bag. Lucas was seated at the end of the table, his face sickly-looking in the blue light of his phone. He appeared not to have changed his clothes since the afternoon.

'Oh, aren't you glam!' Cressida exclaimed, a little too heartily, leaning in for an air-kiss and making Jo more self-conscious as she teetered over the cobbles in her heeled sandals; Cressida was in Birkenstocks and Nina in Stan Smiths. But it was too late to go back and change; Cressida ushered her to a chair as Arlo appeared, a bottle of wine in each hand, and an unforced hush fell over the company.

It was not that Arlo Connaught was especially imposing, though objectively he was a good-looking man: six-foot-four, with a strong jaw and serious blue eyes, you would still notice him in a crowd even now that his hair was thinning. But such extraordinary financial success conferred a kind of celebrity glow; it made him seem separate from the rest of them. Jo knew that Arlo had a once-in-a-generation mind, as a Forbes profile had put it, but since his area of brilliance – Artificial Intelligence – was so opaque to her, she had no objective benchmark by which to measure it. Arlo had always struck her as rather humourless; she used to fear the rare occasions at social gatherings when she would be left to make small talk with him, since he had little interest in discussing travel or children, which left only his work, so that she was always reduced to asking idiotic questions about robots. Oliver had observed more than once that Arlo was almost certainly on the spectrum, and then told her she must never repeat that, as if she might blurt it out like a child. Jo had always considered this to be self-evident, but a posh voice and polished manners went a long way towards smoothing over Arlo's social shortcomings, which could be generously interpreted as the eccentricity of a genius, and Cressida was his greatest asset in that regard; she humanised him, and had become the public face of the charitable foundation he had established to encourage students from under-privileged backgrounds into STEM. Because the one thing everyone knew about Arlo was that he had set up a research company ten years ago, and sold it to an American tech giant five years later for a reported half-billion dollars.

Jo could not even begin to imagine what you did with that kind of money. 'Buy five hundred thousand identical grey T-shirts so you can pretend you're Zuckerberg,' Oliver had said, when she voiced this thought aloud, but Oliver had always tried to hide his envy of Arlo behind snide remarks passed off as banter, even before the Silicon Valley millions.

Arlo was indeed wearing a grey T-shirt and black jeans that evening, as he always did. If it was an affectation, it was an unimaginative one. He lifted one of the bottles and waggled it at them.

'This is a Chateau Léoville Barton St-Julien from 2003,' he announced, as they all looked up at him with encouraging expressions – except Lucas, who remained glued to his phone, a bottle of lager at his elbow. There followed a brief history of the vineyard, the appellation, the grape variety and the specific fermentation process, after which the wine was poured and pronounced to be excellent. Jo privately thought, as she always did, that Arlo enjoyed sharing the information far more than he appeared to enjoy the actual drink, which he hardly touched, but she was in the mood to be forgiving; the wine was rich and velvety and the food – presented with another introduction by Marcel, the resident Parisian chef – equally perfect. Scallops with thin shavings of chorizo and crispy sage, followed by coquelet with julienned vegetables and white beans – though not for Lucas, who loudly declared himself to be vegan now and picked over a beautifully arranged salad that Marcel brought for him, while gazing hungrily at everyone else's plates.

'Are you joking? You know cattle farming destroys 2.71 million hectares of rainforest every year?' he said, when Marcel offered to add some cheese.

Marcel looked baffled. 'This come from goats in Rocamadour.' He returned to the kitchen with a magnificently gallic shrug.

'Saving the world, one salad at a time,' Leo said, reaching out to ruffle Lucas's hair. The boy ducked away, but with a grin; Leo was the only person who could get away with teasing him, because Lucas thought Leo was street, even though he now ran his own TV production company and was a member of BAFTA. Cressida should ask Leo to talk to Lucas, Jo thought, leaning back in her chair and watching them with a smile. She had begun to relax; the food and wine had softened her earlier anxieties and she did not feel as excluded as she had feared. Nina began telling them about a new exhibition she was organising at her gallery for Turkish artists whose work had been banned in their home country; this segued into a discussion about human rights, which naturally led to reminiscences about what a force for good Oliver had been in that regard, and Jo managed to nod and agree without her voice cracking. Everything they said was respectful; she could not detect any insinuation about his accident. She wondered if they had made a pact in advance. Even Lucas looked up from his phone long enough to meet her eye.

'Ollie was a legend, man. He was the best godfather.'

This provoked a mock-indignant cough from Leo; 'OK, triple-tied first place with you and Max,' Lucas modified. Jo laughed with the others. It was beginning to feel almost companionable. Before dinner she had called to speak to Hannah and ascertained that her daughter was happy. 'You concentrate on enjoying yourself,' Emily's mother had said sternly, as if enjoyment were a state Jo might achieve if she strained and focused hard enough. But perhaps she was right, Jo reflected, watching the candle flames wavering in curved glass as moths hurled themselves towards the light. All she had concentrated on for the past year was holding a routine together for Hannah, and it had taken every ounce of focus she possessed; hardening the shell of herself around the bitter truth of Oliver's death, the parts she alone knew, so that their daughter could remain free of that knowledge. Perhaps it would not be the end of the world if she allowed herself, just for a couple of days, to relax her fierce vigilance and let her hair down, as Cressida put it – though she had to wonder what Cressida understood that to mean in this context. Did she hope Jo would get wildly pissed on the Chateau Whatever and leap on Marcel? Given that, for Cressida, self-indulgence meant eating a potato at Christmas, anything was possible.

Elegant, tiny chocolate truffles were brought out, with a silver pot of coffee and a decanter of Armagnac. Soft yellow solar lanterns glowed around the lawns, illuminating the trees from beneath, and a string of fairy lights appeared in the foliage along the wall above their heads. The scent of night blooms drifted across from the gardens.

Cressida stood and tapped a spoon against her glass of sparkling water.

'I wanted to wait until we were all together,' she began. 'Well – almost all. Affairs of state have detained Max, but we'll forgive him, this once. But I have some rather special news. This weekend has actually turned out to be a double celebration.'

She left a dramatic pause; Jo noticed Lucas's eyes flicker in horror to his mother's midriff.

'I have to be the one to tell you,' Cressida continued, 'because my brilliant husband is far too modest to blow his own trumpet, *but*' – she drew the last word out and held a hand towards Arlo, as if introducing him on stage. He shook his head and looked down into his coffee.

'Arlo has been asked to chair a new advisory body for data ethics,' she said, with an air of triumph. Lucas slumped back in his seat with evident relief. The others looked somewhat underwhelmed. 'He'll be reporting directly to the government on everything to do with AI and tech,' Cressida pressed on, determined to rouse them to greater enthusiasm. 'It's a huge deal. It's going to be a world-leading centre, they said. It's not been announced yet, but we wanted to tell you first.'

'*You* wanted to tell them,' Arlo muttered.

'Not sure I'd take advice on ethics from this guy.' Leo jerked his thumb at Arlo and flashed a grin around the table, waiting for the laugh.

'It's not just me.' Arlo didn't smile. 'The board's made up of experts from across the industry – academics, doctors, but there's also a philosopher and a bishop—'

'But they approached *you* to head it up,' Cressida cut in. 'You'll be the public face of it.'

'Well, then,' Leo said, suddenly serious, 'better make sure you keep your nose clean.'

'What's that supposed to mean?' Arlo set down his cup and fixed him with a long look.

Leo shook his head. 'Nothing. Only – if you're taking public money to be the Ethics Tsar or whatever, there'll be people wanting to make sure you walk the walk.'

'I'm not the *Ethics Tsar*,' Arlo said irritably. 'It's about

31

biases in algorithms, that sort of thing. Data privacy. I'm not becoming a bloody priest.'

'Even so,' Leo murmured.

'Well, we've got nothing to worry about,' Cressida said, with a determined smile. 'As long as certain people watch their behaviour.' She darted a pointed glance down the table at Lucas, who rolled his eyes.

'*I* think it's fantastic news,' Nina said, lifting her glass. 'Congratulations Arlo, resident genius. So you guys will be hanging out at Number Ten now, huh?'

'Absolutely not,' Arlo said, at the same time as Cressida, laughing, said, 'We wouldn't turn down an invitation.'

They caught one another's glance in silent rebuke, but before anyone could speak, the company was startled by the sound of an engine close by. Violette emerged from the kitchen, wiping her hands on her apron and peering into the darkness of the drive.

'Madame, there is car. At the gate.'

'Max must have made it after all,' Leo said. Cressida frowned; she didn't like surprises.

'Well, did you ask who it was?'

'They have not press the button,' Violette said. 'You want I go and see?'

The drive curved between the square-cut hedges so that there was no view of the gate from the house. Leo raised a hand to quiet them, and they heard the unmistakable crunch of footsteps on gravel.

Cressida rounded on the housekeeper. 'Why on earth did you let them in, when we don't know who it is?'

Violette's eyes widened, aggrieved. 'I don't open!' she protested. 'Maybe he climb over.'

'Max?' Cressida called, shielding her eyes with her hand.

A figure approached out of the shadows, too slender to be Max, and stepped into the lights of the terrace.

It was a young woman; tall, with chestnut-brown hair that fell past her shoulders under a white knitted beanie hat. She wore an oversized khaki military-style jacket and cut-off denim shorts; her lean, tanned legs ended in chunky biker boots. In one hand she carried a battered leather travel bag; she took a few steps towards the table and dropped it on the ground with a decisive thud. She looked around the company with vivid blue eyes; almost aquamarine, the blue of swimming pools.

Cressida stood and folded her serviette. 'Can I help you?' Her accent ratcheted up several notches when she became defensive, to what Oliver used to call the full Kristen Scott-Thomas.

'Hi.' The girl allowed her gaze to fall slowly on each of them with a half-smile and a private nod, as if confirming what she had expected to find. Her eyes fixed at last on Cressida, who was bristling like a cat, and she thrust out a hand. 'I'm Storm.'

4

'I'm sorry – what exactly do you want?' Cressida's tone turned glacial. Jo wondered if her hostility was provoked more by the stranger's beauty than by the unexpected intrusion.

The girl's smile faltered and she let her hand fall to her side. 'I'm Max's girlfriend,' she said, looking from Cressida to Arlo in search of support. There was a soft lilt to her voice.

'Oh.' Understanding dawned on Cressida's face, vying with something else – fury? Jo had the sense that she had preferred it when she thought this exotic intruder was someone who could be thrown out, but she had been caught off guard; she could hardly acknowledge that she had not even remembered the girl's name, though it was unusual enough to have stuck. The silence seemed to expand.

'Where is he?' Cressida craned around the girl to peer into the darkness, as if Max might have been mislaid somewhere along the drive.

'Max? He couldn't get away. I thought he told you.'

'Yes, it's just – he didn't tell us you'd be coming without him,' Cressida persisted, in a tone that demanded some kind of apology or explanation.

'Did he not?' Storm stuck her hands in her jacket pockets and gave her a guileless smile.

'If you'd let us know you were arriving, we could have sent a car to the airport for you.'

'Don't worry, I got a lift.'

'Oh. From whom?'

'Some guy on his way to Toulouse. I think his name was Philippe.'

'You mean you hitch-hiked?' Cressida was staring pointedly at the girl's bare thighs. 'Isn't that incredibly dangerous?'

She laughed. 'Not if you know how to look after yourself. I do it all the time. Is there any of that coffee left?'

Leo – though he was not the nearest – jumped to grab the coffee pot.

'Is that an Irish accent I detect there?' he asked, twinkling at her.

'That's right,' Storm said affably. 'Galway girl, me. Don't sing it,' she added, pointing a finger in mock-warning as she pulled her hat off and shook out her hair.

'I've got relatives in Ireland,' Leo said, as if this would impress her.

'Really?' She looked politely surprised.

'Yeah, you might not think it. My dad's Jamaican, but my mum's father came over from Cork in the Fifties.'

'Well, then.' The girl smiled. 'We're practically cousins.'

'You know those signs they had in the Seventies? *No Blacks, No Dogs, No Irish?* My parents used to say, when they got married, they bought a dog just so they'd have the full house.' He was talking too fast, eager to keep her attention. Jo watched Nina's face tighten in response.

'Please, come and sit down.' Arlo stood and pulled out a chair. Storm turned to give him an appraising look, head on one side.

'So you're Arlo,' she said, holding out a hand. 'I've read a lot about you.'

'Right.' Arlo took this in his stride as he shook it. 'Would you like a glass of wine? It's a Chateau Léoville-Barton St Julien 2003—'

Cressida clicked her tongue. 'You must be hungry,' she said, across him, determined not to have her role as hostess usurped. 'We've finished dinner, as you see, but I'm sure Violette can knock something up for you.'

'Please, don't go to any trouble. Coffee's good.' Storm turned to Violette and asked something in French. The housekeeper looked first surprised and then delighted; Jo guessed the family never bothered to speak to her in her own language. She disappeared indoors; Storm gulped her coffee and – despite the autumn chill – leaned back to take off her jacket. She was wearing a white silk tank top with no bra, and the evening breeze brushed her nipples stiff. She reached out for a refill of coffee, apparently unaware of the looks trained on her from every side of the table. Arlo, Leo and Lucas were staring, unabashed, mouths agape. Jo glanced at Cressida, and caught a flash of pure loathing, before she smoothed her features back to inscrutable courtesy. In that one careless gesture, Jo saw that the girl had lost any hope of Cressida's goodwill. But how careless was it, really? You couldn't wear a top like that, with tits like those, and not be aware of the effect. Storm seemed otherwise unselfconscious. She was not obviously wearing make-up; she had strong, defined brows and long dark lashes, but both appeared natural. Her nails were cut short and unvarnished, and she wore no jewellery except a couple of ratty bracelets of coloured thread. There was a slightly grubby air about her, as if she had just come from a festival. Jo could see how sexy that looked, beside the effortful polish of the older women. Oliver would have been falling off his chair trying to impress her, she thought, and found herself briefly glad that she didn't have to witness it.

Nina drew hard on her cigarette and ground it out in the ashtray as if she were crushing an enemy. Jo sat back and realised that, with no husband to guard and little personal vanity left to be injured, she was free to enjoy this unexpected drama. Watching Cressida deal with not being the centre of attention at her own anniversary party would be quite the spectacle.

'So, Max is coming tomorrow, then?' Cressida tried, hopefully.

Storm lifted a shoulder again. 'That's the plan.' She turned to Lucas. 'Can I bum one of your smokes?'

He gawped at her, and glanced helplessly at Nina.

'They're mine,' she said, frostily polite, but she held out the packet. 'Help yourself.'

'Thanks. I'll go to the village tomorrow and buy some more.'

In that moment it seemed fully to dawn on Cressida that this was not a mistake, and the girl was really staying.

'Perhaps Max didn't explain,' she said sweetly, 'it's quite a way to the village. Anyway, look – we haven't even introduced ourselves properly. I'm Cressida Connaught.'

'I know. It's lovely to meet you.' Storm raised her coffee cup towards her and leaned across the table for a light, offering Lucas a view straight down the gulley of her cleavage. It took him four attempts to keep the flame alight, his hand was shaking so much. 'And this is our son, Lucas,' Cressida pressed on brightly.

'Ah, right.' Storm tipped her head back and blew out a plume of smoke. 'Max said you had a really cute baby.' She winked at Lucas; he flushed scarlet to his ears.

'Well, he would have meant our daughter, Clio,' Cressida said, with a prissy little laugh intended to shut down any future attempts at flirting. She swept an arm to indicate the rest of the company. 'This is Leo Garrett and Nina Gregorian, and this is our friend Jo Lawless.'

Storm let a gracious smile fall on each of them in turn, as if she were a royal guest. 'You know, I feel like I know you all already,' she said.

'I'm just going to go up and make sure Max's room is ready for you, Storm,' Cressida said, deploying the girl's name with carefully formal emphasis. 'Arlo, could you come and give me a hand?'

Arlo, who had been staring at the newcomer as if she were a troubling calculation, turned to his wife with visible impatience.

'Can't Violette do that?'

'She's busy. I'm asking you.' Cressida's voice was flinty; Arlo must have recognised the tone, because he reluctantly pushed his chair back and followed her inside.

Storm took another drag on her cigarette and cast her eyes up to take in the chateau with its warmly lit windows, before returning her gaze deliberately to Leo.

'Congratulations on your BAFTA, Leo,' she said, giving him that same appraising look.

'Oh, well, that was months ago, but – thank you.'

'Not at all. Well deserved. It's a great show.'

Leo preened a little. His company had made a number of moderately successful shows, but *Paper* was his breakout hit, a family drama set on a fictional estate like the one where he grew up, about a young man who becomes an undercover journalist and has to infiltrate the world of gang crime and drugs that he spent his youth trying to escape. It had won Best Drama Series in the summer; regular laments in the right-wing press about the graphic violence and insinuations that its awards were a matter of ticking boxes had only helped the show's profile.

'It must be great to feel you're making something that matters,' Storm said, resting her chin on her hand and fixing him with an earnest gaze. 'I'd bet half your viewers have never given a thought to characters like those before they saw the show, except to judge them. Because of you, they might actually view them as people.'

Leo's face lit up as if she'd offered him a blowjob.

'That's exactly it,' he said, banging his palm on the table. 'That's what I wanted to do – shine a light on the people who don't normally get a voice. Not to glamourise that life, but to say there are reasons why they've ended up doing what they do. And hopefully tell a good story along the way,' he added, with a rehearsed chuckle, as if he were being interviewed. He stopped, clicked his fingers and pointed at Storm. 'Hey – you should come and audition for us. We're always looking for fresh faces. No previous experience required.'

'Oh, well – I don't know about that. I wouldn't say I'm much of an actor.'

Jo noticed that Nina had placed a hand on Leo's thigh. Storm turned her unhurried gaze to her.

'And *you*, Nina,' she said, levelling her half-smoked cigarette at her, 'were the first person to bring Zehra Aydin to London. Which is unbelievably cool.'

Nina thawed a little. 'You know her work?'

'I *love* her work.' Storm turned to Jo, eyes bright. 'Do you know her?'

Jo shook her head mutely.

'She's a Turkish artist,' Nina said, with a hint of condescension.

'She's this amazing young feminist poet and painter,' Storm cut in, jabbing her cigarette in the air, 'she's been in prison, what, three times? And she's not even thirty. Nina was the first person to show Zehra's work outside Turkey. Four years ago, wasn't it? She sells for tens of thousands now, right, thanks to you?'

'Her work has been recognised, certainly,' Nina said modestly, but she looked reluctantly impressed. 'Weren't you at that opening, Jo? I'm sure Ollie was there.'

'I don't remember,' Jo said. When Hannah was small, Oliver had taken to announcing invitations from his friends at the last minute, making it impossible to find a babysitter, so that more often than not he ended up going alone; this, she suspected, was his intention all along. 'You don't really enjoy these things, anyway,' he always insisted, and it was partly true: she felt out of place at Nina's gallery openings and Leo's private screenings and Cressida's charity dinners, but she would have liked to have been given the option.

'Oh, you'd have remembered if you'd been there,' Storm said, sucking the last life from her cigarette and pressing it into the ashtray Lucas eagerly pushed towards her. 'Am I right, Nina?'

Nina laughed; they exchanged a complicit look and Jo suddenly had the sensation that she was the outsider.

'You'd definitely remember it, Jo,' Nina said. 'Zehra appeared naked with a mural painted on her body.'

'Tanks right across her tits,' Storm said, indicating her own chest. 'Fair play to her. She's a brave woman.'

'Are you into that kind of thing, then?' Leo asked.

'Tits?'

Leo laughed, too loudly. 'I meant – human rights, and, you know, protest . . . art.' He realised Nina was looking at him and subsided.

40

'Am I *into* human rights?' Storm leaned back, amused. 'What am I supposed to say to that? "Nah, I can take them or leave them."' She grinned.

'Jo's husband was a human rights lawyer,' Leo said, floundering.

'I know. He defended those Ugandan activists who were deported. Terrible business.' She turned to Jo. 'I'm so sorry for your loss,' she added, fixing her with a straight look of such expressive concern that Jo – practised by now at deflecting this kind of reflexive sympathy – was ambushed by the prickling of tears at the back of her eyes and found she could not speak. She blinked and looked away, feeling oddly exposed.

'Max has obviously told you a lot about us all,' Nina said coolly.

'Course. I can't believe I'm finally getting to meet you.' Storm reached for the coffee pot. 'He says you guys are his family.'

'That's nice.' Nina smiled, though Jo noticed she kept the restraining hand on Leo's leg. 'So how did you two meet?'

'He didn't tell you?' Storm took a drink and laughed; a full, raucous, throaty sound. It was a laugh you couldn't help liking, Jo thought. It was honest and open and pleasingly unladylike. 'Ah, that doesn't surprise me. He was probably embarrassed.'

Jo caught the swift glance between Nina and Cressida and knew exactly what they were thinking: Cressida's theory about the website was right. She had to acknowledge – to her shame – that the sight of Storm had caused her to wonder the same thing. Max was a lovely guy, they would all agree, but it was hard to imagine quite how he had successfully wooed a girl like this.

'Go on,' Nina said, trying not to look too eager for gossip.

Lucas helped himself to a cigarette without asking; from his scowl, Jo guessed he did not want to think about his forty-two-year-old godfather getting his hands on Storm's golden body.

'I interviewed him for the university paper,' she said. 'About the state of the world, his career, fake news, the death of journalism, all that. We got on, so . . .' she gave a wry smile, as if the rest were obvious.

'You're a student, then,' Nina said, too brightly, over-compensating for the assumptions she had clearly made. 'Where?'

'SOAS. World Philosophies.' Storm turned her gaze idly towards the gardens.

'Wow. Not just a pretty face,' Leo said. Nina flashed him a look. Storm laughed.

'Why, *thank* you.' She held out the hem of her top and bobbed an ironic curtsey.

'Jesus, Leo – you can't say stuff like that any more.' Lucas sat up, spiky with indignation.

'*What?* It was a compliment.'

'Relax,' Storm said, draping her bare arm along the back of the empty chair beside her. 'They've got a lot to unlearn, his generation.' She shot Lucas another wink, and his face flamed again with delight.

'Is your article about Max online?' Nina asked primly. 'I'd like to read it.'

'Nah, they canned it. Someone else got an interview with the thick blonde one from *Love Island* and they thought it read better.'

'Is that what you want to do, after college?' Leo said. 'Journalism?'

'Could be. Haven't decided.' Storm shrugged.

'Max will be useful, then,' Nina said. It sounded more

barbed than she intended, because she quickly added, 'you know, for advice.'

'Ah. I thought for a minute there you meant I must be shagging him to get contacts,' Storm said, and let out that big, robust laugh again.

Jo marvelled at how comfortable she seemed among strangers. She would have been mortified to have turned up among this group without Oliver when they first started dating, but Storm appeared entirely oblivious to any fear of being judged or found wanting, and equally free from any anxiety about offending. Was that the insulating effect of her exceptional beauty, Jo wondered, or some other quality – insouciance or self-possession – that had also been handed out unequally in life's lottery?

Violette arrived and presented Storm with a sandwich and a glass of water; Leo hit back at Lucas by asking why he wasn't giving Storm his lecture about cheese destroying the rainforest, and in the midst of Lucas's embarrassed defence about local produce being an exception, Jo excused herself to go in search of a cardigan. She wasn't sure any of them noticed her leave.

Upstairs, she took off her heels and padded past her room, barefoot and silent on the seagrass matting, until she heard Cressida's voice, raised in protest, from around the turn of the landing. She pressed herself against the wall to listen.

'I can't get through – his phone's just going to voicemail! I've left about seven messages but he's not picking up.'

'Well, the House is still sitting,' Arlo said reasonably. 'I'm sure he'll get back to you when he finds them.'

'Why couldn't he have let us know? Seriously, is that too much to ask – it would have taken a one-line text? What are we supposed to do with her?'

'Put her in their room,' Arlo said. 'Why are you turning this into an issue? It's not as if we don't have space.'

'For fuck's sake, Arlo.' Cressida was trying to keep her voice down while losing her temper; it came out strangled. 'We don't know anything about her! She could be anyone. I mean, how long have they even been together?'

'How would I know?'

'Because he's *your* friend! Haven't you asked him?'

'No.' Arlo sounded increasingly perplexed. 'You wouldn't be making this fuss if Max was here, and he'll be here tomorrow, so what's the problem?'

Cressida clicked her tongue. 'Did you see the way Lucas was looking at her?'

'He's a teenage boy, he's going to look at a girl.'

'Is Leo a boy? Are you?'

'Is that your objection? Because she's pretty?'

'*Pretty?* God, you are so naive—'

At that point, Jo dropped one of the shoes in her hand; it clattered on to the boards and Cressida said, sharply, 'Hello?'

Jo stuck her head around the bend in the corridor, looking sheepish. 'Sorry – I just came up for a cardigan – didn't mean to make you jump.'

Cressida pressed the flat of her hand to her breastbone in a show of relief. 'Thank God – I thought you were her. Did you hear us?'

'Not really. Only the tail end.'

'Jo knows what I'm talking about – right, Jo?' Cressida shot Arlo a look of triumph. 'You saw her clothes, didn't you?'

'Bit revealing,' Jo agreed, trying to steer between sympathetic and judgemental.

'Well, obviously, total slut, but that's not what I mean. Everything she's wearing is designer. You must have noticed?'

Jo gave her a blank look; it was almost flattering that

44

Cressida could have known her for a decade and still imagine she was the kind of woman who would recognise such things.

'Those boots are Jimmy Choo,' Cressida said, breathless with outrage. 'The jacket's Rag and Bone. I didn't get close enough to see her shorts, but I'll bet you they're not from Top Shop. There's well over a grand's worth of kit on her.'

'So? Maybe she has money,' Arlo said.

'She says she's a student at SOAS,' Jo offered.

'There you are, then. What student has that kind of money for clothes? I told you.' Cressida folded her arms across her chest.

'What's your point? You think Max is buying them for her? So what if he is, that's his business.'

'I don't know.' She dropped her voice to an angry whisper. 'But ask yourself – what's a girl like that doing with Max? She must be at least twenty years younger than him.'

'That's very insulting to both of them,' Arlo said. 'If she was just a gold-digger, there are more obvious targets than Max, surely?'

'Like you, you mean?' She jutted her chin at him. 'Maybe she's attached herself to Max as a way of getting to you. You heard her – she said she's read all about you.'

Arlo looked at her. 'What's it like, living in your head? Thinking that way about people all the time?'

'What's it like, being so trusting that you put your family in danger?' she snapped back. They glared at each other for a moment, some unspoken accusation hovering in the air, before Arlo sought Jo's eye over Cressida's head with an appeal to reason.

'This is the level of paranoia we live with,' he said. 'She wanted to get private security to take Clio to a playdate.'

'Yes, laugh it up,' Cressida hissed through her teeth. 'Everyone knows what you're worth, it's the first thing they mention in every profile of you. There are people who target people like us. J.K. Rowling has bodyguards to take her kids to school, I read it somewhere.'

'Oh, well then. By that measure, how do you know Jo didn't marry Ollie for the express purpose of kidnapping our children? She might have been planning it from the off. Should we search her room, make sure she hasn't got Clio in her suitcase?'

'I should probably—' Jo said, taking a step back and nodding in the direction of her room.

'Ignore him, Jo, he's being a dick.' Cressida pulled at her earring. 'He wants it all ways. He wants to go about being just an *ordinary guy*' – she made quote marks in the air – 'but he's not the one feeling sick with panic when a fucking great SUV with tinted windows pulls up a bit too close at the lights and I've got Clio in the car.'

'She watches too much Scandi crime,' Arlo said. 'I'm not having the house full of huge blokes with earpieces – I'm not a rapper. I don't want to live like that.'

'Your father had security when you were growing up,' Cressida said, petulant.

'My father had pissed off the *IRA!*' Arlo exploded, finally provoked enough to raise his voice. 'I think we've got a bit off-topic. You need to calm down. Max's girlfriend is not going to put a bomb under the car.'

'How do you know?'

Jo was wondering how to extricate herself from the cross-fire when Arlo held up a hand for silence; they all froze, and heard footsteps on the landing. Cressida's shoulders visibly slumped with relief when Becca stomped around the corner in a hoodie and sweatpants, her face tight with resentment.

She pointed at the ceiling. 'You lot need to keep your voices down,' she said, glaring. 'The children are sleeping.'

'Sorry.' Arlo hung his head automatically, avoiding her eye. Amazing how ingrained that was, Jo thought; the fear of being told off by Nanny, even when you were the one employing Nanny.

Cressida was less easily chastened. 'You can't hear us through the floor, surely?'

'I promise you I can,' Becca said. 'And if they wake, it'll be me has to get them back to sleep again.'

'Well, yes, that is *literally* your job,' Cressida said sweetly. Becca looked as if she was considering a response; instead she gave them all a last hard stare to make sure they understood, before huffing back to the stairs.

'That's us told,' Jo said, trying to lighten the mood.

'We'd better do as she says,' Arlo whispered, and reached out to stroke Cressida's hair; Jo saw her flinch minutely but grit her teeth and smile.

'Well, I suppose we're stuck with this Storm until Max gets here.' She glared at the phone in her hand as if daring it to ring. 'Do you think that's her real name?'

'I honestly couldn't care less,' Arlo said. He seemed relieved that the tension was defused, for now. 'Can I go and finish my coffee?'

Cressida dismissed him with a curt nod, but she kept her arms wrapped around her ribs, as if holding herself together until she was sure of her composure.

'Do you want a hand getting the room ready?' Jo offered, not knowing what else to say.

This seemed to shake Cressida out of her mood; she gave a brittle laugh and laid a hand on Jo's arm. 'Don't be silly, Violette's done all that. I've put them in Saint-Estèphe, next to you. Oh God – I hope you won't have to listen to them shagging. I should have thought of that.'

'The walls are pretty thick,' Jo said, though she wondered

it hadn't occurred to Cressida earlier – that putting the new couple next door to the widow might be a touch insensitive.

'Exactly. I don't know what that moody cow's making such a fuss about.' She nodded towards the stairs where Becca had disappeared. 'She just likes to stick her oar in.'

'Anyway, it won't be an issue if Max doesn't turn up,' Jo added.

'What do you mean?' Cressida looked stricken. 'Of course he's going to turn up. He said he'd be here tomorrow.' There was a high note of panic in her voice. 'What do you make of her, Jo? Arlo can't see it, because Max is his friend and men always overestimate themselves anyway, but don't you think there's something off about it? A girl like this Storm, with Max? Why *would* she? Or am I just being a massive bitch?' She sighed; apparently she didn't require an answer. 'Arlo's right, I do get paranoid. But this stuff happens, you know? It would be irresponsible to pretend it couldn't happen to us.'

'I reckon we could take her between us, if she tries anything,' Jo said. Cressida cracked a thin smile, just as her phone buzzed with a message; she leapt on it, with a bright nod to Jo as if to say *finally*, before her face defaulted back to a scowl.

'Just the French phone network,' she said. 'Fucking Max – where *is* he?'

5

Jo sat up in bed late that night, her book open unread on her lap, listening to the sounds of the household settling to sleep. She heard an urgent, whispered exchange between Leo and Nina as they passed her room; she couldn't catch the words, but it sounded as if they were arguing. It had been a mistake to drink coffee so late. At midnight, her body exhausted but her mind racing, she finally turned off the light.

The velvet curtains were so thick that the darkness felt solid. Oliver had set tealights in coloured glasses along the dresser, the first time they stayed in this room. The flames had thrown strange, disturbing shadows on his face as he loomed over her, his hand around her throat, whispering his idea of intimacies. And she, so eager to please him, had whispered them back, as he instructed her.

'*You're a dirty little whore,*' he'd said, through his teeth, and in the flickering light she'd seen how his face twisted; not playful but filled with contempt. 'What are you?' When she didn't reply, he had fetched her a sharp slap across the cheek with the back of his hand; don't worry, all part of the game.

'*I'm a dirty whore,*' she had parroted, barely audible, swallowing her shame, because she believed that would make him happy. She had felt so much younger than him, so unfamiliar with her own desires, that she had allowed him to shape them for her, until it was impossible to tell the difference.

Oliver had a trick at the beginning, when it came to getting what he wanted. He would broach the question in a tentative, almost shame-faced manner – hesitant glance from beneath lowered lashes, bashful smile – like a small boy who knows he shouldn't really be asking for an extra treat, but is also confident that he's so adorable you won't have the heart to say no. Could *you* be the one woman open-hearted and generous enough to understand his needs, who was also sufficiently mature and worldly to recognise the separation of fantasy from reality? He presented it as a compliment, with the implication that other women in the past had failed this test, but he had faith that you were different, this was why he had risked everything by offering you such an intimate glimpse of himself. He had laid himself bare; how could you then turn away in disgust, like the others? And the truth was, he made you relish the prospect of being better than your predecessors, of being the one who truly understood him, even as you lay there thinking what a cliché this was, how you'd imagined a man like him might be more sophisticated in his tastes, his language.

She slipped a hand experimentally between her legs, trying to bring to mind those early days, but encountered barely a flicker of a response. It had been like this since Oliver's death; as if that part of her that he had known how to awaken had died with him. She could only make herself come by thinking about him, and that left her so bleak and hollowed-out afterwards that it was never worth it. Better – safer – to shut down altogether, freeze herself numb inside. It was impossible, even after fifteen months, to imagine anyone else igniting her the way Oliver had, despite the years of feeling him withdrawing from her, piece by piece, while she went on convincing herself that there was something left to be saved, if she only tried hard enough.

Two months after that first trip to the chateau, she had discovered that she was pregnant. They never quite knew if it had happened in France, but it seemed likely, and made for a romantic reframing of the story, looking back; they had joked about calling the baby Henri, if it was a boy. She had had the termination booked before she even told Oliver, anticipating his reaction, but after the initial shock he had surprised her, not only by declaring that he wanted this baby, but by proposing so that they could 'do it properly', in his words. Suddenly, at twenty-seven, she appeared to have acquired everything – husband, child – that a year earlier had seemed only a distant dream. How jealous her friends had been, stuck on the treadmill of Match.com! But Jo knew very well that before the pregnancy Oliver had not given a moment's thought to marrying her, not after a mere eight months; even by the time of that first chateau visit, she had worried that he was beginning to tire of her willingness to please. He had been enchanted with Hannah when she arrived, throwing himself into fatherhood with the same competitive rigour he brought to his cases, and for a while Jo had hoped that would be enough to hold them together. Even so, she could never quite shake the suspicion that his friends thought she had trapped him, or that he too had come to believe that version over time.

She was not sure how long she lay awake, snagged in the downward spiral of those thoughts. She was beginning to drift off when she caught the sound of footsteps on the landing outside, a muffled laugh, the scrape of the latch and the soft click of a door. She half-sat up to listen, but there was nothing from next door, not even the running of a tap or the flush of a loo. An owl's distant cry carried from the woods beyond the garden. From Storm's room, silence.

6

Friday

Jo was woken the next morning by birdsong; as she opened her eyes to the dim shape of the canopy overhead, for one strange moment in that land of not-quite-consciousness she thought Oliver was lying beside her, though when she reached out she realised it was only the way the duvet had bunched. Restless, she crossed to the window and drew back the drapes to see a pristine blue sky, still tinged with salmon-pink dawn light. The clock on the mantel said ten past six.

She pulled on jeans and a jumper, negotiated the latch as quietly as she could and crept along the landing, past the closed doors and down the stairs. Sounds of clattering echoed from the kitchen; she hesitated in the hall, tempted to ask for a coffee, but Violette could be brusque when busy and Jo preferred not to be noticed, even by the housekeeper. She slipped out into the courtyard, keeping away from the kitchen windows.

It was a perfect morning, crisp and bright, enough of an edge to the air to remind her that it was no longer summer.

The gardens stretched out pearly and peaceful in the early light, and Jo thought how idyllic it would be if she were here alone, without the prospect of forced camaraderie looming. Cressida was bound to have planned some itinerary, which Jo knew she would find herself agreeing to through lack of resolve and then resent for the rest of the day. But this hour belonged to her; she decided to walk the grounds, make a tour of the places she and Oliver had visited on previous occasions, so that no memories could catch her off guard in company.

As she crossed the courtyard, she caught the sound of rhythmic splashing coming from the pool. Curious to know which of them was up so early, she headed over the lawn and put her head round the gap in the hedge.

The gleaming figure cutting through the water in a graceful front crawl was moving fast enough that, with the water streaming from her skin, it took Jo a moment to realise that she was stark naked. Storm had tied her hair back and moved seamlessly through silver furrows with each stroke, sleek as a dolphin. Jo watched her, mesmerised and slightly guilty, knowing she should leave unnoticed but finding it hard to tear her eyes away. Storm seemed to sense her presence; at the end of her next length she flipped on to her back, breasts pointing at the sky, and gave a cheerful wave.

'Wasn't expecting anyone to be up so early,' she called, laughing, entirely unembarrassed.

'Sorry, I didn't mean to disturb you,' Jo said, though she was not sure why she was apologising. 'I couldn't sleep.'

'Come on in.' Storm grinned and patted the water. 'This'll wake you up.'

'Oh – no.' Jo laughed, and mimed shivering. 'It's too cold.'

'It's gorgeous once you're in. Go on – then you'll have earned your breakfast.'

54

'OK,' Jo said, after a moment. 'Let me go up and get my costume.'

'*What?*' Storm made a face of exaggerated incredulity. 'Whip your clothes off and jump in, Jo, it's not Catholic school.'

Jo glanced back towards the house. 'What if someone comes?'

'They won't be up for hours. What are you worried about?' She caught Jo's creased brow and grinned. 'They're only tits. We've all got them.'

Not like yours, Jo wanted to say. She was having trouble keeping her eyes on Storm's face. It was all very well being so bold about your naked body when it looked like that; Jo felt that her own nudity would be less daring than pitiable. And then, as she looked at the sun glittering on the water, a bolt of rebellion flashed through her and she thought, why the fuck not? Why should she care what this good-natured stranger thought of her stretch marks and cellulite, when there was blue water waiting for her?

Before her rational voice could intervene, she kicked off her Vans and her jeans, pulled her sweater over her head and dived into the deep end, shrieking as the cold water hit her skin.

'Brava!' Storm clapped as Jo came up spluttering and launched into an inelegant breaststroke. Once she started moving, the tingling of her skin and the pleasure of the water on it displaced her fear of the cold and her self-consciousness. She swam four lengths without stopping, enjoying the strength in her limbs, and when she finally paused to catch her breath, she found Storm propped against the corner of the pool, watching her with approval.

'See – feels good, doesn't it?'

Jo nodded, wiping the water from her eyes with the back of her hand.

'This is the secret of life, Jo,' Storm said, and Jo could not tell if her deadpan expression was earnest or mocking. 'Jump in like no one's watching.'

'Easy for you to say,' Jo said, tipping her face to the sun. 'The way everyone looks at you.'

Storm shrugged, as if she hadn't noticed. 'Yeah, but you wouldn't want that all the time, would you?'

Try putting a bra on occasionally then, Jo nearly said, and despised herself, because that voice sounded like Cressida.

Storm laughed. 'You're thinking, I don't act like someone who doesn't want to be looked at, right?'

Jo darted her a guilty glance.

'What I'm saying is,' Storm reached up with both hands and slicked back her hair, her breasts lifting free of the water, 'take up space, Jo. For yourself. And then don't give a shit who's looking.'

'I'll bear that in mind,' Jo said, turning away to hide her irritation; she did not need life coaching from someone who had learned feminism from Instagram quotes.

'Those people aren't better than you,' Storm added, as Jo launched into another length.

She brought herself up short and turned, treading water. 'I never said they were.'

'No, but you think it.' Storm held her gaze, steady. There was no malice in her look, just the clarity of someone who believed herself licensed to speak the truth. 'And I'm telling you you're wrong.'

'You're very blunt,' Jo said. She couldn't think what else to say.

'Yeah, I get told that a lot.' Storm hesitated; Jo thought she might be about to apologise, but instead she karate-chopped the water with the edge of her hand, sending a wave crashing into Jo's face. Jo spluttered, shook her head, swallowed a mouthful; she stared at Storm for a long moment, outraged, on the brink of remonstrating, when she realised – this is supposed to be *fun*. This is what a fun person would do. So she retaliated; Storm whooped with delight, and splashed her back harder, and soon they were engaged in a full-on water fight, all the while a detached part of Jo's brain thinking, I suppose it *is* fun, in a way. They were laughing and splashing with such gusto that they heard nothing until a child's voice cut through the noise, saying, 'It's not *fair!*'

Jo whipped around to see Grace and Oscar standing at the side of the pool; behind them, the nanny with baby Clio on her hip. Grace's pointing arm stuck out at an indignant right angle.

'You said it was too cold for swimming yet,' she said accusingly to Becca. 'Why are they allowed to?'

'I can see that lady's boobies,' Oscar said, eyes fixed on Storm with the air of someone who has stumbled on a dangerous secret. 'And Auntie Jo's.'

Jo ducked under the water, arms crossed over her chest like an effigy.

'Come on – we're going to the swings,' the nanny said with authority. 'Now!' She ushered her small charges reluctantly away from the poolside, shooting a last reproachful look back at the women in the pool as she left.

Storm honked with laughter, flipping on to her back and lying in a star shape. Jo kept her arms folded; she could feel her face flaming.

'I should have realised the kids would be up early,' she muttered, reaching for the ladder, desperately casting around for something to cover her nakedness.

'Here, use that towel under my clothes,' Storm said. 'Sure, they won't mind, they're only little. It's not healthy for kids to have hang-ups about bodies.'

'Nina won't agree.' Jo wrapped the towel around her and turned away.

'She's another one could do with lightening up.'

'Yes, but – I don't think I'd have liked my daughter seeing my adult friends naked. It's just not very—'

'English?' Storm laughed again. 'Did you see that nanny? She looked at us like we were paedos.'

'Cressida will think it's one step away. She'll be furious.' Jo wriggled awkwardly into her knickers under the towel. 'Apart from anything, this is a bathroom towel. The pool towels are kept in the laundry room.'

Storm pushed herself up and out of the pool in one smooth movement and sat comfortably on the side. 'Well, I've got an idea,' she said, with a complicit grin. 'Let's never tell her we used the wrong towel. Seriously, Jo—' She stood and held her arms out for the towel before rubbing herself vigorously. 'Don't look so terrified. You've done nothing wrong. Let's go get some coffee.'

Jo pulled her jumper over her head. 'I think I'm going to have a shower,' she said. Storm was right – but she could not shake off the sense of guilt. There was an obligation, she had always felt, to abide by Cressida's rules when she was their guest, and in her desire to please it had never occurred to her that she had the right to decide those rules were stupid.

Breakfast was awkward. Violette had laid out a buffet on the large island in the kitchen, and the rest of them – with the exception of Lucas and Arlo – were seated at the table in the adjacent dining room. The chatter subsided as Jo entered the room. She muttered good mornings, avoiding eye contact, feeling her face blazing again. Oscar and Grace perched at the table, fingers smeared with jam; Jo smiled at them, but she could sense Nina's frostiness from her clipped greeting. Cressida appeared in the kitchen doorway, wearing a white sleeveless shirt and faded cropped jeans.

'Can I have a word, Jo?' she said brightly, and Jo knew she was in trouble. She followed Cressida through the kitchen, where Violette was taking another tray of croissants from the oven, and out of the opposite door to the yard.

'Well – this is uncomfortable,' Cressida said, with a little high-pitched laugh, digging her hands into her pockets. 'God knows I'm not a prude, far from it. But the children were a bit shocked this morning, and I thought I ought to say something.'

'Sorry.' Jo looked down at her hands. 'We didn't think anyone would be up.'

'Well, that's the point, isn't it? Anyone could have seen you. If it was just us girls here, I wouldn't mind, but what if Lucas had come down? Or Arlo? And the *children* – I mean, what would you think if I ran around naked in front of Hannah?'

Jo bit her lip, gearing up for another apology, and a small spark of defiance ignited.

'I'd probably tell her they're just tits. We've all got them.'

Cressida stared at her, wrong-footed. 'Well – OK. Perhaps you have different standards. I don't think Oliver would have felt the same.'

'He's not here though, is he?' It came out sharper than she'd intended.

Jo watched the warring responses on Cressida's face before she opted for being the bigger person.

'Look, Jo.' She leaned closer and laid a hand on Jo's wrist. 'We can't imagine how much stress you've been under. If you're not quite yourself, that's understandable. I would just really appreciate it if you could stick to certain house rules while you're here, if only for the children's sake.' Her smile stretched tight. 'And perhaps you could have a word with that girl about it? Dressing appropriately, I mean.'

'That might be better coming from you,' Jo said. 'Since they're your rules.'

'I thought, as you're such great friends now.'

She could not miss the waspishness in Cressida's tone. She realised she needed to be careful.

'Hardly,' Jo said. 'Perhaps you should ask Max to say something?'

'I would, if he'd call me back.' She sighed, her irritation transferred to Max. 'He sent a text late last night to say sorry for any inconvenience, they must have got their wires crossed. No other explanation. Did she tell you if she'd heard from him?'

Jo shook her head. Cressida's mouth twitched. She leaned in and lowered her voice.

'What time did she go to bed last night?'

'I didn't ask,' Jo said.

'I thought you might have heard her come in. She's next to you.'

'I was asleep. Why?'

'Oh, nothing. Just – she was down here chatting to Marcel when I went up. Lucas was with them, they were all sitting at the outside table smoking. Then Arlo came to bed about one and said her door was still ajar when he passed. So God knows where she was.'

Jo thought of the footsteps on the landing.

'I've no idea,' she said. 'What are you worried about?'

Cressida chewed the side of her thumb. 'I suppose I was afraid Lucas might be with her.'

'Doing what?'

'I don't *know*!' Cressida tried to keep her voice down and

60

it came out as a panicked hiss. 'I don't like the idea of him hanging out with a girl like that late at night, that's all.'

'She's probably just glad to have company nearer her own age.'

'Well, *exactly*. You saw the way she was coming on to him at the table.'

'I think that's just her manner,' Jo said, trying to sound reassuring. 'She's Max's girlfriend, Cressida. She's not likely to turn up and start hitting on Lucas an hour after she arrives.'

'Right. "Girlfriend".' Cressida made the quote marks in the air, her voice heavy with sarcasm. 'God.' She pressed a hand to her forehead. 'Am I being ridiculous, Jo?'

'I think,' Jo said, carefully, 'that she just has a different kind of lifestyle from us.' She heard how absurd that 'us' sounded; as if she and Cressida lived the same way. 'I mean, of course she does, she's almost twenty years younger. She's a bit flirty, maybe, and she assumes certain liberties that people our age wouldn't.'

'You're probably right.' Cressida seemed deflated. 'It'll be a relief when Max gets here. Well, let's get you some coffee. We'll say no more about this morning. Oh, but, Jo' – she stopped and turned in the doorway – 'the stripy towels are for the pool. It makes more work for Violette if people start taking towels from the bedrooms.' She flashed that tight little smile again and marched back inside.

7

Cressida's plan for the day turned out to involve a group trip to Saint-Émilion for lunch and wine-tasting. It was not presented as optional. After breakfast, Jo encountered her hovering by the stairs, pretending to arrange things on the occasional table and waiting to ambush Jo on her way up to her room.

'Listen, Jo' – Cressida took her by the arm and ducked inside the door to the salon – 'I need to ask you a favour. Would you mind very much staying here today? I'm really sorry to ask, I know you love Saint-Émilion, but' – she lowered her voice yet further, though there was no one in sight – 'it's a delicate situation.'

Jo tried to look disappointed. 'I don't mind. But why?'

Cressida glanced over her shoulder. 'When I told Storm about it, she said she wanted to stay here and read.' Her expression suggested she couldn't parse such a thing. 'I can't force her to come with us, obviously. But I don't like the idea of her being here alone. I don't trust her.'

'What, you think she might steal something?'

Cressida flicked her head impatiently. 'Not that. Although

– as I said, we don't know anything about her. It's more that Lucas will be here. I'd just feel more comfortable if you were around to keep her busy.'

'Right.' Jo didn't know how to take this. 'I mean, I don't know how I can—'

'I can't ask Nina – she and Leo have been looking forward to some time together. And I really need to see the upholstery woman, so . . . That girl seems to like you. Perhaps you could suggest reading by the pool together, or going for a walk into the village – anything to avoid Lucas hanging around her alone. And make sure she keeps her clothes on. Although I'm not convinced I can count on you for that.' She did her falsetto laugh, to show that this was a joke.

'I'll do my best not to let it descend into an orgy while you're out,' Jo said.

Cressida laughed harder. 'Oh, you are funny, Jo. Thanks so much – I really appreciate it. It's only for today – once Max gets here, she's his responsibility. He still hasn't called me, which is a bit bloody rude, don't you think?'

'Perhaps he's embarrassed that he didn't warn you,' Jo said.

'Mm. Or she's lying. About him coming tonight, I mean.'

'Why would she do that?'

Cressida leaned in. 'So we don't ask her to leave. Think about it – what if there's no realistic chance Max can get away this weekend?'

'Then he'd have told you, surely? And why would she have wanted to come without him?'

'Free holiday, for a start.'

'Wouldn't it be a bit weird for her to come away with a bunch of people twenty years older that she's never met, just for a free trip?'

Cressida gave a patient smile. 'I know you never think

badly of anyone, Jo, but I'm afraid not everybody's as innocent as you. Arlo is quite famous, you know, and so is Leo,
and there are ghoulish people who would love the chance
for an inside glimpse of our lives. Didn't that girl say she
wants to get into journalism? She could have wormed her
way in here so she can find something she can sell to a real
paper. And she knows that if she keeps pretending Max is
on his way, then we can't throw her out. But I feel like I
can't relax until he arrives.'

Jo did not know what to say. This was on a par, she felt,
with Cressida insisting to Arlo that people wanted to kidnap
their children; there was a tiny kernel of possibility somewhere in it, but the rest was pure self-absorption.

'I'm sure he'll call. I don't mind staying here if it helps.'

'I googled her, obviously,' Cressida added. 'I dug out Max's
original email to get her surname.'

'OK,' Jo said. 'And?'

'It's Devlin. There's one Facebook account that might be
her, set to private. The profile picture is a shot of lightning
over the sea, for Storm, I suppose, so it could be anyone.
But there's nothing else. I can't find any other social media
for her, or any mention of her anywhere. Isn't that odd?'

'Not really. She's only, what, twenty, twenty-one? She can't
have done that much.'

'But the social media thing,' Cressida persisted. 'Lucas and
his friends have about ten different accounts each, I bet your
students do too.'

'Not all of them.' Jo thought of some of the girls she had
worked with on the estranged students programme. 'Especially
if they've come from a difficult background. Some of them
might have family or ex-partners they don't want to catch
up with them, they try to keep their digital footprint to a
minimum.'

'Oh.' Cressida arched an eyebrow. 'That never occurred to me.'

No, it wouldn't, Jo thought.

'*Storm*, though. It sounds like a porn name. It's got to be fake, right? If she is working for one of those agencies, she could have changed her name to stop her parents finding out.'

Jo fought not to roll her eyes. 'Don't you think Max would have found a way to check up on her, if he was suspicious?'

'Max is not going to look past those tits, is he? Men don't think like that. That's why they let themselves be manipulated so easily.' Her gaze shifted to the window and the snap of anger in her voice suggested she was not just thinking of Max. 'Well' – she shook herself – 'best get on. Let me know what you find out.'

She gave Jo a brisk hug – it was like embracing a rattan chair – and trotted off towards the stairs. Jo tamped down a smile, feeling like a teenager given a last-minute reprieve from a tedious family obligation.

8

Not that Storm was so easy to surveil. Jo wandered the house, but the only sign of activity was Violette bustling around the kitchen, and the girl who came from the village to do the beds hurrying silently down the landings with arms full of sheets. Jo tried a tentative knock on Storm's bedroom door, but there was no reply; she peeked inside to find the room empty and headed for the garden instead.

The sun was high overhead and she wished she had thought to bring a hat; the fabric of her T-shirt stuck to her back and sweat trickled between her shoulder blades. On the other side of the courtyard she saw Violette's husband, Paul, tidying the hedges by the pool, his shears snicking in the still air like a metronome. She raised a hand in greeting and he offered a grave nod in return. She felt a pang of longing for Hannah, and regretted leaving her behind. But at nearly ten, Hannah would have considered the twins too babyish to play with, and was undoubtedly having a better holiday with Emily's family. Jo could not miss the way her daughter was increasingly choosing to spend time at her friend's house; the normality of their big, noisy home, with its full complement of parents, offered her a temporary respite from the silence of her own, where she could not escape the constant reminders of her father's absence. It cheered Jo to see Hannah run up the path to Emily's front door looking almost like a carefree child again, and wounded her that she did not seem able to give her daughter that comfort, despite her best efforts. There had been times over the past year – she hardly dared even articulate the thought – when she had found the weight of Hannah's grief unbearable on top of her own, when she felt she could not go on holding both of them up – but who else would do it?

She followed the path around the end of the house, past the yoga studio, to the gardens at the rear. As she approached the line of trees by the stream, an unmistakable smell of weed reached her and her first anxious thought was: Lucas. If she stumbled on him smoking he would expect her loyalty, and then Cressida would be livid if it came out later that she had known. She was about to turn back when she heard a woman's voice call out.

'Who's there?'

Jo took the last few steps with trepidation; the only thing worse than finding Lucas smoking would be to find Lucas and Storm smoking together.

But as she rounded the stand of birches that hid the brook from view, she saw only Storm, lying back propped on her elbows in the shade, a book open face-down beside her and a thin joint angled between her fingers.

'Hey!' Storm seemed genuinely pleased to see her. 'Thank God it's you – I thought it might be the wee kids. I was getting ready to chuck this in the water. Want some? It's nice stuff, very mellow, not skunk.' She held the joint out to Jo, who shook her head, though after a moment's hesitation. 'I thought you were going out?' She patted the bank beside her.

Jo sat and took off her sandals, curling her toes through the grass. 'I decided to stay after all.'

'Good for you. Did she ask you to stay here and make sure I'm not seducing her menfolk?'

There was a smile in her voice, but Jo snapped her head around so quickly that she knew her expression was an admission of guilt. 'Why would you say that?'

Storm took a long draw of smoke into her lungs and held it. 'Because I can see what Cressida thinks of me. I'm not what she wants for Max at *all*. She's been trying to set him up with women she knows since before his divorce was even through, to keep him in her fold. She's *very* unhappy about me usurping, that much is clear.'

'She was the same with me and Oliver,' Jo said, warming to Storm's frankness.

Storm let out a throaty laugh. 'So you understand. Tell me – does she think I'm a hooker?' She lay back, her hair fanned out around her.

'What? No! Of course not.'

'Ah, come on. I see how she looks at me. When you report back, you can tell her I'm not. Although I wouldn't give a fuck for her judgement if I was.'

'I'm not reporting anything.' Jo plucked a handful of grass. 'She thinks you stayed up late with Lucas last night though.'

'Yeah, I did. We went for a walk, had a smoke and a chat. He's a nice kid. A bit lost. He reminds me of myself at that age.'

'Have you heard any more from Max?'

Storm blew out a plume of smoke. 'He's in Parliament all day, I wouldn't expect to. Relax, he'll be here.' She offered the joint. 'Have a go on this, it'll help you chill out.'

Jo turned her shoulder slightly, affronted; there were few

things she hated more than being told to chill. 'It's not really my thing.'

'Are you afraid she'll tell you off again? She laid into you about the skinny-dipping, am I right?'

'She just mentioned that it's a family holiday, which is fair enough, really.'

'Of course. *Family.*' Storm blew out smoke and her expression turned distinctly sardonic. 'Are you missing your little girl?'

'Yes, although . . . it's nice not to have to worry about someone else for once.'

'Forgive me, Jo, but it strikes me that you worry about other people all the time.' She didn't make it sound like an insult, but Jo was stung all the same; this girl did not have the right, after less than twenty-four hours, to pronounce on what she, Jo, was like – especially not with such precision.

'I suppose I do, a bit,' she admitted.

'Not surprising, after everything you've been through. But it's exhausting, trying to keep everyone happy, don't you think? That's why you should have a bit of this,' Storm said, and held out the joint again. Jo squinted to look at it, considered, then reached out a hand. She hadn't smoked since she was sixteen, on the beach at Newlyn, with some surfer boys she was trying to impress. She took a drag; the smoke scorched her throat and made her cough. When the coughing passed, she felt a slow, pleasant warmth wash through her as the light and leaf shadow rippled overhead.

'It must be hard for you,' Storm murmured, after a while. 'Not knowing what happened. To your husband, I mean.'

'What?' Jo sat up; the sweet easy feeling drained out of her as if flushed by cold water. 'What do you mean? Did Max say something?'

Storm rolled on to her side and gazed steadily up at her.

'Max is really cut up about it, I'm sure you know. He talks about Oliver all the time.'

'What did he tell you?' The only time Max had ever come close to broaching the subject of Oliver's death with Jo was when he had asked her, four months later, if Oliver had left any kind of note. She had told him, truthfully, no; Max had nodded in an ambiguous way, and had never raised it again, but it had been enough to let her know that Max had his own suspicions.

Storm sat up, pinched out the end of her joint and tucked the stub into a battered cigarette packet that she pulled from the pocket of her shorts.

'Max only said there were questions. About the accident.'

'Of course there were questions. That's why there was an inquest.'

'Sure. And they found nothing untoward?'

'No.' She felt her colour rising. 'They think he might have swerved to avoid a deer or something and he went off the road. It was a notorious black spot. Steep hill, tight bends. He'd been going over the speed limit, which wasn't out of character. The weather was bad.'

'Right.' Storm wrapped her arms around her knees and looked down towards the brook. Her tone suggested this was not the version she had heard.

'He was completely sober,' Jo added, knowing she was protesting too much. 'Nothing in his system at all. Only painkillers, a standard dose. He got migraines sometimes.'

'A migraine could mess with your vision, all right. Did he not have a seat belt, no?'

'It malfunctioned. The' – she swallowed – 'the bit that's meant to catch when you jerk forward. There was something wrong with it. The car was ten years old, so . . .'

'God. Just terrible luck, then,' Storm said, her gaze still

distant. 'I'm really sorry, Jo. I shouldn't have asked.' She reached over and pulled a bottle of water from her bag.

'Does Max think Oliver killed himself?' Jo asked abruptly. 'Has he said that to you?' She watched the muscles ripple in Storm's throat as she drank.

'Do *you* think he did?'

Jo almost found herself speaking, but a thought snagged at the back of her mind and pulled her up short: Cressida's comment about the girl being a student journalist. She could not imagine why Storm would have an interest in digging into Oliver's death. It had warranted a few articles in the broadsheet press, little more than that, the obvious speculation about depression and the recent case he had lost – but that was because Jo had managed the facts so carefully. She had lied for him at his death as she had for the ten years of their marriage, to preserve everyone's view of Oliver as selfless, principled, a good man. Which he had been, in many ways.

She flopped back on the grass and let the leaf shadow lull her. There was no easy way to answer that question. Storm rolled down beside her and they lay in silence, listening to the birdsong.

'You know, some men can't live with guilt,' Storm observed, after a while.

'It wasn't his fault,' Jo said automatically. 'He did everything he could for them. It's a dreadful, cruel system.' She pictured them as they had appeared in the news reports, Betty and Jonah, the activists Oliver had represented in his final case, who had been deported back to Uganda because – according to the Home Office – they could not produce sufficient evidence to prove they were gay. She could still picture Oliver's face the day he came home and told her Jonah had been beaten to death less than a week after

71

arriving, and Betty had gone into hiding, her whereabouts unknown. He had retreated into his study with a bottle of whisky and locked the door.

'Sure. But I wasn't talking about them,' Storm said, and in the pause that followed Jo could hear her pulse pounding in her ears as her thoughts scrambled over one another to catch up with Storm's meaning.

How did you know, she almost asked, but the answer was obvious before she opened her mouth. She had convinced herself that she was the one responsible for protecting Oliver's secrets, when all along he must have confided in Max. Of course he had. Shame washed through her, closing her throat. Did they all know? No, she could not believe that; Cressida would have found a way to hint at it by now, and Jo could not imagine Oliver confiding anything so personal to Arlo, they did not have that kind of affinity. Oliver had always been a little in awe of Leo, as if his tough background made their middle-class problems seem trivial, but Max – Max was a sympathetic listener, he didn't judge. Of course Oliver would have told Max about the other woman; she saw that now. And Max had never said a word to her. Perhaps he thought she didn't know; perhaps he, too, believed he was protecting Oliver. But what struck Jo as unforgivable was that Max had obviously told this girl, who he had been seeing for a matter of months. That was a betrayal, and she would make sure Max knew how she felt about it when she saw him.

'What did Max say to you, exactly?'

'Don't blame Max.' Storm's eyes remained closed; snakeskin patterns of sunlight played over her face through the leaves. 'It wasn't your fault, you know. None of it.'

Jo wanted to object; she was too raw and unprepared for this conversation. She felt undefended, furious with Max;

tears slid from the sides of her eyes and ran down into her hairline. Storm reached out and laid a hand over hers in the grass, and as she did so, Jo experienced the strangest sensation; afterwards she would remember it as a kind of heat spreading up through her wrist and along her arm, through her chest, loosening the tightness in her throat, the tension in her jaw and forehead, the ache behind her eyes. The word that came to mind was 'bliss', though that seemed absurd. The silent tears continued to flow and she felt, unusually, no compulsion to stop them.

'Men fuck around,' Storm murmured. 'It has nothing to do with the woman. Not the woman they're cheating on, or the one they're cheating with. It's all about them. Until they have to deal with the consequences – then they run away and leave everyone else to clean up their shit. Don't ever blame yourself.'

Jo closed her eyes and the light rippled pink and gold through her lids. She knew that, for form's sake, she should defend her husband against the charge of cowardice, but it was true. Storm had said the unsayable: he had cheated, perhaps for years, and then driven off the side of a hill to avoid facing up to himself.

'I was going to leave,' she said, and her voice sounded as if it were coming from a distance. 'I'd suspected for a long time, tried not to believe it, and there was our daughter to think of, it seemed easier to let things go on as they were. But then – it was about three weeks before he died, I answered a call I shouldn't have, and I heard something that wasn't meant for me, and after that I couldn't pretend not to know any more. So I made a decision. I even went to see a solicitor.'

'Did Oliver know?'

'I never told him. But I had the solicitor's card in my coat

73

pocket, and one morning I found it on the bedroom dresser. Either it fell out and he picked it up, or he went through my things. But that was his way of letting me know that he knew. Did he tell Max about that?'

Storm ignored the question. 'What, he didn't try to talk to you? Just that little pass-agg gesture with the card?'

'He was in the middle of Betty and Jonah's case and it wasn't going well, so I didn't like to bring it up while all that was going on. I knew he'd broach it when he was ready.' She dug the fingers of her free hand deeper into the earth beneath her. 'I wondered afterwards if that might have had anything to do with – what happened. You know, if he thought I was planning to leave, and he might lose Hannah on top of everything else. But we never did talk, and then he died, and all I can think now is that I would have forgiven him in the end, and maybe it would have turned out differently if he'd known that.'

Storm made a sceptical noise through her teeth. 'The point is, he took that choice away from you.'

Jo considered this. It was true; Oliver had left her with everything unsaid, unconfronted. She would never know if they could have worked things out, or if she would have had the strength to leave, because his death clouded everything with guilt, and left her permanently knotted up with rage at him, while knowing she would do anything to have him back. Storm squeezed her hand harder, and for the first time in a year Jo felt a softening, as if someone had finally understood this. Later, she would put this down to the weed she had smoked, but as she lay there, drifting, it was easy to believe that this wave of comfort washing over her, carrying her away from all her anxieties, was emanating directly from the touch of Storm's hand on hers.

9

Jo dressed more casually for dinner that night: a pale-green sleeveless shirt and beige linen trousers. When she arrived in the courtyard for drinks, the company was depleted, and there was a definite atmosphere. She understood from a brief exchange with Cressida when they returned that Leo and Nina had had a row in Saint-Émilion, causing Nina to come back alone in a taxi, and that the cause was Storm. Now Nina and Cressida stood apart, conversing in low voices. Nina had put on more make-up than usual, and her long black hair fell in a glossy swathe over her bare shoulders. She appeared tense and ill at ease, one arm wrapped across her waist, the other held at a tight angle with a cigarette between her fingers, and Jo noticed how the thinness she had always admired made Nina's face gaunt. At forty-eight, she was five years older than Leo; when he had married her, in his mid-twenties, it was generally accepted that he had won the dating lottery. Nina was beautiful, obviously, but also wealthy, well-connected, already running her own gallery. Her family money had helped to establish Leo's company. Now, on the cusp of menopause, with Leo successful in his own right in an industry that presented him with an endless supply of young women eager for his attention, it occurred to Jo that Nina must be all too aware how the balance of power had shifted.

She took an uncertain step towards the women, reluctant to disturb their confidences, but Cressida spotted her and beamed.

'Hi Jo, we were just wondering where you'd got to. That colour's lovely on you,' she said brightly, gesturing with her glass to Jo's blouse, but Jo caught a hard glitter in her eyes; she was piqued about something.

'Thanks. Is everything OK?'

Cressida's mouth tightened; Nina leaned in and whispered, 'Max.'

'Oh. Is he going to be late?' She glanced back to Cressida, but she had already guessed the answer.

'By another day,' Nina said.

Cressida beckoned Jo closer. 'He waited until six to call me – when he was supposed to be on his way to the airport. Apparently the lobby correspondent has food poisoning and the editor's asked Max to stay and cover for him tomorrow, for the vote. He said he had no choice, there's no one else with the experience to do it.' Her voice vibrated with suppressed fury. 'And all right, he has a job to do – though personally I'd have thought he could explain that he had a prior engagement, I mean it *is* our anniversary. I wouldn't mind so much, except it means we're stuck with—' she jerked her head towards the house to indicate Storm.

'What did Max say about that?'

'He didn't really. He just said he hoped it wasn't too inconvenient and it was awfully good of us. He didn't even apologise. I get the sense he's embarrassed and doesn't know what to do about it himself.'

'What does Arlo think?'

Nina snorted and turned away to stub out her cigarette. Cressida made a face.

'Oh, Arlo can't see why it's a problem, you know him. Besides, he's in his office most of the time, he doesn't have to deal with her. But he won't hear of asking her to leave if Max is coming tomorrow, so what am I supposed to do?' She made an exaggerated gesture. 'Anyway, how was your day, Jo? You seemed a bit distracted this afternoon.'

'Oh – no, I'm fine,' Jo said, a little too brusquely, and added, 'thank you.' She had woken alone by the stream and realised that she'd been asleep for over two hours – enough, she'd hoped, for the effects of the joint to have worn off by the time the others returned, but Cressida had sharp eyes.

'Good. Well, let's get you a drink.' Cressida motioned to Violette, who was standing by the table with a bottle wrapped in a white napkin. As Jo took the glass with a self-conscious *merci*, she saw Cressida's face change and turned to follow her gaze.

Storm half-skipped out of the kitchen door as if she couldn't wait to see them, wearing a pale blue silk playsuit printed with white daisies. Her hair was loose, still wet from the shower, and the tails of it left damp patches on the cloth just above her breasts. There was a girlishness about the floral print – like something a six-year-old might wear to a party – that contrasted indecently with the way the suit fitted her figure, the floaty shorts that emphasised the length of her lean brown legs. She bounded across to them as if oblivious to the hostility radiating from Nina and Cressida, and dropped a packet of Gitanes on the table as she passed.

'Hey, how are you? Did you have a good shopping trip, Nina? Find anything nice?'

Nina muttered a dismissive 'fine', as Cressida's smile grew more fixed.

'How was *your* trip, Storm? You've been out and about exploring the countryside, I hear?'

'Your informants are correct, Cressida,' Storm said, grinning back. 'I fancied a walk to the village, thought I'd look around. Well, truth be told' – she leaned in – 'I wanted to buy some smokes so I don't keep bumming off everyone else.'

'And did you find people friendly?' Cressida asked, with that same pointedness to her voice; Jo wondered what the real question was, the one she was clearly not asking. At least now she understood the source of Cressida's frostiness with her: she had let Storm slip the leash and disappear to the village.

'*So* friendly,' Storm agreed, nodding and smiling like an enthusiastic Labrador. Could Cressida not see the girl was playing with her? 'The lady who runs the tabac, what's her name – Marie-Laure? – she let me have a couple of postcards for nothing—'

'Becca, the nanny, said she saw you chatting to a man in a white car,' Cressida said casually, glancing over towards Lucas and Leo, who had begun edging closer.

'A man? In a *white* car?' Storm frowned, as if the idea were barely credible. 'No, I don't think – oh, I might have asked someone for a light, I forgot to get one. Was the nanny following me?' She smiled as she said it, but there was a steeliness in her eyes that matched Cressida's.

'She had to go to the pharmacy and she just mentioned that she'd seen you, that's all.'

'She should have said hello. I wouldn't have turned down a lift.'

'Apparently you were deep in conversation.'

'Ah, well – I'll take any chance to practise my French.'

A silence stretched between them while Cressida appeared to consider her next angle.

'You've heard from Max, I suppose?' she said eventually. At this, Storm's smile faltered.

'Did he not call you?'

'Oh yes. I was just wondering how long you've known he wasn't coming today.'

'About five minutes after you did, I'd guess. He said he'd already phoned you to apologise.'

'Oh.' Cressida appeared wrong-footed.

'Yeah, bloody bad luck, that guy getting sick. Max is gutted – well, you've spoken to him, you'll know.' She sounded quite insouciant. 'He wouldn't have stayed if it wasn't such an important vote. Ah, *merci*, Violette.' She took a champagne flute and lifted it in a placatory salute. Cressida seemed to be formulating a response when they were inter-rupted by the sudden appearance of Lucas in the doorway to the kitchen.

'Oh, there you are,' Cressida said, relieved to find a diversion. 'Where's your father?'

'He's in his office, he's just dealing with a – a thing. He'll be out in a minute.'

'Oh, for God's sake,' Cressida said, striding towards the door, but Lucas held up a hand to block her.

'No, Mum, honestly, leave him, he'll only get pissed off.' There was a high note of panic in his voice; he looked past her and caught Jo's eye with an imploring gaze. He seemed unusually pale. 'Jo, could I speak to you for a minute?'

Cressida cut a sharp glance at Jo, then back to her son, as if she might be missing some conspiracy between them.

'Is this really the time, Lukey?' she said.

'It won't take a sec,' he said, jiggling one foot and chewing

79

his lip. Jo looked as if for permission to Cressida, who shrugged, and stalked off towards the kitchen muttering about starters.

Jo followed Lucas into the cool of the house. He led her to the end of the ground-floor corridor with hurried gestures and ushered her into the cinema room, throwing a glance over his shoulder before closing the door.

'Something's happened,' he said, half-leaning against the arm of one of the sofas and shifting his weight from foot to foot. When he looked at her from beneath his shaggy fringe, she glimpsed the sweet-faced prep-school boy he had been when she first met him.

Jo smiled and tried to look encouraging. 'You're going to have to give me a bit more than that, Lucas.' Was this about the drugs? But there was none of the bravado he had shown when Cressida had brought it up the day before; the spots of colour on his cheeks and the way he wouldn't meet her eye suggested something else entirely.

'Dad bought Mum a present, for their anniversary,' he said, picking at a loose thread on the upholstery. 'It's a bracelet. From Chatila. Like a sort of snake.'

'Right.' Jo nodded, as if the name meant something to her.

'Yeah, so, God knows how much it cost.' He twisted the hem of his T-shirt between his fingers. 'He showed it to me because he wanted my approval. I have a better idea of what she likes. Anyway, it's gone.'

She nodded again, more slowly this time. She could guess at the next part.

'How do you mean, gone?'

He kept his eyes firmly on his feet. 'He didn't put it in the safe, because Mum would look in there, and it was meant to be a surprise. So he just wrapped it up in a shirt and put it in his underwear drawer, since he only had to hide it for

80

a couple of days. And now it's not there.' He flapped his hands at his sides in a gesture of helplessness.

Jo waited. She may not have been a trained psychotherapist, but she knew from working with the students that if you left enough space they would fill it with words, often not the ones they had come intending to say.

'The thing is,' Lucas said, still not looking at her, 'I told Storm about it.'

'Oh.' Jo felt the weight of this settle. 'When?'

'Last night. After everyone was in bed, we went to the woods to bun a zoot.' His eyes flicked upwards to meet hers. 'To smoke,' he clarified.

'I know, Lucas, I'm not a hundred.' She smiled faintly. 'Your mum said you didn't touch drugs.'

He rolled his eyes. 'That really isn't the point right now, Jo. I don't do ket or anything serious. Storm had some weed. Anyway, we were talking about Extinction Rebellion, and she told me not to be a dick about dropping out of school.'

Jo nodded, surprised. Clearly Cressida had asked the wrong person to do her parenting for her.

'Yeah, she really gave me grief about pissing away my education. Said I didn't know how lucky I was.' He scuffed the toes of his trainers against the tiles. 'But I was chatting shit, you know, trying to show off by taking the piss out of Dad, so I told her he'd just spunked fifty grand on a bracelet that Mum will wear like three times before she's bored of it.'

'Fifty *grand*?' Jo said, in a squeak, despite herself.

Lucas shrugged. 'That might be an exaggeration. It could be thirty. Or ten. I don't actually know. I just wanted to make the point that I thought it was disgusting, so she'd know I wasn't like him. I didn't think it would matter.' He glanced at the ceiling. 'But now – he's going ballistic up

81

there, he was about to accuse Violette or the girl who helps her, they're the only ones who go into the rooms to put laundry away.' He broke off and shook his head miserably. 'But, like, what if it's *not* her?'

'But if Storm was the only other person who knew about the bracelet, apart from you and your dad—' Jo left the thought unfinished. 'Becca saw her in the village this afternoon, talking to a guy in a car.'

She leaned against the doorpost. It all made a bleak kind of sense: Storm staying behind while the others went to Saint-Émilion, discovering that Jo had been left to watch her, so making sure she, Jo, got stoned enough to fall asleep. There would have been plenty of time for Storm to take the bracelet, make the twenty-five-minute walk into the village and pass it to the man in the white car, whoever he was. Then she blinked, and the whole theory fell apart: how could Storm possibly have found, in less than twenty-four hours, the kind of contact who would know how to sell stolen jewellery of that value, in a tiny hamlet of four hundred people? The idea was absurd. But Cressida would latch on to it as confirmation of all her misgivings.

'Shit. There you go, then. We've got to make her get it back.' Lucas looked as if he might cry.

'Is Arlo going to call the police?'

Lucas shook his head. 'Not right away. He doesn't like the local police, he thinks they're anti-English. A couple of years ago some guy from the village pranged Dad's car and the cops totally took the guy's side, even though it was obviously his fault. I stalled Dad for now, I told him I've got it. I said I put it in my room because his hiding place was crap and Mum would definitely find it.'

'Did he believe you?'

'I think so. He was pissed off that I hadn't warned him.

"*Gave me a fucking heart attack, Lucas, do you have any idea what that thing's worth?*" His impression of his father was uncanny. 'Then his phone rang and he sent me out, so I guess he doesn't suspect anything. But if it's not back by tomorrow night he'll have to get the police in, I suppose, for the insurance. I'm telling you because I thought you'd know what to do.'

Jo half-smiled, flattered by his faith and embarrassed that she could only repay it with a blank look.

'But also because you're the only one who's not a total bitch to her,' Lucas added unexpectedly.

'Storm?'

'Mum hates her, she couldn't make it any more obvious. She'd say it's because Storm's not *our sort of people*' – his rendition of Cressida's cut-glass vowels was equally on point – 'even though she'd pretend she was saying it ironically, but really it's because she's jealous. And Nina's salty because Leo can't stop staring at her tits, which is totally gross, by the way. He's old enough to be her dad.'

'Well, so is Max.'

'I know.' He made a face. 'I don't even want to think about that – it's creepy. I mean, *Max.*' He shook his head at the injustice. 'But she likes you. She said you and me are the only ones who talk to her like she's a person. She thinks you're cool.'

'Me?' Jo was beginning to feel increasingly unequal to the task of solving the situation, but she couldn't deny the small flush of pleasure that came from Storm's approval. Ridiculous. She stuck her hands in her pockets. 'So – do you want me to have a word with her?' The idea was monstrous; how could she possibly take Storm aside and confide that they assumed she was a thief?

'Fuck, no. I mean, we can't accuse her to her face, not

83

without evidence. I was thinking – maybe you could search her room while everyone's eating?' He looked up from under his fringe with pleading blue eyes.

'Seriously, Lucas? And how do I explain myself if she catches me?'

'Well, I'll make sure she stays at the table.'

'What about this man in the car? Supposing Storm did take the bracelet – maybe she was getting rid of it as quickly as possible?'

'Then there'll be money, won't there?' Lucas dropped his voice and darted a look at the door. '*Please*, Jo? If the police get involved, it's all going to come out, about me smoking with her, and—' He stopped, his face bright with shame.

'Lucas?' Jo felt the lurch of unease again. 'Did something else happen with Storm last night?'

'No,' he said, too quickly, refusing to look at her. 'But it's all my fault. I should never have said anything about the fucking bracelet. If you find it, Jo, we could put it back before anyone knows it was her.'

This seemed like wishful thinking, but Jo could not think of a better solution. She felt obscurely cheated, as if her determination to think the best of Storm in the face of Cressida's unsubtle prejudice had been abused. Because she couldn't see another explanation. Violette had worked for the family for years; she and her husband lived in the gate-house lodge, surely she wouldn't risk her home and her employment? Besides, she could have lifted half the orna-ments in the house before now if she'd been so inclined, it was full of valuable antiques, and it would have been noticed long ago if things were going missing. No – this could only have been Storm, and what Jo resented most was having to concede that Cressida had been right.

'OK,' she said to Lucas. Cressida might have relished the drama of the gendarmes coming after Storm, but Lucas had a point; if they searched the house they might find her drugs, and then it could come out that Jo and Lucas had been sharing them too. She didn't think it likely that the local police would bother much on that score, but it would be preferable to avoid any incident that might potentially leak back to her in-laws.

'Great. I knew you'd help.' His face crumpled with relief, and he gave her an impulsive hug; she caught his scent of sweat and body spray and recalled one interminable Sunday lunch at the Connaughts' house in Richmond, four or five years ago, when he had patiently let Hannah help him build his Lego Death Star, even though she was only little and insisted on putting all the pieces in the wrong place. Jo felt an unexpected rush of affection as she squeezed his skinny shoulders; he had been a kind boy, and was still, under all the swagger.

She nearly collided with Cressida in the corridor that led back to the courtyard.

'There you are! Marcel wants to bring out the starters. Is Lucas OK? Did he talk to you about the drugs business?'

Jo stared at her for a panicked moment before she understood Cressida's meaning. 'Oh. Yes. I mean – he asked if we could have a proper chat later, after dinner.'

'Well, that's something. I didn't think he'd actually be willing.' She looked at Jo, almost impressed. 'Is everything OK, Jo? You look—' She thought better of whatever she had been about to say; presumably it would not have sounded flattering.

'Yes, I just—' Jo searched her scattered thoughts for inspiration. 'I had a message about Hannah.'

'Oh. Nothing wrong, I hope?' Cressida's nose wrinkled

minutely in concern, though Jo suspected she was more worried about any further disruption to the weekend than Hannah's welfare.

'She's just a bit upset without me. I should give her a quick call.'

'Really – now?' Cressida could not help the tiniest note of pique. 'We're about to sit down.'

'I know, I'm sorry, but she'll be in bed by the time we've finished,' Jo said. 'I won't be long.'

Cressida mastered her annoyance, perhaps in the interests of keeping Jo on side for dealing with Lucas. 'No, of course, take as long as you need. Poor Hannah. Is this the first time you've left her since . . .?' She made a face that circumvented the need to mention death.

Jo nodded, and Cressida patted her arm with a sympathetic murmur. 'Pity you couldn't bring her while we've still got the nanny.'

'Oh – is she going?'

'Yes, before Christmas. It's time for her to move on.' There was a stiffness to the way she said this. 'Childcare – such a nightmare, isn't it? Give Hannah my love, won't you,' she added over her shoulder as Jo reached the stairs. 'I'm sure Marcel can keep your food warm.'

On the first landing she met Becca the nanny with her entourage: the twins, squeaky-clean in matching pyjamas, damp-curled and smelling of bubble bath; baby Clio on her hip, flushed with tiredness, eyelids drooping, pink rabbit dangling by an ear from one small bunched fist.

'We're off to say night-night to the mummies and daddies,' Becca said briskly, marching her charges past Jo, who reached out impulsively and ruffled Clio's soft blond hair. The baby favoured her with a sudden beaming smile and tucked her face into the nanny's neck in mock shyness.

'Auntie Jo, did you know this house is haunted?' Grace said, pirouetting. 'Storm says.'

Becca laid her free hand on the girl's head. 'You know that's just a silly old story, don't you?' She fixed Jo with a meaningful look.

'The white women come out of the forest and steal children,' Oscar announced solemnly. 'They make you dance with them. Storm says.'

'White women?' Jo looked at him anxiously.

'Yeah, they're French,' he said, and Jo was none the wiser.

'There's no white, red, blue or green women coming to steal children in this house while I'm here,' Becca said firmly. 'Now let's go down or it'll be midnight before we get you in bed. Tell your friend from me,' she said to Jo, under her breath, 'that if she fills their heads with any more of that crap, she can get up in the night and deal with their nightmares. I don't need things made any more difficult right now.'

'Sorry,' Jo said, though she was not sure why she was apologising. 'I'm sure she didn't mean any harm. She probably doesn't have much experience with children.'

'Then tell her it would be better if she kept away from them.'

Jo watched her shepherd the children to the stairs. *It's time for her to move on*, Cressida had said, though Becca seemed good with the little ones. Jo wondered how Becca felt about that, especially since she seemed attached to Clio; it might account for the girl's general air of resentment. Perhaps she had picked up on Cressida's antipathy to the newcomer and seen a chance to curry favour by reporting Storm's trip to the village and the man in the white car. Jo crept along the landing past her own room to Storm's.

Because the chateau was only rented out to groups for weddings and house parties, there were no locks on the individual doors, based on the charming assumption that friends and families could have no secrets from one another. Jo cast a guilty glance towards the stairs, but through the open windows on the landing she caught the buzz of conversation from the courtyard, the children's high, bright chatter, the indulgent exclamations of the adults. She pushed open the door to Sainte-Estèphe and slipped inside.

10

Besides the bottles laid out on the bathroom shelf and the toothbrush on the sink, there was little visible sign that the room was occupied. Jo was not sure why she was so surprised to find it neat; perhaps Storm's casual manner and her disregard for propriety had implied a more general carelessness, but the room was clinically tidy. Jo moved to the chest opposite the bed and pulled open one of the top drawers, feeling an odd constriction in her ribs, as if she were the wrongdoer here.

The first drawer revealed only underwear. Jo plunged her hand into a froth of lace and silk, groping for a jewellery box, and encountered nothing but soft fabric. She plucked out an item and held it aloft: a flimsy pair of knickers in midnight blue silk, with translucent panels at the front, the kind of lingerie that cost a small fortune though it barely existed. She wondered if Max had bought them for her, and why the idea bothered her so much. Jo was deeply fond of Max, but it was hard to think of him as *sexual*, somehow. He always wore an air of slight neglect since his divorce from Fran – a button missing from his suit jacket, a patch he had missed while shaving that no one had pointed out – that would have excited pity in some women, and a desire to take charge and sort him out, but Jo could not imagine that was Storm's thing at all.

By the time she had been through all the drawers, Jo found she was willing the bracelet to appear, if only to justify her intrusion. But there was nothing here except clothes. She searched the pockets of every item hanging in the wardrobe, and even stuck her hand inside the trainers and boots paired neatly on the shoe rack. The canvas bag Storm had had with her that afternoon by the brook was slumped at the bottom of the wardrobe, empty. So were both bedside tables. In the bathroom cabinet she found a plain black make-up bag containing a small medicine bottle whose label had been torn off. Intrigued, she cracked open the lid and sniffed; it was three quarters full of a thick milky liquid that smelled faintly of mint.

Jo replaced it carefully and closed the cabinet, feeling foolish and guilty; what good was she doing anyone by poking around in Storm's medication? She ought to go downstairs and join the others before Storm decided she needed a jacket and caught her in the act. But her instinct to get out as quickly as possible bumped up against a troubling sense that something was not quite right. The bracelet was not there, she was sure – but neither was anything else of value. Money, phone, passport, the drugs Storm had had with her that afternoon – all these must be somewhere. Storm was not a handbag sort of person; she had been holding her pack of cigarettes in her hand when she came down for dinner, so where would she keep her most personal things? Jo crouched and looked under the bed, to see the leather travel bag Storm had been carrying the night she arrived. It was folded flat; Jo edged it out and found nothing inside.

Closer inspection revealed a zip pocket set into the lining. She opened that and slipped her hand inside.

First out was the old tobacco tin she had seen Storm holding by the stream. Jo flipped it open, but found nothing except the drugs in a clear plastic bag, a packet of rolling papers and a couple of pre-rolled joints. She reached into the inner pocket again and pulled out what looked like an old washbag, blue canvas, contents bulging. This was more intriguing; she slid the zipper and bit down a gasp. It contained fat rolls of notes, bound tight with elastic bands. She worked one free and spread the money flat: twenty and fifty euros, to the value of five hundred. A quick count suggested that, if all the rolls were equal, Storm was keeping four thousand euros in cash under her bed. Jo ran her tongue around dry lips. Perhaps Lucas had been right after all, and Storm had sold the bracelet straight on. Could she have planned this? But she had only found out about the bracelet last night, when Lucas, wasted, as good as dropped it into her lap. Jo rolled the notes tight again and snapped the band around them. She couldn't make this theory credible; for one thing, Storm was not stupid. If Lucas had told her the bracelet was worth fifty thousand, surely she would never have let it go for four. She wished again, fiercely, that Lucas had not involved her. Whether it was connected to the bracelet or not, this was not a normal way to store your spending money for a weekend house party; something odd was going on with Storm, and Jo would have preferred to remain ignorant. She stuffed the washbag back into the pocket and her fingers brushed up against another object, small and square. She drew out a Moleskin notebook and, with a glance at the door, slipped off the band and flicked through. The pages were mostly blank; she found only a French phone number with the initials B.L., and some numbers that might have been flight or train times. It was not an intimate diary, at any rate.

A tumble of water in the pipes overhead snapped her back to herself; someone was flushing a toilet on the floor above, presumably the children on their way to bed. Fumbling in her haste, she shook out the little concertina pocket at the back of the notebook and a square of shiny white paper slipped to the floor. Jo picked it up and saw that it was an old Polaroid of the four boys – Arlo, Oliver, Leo and Max – taken around the same time as Arlo's wedding, or perhaps even earlier. It showed them crowded around a pub table of dark wood, pints on cardboard beer mats, faded upholstery on the banquette behind, flushed faces and self-conscious grins (all except Arlo, who was scowling and looking off to one side), Nineties hair hanging in their eyes. Over the previous six months, since Max had finally bought a new house and taken all his boxes out of the storage unit where they had languished since the divorce, he had sent Jo various photos he had unearthed of Oliver, usually by email, although occasionally he dropped by with a stack he had printed out and a gift for Hannah. But she had never seen this one; she felt a little stab of envy at the thought of him giving it to Storm instead. And why would he choose to do that – give his young girlfriend a twenty-year-old photograph that would only remind her how much he had aged? Why would Storm carry it around with her instead of a current one? Jo turned it over to look for a date and saw their four names listed on the back in faded ink:

Arlo Connaught
Oliver Lawless
Leo Garrett
Maxim Steadman

The handwriting was not Max's. There was a pinhole in the top of the photo, as if it had once been displayed on a noticeboard. Jo peered again at the picture, trying to divine its significance, when some instinct made her sit up, alert, senses quivering like a hare. Someone was coming. She scrambled to pack away the photo, the notebook, the bag, and once they were safely stashed under the bed she slipped out.

She was closing the door to Storm's room when she heard the clang of a latch and hurried footsteps approaching along the corridor from the other end. There was nowhere to hide; in the moment that she dithered, Becca appeared around the corner, pink-cheeked and flustered, head down. When she saw Jo she started, with a fast glance over her shoulder.

'Oh. Didn't realise anyone was still up here. Isn't that Storm's room?'

Jo hesitated. 'Yes – she asked me to get her jacket while I was here. I didn't hear you guys come back in.'

Becca glanced at the ceiling. 'They're all being quiet for once, I think they're ready to drop. I'm just getting Grace some water,' she added, with a defensive air, as if Jo had challenged her. She looked away as she said it and Jo had the odd impression that she was trying not to cry.

'Are you OK?' she asked, concerned.

'Yeah, fine, honestly,' Becca said, pushing her way abruptly past and avoiding Jo's eye.

Jo watched her hurry towards the main stairs, wondering if she should check on her; the girl was clearly upset. There was a smaller, servants' staircase at the far end of the house, so if Becca was coming from the second floor to the kitchen she had chosen an odd detour. On this floor there was nothing past the bend in the corridor except Arlo and Cressida's room and, beyond it, the long wood-panelled gallery where the wedding ceremonies took place in the winter months.

As she stood havering about whether to follow Becca, Arlo strode around the corner. He too jumped at the sight of her.

'Jo! Did Cress send you? I already told Lucas I'd be down in a minute. I had some things to sort out.'

He sounded terse. Jo offered an apologetic shrug, grateful that she didn't have to come up with an excuse.

'Well, better not keep them waiting any longer,' he said, holding out a hand to usher her ahead of him, and Jo found herself rapidly revising what she thought she'd seen. If Becca had been in the room with Arlo, perhaps there had been an altercation; that might explain why she had looked close to tears. Could *she* be the one stealing from them? Or maybe she wanted him to reconsider her dismissal. Whatever was going on, Jo did not want to be drawn into it any further; she should never have agreed to search Storm's room. She wished she did not have to think about the money under her bed, and what it might mean.

11

Dinner was a tense affair. Nina was snippy with Leo, contradicting him or putting him down every time he spoke. Lucas barely said a word, and spent the meal hunched into himself, stealing furtive looks at Storm; he was so preoccupied he forgot he was vegan, and was halfway through Marcel's rib of veal before Leo noticed and laid into him mercilessly, until Lucas scraped his chair back and stomped off indoors. 'Leave him, don't indulge it,' Cressida snapped when Leo made to follow, protesting that he was just having a laugh. Only Storm seemed relaxed; in fact, the tighter the others wound themselves, the more expansive she became, in her talk and her body language, until you would have thought she was the hostess, pouring the wine and putting everyone else at ease.

'Are you with us, Jo?' Cressida said, cutting into her thoughts, and Jo snapped her attention back with a murmur of apology. 'Was everything all right with Hannah?'

It took a moment for Jo to remember her own lie. She set her glass down, registering with a sense of puzzlement that it was her fourth. She was usually so careful of how much she drank around Oliver's friends; not so much that she would say or do something to embarrass herself, or him, but not so little that she would come off as prudish, or uptight, or someone who didn't know how to have fun. But tonight's wine, whatever it was – she had sadly missed Arlo's introductory lecture – was slipping down so easily that she now realised she was teetering on the edge of drunk, a bad idea when the fraught atmosphere required her to be alert and sure-footed.

'Oh, she's fine,' Jo said, twisting the stem between her fingers. 'She was just missing me.'

'You know,' Cressida said, pouring herself a glass of water, 'this will actually be really good for Hannah. For both of you. This past year must have been unbearable, I can't imagine, but you need time away from each other too, to heal.' She nodded at the rightness of her own point. How could you possibly know what we need, Jo thought. 'Well, you're the psychologist, of course—'

'I'm not,' Jo said, to no avail.

'—so you'll know better than me, but you can't let Hannah cling to you because you feel you have to make up for Oliver's absence. It's not healthy for either of you.'

'She doesn't.' If anything, Hannah had withdrawn from her since Oliver's death. Jo might have welcomed clinging. As it was, she felt Hannah had placed herself out of reach, somewhere inside the fortress of her grief; it was rare that her daughter voluntarily approached for a hug or to offer a glimpse of her inner world.

'Have you thought about dating yet?' Nina asked, meticulously paring a vein of barely visible fat from her veal. Jo stared at her.

'Oh – God, no. Not at all. I haven't really felt—'

'My advice is, get out there. Even if you don't feel ready – it'll give you an incentive.'

'To what?' Jo asked. It occurred to her that Nina was quite drunk too.

'You know.' Nina made a circling gesture that seemed designed to encompass Jo's whole person and the petal-thin slices of potato on her plate. 'Get back in shape, take care of yourself.' She pointed a fork with sudden focus. 'Because you're still – what are you, thirty-nine?'

'Thirty-seven.'

'Right.' Nina looked grudgingly impressed. 'But you don't want to wait till your age starts with a four. Trust me. I look at my girlfriends who are divorced now and they all tell me the same story – no one's going to swipe right on you after the big four-oh, except guys with a bus pass. You're still young – you could even have another baby.'

Jo strained to smile. She wondered what would happen if she answered that, if she said aloud – actually, Nina, I almost certainly can't have another baby. We tried for the best part of five years. That was just one of the many things that went wrong with my marriage. There was a chance that Nina – who had been forty-two when she had the twins, after years of expensive intervention – might understand, even offer sympathy, but Jo had never felt close enough to share confidences with the wives, and now was hardly the time to start. She could see Storm following the conversation with an expression of mounting indignation.

'Are you shitting me?' she said now, setting her fork down, her gaze pinballing between the three of them.

'I beg your pardon?' Cressida's voice iced over.

'Did you just tell a woman who is *grieving* to lose a bit of weight otherwise no one will fuck her except pensioners?'

'It's fine, Nina didn't mean—' Jo muttered, holding up a hand; Storm clearly thought she was helping by riding aggressively to her defence. She could not know it would only make things more difficult.

'Right, that's not what I meant—'

'It's what you *said*.' Storm's eyes blazed at Nina.

'Jo is our *friend*,' Nina said, leaning back in her chair. 'We're just looking out for her.'

'Oh, *right*,' Storm said, in that way that suggested she had seen straight through you. 'So how many times have either of you been round to see her in the last year?'

There was a long, pregnant silence, in which fury and guilt fought on Nina and Cressida's faces. Jo found herself blushing to the tips of her ears, mortified; now it would sound as if she had been bitching to Storm about the lack of attention. It was true, of course; neither of them had made a single visit to her in the months after Oliver's death. Instead, they threw money at the problem: Leo and Nina sent flowers and, once, a box of expensive macaroons (and now here was Nina giving Jo side-eye about her weight); from Cressida and Arlo they had received an exquisite hand-made doll's house for Hannah, which barely fit in her bedroom and probably cost more than Jo's car. And while Cressida had invited Jo to plenty of events, which in her eyes counted as being attentive, they were always things she was doing anyway: parties, fund-raisers and, once, a West End show which she had texted Jo about on the morning of the performance, so that it was obvious her original guest had just cancelled. Jo had usually made excuses about babysitters. But coming round just to sit with her and let her talk, or watch a film together, turning up with a home-made casserole or a cake, offering to help her clear out Oliver's clothes and take the bags to Oxfam, all the small gestures she had needed from a friend – none of them had done those things except Max. The very idea of Cressida driving out to Lewisham to make Jo tea and sit beside her while she cried through an old film was almost comical, and would have been painful for both of them if it had ever happened. But now that Jo thought about it, she might at least have offered. How was Storm so perceptive? Seeing the expression on Nina and Cressida's faces, she realised that they had in fact let her down, and she could be angry about it if she allowed herself; she understood that they knew it too, and felt ashamed, and their shame was already manifesting as resentment against Jo for apparently ratting them out to a stranger at the first opportunity.

'Everyone's been very kind,' she said quickly, flashing Storm what she hoped was a warning look. 'We're all busy.'

Storm gave a short, dry laugh.

'Look.' Cressida placed her hands flat on the table, her expression glacial. 'I really don't think it's any of your business. If Jo has a problem with us, she's perfectly well able to speak for herself—'

'I don't have a problem,' Jo said, alarmed. Storm shot her a look that said, *Seriously?*

'I don't know who you think you are,' Cressida continued, louder, determined to reassert control. 'You don't know any of us, you barely know Max, you invite yourself here—'

'You invited me,' Storm said calmly, refilling her glass. Jo half-expected Cressida to dash the bottle out of her hand.

'We invited you here *with Max*!' Her voice had risen an octave; at the other end of the table, Arlo and Leo broke off their conversation, alert to a potential scene.

'Ah, I see.' Storm set the bottle down. 'Would you like me to leave? You should have said.' She pushed her chair back. 'It's fine, I can hitch to a hotel. I'll get my stuff.'

Cressida hesitated; she would clearly have loved nothing more than to watch Storm walk down the drive.

'Don't be bloody ridiculous,' Arlo said, with a sharp glance at his wife. 'It's nearly ten and we haven't had pudding. No one's hitching anywhere. We'll get another couple of bottles. I'll call Violette.'

They sat in a tense silence, until Lucas slouched out of the main door and pulled up a chair, oblivious to the atmosphere.

'What's for pud?'

'Horse,' Storm said. 'Horse profiteroles. It's organic, you'll barely know you're eating it.'

Lucas laughed self-consciously, but his face fell as she stood up.

'Think I'll turn in,' she said, with a diplomatic nod to the company. No one objected. 'I need to give Max a call anyway. Thanks for a lovely dinner.'

'Tell him to get his fat arse on a plane as soon as possible,' Leo called as she reached the door and she lifted a hand in acknowledgement.

A pause stretched out after she left, as if no one quite trusted her to have gone completely.

'My God, she's a piece of work,' Cressida muttered, picking at a loose thread on the tablecloth.

Lucas flashed a look of panic at Jo. 'Did I miss something?'

'Jo – I'd have come round if you'd asked, you know,' Nina said, suddenly solicitous. 'You never asked. We thought you wanted to be left alone. We thought—'

'It's fine,' Jo said, 'I don't know where she got all that from, I didn't expect you—'

'She's a little shit-stirrer,' Cressida cut in, spitting the words. 'She wants to set us against each other, can't you see? She's been doing it since she arrived. I'm sorry, Arlo – I want her to leave. First thing in the morning, if it's too late now. I'll ask Violette to call that guest house in the village.'

'You can't just throw her out, Mum,' Lucas said, half-standing in protest. Jo heard the note of alarm in his voice; he was thinking about the bracelet.

'I'm not having her in my house if she's going to speak to me and my friends like that. And by the way, sweetheart – your little crush on her is adorable, but it's getting embarrassing now.'

Lucas turned to his father. 'Dad? What's Max going to say?'

Cressida snorted. 'At this stage, I'm not convinced Max is even likely to turn up. Arlo, I mean it – I've had a bad feeling about her since she arrived. She's running around naked, she's monstrously rude to all of us—'

'Oh my God, Mum – she's not *rude*, she's just honest. You're so used to people sucking up to you all the time, you take offence if someone doesn't fall at your feet.'

'You know, Lucas,' Nina said, leaning in with tipsy earnestness, 'it's not a virtue to go through life saying whatever you think without any regard for how people might feel about it, or how it makes you sound. Only populist politicians believe that.'

'I think, playing devil's advocate,' Leo said, twisting a serviette around his fingers, 'it's going to look pretty bad if you send her away now. If Max is serious about her, it'll make things very awkward—'

'Max can't possibly be serious about a girl like that,' Cressida said. 'How could he?'

Nina rounded on Leo. 'Why are you defending her? What do you care if she leaves?'

'I'm just thinking of Max,' Leo protested. 'If he gets here tomorrow and she's been exiled to a B and B, then he's got to pick a side. And where do you think he'll choose to stay, if his girlfriend's in the village?'

'Well, then, he'll have to think long and hard about where his loyalties lie.' Cressida cast her gaze around the table and huffed out an angry sigh. 'Look at us. This was supposed to be a nice relaxing weekend with old friends, and she's got us all bickering like children.'

'Murder at the Bickerage,' Lucas said, slumping back in his chair.

Cressida gave an icy little laugh. 'Well, I'd draw the line at murder, but I don't think it's outrageous to say I can't see why we should have to put up—'

'For God's sake,' Arlo said, slapping his palm on the table so that Cressida jumped, mid-sentence. It was so rare for him to raise his voice that everyone stared. 'Stop, all of you. No one's being exiled. She came here as our guest and I'm not going to kick her out and have her staying in a B and B down the road for one day.'

'And what about dinner tomorrow, Arlo?' Cressida fixed him with a look that contained some unspoken message. 'You want to risk her causing a disruption then, do you?'

'Max will be here tomorrow,' Arlo said firmly, pushing his chair back. 'I'll make sure of it. If you'll excuse me, I've got a lot to do before then.'

Overhead, a window slammed shut. They all snapped their heads up to the facade.

'Shit,' Lucas said quietly. 'Do you think she was listening up there?'

'Her room looks out over the other side,' Jo said. 'Towards the woods, same as mine.'

'But the landing's on this side,' Nina said, peering up. 'She could have been standing there eavesdropping.'

'Well, good.' Cressida gave a small shiver and reached for the water bottle. 'Won't do her any harm to know she's on her last chance.'

12

Later that night, lying in the dark, Nina's words came back
to Jo: 'You should have asked.' Perhaps she was right. She
could have called Cressida or Nina herself and invited
them over – why had she assumed she couldn't do this?
She could have asked Oliver's parents to stay with Hannah
so that she could have a weekend away long before this;
maybe they would have liked to help more but had been
waiting for her to reach out. Why had she been so reluctant to ask anyone for support after Oliver's death – out
of a fear of being pitied? Or because of some misplaced
determination to prove that she would not be crushed by
what Oliver had done to them, to her and Hannah? Her
father had been the same when her mother died, she
recalled, pushing everyone away. He had gone back to
work at the post office in Penzance less than a week after,
leaving thirteen-year-old Jo to run the home. You kept
your problems behind your own front door, that was his
view; he wouldn't have the neighbours saying he couldn't
manage. His pride had baulked at the idea of sympathetic
glances, people interfering. Somewhere along the way, Jo

had absorbed his belief that to accept help would be an admission of weakness.

The house had fallen into its creaking night-time stillness. She turned on her side, infuriatingly wide awake, yanking the duvet with her. Storm's outburst had distracted Cressida in the short term, but Jo knew there would be a price to pay for her perceived disloyalty in supposedly complaining about the wives to Storm; Cressida's *good night* had been distinctly frosty. She wished Storm had kept her mouth shut.

She got up to use the bathroom, drank a glass of water and was groping her way back to bed when she caught the sound of a voice drifting faintly from beyond the window. Pulling back the curtain, she could make out a figure in the sheen of moonlight, standing at the edge of the back lawn, hunched and talking into a phone. The glowing tip of a cigarette traced quick patterns through the dark as they gestured; a flick of long hair, and Jo realised it was Storm. Who was she talking to so furtively in the middle of the night? Max? She watched Storm slip the phone into her pocket and dart a fast glance back at the house, as if she could sense eyes on her. Then she disappeared over the rise and out of sight.

Afterwards, Jo could not quite say what made her decide to follow. There was reason enough to be suspicious of Storm – the money in her bag, the missing bracelet – and in the back of Jo's mind lingered the possibility that she might witness some exchange that would confirm Storm's guilt. But that was not the whole of it; the truth was that she was intrigued by Storm, curious to know what she was up to, running around the gardens while the rest of the chateau was asleep.

She rolled out of bed and threw on clothes at random, grabbing her phone on her way out. Downstairs in the entrance hall, she could see that the main door to the court-yard was still bolted from the inside; the back door from the kitchen to the yard and car park behind showed the same. Storm must have found some other way out. Jo crept along the ground-floor corridor, glancing in at the rooms that had French doors leading on to the terrace, until she came to the small library at the turn of the L and saw that one of the curtains had been pulled back. She found the key still in the unlocked patio door and tucked it into her pocket, just in case, before slipping out into the night.

A fat moon hung low in the sky, almost full, bright as a searchlight; the garden stretched out silvered ahead of her. She followed the route Storm had taken across the terrace and down the steps until she felt the soft tread of earth and grass beneath her feet. A glance back at the chateau showed a rhomboid spill of light from a ground-floor window on the far side; Arlo must be up late working. The rest of the facade lay in darkness, save for the soft glow of a nightlight on the nursery floor. Jo took care to keep out of the study window's line of sight as she hurried down the whitened slope of lawn towards the brook.

Away from the house, she switched on her phone's torch and let the wavering beam illuminate the way between the trees. When she reached the place where the path ran out and the bank gave way to a narrow thread of water, she paused, straining to listen. Overhead, the branches had come alive with strange whispers and flutterings, sounds of night creatures going about their unseen business, but she could not make out anything that might indicate Storm's presence. There was nowhere to go from here except over the stream and into the forest, and why would Storm choose to go wandering out there in the dark? It was hard enough to find a viable path in daylight. Much more likely that she had sought out a quiet place at the bottom of the formal gardens for a smoke. Jo felt suddenly foolish, stalking the girl through the grounds in the middle of the night. She turned to retrace her route; with luck she could make it back to bed without anyone knowing.

She had barely taken a step when she caught the breath of a movement behind her; before she could register what was happening, a hand clamped over her mouth and another arm wrapped around her chest, pinning her arms to her sides. The beam of her phone skewed wildly into the trees as she dropped it, and Storm's voice hissed in her ear, 'What the fuck, Jo? Are you following me?'

She tried to pull free, shaking her head as emphatically as she could with Storm's hand holding her face. She could feel the girl's strength, belying her slender arms. When she seemed satisfied that Jo was not going to make a noise, she released her and picked up the phone, holding it with the light pointing down towards the water.

'So?' she said.

'I couldn't sleep,' Jo mumbled, rubbing the side of her neck.

'And by an amazing coincidence you wandered in exactly the same direction as me.' Storm cocked her head to one side.

'I wasn't to know you'd be here,' Jo said, shifting her gaze away. 'What are you doing, anyway?'

Storm gave her a long look. 'Ah, I'm a terrible sleeper too, especially in a new place,' she said, evidently choosing to drop her suspicions about being followed. 'I'm always roaming around at night. I like to explore. Talking of which – come here and I'll show you something cool.' She nodded in the direction of the trees opposite.

Jo hung back – not afraid, exactly, but apprehensive. She

had never liked the forest, even in daylight; she and Oliver had tried walking there a few times on early visits and had always been obliged to turn back, finding the trails so indistinct and overgrown that they had feared losing their way back to the chateau completely.

'Come on, now.' Storm smiled and beckoned as if coaxing a wary animal. 'You like history, don't you? Wasn't that your degree?'

Jo looked at her, surprised that she should know this. 'Yes, but—'

'Well, then, you'll want to see what's in the woods.' She swung her canvas satchel around to her front and pulled out the neck of a bottle, grinning. 'Besides, I can't drink all this on my own.' Without waiting for an answer, she grabbed Jo's hand and pressed her phone into it. 'Keep the light shining down there.'

Before Jo could protest, Storm swung her arms back and leapt the stream, teetering for a moment on the edge of losing her balance and righting herself on the other side with a breathless laugh. 'Now you. Don't fall in.'

Jo gathered herself. The brook was not deep, but its span was at the outer limit of her range and the light unsteady; she could not really see where she needed to land. But it seemed too late to turn back; she took a deep breath and launched across the water, her feet slipping under her, until Storm caught her arm and pulled her up the bank. They pressed on, laughing like children at their own daring, as the path began to climb and the forest grew dense around them. Night air with its edge of frost slid down her throat like spring water, and she felt wired with crackling energy, alive to every rustle in the leaves around them, every twig that snapped under unseen feet.

They reached a high chicken-wire fence, where Storm

shone the torch along the ground until she found what she was looking for: a gap where the wire had been torn away from its post at the bottom, just large enough for a person to push through. Jo followed her, loose strands catching on her jacket; they were no longer on Arlo's land, but had crossed a boundary into some wild, unknown territory. They continued between the shadows of trees on a path only Storm could see, until she ducked under a low-hanging branch and led Jo into a clearing where the moon stared down on the hollowed-out ruins of an old chapel. One gabled end was still standing intact, its two narrow arched windows and low doorway disturbingly like eyes and a mouth. An owl called a warning, startlingly close. Jo felt a prickling sensation along her scalp.

Storm released her hand and whirled around with her arms spread wide, offering the scene for Jo's approval.

'Did you know this was here?' She dropped to her knees in the centre of the clearing and began to rummage in her bag again.

Jo shook her head. 'I've never seen it before. It's creepy. Does it belong to the chateau?'

'Supposedly it was attached to a leper colony outside the walls. Thirteenth century. It's the only part left.'

'How do you know that?'

'Lucas brought me last night. It's where he comes when he wants to get away from the fam. Hold the light over here, will you?'

Jo wanted to ask how long Storm had been out here with Lucas last night, what had happened between them, but she did as she was told and saw that the beam was pointing to a heap of charred wood where someone had recently laid a fire. A small pile of broken branches had been stacked beside it; Storm arranged these over the ashes and brought out from her bag a handful of screwed-up balls of paper, which she stuffed into the gaps between the sticks. When she was satisfied, she took out a Zippo, lit a twist of paper and held it to the pile until the flame caught.

'Are you allowed to do that?' Jo asked. She saw the glint of Storm's eyes in the firelight.

'Am I *allowed*?' She took the phone from Jo and clicked off the light, her face with its wicked grin plunged suddenly into shadow, like a carved mask. 'Who's going to tell me off? Cressida? Oh no – will I be expelled?'

'I just thought there might be regulations, in the forest,' Jo said, as her eyes adjusted to the gleam of moon and fire. 'It's so dry – what if it catches?'

'Ah, Jo.' Storm sat back on her haunches, watching the flames with satisfaction. 'The forest belongs to everyone, relax. Here, this might help.'

She brought out a slim bottle and held it out. 'Now, this is a very expensive vintage from the Haut-Armagnac region, bottled in 1970, blah blah blah zzz,' she said, in a surprisingly good imitation of Arlo. Jo took the bottle, and tilted it to her lips; the brandy slipped down, pure and silky.

'That's nice.'

Storm reached for it and gulped generously, wiping her lips before replacing the cap. 'So it should be. This stuff is like four hundred quid a go, Marcel told me. It's wasted on Arlo, he barely even drinks. Tomorrow we'll fill it up with supermarket brand and Arlo won't know the difference – he just likes collecting it and wanging on about it. Our secret.'

Jo eyed the bottle, feeling tawdry; the thought of stealing from Arlo's premium drinks cabinet took the shine off the adventure. It was not that he would miss it, but how shabby they would look if they were found out. She could almost hear Cressida saying, in her best disappointed voice, *Oh Jo, you should have asked for a glass, we'd have been happy to share it.* Cressida would probably give her the whole bottle, to make a point; there was no need to sneak about like teenagers, except for the kick of feeling they were getting one over on their hosts. But maybe that was the thrill, for Storm. Maybe when Jo was Storm's age she too would have been excited by the idea of stealing from millionaires, sticking it to the man – although she would never have dared to do it. But if Storm could be so blasé about helping herself to a £400 bottle of brandy, would she be equally at ease pocketing a £50,000 bracelet? You could hardly replace that with a cheap knock-off and hope no one noticed.

'Were you planning to come out here and drink it by yourself?' she asked.

Storm eyed her. 'Why, who else would I be drinking with?'

'I don't know. Lucas?'

Storm shook her head. 'I don't think he's that keen to hang out with me, after last night.'

'What happened?'

'Ah, it was nothing. He tried for a snog. I put him straight, it's no big deal. But I think he's feeling a bit awkward.'

She brought out the little silver tin where she kept her weed, balanced it open on her knees and began assembling a joint. Jo watched the tip of her pink tongue trace delicately along the gummed paper and a small charge zipped through her lower belly. She pushed the sensation away, shocked. Storm shook the joint into shape and held the lighter to it.

'Tell you what, I thought I'd be spending the night on Marcel's sofa,' she said, inhaling and holding the smoke in, her voice coming out deep and throaty. 'Her ladyship was *this* close to kicking me out at dinner, am I right?'

'I don't think she'd dare, really. Was that what you were telling Max?'

'Max? When?'

Jo dipped her head, glad the dark hid her flush. 'I saw you from my window, on the lawn. You were on the phone.'

Storm's lips curved into a sly smile as smoke leaked between them. 'So you *did* follow me?' She seemed amused rather than annoyed now. 'So go on, tell me – what did she say about me after I'd gone?'

Her eyes shone, and Jo saw that she was delighted by the mischief she was making; it put her in mind of some puckish Shakespearian sprite, prancing through the house while mortals were sleeping, switching things around and whispering devilment in their ears, for the fun of watching them flounder when they woke to confusion.

'It all turned into a barney. Cressida wanted to make you leave, Arlo wouldn't hear of it, Leo defended you and Nina had a go at him. They're all a bit thrown by you coming here without Max. But then you know that.'

After a moment, Storm gave a dry laugh and handed the joint to Jo.

'It was only supposed to be one night. Max has spent the last four months telling me how amazing his friends are. I wasn't anticipating quite so much hostility.'

'You don't exactly help yourself,' Jo said, taking a drag. 'The skinny-dipping, and—' she waved at the brandy bottle – 'all this. Having a go at Nina. You set out to provoke them, to get a reaction.'

'Well, maybe I do, a bit. But you know that's not the issue. I could make myself small as a mouse, never offer a contradictory opinion, the way you do, to be liked, and it wouldn't make a blind bit of difference. Those women – they talk about empowerment but they don't like other women, not really.'

'I don't do that,' Jo said, stung.

'Sure you do. I was right, wasn't I, at dinner, about Nina

111

and Cressida? They haven't lifted a finger to help you, since Oliver died, not the way friends should?'

Reluctantly, Jo murmured her assent. 'But it wasn't for you to have a go. I suppose Max told you that?'

'No.' Storm reached over to take the joint. 'I have eyes and ears. I've been hearing the way they talk to you since I got here – the little digs, the pass-agg reminders that you're not coming up to their standards. Why'd you put up with it, Jo? Those women don't care about you. Why'd you even want to spend time with them?'

Jo let out a sigh and felt it whisper through the grass, into the silence of the trees surrounding them. 'I suppose they're all I have left of Oliver.'

'You have your daughter, no?'

'Yes, but—' How could she explain it to this young woman, whose life was still a map of paths not taken? 'They know his history, in ways that I don't.'

'Do you ever think there might be things you'd be better off not knowing? About their history?'

Jo propped herself up on one elbow. She felt her stomach contract. 'Like what? What has Max told you?'

Storm lay on her back and blew smoke in a straight line into the sky. 'Are you a vengeful person, Jo?'

'How do you mean?'

'You told me you answered a phone call, that's how you knew Oliver was unfaithful. Was it the other woman?'

Jo hesitated. She had never told this story to anyone, not even Max. 'It was one Sunday, about three weeks before he died. We'd visited his parents for lunch in Sussex. We got in the car to go home, Oliver plugged his phone into the CarPlay, for the music. Then his mother came out and called him back into the house, something she'd forgotten to tell him or she needed his help, I don't know. She always did that at the last

112

minute. So Hannah and I were sitting in the drive with the engine running, waiting for him, and a call came on his phone.' She paused to gather herself. 'On the screen, it said 'John W (work)'. So I left it to ring, I thought John W would leave a voicemail for Oliver to call back. But he didn't – it rang again straight away. I thought it must be something urgent, if he was trying this hard to get through on a Sunday, so I pressed answer. And before I could speak, this woman's voice, very posh, said – well, she said something that made it clear she was involved with Oliver.' She sat up and reached for the brandy. 'I just hung up and I didn't mention it to him, but he saw the missed call. She must have told him what she said, though, because I looked through his phone a few days later and John W wasn't in his contacts any more.' She tipped the bottle back and took a long gulp.

'And you never found out who she was?'

Jo shook her head. 'I went through everything after he died, in case he'd kept letters, or, I don't know. The only thing I found was a second phone, in his desk drawer.'

Storm's eyes widened. 'A burner?'

'I suppose. He must have got it after that call happened, because he started leaving his main phone lying around on the kitchen counter, unlocked, like he knew I was going to check it. Which, obviously, I did, even though I felt really low doing it. And all the time he had this other, pay-as-you-go one. I never thought of that.'

'Jesus. What was on it?' Storm sat up, hugging her knees.

'Nothing. I mean, he must have deleted everything. There were no messages, no contact names. Just a couple of outgoing calls to one number, on the morning of the day he died. When I called it, I got a voice message saying it was no longer in use. But I'd bet any money that was her. The woman. She must have had a secret phone too.'

113

'Didn't the police look into that? I mean, if he was calling her on the day he died, they must have thought it was significant?'

Jo picked up a stick and threw it into the fire, listened to it pop and crack for a few moments before she answered.

'They didn't know about it. I got rid of the phone.'

Storm stared at her and laughed in admiration. 'Jo! You're an actual badass criminal. What did you do with it?'

'I deleted the calls and threw it off Southwark Bridge when I was walking into town early one day. I didn't think it was criminal, I just – I didn't want anything coming out about this lover. For Hannah's sake – I didn't want that in the papers. I wondered if the woman would come forward when she read about his death, if she'd feel guilty, but she never did.'

'And you really have no idea who she was?'

Jo shook her head, making the firelight swim in patterns. 'No. I was obsessed with it for a while – like, if I could confront her, I could, I don't know – make sense of what happened, I suppose.'

'Because you'd have someone to blame?'

'Yes. But after a bit I realised it wouldn't change anything. If I'd really wanted to know, I'd have let the police trace her.'

'It wouldn't *change* anything?' Storm swivelled to fix her with an incredulous stare, eyes blazing in the dark. 'Are you serious? You're telling me if you found out tomorrow who that woman was, you wouldn't want to make her pay?'

Jo took the joint from her hand while she considered her answer. 'There was a time, in the first few months, when I'd have torn her limb from limb. I'd have been capable of any violence. I'd never had those kind of thoughts before, it was frightening. But' – she exhaled smoke, shrugged – 'that passed.

114

It wasn't that woman's fault that Oliver died, any more than it was mine, or the court case, or anyone's but his. So it's for the best that I don't spend my time fixating on her. Like you said yesterday – if it hadn't been her, it would have been someone else sooner or later.'

Storm nodded slowly, shadows chiselling her face to sharp planes. 'Well, you're a better woman than me, Jo, I'll give you that. If someone had taken the person I loved most from me and left me with half a life, and I found out who they were, I'd hunt them down and rip everything they cared about from their bleeding hands until there was nothing left.' She laughed, and took a drink.

The firelight had turned her profile to hammered bronze, transfigured her into something noble and ancient, from another age: a Celtic warrior queen or an avenging Greek goddess, all wild hair and blazing eyes.

'I'll bear that in mind,' Jo said, trying to make a joke of it. She wanted to protest that she didn't have half a life, but there was truth in it. A thought struck her. 'Wait – you said just now there were things I'd be better off not knowing, about Oliver's past. Does Max know, about the woman? Was that what you meant – does he know who she was?'

'If he does, he hasn't told me,' she said, but Jo thought she hesitated a moment too long. 'You should talk to him. You guys are good friends, it's mad that you've been tiptoeing around this for a year because you're both trying to spare each other the knowledge that Oliver wasn't such a great guy after all, when you already know. But it's not fair to ask me stuff you should be asking Max directly.'

'What's not *fair*,' Jo said slowly, closing her fingers around the cold grass beneath her, 'is Max telling you what he knows about my husband's private life, when he hasn't said a word to me.'

'So ask him. Maybe wait till after this weekend, though, when you'll have time to talk properly.' She drank again and set the bottle between her feet. 'I suppose I should apologise to Cressida for the dinner debacle?'

'Couldn't hurt. For Max's sake, as much as anything.'

Storm shot her a look. 'That's what you'd do, eh?'

'It's the simplest way to keep the peace.'

'What, let her think she's always in the right?' Storm shook her head as if she despaired of them all. 'Jesus. Well, I'll do it for Max, this time. Otherwise I'd get out first thing tomorrow. These fucking people. Someone's been through my room, you know,' she added abruptly.

'What?' Jo turned to look at her. 'How do you know?'

'I could just tell something was a bit off when I went to bed. Things not quite where they should be.'

Jo felt the cold rising up through the ground and along her spine. She couldn't tell if she was being toyed with.

'Why would they do that?'

'I dunno, Jo. You tell me.' Storm twisted her head and Jo caught the glitter of her eyes. Her breath stuttered; things stirred in the forest and in the shadows of the ruined walls, pacing, watching. The warm buzz of the brandy slid away, replaced by a spark of danger; the clearing had turned hostile and Storm was not her ally but an unknown quantity, a shapeshifter she should never have trusted. She had time to think how little it took to get her stoned these days as she opened her mouth on an explanation, but Storm cut across her, aggrieved.

'I mean, do they think I'm robbing them? They think I'm a hoor *and* a thief now? I've got the family silver in my knicker drawer, is that it?'

'No one thinks that.' Jo could feel her heart beating too fast in her throat as she bit down on what she had been

116

about to confess. She refrained from pointing out that Storm had in fact stolen a £400 bottle of brandy that was right there in her hand. 'Maybe you imagined it?'

'I didn't. It's something else, then. Maybe they wanted something of mine.'

'Like what? Was anything missing?'

'Not that I could see. But I've nothing worth taking,' Storm said, gazing up. Her face had assumed a wounded expression.

Four thousand euros in cash under the bed, but nothing worth taking. Jo wanted to ask about the money, but realised in time that might be exactly what Storm was fishing for. Talking to her was like feeling for a trip-wire.

'I wondered,' Storm said, as if to herself, 'if it mightn't be that nanny.'

'Stealing from you?'

'No, the opposite. Putting something in my room that would cause aggro.'

'Why would she want to do that?'

Storm leaned forward and poked the fire with a stick, so that a shower of sparks cascaded through the gaps.

'Well, come here and I'll tell you a story,' she said, settling back against the fallen masonry. 'I was in my room this afternoon, after you fell asleep by the stream. I could hear the baby crying from the floor above, properly screaming her little lungs out. It went on for fifteen minutes or more, it was wrecking my head, so in the end I went up there. No sign of the nanny. I picked up the baby and she stopped, thank Christ, so I went looking for Becca, thought maybe she'd put Clio for a nap and taken the twins outside. I walked all around by the pool and the swings, not a hair of her. Eventually I went back inside and saw her coming out of Arlo's office on her own. She nearly hit the ceiling, grabbed

117

the baby off me like she thought I was stealing her. I told her Clio had been crying all that time – Becca went bright red and started gabbling about how she'd had to have a word with Arlo about her references while the kids were watching a film or some bollocks. I'd say she's fucking him, by the look of her when she came out. She was all flushed and shifty. So that business with the white car, I reckon that's her going on the offensive in case I say something.'

Jo considered what she thought she had seen before dinner; Becca coming from the direction of Arlo's bedroom on the verge of tears, Arlo's defensive manner, Cressida's pursed lips when she talked about Becca moving on.

'So – the man in the white car isn't real?'

'Oh, he's real, all right. He sold me this.' Storm laughed and waggled the joint at Jo. 'He's a friend of Marcel's. An *associate*, if you know what I mean. So, yeah – I wouldn't put it past the nanny to try and discredit me in advance.' She took a last deep drag and pinched it out between her fingers. 'Maybe I'm just being stupid. Forget I said anything.'

In fact, Storm had been extremely clever; Jo saw that now. If the bracelet should turn up in her room, Storm had already provided herself with a plausible cover story, with Jo as witness to her suspicions.

'You really think Becca's that manipulative?' Jo said, her tongue fumbling over the syllables.

'Well, if she's fucking her married employer, that would indicate a certain level of deviousness.' Storm was over-enunciating; it was impossible to tell if she was drunk or not. 'And look how she went running straight to Cressida to tell her I was talking to a guy in a car – what business is that of hers? She obviously wants a reason to make me look bad.'

'We don't know that she's having an affair with Arlo.'

'Well. I didn't see his cock in her mouth, but I saw her face when she came out of that room. Something was going on in there that she did not want people knowing about. And she didn't like that I saw it.'

Jo watched her, aware again of the gulf between them. Storm was the age of the students she worked with, for whom everything was a matter of high drama, all the time; Jo had temporarily forgotten how exhausting that could be. It was absurd that she should be out here skulking in the woods in the middle of the night smoking like a truant teenager. She suddenly wanted, more than anything, to be in her own bed.

'I should go,' she said, though she knew the words lacked conviction; she was not confident she could find her way back without Storm.

'No, not yet,' Storm said, leaning in to throw another stick on the fire, her eyes shining in the brief shower of sparks. 'We haven't even started.'

'Started what?' Jo drew back, apprehension worming its way back up her spine.

Storm swivelled to face her, and her expression was deadly serious. 'I can help you, Jo.'

'Help me how?' For an awful moment she feared Storm would offer to exact some kind of revenge on Cressida and Nina, teach them a lesson for their failures of friendship.

'You're grieving,' Storm said, matter-of-factly. 'And it's not getting any better. In fact, it's festering, because you can't talk to anyone about what you know. Am I right?'

Jo felt herself brace against the presumption. 'I don't think that's any of your—'

'I can see it for myself, Jo. It's because you're angry. And that's not allowed.' She had taken on the over-earnest conviction of the stoned. 'The rituals we're permitted – the

119

funerals or scattering the ashes or whatever – they're not enough. They don't give us room to deal with the sheer fucking anger at the dead person. You can't say any of it out loud. You can't scream and smash things like you want to. You know what I'm talking about?' She pushed herself to her knees and reached again for her bag, drawing out the Moleskine notebook. 'Listen to me,' she said, when Jo didn't respond. 'I read this article in a posh magazine a few months ago, *Bazaar* or one of those, about a retreat that women go on to heal their psychic wounds or some shit, and it costs like six grand for five days, and I was reading all this thinking, fuck me, this is exactly what my grandmother used to do for people, except she never knew to charge that kind of money for it.'

'Your grandmother? What did she do?'

'I'll show you. Here, take this.' She passed the notebook across. 'They've done experiments on this stuff, you know,' she added conversationally, rooting in the bag and bringing out a pen. 'Psychologists, I mean. The power of belief and ritual. But my grandmother knew it instinctively. People used to say she had *gifts*. But what it was, really, she listened, that was her secret. There's magic in that, if you've spent your whole life not being heard.' She sat back on her haunches and peered into the fire. 'My grandmother came from a small community in the west of Ireland where women weren't supposed to complain, so they didn't. They kept it all inside.' She bunched a fist and held it to the centre of her chest to demonstrate. 'That'll kill you in the end. My grandmother gave them a safe place to let it all out. They'd come to her – mostly women of a certain age – and she'd make some kind of tea that was supposed to help with their hot flushes or whatever, but really they just came to talk to someone who wouldn't judge. They'd tell her things they'd never say to the priest, and she'd let them rant. I used to listen at the door when I was a kid. Sometimes she'd take them out to the back garden and do this ritual. And after, they felt lighter for unburdening themselves, so they credited her with making them better, and she got a reputation for being some kind of a healer. So many angry women, just wanting to be told it was normal to feel like that and they weren't bad people.' She gave a soft laugh. 'She was basically a shrink for people who would never in a million years consider seeing a shrink, and she hid that behind the hawthorn tea or whatever, because that's easier for some people to understand. That's my take, anyway, looking back. But it's a blessing and a curse when people believe you have gifts. Two hundred years ago they'd have burned her for sure.'

'Were you close to her?'

'She raised me. My mother died when I was two, so she was stuck with me.'

'I'm sorry.' Jo hesitated. 'My mother died when I was thirteen.'

'Worse for you, then. I don't remember mine.' She leaned across and tapped the notebook in Jo's lap. 'Now. Here's what we're going to do.'

Jo could feel her head beginning to swim. She pushed the book towards Storm. 'I'm going back.'

'Jo.' She had moved closer, so that she was kneeling in front of Jo, her eyes wide and intense, the light dancing in them in strange patterns. 'You're really fucking livid with Oliver, and you've not been allowed to say so to anyone, because that would be disloyal, because you have to keep pretending for your daughter's sake and all your friends that it was an accident. But he abandoned you twice, once when he had the affair and once when he killed himself, and you're raging about it inside. Aren't you?'

Jo closed her eyes. How could she begin to explain to this girl the compromises you learned to make with yourself? That it was not weakness to keep your feelings locked away, but a feat that had demanded a superhuman show of strength over the years; that you couldn't simply start emoting on demand when you had been conditioned your whole life to believe it was your job to smooth things over, keep everything nice, submerge your own anger and frustration and desires for the greater good of keeping a home running. What would Storm know of that?

'What you do,' Storm continued, as if Jo's participation were agreed, 'is you write down everything you wish you could say to them. Don't hold back. Everything you bottled up, everything you'd say if you could see them now and the brakes were off. Just write it all down, as if you're writing a letter to him.'

'I wouldn't know where to start.'

'So start with – how did he make you feel?'

Jo smiled. 'I couldn't believe my luck, at first. He sort of swept me off my feet when I was at a pretty low point.' She shifted position, stretching her legs out towards the fire. 'I trained to be a teacher, you see. Maybe Max told you. But I got signed off sick with stress in my first year on the job and never went back, I couldn't hack it. I'd lost my direction, I think, when I met Oliver, and he made me feel – if a man like him wanted me, maybe I wasn't a complete failure after all.'

'So he seemed like a real catch, eh.' Storm's curled lip betrayed scepticism.

'But he *was* a catch,' Jo said, throwing a twig at the fire. 'He was successful, handsome, romantic. I never understood what he was doing with me – I always thought he could have found someone who was more his equal. I think if I hadn't got pregnant with Hannah he would have.'

'So you spent your whole marriage thinking you weren't good enough for him?'

Jo turned her head to find Storm's level gaze fixed on her.

'He was a good father. I wouldn't have stayed so long if he hadn't been.'

'No doubt.' Storm pressed her lips together so tightly they disappeared. 'You haven't talked to anyone about him like this since he died, am I right? Or even before?'

Jo shook her head and gripped the pen.

'So write it down.'

'Do I have to read it out?'

'God, no. Not unless you want to.'

So Jo started to write – self-consciously at first, aware of Storm watching her at a distance, tip of her tongue caught between her teeth as she rolled another joint precisely in her long fingers. But as the words began to flow, Jo quickly forgot her audience and pictured Oliver instead. Looping, illegible script poured across the page; long-buried instances of hurt and humiliation rising to the surface like debris from a wreck disturbed, and though she couldn't see what she was writing, her pen seemed possessed by a furious energy of its own. When she had exhausted all the words, she looked up at Storm, at the small red dot of the joint glowing in the dark, and found her vision blurred; she had not even realised she was crying. She swiped at her eyes with the back of her hand, and Storm nodded her approval.

'You done?'

'I think so.' Jo had no idea how much time had passed. The fire was burning lower and smoke drifted low across the clearing.

'Good. Now tear out the pages.'

Jo looked down. She appeared to have covered half the book with her wild script. She gripped a clump of pages in her hand and ripped until all her writing was bunched in her fist.

'OK. Now you throw them in the fire, one by one, and you imagine yourself saying all that to him, and you let your anger burn up with it. What?' Storm caught her expression. 'Yeah, I know it sounds like bollocks. But remember people pay six grand to do this. Pretend I'm not here. Picture him.'

She backed away until she was hidden in shadow, and Jo began feeding single pages into the flames, slowly at first, then more rapidly, as she imagined saying all those furious words to Oliver; some were caught by invisible currents and whipped away into the darkness, but most flared and sparked brightly before curling to ash, and it was as if something burst in her throat; it took her by surprise, the noise that came out of her, as everything that had been stuffed down and silenced for so long burst its bounds and she found herself on her knees, sobbing, papers clutched in each fist, vanishing in flurries of sparks. Storm let her cry herself out, until all the pages had turned to ash, then she quietly knelt beside her and pulled Jo's head to her shoulder.

'I just miss him,' Jo mumbled, through her hair, into Storm's jumper.

'I know.' She rocked her gently. 'It's done now. Here.' She wiped the top of the bottle with her sleeve and passed it to Jo. 'Drink up and then hurl this as hard as you can at that wall, and smash it to pieces.'

Jo looked at the bottle in her hand. 'Why?'

'Because sometimes you just need to break something.'

So Jo stood, swiping at her snot and tears with her knuckles, knocked back the last dregs and threw the bottle with all the force she could muster so that it shattered against the wall of the old chapel.

'Feels good, huh?' Storm looked at her and in the firelight

the glint of mischief in her eyes had turned wild and dangerous. 'Come here to me now.'

She held out her arm and Jo settled comfortably against her shoulder again while Storm stroked her hair. It should have felt awkward, to be held so intimately by a stranger, but Jo had nothing left inside to register self-consciousness or shame. She felt entirely scoured, and besides, it was such a long time since anyone had put their arms around her like that; she gave up her resistance and let herself fall loose against Storm's side as Storm rested her cheek against Jo's hair.

'You'll feel lighter now,' she said, 'you'll see,' and Jo, feeling her shoulder move gently up and down with the rhythm of Storm's breathing, thought how nice it would be to believe that.

'We were supposed to refill that bottle and put it back so Arlo wouldn't notice,' she murmured.

'Ah, they'll have other things on their mind tomorrow,' Storm said. 'Trust me.'

13

Saturday

Jo woke at eleven, head tender, mouth claggy, and realised she had missed breakfast; Cressida would be annoyed. As she showered, letting the hot water sluice away the excesses of the night before, she realised she felt considerably better than she had been expecting; her head, though sensitive, lacked the usual fog she associated with hangovers. Perhaps there was something in Storm's ritual after all, she thought, or more likely the solution was to only drink £400 brandy. Instead of feeling guilty, she found herself laughing.

As she headed down the stairs, she heard the old-fashioned ring of the telephone in the hall, followed by the brisk squeak of rubber-soled shoes and Violette's harassed, '*Allo?*'

After a moment's silence Violette called, 'Madame?'

There was no reply; as Jo reached the hall, the housekeeper's gaze alighted on her.

'Madame Connaught, *elle est où?*'

Jo held out empty hands. 'I haven't seen her, sorry.'

Violette puffed a stray wisp of hair out of her face. 'She

126

is not upstairs. You can find her?' She mimed a telephone receiver and gestured towards the corridor. 'There is a woman want to speak – my English is not, uh . . .' she shrugged. 'I have to help Marcel.'

'Oh – of course.' Jo nodded. If Cressida was not upstairs, then the most likely place was the gym or the yoga studio, though she decided to go via the ground floor, poking her head into the salon and the cinema room along the way just in case. But as she passed the closed door to Arlo's office, she heard Cressida's voice inside and paused, about to knock, when she realised they were arguing.

'I don't care, I want her out this minute, Arlo. I'll book her a plane ticket and drive her to the airport myself if I have to. I told you this would escalate.' Cressida was high-pitched with anger.

'I think,' Arlo said, trying to sound reasonable, 'that we would be making more problems for ourselves if we kick her out now. She's likely to be more of a danger.'

'That's what she's counting on, isn't it? She thinks she's got us over a barrel. And I'm not having it – I won't be manipulated by someone like *her*.'

'I think we just sit tight for another day and keep calm. There's nothing to be gained by using the nuclear option. She wants a reaction from you. Don't give it to her.'

'And what's the alternative? Does she think we're just going to let her stay on as if nothing's happened? What about tonight – suppose she decides to cause a scene?'

'She won't. Let me find a solution.'

Cressida snorted. 'Forgive me if I don't have much faith in your solutions. This is on you, Arlo, all of it. You need to deal with her, or I will.'

Furious footsteps clicked towards the door; Jo barely had time to duck into the neighbouring room before Cressida slammed her way out of the office and marched off down the corridor. Jo crept away in the other direction and into the courtyard, hoping to avoid her; Violette could tell her about the call. Cressida had clearly not softened towards Storm overnight; in fact, it sounded as if her anger had been fuelled by some further incident. What had she meant by 'as if nothing's happened'? Why did Arlo think Storm would be a danger? She wondered if they could have found out about the bracelet, or the brandy, and was surprised to find that she felt a pang of loss at the thought of Storm being ejected from the house. She had shaken them all up, made them look at themselves and each other with fresh eyes; without her, they would too easily fall back into their old roles, and Jo had begun to feel the constraints of it chafing at her. She wondered if she ought to warn Storm of Cressida's threats, and turned her steps towards the pool, thinking vaguely that she might find the girl there.

As she passed the gym and studio she glanced up and saw, through the floor-to-ceiling windows, the flash of Leo's neon orange running vest. A second glance caused her to shrink back; he was standing behind Storm, his hands firmly on her hips, steadying her as she braced under the weight of a barbell. When she dipped into a slow squat, he didn't move back, so that her buttocks pressed against his groin. As she pushed up, he caught the weight and replaced it in the frame; Storm turned to him, laughing and breathless, her fingers resting on his forearm. Leo said something to her, then angled her again, holding her hips, apparently guiding her into a better alignment, though if they hadn't been clothed, it would have looked as if he were preparing to take her from behind. Jo felt the heat rush to her face and hurried away before they spotted her loitering like a voyeur. She was not sure exactly what she had accidentally witnessed – a bit of harmless flirting, or something more sinister? She thought of Cressida's accusation at dinner, that Storm was intent on setting them against one another, and wondered again if she had been a willing dupe. She wished she had not been so quick to expose her vulnerabilities in the woods the night before; she now felt as if she had given Storm a part of herself that she could not take back.

In her confusion, she kept walking and found herself at the pool, where Becca and the children splashed in the water while Nina lay impeccably arranged on a lounger with a copy of *Vogue* as if they were nothing to do with her.

'Hey Jo,' she called, patting the bed next to her. 'You look well.'

'Do I?' Jo's cheeks burned as she imagined how Nina would react if she knew about the scene in the gym.

Nina lifted up her glasses to examine her.

'Sure. You've got some colour in your face. Nice to get away without kids, huh?'

Jo glanced at the pool, where less than six feet away someone was being paid to entertain Nina's kids, despite their frantic shouts of 'Mummy, watch me!'

'Listen, Jo.' Nina swung her legs off the sunbed and sat up to face her. 'About Storm.'

'What?' Jo snapped her head up, certain Nina must be able to read it in her expression.

'What she said yesterday – I'm sorry if you feel like we haven't been around for you since Oliver – you know. I just wish you'd talked to us about it, instead of . . .' She gave a loose, one-shouldered shrug. It was impossible to tell from her tone whether she was genuinely upset at the idea of having let Jo down, or at the thought that Jo had been bitching about it to someone else.

Jo let out her breath, lay back and closed her eyes. 'I didn't say anything to Storm, if that's what you mean. That all came from her. Anyway, it's fine. I didn't expect you to be turning up on the doorstep with casseroles. It's not as if we were ever . . .' She let the sentence hang, unfinished, enjoying the sun on her face and Nina's palpable discomfort at her side.

'OK, I know we weren't, like, *best friends* or whatever, but we tried, Jo. You were hard to get to know. We always felt you disapproved of us.'

Jo sat up, shielding her eyes with her hand. 'Why on earth would you think that?'

'Well.' Nina rubbed the back of her neck. 'Because you thought we were superficial, or something. Because we have, you know . . .' She waved a hand to take in the pool. 'A different lifestyle. Like – Oliver mentioned that thing about Cressida's swimsuit.'

'What swimsuit?' Jo stared at her, uncomprehending, and then it clicked into place: one of their early visits to the chateau – eight years ago, maybe, nine? – and they'd all been out here, beside the pool, when Cressida had started complaining about some diamanté embellishment coming off her new swimming costume, and how she expected better for four hundred quid. Later, in their room, Jo had commented on it to Oliver. Four hundred pounds for a swimsuit! She hadn't even known that was possible. When only the week before she'd had a first-year boy come to her in tears because his single mother had lost her job and was insisting that her son abandon his course and start earning a wage so they didn't lose their home. Cressida's swimsuit could have wiped out that boy's overdraft, Jo had said, and Oliver had calmly pointed out that he understood, he too worked with people in desperate need, and yes, it was obscene, but she had to accept that his friends thought of

130

money differently, and they also gave away far more in real terms than anyone else, so it was not worth getting worked up about individual price tags. 'It's just a different world,' he'd said, and then apparently repeated her criticisms to the others at the first opportunity.

'So all this time you've thought I'm some kind of Puritan who believes everyone should walk around in fair trade sackcloth?' she said. She was not angry; more curious, that she could have so much to learn about Oliver, even now.

'Not exactly.' Nina looked uncomfortable. 'But – so often we'd invite you to parties or openings and then Oliver would turn up by himself and say you didn't feel well, or it wasn't your kind of thing, or you were seeing your own friends. After a while it was so obviously bullshit, we thought you just really didn't like hanging out with us. So, after he died, Cress and I figured you'd probably be relieved you didn't have to see us to be polite.'

Jo took a moment to digest this. 'Oliver said that?'

'I mean, he never said outright that you didn't want to see us, but the way he made excuses for you, it was implied.'

'No, that was never—' Jo felt the old weariness creeping up on her. 'Oliver had this thing about not leaving Hannah with babysitters, so I could only come out if his parents were free. He always assumed I'd stay home with her so he could go. After a while, it didn't seem worth arguing.'

She almost wanted to laugh at the idea that she had been busy with a separate social life of her own. It had been an unspoken assumption from the beginning that she would fit herself into Oliver's world, with little or no attempt on his part to accommodate hers, so that she had found herself gradually losing touch with her old friends over the course of their marriage. It was not that he explicitly stopped her from seeing them, just that his commitments made it so difficult for her to find a free weekend or evening that she feared her friends would lose patience with her last-minute cancellations. It had become easier not to bother.

'Huh.' Nina paused to process this. 'He could have told us that.'

'Yes. He could.'

'You know, Leo and I always thought you and Hannah were the best thing that happened to Oliver.'

'Really?' Jo could not hide her surprise.

'For sure. He was pretty cavalier with women before he met you. Kind of status-obsessed. You were different. Normal. Leo said you grounded him.'

'Oh.' Jo wasn't sure how to take this.

'Yeah, so.' Nina glanced in the direction of the house. 'Listen, I'm glad we talked. I should see where Leo's got to.' She stood and wrapped a floaty robe around her. 'What do you make of her?' she said, in a low voice, making clear the way her thoughts were tending.

'Storm?' Jo shrugged, but she kept her eyes fixed on the pool. 'She's just young. She doesn't think before she speaks.'

'OK, but – do you think she's dangerous?'

'*Dangerous*?' Was Nina testing her? Arlo had used the same word to Cressida. 'How do you mean?'

'Like . . .' Nina twisted her wedding ring and her gaze flicked again towards the house. 'Don't you think it's weird how she knows so much about us all?'

'Not that weird – you're all high profile, easy to google, and I suppose it's normal for Max to tell her about his friends.' But she understood Nina's misgivings; she remembered again Storm's frank discussion of Oliver's infidelities, her blunt questions about his death, and the same sense of unease came creeping back.

132

'I don't know,' Nina said, a dark note in her voice. 'I think she's after something.'

'Like what?' Jo half-expected her to say, *my husband*.

'You tell me. But she decided to come here without Max for a reason. Cress agrees, she doesn't trust her an inch. Look at the way she's schmoozed up to Leo. I'd say she's one of those girls that has to play up to male attention, but she's got you eating out of her hand too.'

'She hasn't,' Jo said, and looked away before Nina could read her face. But Nina was still looking towards the house, her thoughts following another track.

'You know, I have this bizarre feeling that I've seen her before somewhere. I just can't place it.'

'She could have been to the gallery. She knew your Turkish artist.'

'Yeah. Maybe.' She turned back to the children. 'You guys be good for Becca, OK? I'm just going to find Daddy, see if he wants a swim.'

Jo wondered if she should warn Nina about the gym, and immediately realised the best thing she could do was pretend she hadn't seen it. The twins yelped after their mother with pleas for Leo to hurry up, and when she had rounded the corner of the hedge, they turned their supplications on Jo.

'Come in and swim with us, Auntie Jo,' Grace called, holding on to the side and bouncing herself up and down.

Jo watched Becca towing Clio along in an inflatable duck, tickling her and murmuring nonsense while the baby giggled and splashed. She seemed to have eyes only for Clio; it was no wonder the twins were feeling neglected.

'In a minute,' Jo said, sitting carefully on the decking at the edge of the pool and letting her feet dangle in the water. 'Besides, you've got Becca to play with.'

133

The nanny raised her head at the sound of her name and padded over, with Clio in her duck trailing behind; Oscar pointedly swam away to the other side, followed by his sister.

'Did you have a word with your friend?' Becca said. 'About the' – she jerked her head towards the twins – 'horror stories.'

'Oh. Yes.' Jo had completely forgotten Becca's indignation over Storm's tales to the children. 'I'll remind her.'

'Good.' Becca flashed a glance back at the twins and gave Jo a sly look. 'So, what were you up to last night?'

'What do you mean?'

'I saw you out the window, you and her. On the back lawn, arm in arm, about two in the morning, laughing your heads off. It stank of spliff on the stairs when you came in.'

Jo took in the girl's calculating expression. She was quite pretty, in a wholesome, scrubbed kind of way, except that her eyes were on the small side, which gave the impression that she was sizing you up.

'We went for a walk,' she said, trying to keep her voice even. 'I couldn't sleep.'

Becca pushed the baby gently back and forth. 'Cressida's really uptight about drugs,' she said, her gaze on Clio. She'd adopted a regretful tone, as if she were forced to have this distasteful conversation for Jo's own good. 'Even more than she is about skinny-dipping. And she's got quite a temper on her. But you probably know that. Don't worry, I haven't said anything,' she added.

The implication was clear. Jo braced herself wearily for some crude attempt at coercion. 'But you might, is that it?'

Becca cut a quick glance at her. 'You know yesterday evening, when I saw you on the landing . . .?'

'Outside Arlo and Cressida's room, you mean?'

'I wasn't in their room, I was getting the kids a glass of water, I told you. But yeah.'

Jo remembered what Storm had said about finding Becca in Arlo's office earlier the same day, and her theory about the nanny's reason for being there. Perhaps she was not so far off the mark after all.

'I heard a door slam on that landing,' she said. 'You were crying.'

'No, I wasn't. I get allergies.'

'In October?'

Clio splashed her fat little hands in the water and gasped with delight when the drops hit her in the face. Becca watched her, considering. 'How about, you don't say anything to anyone about what you saw, and neither will I?'

'You told Cressida about seeing Storm in the village.'

'She was in a car with some random French lad, I thought it was dodgy.'

'*In* the car? She said she was asking for a light.'

'Yeah, right. Don't know why she'd have to get into the passenger seat to do that. Unless she was buying something off him.' Becca cocked a knowing eyebrow.

Or selling, Jo thought. 'Fine.' She pulled her feet out of the water. 'You mind your business, I'll mind mine.'

'And tell *her*,' Becca added, as Jo stood. 'Storm. Same goes for her. I saw her out there the night before too, with Lucas. She'd be out on her arse if Cressida knew about that.'

'You should join MI5 with your surveillance skills,' Jo said pointedly, settling back on her lounger. She picked up Nina's discarded *Vogue* to make clear the conversation was over, but her eyes skittered over the pictures, unable to focus. She couldn't really care less if Arlo had something going on with the nanny, unlikely as it seemed, but it rankled

135

that Becca thought she was that easy to manipulate. She would have liked to tell her to grow up, but Becca was sharp enough to be sure of her bargaining power; there was no question that Jo would be *persona non grata* if Cressida knew about her night-time expedition with Storm. Worse, she had a nasty suspicion that Cressida, who remained on good terms with Oliver's parents, would find a way to drop hints to them about drugs out of faux-concern, and she could not afford to lose their trust or have them doubt her mental state and her fitness as a mother. Stupid to imagine she and Storm could run around the grounds at night without being seen. She had to hope Becca didn't know about the brandy.

A squeal from Grace interrupted her thoughts.

'Storm!'

Jo glanced up to see Storm loping down the steps between the box hedges, waving at the children, still dressed in her workout gear: shorts and a loose vest over a sports bra, hair tied back in a ponytail that bounced as she moved, a sheen of sweat glazing her skin.

'Did they not come for you in the night, the white women?' Storm called to the twins, circling the pool to their side and kneeling on the decking to lean in and splash them. They shrieked and giggled, jostling one another for her attention. 'I was sure they'd have stolen at least one of you.'

'I would fight them,' Oscar declared, thumping the surface of the water so that a spout rushed up and hit Storm in the face; she roared and made as if to dive in after him, and the children paddled backwards, hysterical with laughter.

'Fuck's sake,' Becca muttered audibly, giving Jo a dark look.

Storm pushed herself upright and jogged round the pool to throw herself down on the bed next to Jo.

'You look well,' she said, wiping her forehead with the hem of her vest. 'Rested. Last night did you good, eh?' She winked.

Jo smiled, embarrassed. 'I think so. I didn't quite feel up to the gym this morning, though.' She gestured to Storm's trainers.

'Thought I'd better do something or I'm going back fat as a house with all Marcel's food. Have you seen the kitchen? Looks like they're feeding the five thousand.'

'Let's hope Max makes it,' Jo said, leaving a pause for Storm to offer an update on Max's progress, but she didn't.

'Listen' – she leaned in and lowered her voice, though over her shoulder Jo could see Becca watching them intently. 'We've got a mission. I need you to come to Saint-Émilion with me.'

'What for?'

'Marcel spotted the brandy missing. He thought it was Lucas, so I had to fess up. But Marcel's pissed off – he says Arlo will notice sooner or later, he's quite OCD when it comes to his bottles, so we need to replace it. He's given me his car keys and told me where to go, there's only this one place that sells it, but I thought it would look less suspicious if we went together. I'll get Cressida an anniversary present while we're at it, that should stop her moaning for a bit. You up for a road trip?'

'Uh – sure, but . . .' Jo swallowed. She was perturbed by the use of 'we'; she had not banked on paying out two hundred pounds for a bottle of stolen brandy. Storm read her expression and laid a hand on her arm.

'Don't worry about the money, I've got that. Just come with me so her ladyship doesn't start accusing me of meeting strange men again. Anyway, it'll be fun.' When Jo continued to look hesitant, she cuffed her lightly on the shoulder. 'What else are you going to do all day – lie here with Wednesday Addams over there looking daggers at you?' She jerked her head towards the pool, and Jo stifled a laugh; there was more than a hint of Wednesday in Becca's broad forehead and baleful stare.

'She wants you to stop telling the children stories about white women kidnapping them,' she whispered. 'It's insensitive.'

Storm stared at her, open-mouthed, then let out that pleasing rough-edged guffaw and fell back on the lounger, clutching her stomach, convulsed with laughter.

'Oh my God, I never thought of that. The *dames blanches*, it's a French folk-tale, a version of the women in white, you know? It's centuries old, they have it all over France. They're wraiths who lurk at crossing places – bridges or ravines, rivers, the like. They hold out their hand to strangers for a dance. If you stop and dance with them for a while, they let you pass. But if you reject them, they throw you into the ravine or drown you.' She shook her head, still laughing, and began to unlace her trainers. 'In some versions, they're women who've been abused and mistreated in life, so they come back for revenge, to lure men to their deaths. It's very moral really. Is that why Wednesday's being so arsey with me, she thinks I'm a massive racist?'

'It's not exactly a fun story for children,' Jo said.

Storm shrugged, and stood to pull off her vest top. 'You should hear the stuff my grandmother filled my head with when I was their age. So you'll come with me later?'

'OK.'

'Grand.' Storm gave her a thumbs up, slid down her shorts and ran to the poolside in her bra and pants, leapt in the air and bombed into the water, sending a wave crashing over the side and the children into paroxysms of delight. Jo brushed droplets of water from the glossy bodies of the magazine models and thought about women mistreated in life, seeking revenge from beyond the grave. Such a commonplace, age-old story that myths had grown up around it, presumably to give women some faint hope of justice, even if they never lived to see it.

14

Marcel's car was an Audi convertible; Storm drove it fast along the narrow lanes with the top down and the radio blasting French bubblegum pop. The road north unrolled through acres of vineyards to either side, dotted with clusters of cottages and farm buildings in the region's pale blond stone, neat rows of vines fanning away to low wooded hills, tinged red and gold against the blue sky. Jo tilted her head back against the passenger seat to feel the sun on her face and the breeze raking through her hair, and laughed aloud. She caught Storm looking at her sidelong with a wide grin.

'Penny for them?'

It was something her mother used to say; the old-fashioned phrase was oddly endearing. Jo found herself blushing; she could hardly tell Storm that she had been imagining they were a couple of friends on holiday together, carefree, at liberty to go anywhere with the music loud and the wind in their hair. For the first time in a year, she had remembered that she was still young.

'I was thinking how we should just keep driving,' she said,

holding a hand out to feel the air rushing between her fingers. 'All the way to St Tropez and keep going to the sea.'

'What, like Thelma and Louise?' Storm laughed.

'Not *exactly* like that, no.'

'Fair play to them, Thelma and Louise. That's what I'd do, if I was ever cornered. One last blaze of glory, or the banality of facing the music – it's no choice, is it? I hate to tell you this, Jo, but we're going the exact wrong direction for the sea. Plus I think Marcel might have something to say if his car doesn't come back. I like your thinking, though. You know what you look like?' She drove one-handed, the other resting easily on the gear stick. 'You look like your whole body has *unclenched*. When I first saw you, you were all tense and knotted up. Now you look ten years younger.'

Jo smiled, still self-conscious. 'I thought I'd feel like shit this morning, but I actually feel fine. Maybe your grandmother's magic does work.'

'Told you. Plus everything we had last night was pure as the driven snow. They don't put any additive crap in four-hundred-quid brandy. That's what gives you the hangovers. It's not the alcohol.'

Jo was not convinced by the science of this, but she didn't argue. 'I don't think I'd better get used to drinking that,' she said, leaning her elbow on the door and gazing out across the landscape. 'Not if I have to pay for it.'

'Don't worry about that,' Storm said, slowing for a mini-roundabout, 'I've got it.' Then, off Jo's look – 'What? I'm not a *thief*, Jo. I have no problem taking what's fair, but not if it means Marcel or Lucas get in trouble. You were right, we shouldn't have smashed the bottle. It was worth it though, eh?'

Jo glanced at her, unsure how to respond. Storm's expression was hidden behind mirrored aviator sunglasses. What did she mean by *fair*? Stealing from your hosts could be many things, but fair was a stretch, unless Storm thought of herself as some kind of class warrior, taking down the one per cent one bottle at a time.

'Go on, ask me,' Storm said after a while. 'I know you're dying to. I don't mind.'

'Ask what?'

'You want to know where I got the money.'

Jo felt the heat surge to her face; she could only assume Storm was talking about the rolls of cash under her bed, and that she somehow knew Jo had been through her room.

'I don't – I mean, it's none of my—'

'You want to know how come I have money? I'll tell you.' She reached over and turned the radio down. 'My grand-mother died two years ago, when I was nineteen. She left me her house. It was worth a fair bit.'

'Oh.' Jo didn't know what else to say. They passed through a small town with an abandoned petrol station and a cluster of warehouses and builders' yards on the outskirts.

'Yeah, I was more surprised than anyone,' Storm said, keeping her eyes on the road. 'I ran away from home when I was fifteen, I hadn't spoken to her since. It wasn't even her house, really – it belonged to her second husband, my step-grandad, he'd inherited it. He'd no kids of his own, so I thought there'd be a gazillion cousins on his side fighting over it. But it turned out he'd put it in her name and she left it to me. It was a big old house right on the bay, with land. They did it up all fancy, it's a boutique hotel now.'

'You sold it?'

'Yup. And with the money I bought a flat in Dalkey which I rent to a lovely hipster couple. And that's what puts me through uni and buys me nice clothes. Max isn't paying me to fuck him.'

142

'Storm, I never thought—'

'Cressida did. I know she did. Nina too, probably. And I bet you've wondered. So, as long as we're clear?'

Jo nodded, chastened. None of this explained why Storm had four thousand euros in cash under her bed, though Jo was glad she hadn't blundered in and mentioned it.

'I see their judgy faces, and it pisses me off. Women who've never had to want for anything in their lives. Here, this is us.'

She swung right at the roundabout and the road narrowed between houses, rising up a gentle slope to the outskirts of the town. Storm parked in a shady bay outside a café and put the roof up.

'Coffee first, right?' She set off up the rise without waiting for an answer; Jo quickened her pace to keep up with her long-legged stride. Storm hooked her arm through Jo's and led her to the square in front of the church. They took a seat under the bright awnings of the little café opposite the facade and ordered coffees. Storm, preoccupied with her phone, did not seem inclined to talk, so Jo leaned back and watched passers-by crossing the square; old women with stiff hips, small dogs and baskets of shopping; tourists in hiking boots, crouching to photograph the bell tower; middle-aged Frenchmen in open-necked shirts, with comfortable bellies and expensive shoes, who greeted one another with the ease of people who own the place. She had sat here with Oliver, she remembered; he had made her laugh by inventing a story in which every person who passed was a character in a local murder mystery. Even now, recalling that conversation felt like pressing on a bruise.

'Everything OK?' Storm asked, looking up, as the coffees arrived. Jo nodded.

'I was just thinking about Oliver. We were really happy here once. I keep wondering how we lost that.'

143

'Because they all try at the beginning.' Storm glanced down at her screen. 'You never did tell me what she said.'

'Who?'

'The woman on the phone. John W.'

Jo looked away, across the square. 'Doesn't matter. It was something that only someone who was sleeping with Oliver would have known.'

'Ah. He liked the old dirty talk, eh?'

Jo made a non-committal noise and Storm nodded, with an air of understanding. She pulled her crumpled pack of cigarettes from the pocket of her shorts and shook one out before pushing them across the table.

'Did you really run away from home at fifteen?' Jo asked, spinning the pack under her forefinger without taking one. 'Where did you go?'

'Dublin first. Then London.' Storm blew out a stream of smoke and turned her gaze away to the church.

'How did you manage?'

Her eyes slid slowly back to Jo. 'How'd you think? Same as any pretty girl who needs to get by. I found an older man who said he'd take care of me. Learned the hard way they don't always mean what they say, and then I was stuck there with no money of my own and too proud to go home and admit I'd been wrong. Which was stupid, I realise now, but I was young. You always think there'll be time to sort things out, until there isn't.'

'So you never saw your grandmother again?' Jo wanted to smile, the way Storm talked about being young as if it was years ago. 'Didn't she call the police when you ran off?'

'I sent her postcards to let her know I was all right. I knew she wouldn't come after me. She blamed herself.'

'Why?'

She took a long drag, considering. 'I went a bit wild when

144

I was young. Like, from when I was barely in my teens. Booze and bad boys, bit of drugs, whatever I could get my hands on. Run-ins with the police, pregnancy scare – you name it. My grandmother didn't know what to do with me. She started talking about getting me put in care, you know? I think about it now, and there's no way she would have done it, because everything would have come out. She just wanted to frighten me. It worked too well, because I saw a chance to get away and I took it.'

'What would have come out?'

'Oh.' She gave a small, private laugh and stubbed the butt hard in the ashtray. 'Well, you won't credit this, Jo, but it was still pretty conservative where I grew up, even at the end of the Nineties. My grandmother was forty-five when I was born, her husband was still alive. They registered me as theirs. God knows how they got away with it, but they did. My grandmother never went to the doctor from one year to the next, she was strong as a horse, so I suppose it was just about plausible that she could turn up one day with a late baby she'd popped out at home. They did it to spare my mother and me the shame, but people aren't thick, especially in small towns. I wasn't the first kid to grow up with a much older "sister". Things were said in my hearing before I even understood what they meant.'

'That's awful. What about your father?'

'He was not around.' This was said with the finality of a slammed door.

'When did you find out? I mean, that your grandmother wasn't your mother?'

'I was twelve when she told me the whole story.' She picked up her phone and turned it over between her hands. 'I was walking home from school one day. This group of lads outside the pub, they were all looking at my tits and

145

making comments. I kept going with my eyes down, trying to pretend I couldn't hear. And this old woman from the village, she must have been in her eighties – she watched it happen, and as I walked by her she said to me, "Fifty years ago they'd have put you in the laundries, same as they would your mother, keep girls like you from making trouble." And I couldn't get my head around that. I was a child, doing nothing except having a body, what trouble was I making? But the way she saw it, the fault was mine, not theirs.'

'What laundries?'

'You know – the Magdalene laundries.' When Jo looked blank, she clicked her tongue, impatient. 'These places they had in Ireland back in the day for single mothers and fallen women and bold girls who were in danger of tempting men by being too sexy. She was basically saying my mother had been a slut and I was heading the same way. Nothing more brutal than the judgement of women, eh. So I asked my grandmother, who I thought at the time was my mother, what this woman had meant, and she told me the whole story. Well, not the whole story, but enough.' She set the phone down and picked at the edge of her cigarette packet with a fingernail. 'I'd always known I had a dead sister, and then I found out she was actually a dead mother. It was a lot to deal with.'

'Didn't your grandmother try her healing rituals?'

'I didn't give her the chance. I was having none of it – I was too wrapped up in raging at her for lying to me. It's a shitty age for girls at the best of times, isn't it? You've got a daughter, you must have thought about it. One minute you're a kid wheeling around on your bike, then you wake up with these fucking things' – she grabbed her breasts with both hands – 'and suddenly grown men are shouting out of vans that they'd fuck you, and boys at school are pushing you up against the lockers to touch you, and you realise your body will never belong solely to you again, it's there to be rated and commented on and judged for what it makes other people think. Do you want another coffee?' She seemed unusually jittery; without waiting for an answer, she hailed the waiter and held up two fingers. 'So listen – what am I going to get the people who've got everything for an anniversary present?'

The abrupt change of subject was enough of a cue for Jo not to press any further, though she was bursting with questions: how did a teenage runaway get herself to a top university? With that and the sudden inheritance of a valuable house, Storm's life story had taken on aspects of a fairy tale; there was a small pinch of doubt at the back of Jo's mind that left her wondering how much of it was actually true.

'You could do with giving Cressida some of what we were smoking last night,' she said, lowering her voice.

'Ha! Fuck, yeah. Can you imagine? If ever someone needed to chill out. But I don't think that was her drug of choice. She preferred something a little more stimulating.'

Jo smiled. 'She doesn't like to talk about those days.'

'I'm not surprised. Doesn't really fit with the *brand*, does it? And Cressida's all about looking after the Connaught brand. You know they got an injunction a few years ago to stop one of the tabloids publishing teenage photos of her flashing her knickers as she fell out of Annabel's? She was quite the *It* girl back in the day, by all accounts.'

'That was long before I met her.'

'Oh yeah. Before she married Arlo and straightened out. Did you know her family sent her off to rehab in the States to get her out of the way? And when she came back, the first thing she did was become a nice respectable wife.'

She leaned back in her chair, amused, one hand resting lightly on her phone. Jo had known the bare details of what Cressida glancingly referred to as her 'misspent youth', but rarely given it much thought; she presumed that was just what girls like Cressida did: dabble in rebellion for a few years until their parents bailed them out. Now she recalled Nina's remark about Storm's unusual level of interest in their pasts.

'What are you saying?'

'Ah, nothing. Only – I don't totally buy that marriage, do you? Feels like a performance to me.' When Jo didn't answer, Storm waved a hand. 'Sorry – not fair of me to ask you that, they're your friends.'

'I think,' Jo said, 'all marriages can seem like that from the outside.'

'Fair point. I just don't see any sex there, do you know what I mean?'

'I haven't considered it,' Jo said, a little primly.

Storm tilted her head and laughed. 'Really? It's the first thing I notice when I look at a couple. You can always tell. Like, Leo and Nina, they're still fucking, even if he's . . .' She stopped to take a drag of her cigarette.

'If he's what?'

'Nothing. What about you and Oliver? Was the sex good, even when he was seeing this other woman?'

She asked as if this were the most normal conversation in the world. Jo shifted uncomfortably in her seat; she didn't want to discuss any of that with Storm in a market square. All the intimacy of the previous night, the joint and the campfire, now seemed like the stuff of adolescent sleepovers and she was embarrassed. More than that, she didn't want to revisit all the ways she had humiliated herself trying to win Oliver's attention back, long after she had realised that what excited Oliver was the illusion of something transgressive; he liked the idea of persuading a woman into doing things she wasn't entirely sure about. There was little thrill for him in someone offering it all on a plate, someone whose novelty value had long since expired. She had assumed this happened in all marriages, but she had nothing to compare it to; she never talked about her sex life with other women, partly out of loyalty and partly from shame.

She was spared from answering by the waiter arriving with the coffees; Storm flashed him a dazzling smile and he retreated a few feet away, his eyes glued to her. Storm's phone buzzed and she lurched for it with obvious urgency. Her face remained neutral as she read the message, but she pushed her chair back and stood, stretching her arms over her head in a show of nonchalance. Her linen shirt lifted and Jo glimpsed the edge of a money belt beneath the waistband of her denim shorts.

'Listen, Jo – I have to make a couple of phone calls. Just – personal stuff. Will you be all right having a little mooch for a while? Maybe you could check out the shops, see if there's some tat we can get them for tonight. I'll meet you back here in an hour, OK?'

Jo was taken aback at the sudden desertion.

'Was that Max?' she managed.

'What?' Storm glanced down at her phone in her hand. 'Oh – no. Just some business I have to deal with.' She picked up her cup and downed the espresso as if it were a shot, then fished in her pocket, drew out a crumpled twenty and dropped it on the table. 'That'll cover it. I'll see you later, yeah?' And with a brisk wave, she was striding up the hill, past the church, eyes on her screen, tapping out a message as she went.

Jo stirred her coffee as it grew lukewarm, to try and look

casual. Across the square, two old men in identical grey cardigans and baggy trousers started up a loud and amiable argument in a shop doorway. The air smelled of hot pastry and cigarettes. She had fondly supposed that Storm had asked her to come because she wanted Jo's company, because after last night they were friends; now she began to suspect that she had been used as a cover for something, and the sting of rejection curdled her earlier good mood. How would it take Storm an hour to make a couple of phone calls? The town was tiny, and consisted almost entirely of wine merchants; even for tourists it would be hard to fill the time. There was no escaping the sense that she had been banished, and had no choice but to wait for the appointed time; she realised she didn't even know Storm's number to message her.

Berating herself for not seeing the obvious, Jo pushed the cup away so abruptly the coffee sloshed over the table. Storm had come into Saint-Émilion not to replace the brandy or buy a present, but because she had arranged to meet someone. She had been waiting for a message. Possibly she was buying more drugs, but there was the matter of the bracelet, and the mystery of the four thousand euros. Before she even knew she had made a decision, Jo tucked the twenty under the edge of a saucer, grabbed her bag and headed off up the cobbled lane that Storm had taken.

15

The little town was a maze of winding streets fanning out from the old church, all identically narrow and cobbled, between buildings of weathered limestone garlanded with creepers, the shopfronts all painted in deep red, slate grey or racing green with gold lettering. Jo climbed the hill away from the square and reached a junction, where she havered; Storm clearly did not want to be observed, so if she had told Jo to mooch around the town, it was unlikely that she would be anywhere near the centre. Jo turned away from the shops, following the lane past cafés open to the street, where bored men in white aprons lounged in doorways, scanning for tourists. The gift shops began to thin out; there was no sign of Storm's bright coral shirt. Sweat trickled down her back and she wished she had brought water; the coffee had made her shaky and she began to feel like an idiot, wandering around in the heat after Storm, playing detective. She turned into the grounds of the ruined castle and climbed the steps to the viewpoint at the top. The ascent left her hot and dusty; when she reached the stone benches on the ridge above the tower, she sat looking out over the town, picture-perfect from here with the low sun striking gold off its stones. All the bright promise of the drive in seemed to have evaporated. She was mustering the energy to head back to the shops and turn her attention to choosing a present for Arlo and Cressida – always a thankless task – when she heard a woman's voice raised as if in protest over a man's from further down the street, and some familiar note in it caused her to jump to her feet.

She moved cautiously towards the sound. She had reached the edge of the town here, with only vineyards beyond; if Storm should see her, it would be hard to make it look like a coincidence. On her right was a derelict house with a forlorn *A Vendre* sign hanging lopsided from the gatepost. Its front garden formed a triangle in the fork of two roads and at its apex, straight ahead, was a curious garage that had been built out of the limestone cliff. Parked in front she saw a grey Renault van, and there was Storm, leaning with one hip against the bonnet, talking to a man. Jo ducked through the open gateway and crouched behind the garden wall of the empty house under the shadow of a pine tree.

She was not close enough to catch their conversation, though from the cadences she could tell it was in French. Nor could she see the man clearly; he was tall and broad-shouldered, dressed in a white T-shirt and loose jeans with what looked like oil smears on the leg, and a dark blue baseball cap pulled low. He stood with his feet planted apart and one hand in his back pocket, and his easy stance made Jo think he was young, though she couldn't see his face. But it was Storm's body language that caught her attention and made her lean around the tree for a closer look.

Her usual frank, shoulders-back manner had been replaced by a hunched posture, as if she were trying to make herself smaller; she looked up at the man with a hesitancy Jo had not seen before, seeming fearful of his reaction. As Jo watched, she saw Storm reach up and swipe at her eyes with the back of her hand, and realised with a delayed shock that the girl was crying. Her thoughts raced ahead to probable conclusions: this was the drug guy, he was bullying Storm, he was pressuring her for something, she was afraid of him. But as she stepped out from behind the tree, on the point of intervention, she saw the man reach out and touch Storm's shoulder with unexpected gentleness. Storm lifted her eyes to him, her smile brave and grateful, while he stroked the top of her arm tenderly with his thumb. Jo shifted back to her hiding place, uncertain. At a second glance, Storm did not appear threatened or fearful; she looked, if anything, beautiful and tragic, and the man – whoever he was – appeared to be comforting her. He had his phone out now, and was typing something fast, seemingly in response to what Storm was telling him. Storm smiled, brushing away the last traces of tears; as Jo watched, she reached up to kiss the man on each cheek in the usual French salutation. He squeezed her arm one last time, and watched her as she walked away down an alleyway opposite, before getting into the van. Jo glimpsed a beard and sunglasses as he turned his head. She remained crouching behind the wall, but on a sudden impulse, as she heard the engine revving, she grabbed her phone and poked her head up, half-hidden by the tree, to take a photo of the licence plate. Just in case, she told herself; something about the meeting she had witnessed seemed off, but she could not quite say how.

'You're very quiet, Jo,' Storm said, on the drive home. Jo was watching the vineyards flashing past, her head propped on her hand. The caffeine buzz had worn off, leaving her

153

with a headache that seemed a fitting price for the night before.

'Just tired.'

'Are you pissed off with me? For going off?'

'Of course not,' Jo said, though she hesitated a beat too long, and she knew Storm had caught it.

'Sorry. I thought you'd want a chance to get away from that lot and have some time on your own. At least we've got gifts, even if she hates them.'

After they reconvened in the main square, Storm had suggested a craft collective that sold work by local artisans, where they had bought a pair of impractical vases. Storm had not mentioned her mysterious assignation, and Jo had not asked, but she could find no trace of the distress she had witnessed less than half an hour earlier, during Storm's conversation with the grey van man.

'She'll approve of the fact that we have them,' Jo said. 'That's the best you can hope for with Cressida.'

Storm made a sucking noise through her teeth. 'If I was that rich,' she said, 'I'd just tell my friends to give a donation to charity and never bother with a present again. Wouldn't you? Like, what is the point of making people waste their money on something she'll never even look at?'

'She needs to feel that people value her, I suppose,' Jo said.

'It's disgusting. Lucas told me Arlo's bought her a bracelet that cost fifty grand or something insane, and she'll wear it three times and then put it in a safe with the rest. Can you imagine?'

She said it so casually that Jo whipped around to stare. Storm laughed at her expression.

'What? Why've you got a face like someone just gave you a wedgie?'

Jo stalled. If Storm had taken the bracelet, would she have mentioned that she knew about it?

'It's gone,' she said, finally.

'What has?'

'The bracelet. Arlo couldn't find it last night. Lucas is in an awful state. He's terrified that—' She stopped, aware of the way Storm was looking at her. She wanted to tell her to keep her eyes on the road.

After a pause, Storm turned her gaze pointedly ahead and switched the radio off.

'He's terrified it was me,' she said. 'That's what you were going to say, isn't it? And he'll be in the shit because he was the one who told me.' She kept her voice level, but Jo saw her hands tighten around the wheel. 'I *knew* someone had been through my room. Was that Lucas? Has that little fucker been rummaging around in my underwear looking for stolen jewellery?'

'I'm sure he wouldn't—' she began, but Storm cut her off.

'And what do *you* think, Jo? Do you think I'm a thief?' When the silence stretched long enough to make the point, she let out a sharp bark of a laugh. 'Wow.' Then, after another beat: 'I thought we were friends.'

When it's useful to you, Jo wanted to say, but she bit it back.

'I barely know you,' she said, instead. 'I mean – no, I didn't really think you'd take it, but Lucas said he told you on the first night, and no one else knew about it, so . . .' She held out her hands in a show of helplessness. 'Then when you took the brandy, I thought maybe you didn't have a problem stealing from the rich.'

'What, like fucking Robin Hood?' Storm let out a ragged laugh. 'Did you think I was going to sell the bracelet and give the money to the poor?' She shook her head in disbelief.

155

'I didn't think anyone would notice the brandy, is the truth. Didn't like to think of it going to waste. And now I've replaced it, for fuck's sake.'

'I know – when I saw that you wouldn't let Marcel or Lucas get into trouble over the brandy, I didn't think it was likely that you'd let anyone take the blame for the bracelet.'

'Well, that's big of you, Jo. Appreciate the vote of confidence.' She set her jaw and they drove on in silence. Afternoon light slanted golden over the vineyards, illuminating the water towers on the horizon. Jo couldn't think of anything useful to say; the accusation was out there, and hung in the air between them.

'Apart from the obvious,' Storm said, after a while, 'it's just insulting. Like, how stupid would someone have to be to take a bracelet worth that much? It would be traced in an instant. What do you imagine I would do with it – try and fence it to some guy in the village café? The idea that you'd think I was that thick is almost more offensive than calling me a thief.'

'Becca mentioned that man in the grey van, so—' She stopped, realising her mistake. She could feel Storm looking at her.

'Car. Becca said a white car. Where d'you get a grey van from?'

'I must have got mixed up.'

'Huh. I told you what that was about. I was picking up the stuff you've been so happy to partake in.' When Jo didn't respond, she banged the side of her fist against the door. 'How would you think I'd have the contacts to get away with that? Do you think I'm some kind of international criminal mastermind?'

'No,' Jo said, pressing herself back in the seat unhappily

156

as Storm took a corner too fast. 'But if it doesn't turn up by tonight, Arlo will get the police in.'

'Fuck,' Storm said. 'Well, that can't happen.' She appeared to be talking half to herself. Before Jo could ask what she meant, she turned sharply to face Jo. 'You know, I'm not the one who's in and out of Arlo's bedroom when no one's looking.'

It took a moment for Jo to catch up. 'You mean Becca?'

'Why not? I don't imagine she's planning on keeping it, or selling it, or anything serious. But think about it – if she's got something going on with Arlo, it might suit her to sow a bit of strife. If Cressida reckons Arlo didn't get her a gift, she'll be pissed off, it'll wreck her special night, maybe force those cracks in the marriage a bit wider.'

'I can't see Becca doing something like that without thinking it through. What would she hope to gain if the police turn up?' Even if Becca was angry about leaving the Connaughts, she would still need references for her next job; surely she could not afford to have her employers suspect her of theft.

'I don't know. We just have to make sure no one brings the police into it.' Storm's knuckles had turned white as she gripped the wheel. Jo presumed her aversion to the police was on account of the large amount of drugs in her possession, but there was also the question of the cash under the bed. The difficulty was that Jo had no idea if Storm was lying to her; she had enough secrets to make everything on the surface appear doubtful.

Storm glanced at the car clock. 'We should be back by five. What time do the kids have their tea?'

'About then, I think, or five-thirty. Why?' Cressida maintained a Victorian regime where the children ate early with the nanny so the adults didn't have to be bothered by them at dinner. It had been another argument against bringing Hannah; she'd have been furious at being consigned to teatime with the little ones.

'Right. When Becca's in the kitchen with the kids, I'm going up to search her room. You can help me if you want.' This last was thrown out casually, but Jo heard the edge in it. Storm was offering her a way to atone for thinking the worst.

'Wouldn't it be more discreet if there was just one of us?'

'Yeah, but if that bracelet's in her room, the first thing she'll say is that I planted it there to get her back for spying on me yesterday,' Storm said. 'I want a witness on my side. Plus, I'd quite like to put your mind at rest about me. There's still a kernel of doubt, isn't there, Jo? If I say I found it under her bed, there's going to be a little voice in the back of your head going, "Did she, though?"'

Jo shifted in her seat. It troubled her that Storm appeared to be able to read her so easily. 'I don't think Becca likes me any better than she likes you,' she said. 'If we do find it, she'll say we both cooked up a plan to accuse her.'

'Yeah, but Cressida won't believe that of you. Whereas we know what she thinks of me. Anyway, we don't have to accuse anyone. We find it in her room, we slip it back to Lucas, Arlo gives it to Cressida tonight, Becca won't dare say a word because she'll know someone knows.'

Jo was not convinced it would all go so smoothly, even if Storm's version of events were proved true, but she nodded unhappily as they approached the village.

'Hey, you want to see something else?' Storm said, more brightly, after they had passed through the village in silence. Jo turned and saw that she was grinning. 'Get my phone out of my bag, I'll show you.'

Jo twisted to reach for Storm's canvas satchel on the backseat and held it open towards her.

'You get it, I'm driving,' she said. Jo rummaged in the bag; beneath the rectangular box containing the replacement brandy, she found a hairbrush, a small leather wallet and a lip balm. 'Inside pocket,' Storm said, and Jo pulled out an old model of iPhone. She could see from the screen that there were three missed calls from Max. Storm took the phone from her, unlocked it one-handed, found what she was looking for, her eyes flicking between the screen and the road, and handed it back to Jo.

'Check that out.'

It was a text from Leo.

Enjoyed our chat this morning, would love to talk more about it. Let's have that dinner when we're back in London and see if we can find an arrangement that works for both of us x

Jo looked up at Storm, who waggled an eyebrow triumphantly.

'Is that about the show?'

'Supposedly.' She snorted. 'This is sleazy though, right?'

'Depends how you read it, I guess.'

'Ah, come on, Jo. He followed me into the gym this morning. Started all this again about how I had the right look for this character he had in mind, did I want to come and screen test for him, ended up suggesting we have dinner and discuss it. Wonder what that audition would involve, eh?'

'So you gave him your number.' Jo couldn't keep a sceptical note from her voice; she recalled the scene in the gym, Leo's hands on her hips, Storm smiling up at him wide-eyed, pressing herself against him as she squatted.

'I wanted to get something in writing.'

'Why?'

Storm gave her an exasperated look. She reached out and jabbed a finger at the phone in Jo's hand. 'He's basically propositioning me, on a weekend away with his wife and my boyfriend. Look at that kiss there, at the end.'

'Lots of people put kisses without thinking,' Jo said. 'I've done it on work emails by mistake. I don't think this is conclusive evidence of harassment. He could easily argue that you've misread it.'

'What, misread an invitation to dinner? That bit about working out an arrangement – what do you think that means?'

'The dinner is a bit . . .' Jo conceded. 'But he'd just say that's how he does business. You must have given him the impression you'd be interested, for him to have sent that. Especially giving him your number.'

'Oh, so it's my fault? I've encouraged him? Are you serious?' Storm bristled at her like a dog with its hackles up. 'He's got a rep for this sort of thing, you know,' she continued, slowing as they reached a junction.

'Leo has?' Jo was taken aback. 'I always thought he was—'

'Such a great family guy? I know, he makes sure everyone thinks that. I'll tell you a story. This girl I know in London, Sooz, she's an actor. About a year and a half ago she was in a play, a two-hander, one of those little fringe theatres above a pub. The guy she's in it with, they have the same agent, friend of Leo's, and the agent invites Leo one night, talent-spotting. They all have a drink together after, everyone gets along great. A couple of days later, Leo calls Sooz directly, says he's interested in talking about a screen test for his show, wants to arrange a meeting. So she's thrilled, naturally – doesn't stop to think whether it's odd that he wants to meet in a bar or that he's got her personal number, she thinks that's just how it's done. Anyway, they meet, he's asking her about herself, telling her all about the show, this part he has in mind for her, more or less sets a date for an audition, it all seems good, and then suddenly, after the second drink, Leo leans in and he asks her if she'd be prepared to do a nude scene, if it was in the script.'

'Ah.'

'Yeah. She doesn't want to wreck her chances, she wants him to think she's a pro, so she says that wouldn't be a problem. And he says, like he thinks this is really cute, I don't imagine it would be with a body like yours. He tells her it's been almost impossible to concentrate on a word she's been saying because she's so gorgeous.'

'OK. I mean – that's unprofessional, but—'

'It was a come-on. It was an invitation to respond.'

'Maybe he just has a very dated view of what's flattering. I'm not sure you could build a court case on it.'

'Wait, it gets better. So she's panicking, doesn't want to offend him because she really wants the show, right, so she laughs it off, pretends she thought he was kidding, makes up some shit about having to get home to her boyfriend. He goes very frosty. They shake hands, she says again how nice it was to meet him, how much she's looking forward to the screen test. She never heard another word about the show. She got her agent to chase up and he told her they'd decided she wasn't right for it.'

'Oh. That's—'

'I know. And the real kicker is that the guy she was in the play with – he got an audition. A proper formal approach, through the agent, no meeting privately in bars, and he ended up with a small part.'

'Did your friend complain?'

Storm let out an incredulous laugh. 'To who? She's just out of drama school. The only thing that would happen is she gets a reputation in a very small industry for being difficult, not someone you want to work with. Her career would be screwed – it wouldn't touch him. And she had no proof that he was hitting on her, only her instinct. She even started second-guessing herself after. Like – maybe I over-reacted, it was just a compliment, if only I'd been a bit less uptight, flirted back, maybe I'd have that job now. She ended up blaming *herself*, for fuck's sake. And that's not the only story like that. Some of them are a lot worse. Now here he is, at it again' – she pointed to the phone in Jo's hand – 'with his best friend's girlfriend.'

Jo looked down at the screen, revising the scene in the gym. So it had been a deliberate honeytrap.

'Are you going to say something to Max?'

'Haven't decided yet. What do you think Nina would do if she saw that text?'

'Truthfully?' Jo squinted into the low sun as they turned on to the one-track road towards the chateau. 'I think she'd say you'd misunderstood.'

'That's what I thought. She'd have to exonerate him, for the sake of her dignity. And Max would brush it off too – they always defend each other, those guys.'

Jo thought uncomfortably of Max knowing all along about Oliver's affairs. 'So what would be the point in telling him?'

Storm didn't reply until the chateau gates swung open and she eased the car around the curve in the drive.

'Maybe you're right,' she said as they pulled up in the car park behind the house. 'Maybe I should keep my mouth shut, let Leo get away with it as usual.'

Jo pressed the home button on Storm's phone to close the text; as she did so, her thumb accidentally brushed the call log icon and a list of recent numbers flashed up on the screen. She had time to see that there were two missed calls from

Max that morning, but what caught her eye was a French number, called at 12.14 a.m. That was when she had seen Storm out of the window, on the back lawn; Jo had asked her if she'd been speaking to Max, and Storm had dodged the question. Jo couldn't remember if it was the same number she'd seen written in Storm's notebook, but she wondered if it was connected with the man in the van.

Storm switched off the engine and held her hand out for the phone; Jo fumbled to close the screen, but the quick glance Storm gave her suggested her sharp eyes had not missed what Jo had been looking at.

'I'd better get this bottle to Marcel without anyone seeing,' Storm said, reaching for her bag. 'I'll come fetch you when the kids are downstairs, OK, and we'll go sleuthing.'

Jo walked around to the courtyard with the crisp white bag from the boutique swinging from her wrist, and found Cressida in the entrance hall arranging photos on the occasional table by the stairs. Jo had the impression that she had been arranging them for quite some time so that she could happen to be there when they returned.

'Oh, Jo, you're back. How was your day?' Her eye slid to the bag. 'Ooh, intriguing.'

'Not for you to look at, I'm afraid,' Jo said, with a knowing twinkle, hoping that this exchange would be short.

'Now I'm dying to find out.' Cressida arched an eyebrow. 'I love that shop,' she added, 'all those clever little pieces,' which was her way of telling Jo she knew the price of every-thing in it and would already have bought it if she'd wanted it. 'Listen – about tonight. We're going to eat a bit later, dinner at nine, hope that's OK. Drinks from eight in the courtyard. Smart casual.'

'Because of Max coming?' Jo asked.

Cressida pulled at a strand of hair behind her ear. 'Partly Max, yes. But also we've got a guest of honour this evening. A last-minute surprise.' Her smile was so stretched and her tone so breezy that it was immediately clear that this was neither a surprise nor her choice.

'Sounds exciting,' Jo said.

'Well – it is, rather. It's the French Minister of State for Technology and Digital something-or-other.' She leaned in, as if sharing official secrets. 'Obviously don't repeat this, but Arlo's company wants to open a research lab in Paris, as a European hub. He's been planning it for a while, but these things are always delicate, huge amount of red tape in France, especially now. Arlo would like to move things along and there's a bit of resistance at the top, so this guy would be a useful ally, he's very keen on Arlo's work. And they have a house in the Dordogne, so Arlo thought it made sense if they dropped in for a meal on their way, just a social visit. Not the occasion I'd have chosen, but here we are. But it does rather mean we'll all have to be on our best behaviour.' She said this with her extra-bright laugh, but there was no mistaking her expression.

'I'll try not to get drunk and dance naked on the table,' Jo said.

'I was thinking more of our friend Storm.' She glanced past Jo. 'I don't know how to broach this with her, but it's really important we don't have any scenes at dinner like we did last night. But I have a feeling that if I say so, it's more likely to make her provocative, don't you think?'

Jo pictured Storm standing up to denounce Leo as the main course was served.

'I don't think she'd appreciate being told how to behave, no.'

'No. And in an ideal world one wouldn't have to tell

164

someone of her age not to act up,' Cressida said drily. 'If Max were here, I'd ask him, but we can't expect him until ten at the earliest, and that's if he makes his flight. Maybe you could ask her to dress more appropriately too. She'll listen to you.'

'I don't know about that,' Jo said. 'I don't really think it's for me to tell her what to wear. Can't you explain that there's a dress code?'

Cressida nudged one of the silver-framed photos a millimetre to the left with the tip of a forefinger. 'Between you and me, Jo, I'm bloody furious with Arlo. The whole point of doing a weekend away with old friends was precisely so we could relax and not have to perform for anyone with multimillion-euro deals riding on the outcome. He sprung this on me the morning we came out – it's lucky Marcel always over-caters. Arlo says it's too good an opportunity to miss. But with things the way they are – Lucas has been in an impossible mood all day, the nanny's being bolshie, and Storm clearly enjoys winding people up – I'm going to be on a hair-trigger all night waiting for one of them to kick off.' She sighed, and moved the frame back. The wedding pictures on the side table had proliferated, presumably with contributions from Leo and Nina. A handful of photos showed the four boys on Arlo's stag weekend, an incongruous hunting party in the Highlands organised by Cressida's hearty brothers, who appeared not to have noticed that Arlo was not the outdoorsy type. Cressida followed Jo's gaze and smiled distractedly.

'Wasn't that ridiculous? Ollie and Max and Leo couldn't agree on what to do and time was running out, so my brothers just went ahead and booked a hunting trip. They couldn't conceive of a bunch of guys not wanting to shoot things. I think they all quite enjoyed it in the end, though. Max looks like he's been forced to do a cross-country run.'

'Not really Arlo's cup of tea, I'd have thought,' Jo said, looking at the picture of Oliver with the sun in his eyes, rifle cocked jauntily over one shoulder.

'Actually, my brother Raf said Arlo could have been an excellent shot if he'd practised, he had a natural eye. I've been meaning to ask you, Jo . . .' she lowered her voice, 'you didn't hear anything odd in the night, did you?'

Jo felt the colour burn across her cheeks to her ears. 'Like what?'

'Well, the nanny said she was up with Clio some time in the early hours and thought she heard people moving about downstairs.'

'Probably just someone getting a glass of water,' Jo said, wondering if this was a trick question.

'It wouldn't be the first time Lucas has got up in the night to raid the booze cabinet,' Cressida said darkly. 'I only wondered if you'd heard anything, you know, from Storm's room.'

'Not a peep,' Jo said, hoping Storm had managed to replace the brandy before Cressida decided to take an inventory. 'Maybe Becca imagined it?'

'Hm. Wouldn't put it past her. She does have an overactive imagination.' She flicked a tense glance at the stairs before giving herself a little shake. 'You know, it'll be a relief to see the back of her,' she muttered as she moved towards the kitchen, and it was unclear which of them she was referring to.

16

The second floor, once the domain of the chateau servants, was now given over to children. The colours were brighter up here, the floors softly carpeted, the furniture chubby and smooth-edged. At the top of the stairs was the room Hannah loved, painted eggshell blue with cabin-style bunk beds built into the wall; through the open door Jo could see the twins' clothes strewn over every surface. At the far end of the corridor was a green and pink bathroom, and to the right of the twins' room, a neat little white-painted nursery with a cot, changing table and basket of toys. The nursery had a comforting, powdery smell, of clean towels and baby lotion, that pierced her with nostalgia. She followed Storm into the nanny's room through the adjoining door.

On the bedside unit there was only a lamp, an almost-full plastic bottle of Orangina and a creased copy of *Glamour* magazine. Storm picked up the bottle, unscrewed the lid, sniffed the contents and replaced it. Jo crouched and opened the door of the cabinet, feeling ashamed of herself, as she had when looking through Storm's room the day before.

Inside she found a washbag with a design of pink lipstick prints. She poked it open with the tip of a fingernail and found a blue plastic inhaler and six condoms in gold foil tucked in the back compartment.

'Looks like you might be right,' she said, holding one aloft. Storm raised an eyebrow, delighted.

'Well I never. No other reason she'd need those on a family vacation, is there – who else would she be doing? Poor Cressida.' She opened the wardrobe and cast an eye over Becca's few clothes. 'I mean it, I feel sorry for her,' she said, glancing over her shoulder and catching Jo's expression. 'All that time and money and sheer bloody effort she puts into holding on to her looks, her and Nina, and none of it's keeping their husbands in their beds, is it?'

Jo replaced the condom and closed the cabinet. 'Maybe that's not why they do it.'

'I suppose not. God, I'm never pumping that shit into my face. I can't wait to get old. I'm going to embrace every wrinkle. I'll be one of those proper eccentric old women who wear cloaks.' She lifted a pile of T-shirts and ran her hand over the shelf.

'Easy for you to say. Looking like you do.'

Storm kept her back to Jo. 'Yeah. People always think that, and no one wants to hear any different. But believe me – whatever advantages Nature gave me in that department come at quite a cost. Women hate me.'

Jo opened her mouth to argue and realised it was probably true.

'You've seen a bit of it.' Storm gestured downstairs. 'Those two. That's what it's been like for me since I was twelve. I don't have female friends, not really. Women don't want to be around me – even if they like me, even when I haven't done a thing to give them cause, they think I'm competition.

They don't want their men paying me attention. It's pretty lonely, actually.' She crouched on her haunches and wrapped her arms around her knees, and for a moment Jo wanted to comfort her. 'But it's not something you can complain about, because it's what everyone thinks they want, isn't it? My mother was outstandingly beautiful, and it brought her nothing but grief.'

She fell silent and Jo wanted to ask – how, why? – but before she could speak, Storm continued:

'When I ran away from home, it was because me and another girl from school met these two fellas in a bar in Galway city – they'd come up from Dublin. We were all done up in our best gear and we told them we were nineteen. I don't know if they believed us, but they bought us drinks and one of them, he said he was a fashion photographer. He told me I could be a model and gave me his number. I know, right?' She offered a rueful grin. 'So the next time I fell out with my grandmother, I got on the bus and called him. Ended up living in his flat for a year. He took photos, all right. I was *fifteen*.' She shook her head, though whether her dismay was for her own naivety or the state of the world was hard to tell. She dropped her gaze to the floor again and examined the ends of her hair between her fingers; she looked suddenly very young. 'But you live and learn, I guess. You know, you're the first woman who's been straightforwardly nice to me in a long time, Jo, and I can't help wondering whether you'd be as friendly if you had your man here. That's no shade on you, it's just my experience.'

Jo didn't answer. Storm was right; if Oliver were here, she would have bristled at every word he spoke to her, every glance that slid her way, and done everything in her power to steer him out of Storm's orbit.

'We should go,' she said, instead.

169

'Hold your horses. Try the bed.' Storm leaned over her to press the pillows, her face lighting up as she found something. 'Ah-ha. Let's see what we've got here.' She looked triumphant, though what she drew out was not a jewellery box but a red iPhone in a white plastic Hello Kitty case. 'Why's she got this hidden away, I wonder?'

'Stop the children playing with it?'

The screen was cracked at the bottom; spiderweb lines spread out in a perfect fan shape across the lower half of the screen.

'Maybe. Let's think.' She tapped her thumbnail against her teeth. 'What's Arlo's birthday?'

'Seventeenth of September,' Jo replied automatically. She knew the whole group's birthdays by heart, including the children; she had assumed the responsibility of remembering and organising cards and flowers on behalf of her family, and it was one she had felt proud to discharge efficiently, long before everyone was sharing that article about women and emotional labour.

'Bingo!' Storm looked up and grinned. 'We're in.'

'How did you know?'

'Girls are predictable. It was either that or the date of their first ride, which would have been trickier – oh my Jesus. My *eyes*. Look at this.'

She had clicked through to the videos, where a fuzzy recording played what were unmistakably the sounds of amateur porn. Reluctantly, Jo looked over her shoulder at the screen and saw jerky limb movements in a dimly lit room, the occasional flash of white flesh. Storm scrolled to the next video, which showed Becca more clearly, propped face-forward on the end of a bed with her arse in the air, a man standing behind her, diligently pistoning in and out. The man was too tall for his face to show in the film, but he was wearing a grey T-shirt and had his jeans and boxers pulled down to his knees. You couldn't say for certain that it was Arlo, but the physique and the clothes certainly suggested it. As they watched, Becca's eyes flicked deliberately upwards to meet the camera. Jo looked quickly away; it felt disturbingly as if they'd made eye contact. Storm laughed aloud.

'Well, well. Girl's not as dumb as she looks.'

'What do you mean?'

'She's trying to stitch him up. Don't you see? This isn't them filming themselves for their sexy funtimes. She's stuck her phone on a shelf or something to record it without him knowing. I reckon she wants some leverage in case she needs to blackmail him. Trouble is, she can't get the angle right.'

Jo looked at the screen. Arlo's performance was exactly as she would have predicted; brisk and methodical, as if he were aiming to meet a series of targets. Becca's moans had a ring of artifice about them.

'Neither can he, by the looks of it,' she said.

Storm honked and clapped a hand over her mouth with a glance at the door. '*Joanna!* What are you like. You're right, he fucks like he's on a deadline. Rather her than me. Let's see what else we've got.' She swiped out of the videos and began to scroll through messages. 'No – there's nothing here from Arlo. Cressida WhatsApps her with instructions about the baby, but never him.'

'She might have him saved under a different name,' Jo said, with a touch of bitterness.

'Nope. She doesn't have that many contacts. Can't see any sexts or dirty pics. She's not sending horny messages on this number. Makes sense.' She looked up at Jo. 'He's been careful not to leave a trail that she could show. That's why she's trying to get something on film. Bit of insurance in case she gets dumped or sacked, I'd bet.' She opened the photos. 'Oh. OK, now this is weird.'

Jo peered at the screen. There were a handful of selfies: Becca pouting into a mirror with a full face of make-up, squeezing her arms together to push up her cleavage, but apart from those, all the photos were of baby Clio, rows and rows of them: on a swing, on a blanket, in the bath. Storm's thumb whizzed through the albums.

'There's got to be two hundred pictures of that baby here,' she said in a low voice. 'Don't you think that's creepy?'

'I don't know.'

'Seriously? If you found your daughter's babysitter had a phone full of pictures of her, that wouldn't trouble you at all?'

'Well, it's different. Becca lives in their house, she takes all her holidays with the family. I don't suppose she has much of a life outside of Clio.' But Storm was right; it was a little creepy. A thought occurred to her. 'I wonder if Cressida knows. About Becca and Arlo, I mean?' Was this why she had decided it was time for Becca to move on?

'Maybe we should tell her over dinner. Happy anniversary, we've looked through your nanny's phone, turns out she's obsessed with your baby and she's doing your husband. Let's throw that in during the toasts.' Storm grinned at Jo. 'It's like one of those movies where the stalker starts taking over the woman's life.'

Jo giggled, despite herself. 'Do you think she dresses up in Cressida's clothes when they're out?'

'She wouldn't get one arm in any of Cressida's gear. I bet she rolls around on their bed though. I bet she's got a secret diary where she's written "Mrs Becca Connaught" a hundred times to practise her signature.' Storm was trying to stop herself laughing too loudly. 'Maybe she's planning to bump

Cressida off so she can steal the husband and child as well as the jewellery.'

Jo stifled another fit of laughter. 'All right, Miss Marple. Anyway, the bracelet's not here.'

'No. That's a flaw in the theory. Have you got your phone on you?'

Jo's hand moved to her back pocket, a flare of anxiety displacing the giggles.

'Yes. Why?'

'Bring it here, I'm going to AirDrop those videos to you,' Storm said, scrolling back to find them.

'What? No.' Jo jumped back as if she could physically dodge them. 'I don't want that on my phone.'

'Well, I don't have time to go and get mine. You can forward them to me later and delete them.'

'But Becca will see you've sent them.'

'Not with AirDrop, it doesn't leave a record. That's why we need to drop it to yours quickly, it's right here. Mine's not set up for it.'

'But why do you want them?'

'Same reason she does. Insurance.'

'You want to blackmail Arlo? I'm not going to be part of that.'

'I'm not planning to blackmail anyone. But if they try accusing me of stealing, these might come in useful for bargaining. Come on, we don't have much time.'

Reluctantly, Jo found herself accepting a cache of unwanted sex tapes. Storm glanced over her shoulder to check they'd arrived.

'Thanks. We'll sort it out later. Let's get this put back, they'll be finishing their tea any minute. She must keep wipes around here somewhere?'

Jo nodded towards the connecting door to the nursery.

While Storm cleaned the phone, which seemed unnecessarily scrupulous (did she think Becca would be dusting for finger-prints?), Jo's eye was caught by the handle of a pink wheelie case sticking out from under the bed. For the second time that weekend, she found herself crouching to poke through someone else's luggage.

'Good thought,' Storm said, leaning over her to slip the phone back inside Becca's pillowcase. 'Anything?'

Jo shook her head. 'Empty.' She made to zip the case again, but Storm knelt beside her and slipped her hand in, feeling around the lining with a practised air, like a customs officer. She stopped very still and her eyes widened.

'There's something under here.' She pulled apart the Velcro fastenings that held the lining in place and drew out a slim oblong box, which she flipped open to reveal a white-gold bracelet studded with tiny stones, its glimmering coils ending in the head of a serpent with two emeralds for eyes. She looked up at Jo with a thin smile.

'I'll accept your apology any time.'

'Sorry. I—' Jo stared at the snake; for the briefest moment she wondered if there was some way Storm could have engineered this discovery. She couldn't make sense of it. 'I don't get it,' she said. 'Why would she – what good could it do her?'

Storm removed the bracelet from its satin cushion and slipped it over her wrist, twisting her arm to admire it from different angles.

'Fifty fucking grand,' she said, shaking her head. 'That's more than he paid for—'

She broke off, head lifted; they both heard the skittering of small feet on the stairs. Storm hastily replaced the bracelet and tucked the box into the back waistband of her shorts, under her loose shirt. Jo zipped up the case and shoved it under the bed; over the twins' excited chatter came Becca's voice telling them to choose a book. Storm grabbed Jo's arm and pulled her through to the baby's room just as Becca appeared in the doorway with Clio on her hip, and froze at the sight of them.

'Oh, hey,' Storm said pleasantly, 'just the woman. I got an almighty blister on my foot walking around today and Jo said there might be first aid supplies in the nursery. Do you have any plasters?'

Becca looked from her to Jo, her brow drawn low. 'Under the changing table,' she said, after a pause.

No one moved. Storm and Becca continued to face off; Jo, feeling someone ought to maintain the charade, opened the cupboard and rummaged for a Band Aid.

'Hey bubba,' Storm said, tickling the baby's cheek. Clio giggled and held her arms out to her. 'Can I have a wee cuddle?'

Becca grudgingly passed her the baby. Storm studied Clio's face intently while chubby little hands clutched at her hair.

'She's a dote, isn't she? Can you imagine being this little princess?' she murmured. It was not clear who she was addressing. 'When she's fifteen, she'll have tennis lessons and prom dresses, and holidays in the Maldives, and private tutors, and she'll never have to fuck some perv twice her age to keep a roof over her head, will you, chicken?' She plinked the baby on the nose with the tip of her finger and Clio let out a peal of bright laughter.

'All right, that's enough,' Becca said, grabbing the child from her arms. Clio clung on to Storm's shirt with both fists, Becca pulled at her less than gently and Storm let out a yelp; in the scramble her long hair had caught in the zip of Becca's cardigan. Storm swore at her; Jo had to step in and disentangle them as Clio began to howl.

175

'Let's go,' she said, when she had finally unravelled the tangle and Storm stood glaring at Becca, smoothing the ends of her hair while Clio strained out of the nanny's arms towards Storm. Jo took Storm by the elbow and steered her towards the door just as the twins crashed through and shouted 'Storm!' in perfect unison. The effect was quite uncanny.

'Ah, here's trouble,' she said, swooping down to tickle one twin with each hand as they shrieked and twisted away in delight.

'Will you tell us another story?' Grace asked, hanging on to her hand.

'A *ghost* one,' Oscar said with relish.

'No, these ladies have to go now,' Becca said, straightening her cardigan and sending Jo a meaningful look. 'I'll be in to read to you in a minute.'

'We want Storm.' Oscar bunched his fists mutinously on his hips.

'I don't mind,' Storm said with a shrug. 'Now, have I told you the story of the Dearg Due, who walks out of her grave and goes about luring young men to their deaths to drink their blood?' She bared her teeth and widened her eyes; Oscar yelped in delight and Grace looked nervous.

'Definitely not,' Becca said firmly. 'Seriously, you need to leave now, if you have what you came for.'

'Oh, I think we absolutely do,' Storm said, smiling sweetly. 'I hope you sleep better tonight,' she added to Becca, ruffling the twins' hair on her way out.

'Likewise.' Becca caught Jo's eye with a look that implied all kinds of undercurrents. Oscar stamped his feet and demanded the ghost story; Clio began to cry, stretching her hands out to the door where Storm had disappeared.

'Hey,' Becca hissed, as Jo made to follow. 'Have you been poking around up here before?'

'What? No.' Jo glanced through the open door into the nanny's room and noticed that she hadn't pushed the suitcase far enough under the bed.

'Has *she*?' Becca nodded towards the landing.

'Not that I know of. She wanted a plaster, like she said.'

'Only, stuff's been going missing since yesterday,' Becca said, giving Jo a long look.

'What stuff?'

'Stupid things. Calpol. Nappies. Clio's dummy.'

Jo laughed. 'What would Storm want with those? Do you think maybe Clio could have lost the dummy? They're pretty easy to drop.'

'Clio hasn't been taking nappies out of a new pack, though.'

'Are you sure? My daughter used to love pulling things out of packets when she was a toddler.' She turned to leave; Becca was clearly paranoid or looking for things to complain about. She has an overactive imagination, Cressida had said.

'Her little red coat's gone,' Becca said belligerently.

'Perhaps you've misplaced it,' Jo said, at the door. 'It's understandable, if you've been distracted this weekend. Looking for a new job takes up a lot of time, I remember it well.'

She regretted the words even as she heard them come out of her mouth. It was a stupid thing to say, a way of pushing back against Becca's attitude, a mean reminder of how little power the girl really had. She realised immediately that it was a mistake. Becca's expression tensed; her eyes narrowed further still.

'I don't know where you got that idea,' she said in a hard voice. 'I'm not looking for another job. I wouldn't dream of leaving Clio, would I, pumpkin?' she added, nuzzling the side of the baby's head. 'She needs me.'

'OK.' Jo took a step backwards on to the landing; she had no wish to prolong the conversation. 'I must have got the wrong end of the stick.'

'I'll be keeping my eyes open,' Becca said. She made it sound like a threat.

17

The courtyard had been done up for the anniversary dinner like a scene from the last days of Versailles: torches flamed in the flower beds and planters, silver chandeliers swayed from the lowest branches of the great horse chestnut, blazing with candles against the blue dusk. The effect was extravagantly magical, and – Jo couldn't help thinking – a colossal fire hazard among all the dry leaves. The long table was set in the centre of the lawn, beneath the tree, gleaming with pristine white linen and silverware. Standing heaters, not yet lit, had been placed at each end. A string quartet, dressed in white shirts and black skirts or trousers, played softly from the far side of the courtyard. Chastened by the reaction to her green formal dress on the first night, Jo had opted for her fallback outfit, black crepe trousers and a cream silk blouse, and now saw that she was indistinguishable from the musicians and waiters. She had unwittingly adopted Cressida's staff uniform; she wondered what Storm would make of that.

Cressida moved along the table, making adjustments to the settings while arguing with Lucas, who was complaining about being asked to leave his phone in his room. A diamond collar around her neck reflected the candlelight and when she moved her head, the matching stones in her ears flashed tiny strobing glints.

The Garretts were putting on a show of solidarity; they walked across the lawn in perfect step, arms around one another, looking as if they were ready for a red carpet. Jo couldn't help wondering if this had anything to do with Leo's gym session with Storm that morning, which Nina could not have failed to guess at. Leo appeared tense, despite the broad smile. Nina wore a midnight-blue shirt dress that had no shape and hung straight down from her shoulders to her ankles; on anyone else it would have looked like maternity wear, but Nina's height made it shimmer elegantly around her spare frame like a curtain of dark water. She kissed Cressida on both cheeks.

'Happy anniversary, darling. Any word from Max?'

'Yes! Finally. He texted about an hour ago to say he was at City airport. He's going to pick up a rental car and drive from Bordeaux, which I think is madness, but he and Storm want to go on to the coast for a couple of days tomorrow, he says. Apparently he can manage to take the time off for that,' Cressida added waspishly.

'I hope he won't talk to the French dude about the EU all night,' Lucas said, knocking back his champagne.

'The subject is banned,' Cressida said firmly. 'The minister's coming for a nice family meal, that's all. And you've got a three-drink limit, young man, so you might want to make them last.'

Lucas's protest was cut short by the sight of Arlo striding over the lawn towards them, his face taut.

'Everything all right, darling?' Cressida called out breezily, when he was still several metres away, as if she might ward off trouble by pre-empting it.

Arlo was flapping a small piece of paper in his left hand; as he approached, Jo saw that it was a Polaroid.

'What the fuck is this?' The question appeared to be addressed generally.

'What? I can't see it from here.' Cressida held out her hand but Arlo seemed reluctant to part with the picture. He turned it outwards towards Leo; Jo realised with a jolt that it was the photo from Storm's notebook, the one of the four boys at a pub table. Leo peered at it, frowning, then raised his eyes slowly to Arlo and a complicated look passed between them.

'Where did you find that?' Cressida asked, looking from one to the other.

'On the table with the wedding photos.' Arlo was still staring at Leo as if expecting an explanation. 'Our *names* are on the back.'

Nina peered over Arlo's shoulder and let out a peal of laughter.

'Oh my God, Leo, your hair!'

'Is this a Cambridge one?' Cressida joined her. 'I haven't seen this before – did you bring it, Leo? Look at your little faces, you scamps.'

'Not me,' Leo said, shaking his head and taking a step back. 'It was Jo, surely?'

Arlo switched his laser-glare to Jo and his shoulders twitched. 'Of course. Stupid of me. Of *course* Jo had it.' But he was looking at her as if she should have known better.

'Well,' Cressida said lightly, before Jo could speak, 'it was just meant to be a bit of fun, to remind us of how many years have passed. Darling, are you going to change? They'll be here any minute.'

Arlo looked down at himself. 'I am changed.' He was wearing black jeans and a grey T-shirt.

181

'Do you think you might put a collared shirt on? I left the Paul Smith one on the wardrobe door,' Cressida said, plucking the Polaroid from his hand and shepherding him back to the house.

'Why's Dad so freaked out about a picture?' Lucas asked, watching them walk away.

'If you'd had curtains like his in the Nineties, you'd want to hide the evidence too,' Leo said. 'Not that I can talk,' he added, passing a hand over his buzz cut. He rolled his shoulders, trying to appear relaxed. Nina continued to look at him sidelong.

'But there are loads of old photos on that table,' Lucas persisted. 'He reacted to that one like someone had published a picture of him naked.'

'Lukey, those other photos are from the wedding and the stag do,' Leo said, slipping an avuncular arm around the boy's shoulder. 'That Polaroid was from the last year of college. And I don't know if your dad's ever talked to you about this, mate, but he didn't have a great time of it in his final year.'

Lucas's eyes widened. 'Why not?'

'Oh, you know. There was a lot of pressure on him, he was this phenomenal computer genius, expectations were sky-high. It's an intense environment, especially around finals. Your dad was pretty stressed, he wasn't handling it all that well.'

'What, like a breakdown?' Lucas seemed amazed; perhaps he had never considered his father as a person, prone to ordinary human weakness.

'Not exactly. Just . . . like I said, it was a stressful time, finals – you'll find that out soon enough.' He gave Lucas an encouraging little shake. 'So, that picture probably brought back memories he didn't want to think about.'

'Oh.' Lucas scratched the back of his neck as Leo moved away to pour more champagne. He glanced at Jo. 'Bit insensitive to bring it, then.'

'I'm sure Jo wouldn't have known. It probably got caught up with other photos from the same time, right? Easily done,' Leo said, smiling, as he took Jo's glass. There was nothing she could say to absolve herself without revealing that she had been through Storm's bag, though she couldn't help wondering if Storm had had some inkling of the photo's likely reception. But Max would surely have known; why then had he given it to her?

She was saved from answering by the growl of a car engine. Everyone moved for a better view of the black Mercedes as it slid between the box hedges and pulled to a halt. A uniformed driver stepped out and held open the rear door; at the same time, Cressida hurried out of the house towards it, arms held aloft, followed closely by Arlo, now wearing a button-down chambray shirt in exactly the same shade of grey, which he was still tucking in at the back.

'Best behaviour, children,' Nina murmured, watching the guests of honour descend.

'Let's all moon them, on the count of three,' Leo whispered. He turned round and looped his thumbs into his waistband. 'Ready?'

Lucas snorted with laughter and the Polaroid appeared to have been forgotten.

The minister was in the same mould as the current French president: mid-forties, ski tan, designer suit, looked as if he played a lot of tennis. His wife would have stood out as Parisienne from a hundred paces: tall and slim, with a glossy bob that swung in perfect sync as she walked, wearing a white linen shift dress with a cropped navy jacket around her shoulders and discreet gold earrings. She was a similar age to her husband and had smoker's lines around her mouth, though she was soignée and self-possessed in a way that made Jo think of French cinema. The minister's wife bent to kiss Cressida on both cheeks with impeccable politeness and a faint air of boredom. Her husband shook Arlo's hand, clasping both of his around it, and the party moved towards them across the lawn. A slab of a man in a dark suit, shoulders straining the fabric of his jacket, positioned himself like a sentry at the edge of the grass, staring straight ahead, legs planted apart, a curly wire disappearing from his ear into the collar of his shirt.

Champagne was poured and handed around; a girl dressed exactly like Jo brought out bottles of water; two young men appeared with trays of canapés: scallops in their shells with twists of crisped ham; tiny glasses of gazpacho; halved quail eggs on thin slivers of toast; a plate of oysters glistening indecently. The minister took one of everything, balancing it in his hands while Arlo outlined his ongoing efforts to buy one of the local vineyards. He seemed distracted; he kept losing his train of thought mid-sentence, darting troubled glances back at the house.

Cressida turned to the wife, whose name was Alice. 'So, you used to work in television?' she asked.

Alice tilted her head. 'I was a producer. Current affairs. A long time ago,' she said, casting her eyes around to take in the chateau, the table, the trees, with no obvious reaction.

'Is that how you met your husband?' Cressida continued valiantly, as Alice drew a packet of slim white cigarettes out of her bag; when Nina leaned in to offer her a light, her face broke into the first real smile since she arrived.

'My children think I've stopped,' she said, with a guilty glance over her shoulder, as if they might suddenly appear. 'I can't smoke anywhere I might risk getting photographed.'

'Mine too,' Nina said, and Jo watched them exchange a moment of mutual understanding that only happens between mothers.

'Well, I can promise there'll be no photos tonight,' Cressida said, but Alice's attention had already moved on; she was staring in the direction of the house with a pointed expression. Cressida's face darkened and Jo turned to follow their gaze.

Storm approached across the grass, hips swaying, her hair loose in a twist over one shoulder. She wore a long, bias-cut dress in grey silk with spaghetti straps and black lace trim that looked like lingerie. She was wearing more make-up than usual, her eyes ringed with smoky navy kohl, and was clearly not wearing a bra.

'Sorry, bit late, had to make a phone call. Hi,' she said, walking straight up to the minister and thrusting out a hand. He took it with an expression of wonder, as if he'd been handed a rare and breakable museum exhibit.

'And this is . . .?' He addressed the question to Arlo, as if a vital piece of information had been deliberately withheld from him.

'I'm Storm,' she said. 'And you are?'

He chuckled, assuming this was a joke. '*Storm*,' he repeated, savouring the word. 'This is your real name?'

Storm laughed easily. 'Well, it's the name my mother gave me, doesn't get more real than that.'

'It suits you,' he said. 'I imagine you create *une tempête* wherever you go.'

'Actually, it's because there was a terrible storm the night I was conceived, according to my mother,' she said.

185

'Storm is Max's, uh . . .' Cressida began, then faltered on the right word.

'Lover,' Storm offered cheerfully. The minister still had her hand clasped between both of his.

'A lucky man.' He beamed, then looked to Arlo with a wrinkle of concern as the name registered. 'Max is the journalist, yes?'

'You don't need to worry about him,' Arlo said.

'You're sure? Because' – the minister gestured to himself and Arlo – 'this would be a good story for him.'

'Max is not that sort of journalist,' Cressida said. 'He's an old friend. He knows how to be discreet.'

'Of course,' Storm said. 'Max is good at keeping secrets, eh.' She looked at Arlo as she spoke; Jo saw him frown, as if he realised there was a subtext but couldn't decipher it.

'Now, now,' the minister said, placing his hand carefully on Storm's bare shoulder, 'we have no secrets here. Just a pleasant dinner among friends in this magnificent part of the country.'

'Then you've no need to worry about Max, have you?' She smiled demurely.

Alice leaned over to Nina. 'Call girl?' she murmured.

'We think so,' Nina whispered back.

'She's a philosophy student,' Jo said.

'The two are not incompatible,' Alice said, waving away another tray of canapés. She watched her husband for a moment and curled her lip in beautiful disdain. 'Men. So predictable.'

Despite Cressida's best efforts at imposing a seating plan, the minister pulled up a chair opposite Storm and the others had to configure themselves in their orbit. Jo turned to Lucas on her left, who was picking at something brown on his plate. He had hardly spoken since they had sat down.

'You OK?' she said in a low voice. 'You got the bracelet, right?'

'Yup.'

'What, then?' She had assumed this development would have lifted his mood, but it seemed only to have darkened. 'You know Storm didn't take it?'

'I know. I feel shitty for even thinking it. You shouldn't have told her.'

'You wouldn't have it back if I hadn't.'

'Yeah, but it was awkward enough with her already.'

'Because of what happened the first night, you mean?'

'She told you?' He let out a long sigh. 'I didn't mean to. It was so dumb – I showed her the chapel in the woods, I was totally baked and she's lovely and I got carried away and sort of tried to kiss her. Do you think she'll tell Max?'

'I'm sure she won't.'

'She was pretty angry at the time – she jumped away from me like I had the plague. But the next day, I apologised and she was really nice about it. Said we'd forget it ever happened.'

'Well, then. I don't think you need to worry.'

'But now I've pissed her off again by calling her a thief. When I should have realised . . .' He fell silent and poked at his food with a knife.

'What *is* that?'

'I think it's aubergine.'

'Is it nice?'

'It's aubergine.'

'Do you want some of my pigeon?'

He shook his head and stabbed at the vegetables again as if punishing them. Arlo laughed too loudly at something the minister said, and she saw Lucas dart a furious glance down the table at his father; in that moment she understood the source of his discontent.

'Did Storm tell you where she found the bracelet?'

Lucas's jaw tensed. 'She didn't have to. I guessed.'

Jo set her cutlery down. 'Oh.'

'Don't worry, Jo – it's nothing I hadn't suspected. I didn't think she'd be stupid enough to try stealing, though. I suppose she feels she's got nothing to lose.'

Jo felt a momentary flash of anger at Arlo; if you were going to have an affair, at least be discreet enough that your child doesn't notice. Even Oliver had managed that. 'Have you said anything? To your dad, or Becca?'

'Not yet.'

'Maybe – don't? Not this weekend, anyway. Now that you've got the bracelet back, it's not worth making a scene.'

'You don't know the first thing about it,' Lucas muttered.

'Think how your mum would feel,' Jo persisted, despite the tension radiating from him.

'I said leave it, OK?' he snapped, loud enough for the others to hear. Seeing them all looking, he reached defiantly for the nearest bottle, poured himself a large glass of red and drank it straight down.

The awkward silence was broken by the ring of silver on glass as Arlo stood, tapping his champagne flute with a spoon.

'If you'll indulge me for a moment,' he began, looking down the table, 'I want to pay tribute to my amazing, beautiful, talented wife, who has been my rock for twenty-one years, and taken care of our children while also running her own business.' He sounded as if he were reading the words off a teleprompter, but that was how he always sounded. 'It's wonderful to have our oldest and dearest friends here

188

to celebrate with us, as well as new friends . . .' He lifted a glass to the minister, who raised his in return. 'You all know I'm not one for long speeches, but – thanks to Cress for putting up with me all this time. I couldn't have done any of it without you. And you're dazzling enough without adornments, but this is just a little token of my devotion.' He left his place and circled to the other end of the table, where he knelt and presented Cressida with an oblong parcel wrapped in silver paper.

Her eyes snapped up to meet his, and for a heartbeat her face froze in an expression of – what? Confusion? Disbelief? It was there and gone so fast Jo could not be sure, but she saw Cressida shake it away with a toss of her hair, her smile back in place by the time she turned to face the company. She had not been expecting this, Jo thought, as a suspicion began to form in the back of her mind.

Cressida opened the package carefully and lifted out the bracelet.

'Oh, darling, too generous. What a lovely surprise.' She tilted her face up for a kiss; Arlo obliged and there was a smattering of applause. Gratified, Cressida fitted the serpent to her wrist and held her arm out for Alice and Nina to exclaim over.

'To Monsieur and Madame Connaught!' the minister said, standing and raising his glass. The others dutifully echoed the sentiment, though Leo looked a little put out to have the newcomer usurp the first toast.

'And to absent friends,' Arlo said, turning to Jo. 'To our dear Ollie. There's not a day goes by I don't miss him like hell.'

'Hear, hear,' Leo said, 'to Ollie,' and the murmur rippled around the table as they clinked glasses.

She tried to smile, but a rush of emotion caught in her throat.

'Oliver,' she managed, blinking hard.

Lucas pushed his chair back and lurched to his feet, glaring at his father. For an awful moment, Jo thought he was about to denounce Arlo in front of the company, but he merely shook his head in disgust and began to walk away.

'Sit down, Lucas,' Arlo said.

Lucas spun on his heel. 'No, I don't think I will. I've had enough. There's something I need to do.'

'Lucas!' Cressida called as he stalked away towards the house, but he didn't turn around. She gave Jo a sharp look. 'What's the matter with him?'

'I think he's not feeling well,' she said.

Cressida tutted. 'I'm not surprised, the way he's been going at that wine. You might have stopped him, Jo.' She turned to the minister before Jo could respond. 'I do apologise for my son.'

He waved a hand airily. 'Please, no apologies needed. My daughter is fourteen, I promise you girls are worse.'

'You have that to look forward to,' Alice said drily.

'Should I see if Lucas is OK?' Storm asked, gesturing to the house.

'No thank you, Storm, that's not your responsibility,' Cressida said, clearly meaning 'not your business', but as she spoke, her attention was distracted by the sight of Violette hurrying towards them at an ungainly half-jog, looking flustered.

'Monsieur Leo, téléphone,' she said, breathless. 'I tell him you're having dinner, but he have called three times now. He say it's an emergency.'

'Who?' Leo half-rose, setting his serviette on the table. 'What emergency?'

'*Dan*. He don't say, but he want you to call him immediately.'

Leo's eyebrows shot up. 'Dan? OK – excuse me, everyone.'

'Dan's his agent,' Nina said, her face tense as she watched him lope across the lawn.

'Oh dear, is there a problem with the show?' Cressida said.

'I'm sure it's nothing,' Nina said lightly. 'Dan's one of those people who literally never stops working, so he can't imagine anyone else having a holiday. He'd think it was an emergency if he couldn't find somebody's email address.' She held out her glass to a waiter for more champagne.

Storm looked up at Jo with a small, private smile. 'Yes, it's probably nothing,' she murmured.

Leo didn't return for dessert, and after picking at the exquisite, tiny chocolate petits fours, Nina excused herself to look for him. Lucas had not come back either. Arlo and the minister announced that they would take coffee in the library; Alice produced a theatrical shiver and Cressida suggested that 'the ladies' should decamp to the indoor bar.

'Like a Jane Austen novel!' Storm exclaimed, delighted. 'That's a beautiful bracelet, by the way.'

Cressida glanced at her wrist warily, as if she might have missed a hidden jibe. 'Isn't it? I wasn't expecting this at all.'

'Well, you'd better put it somewhere safe. Something that valuable – you never know if you might have thieving tinkers in the house. Isn't that right, Jo?'

Jo mumbled her assent, feeling the heat mottling her neck. Cressida gave her an odd look.

'Well, we wouldn't employ staff we didn't trust, Storm,' she said, with a self-conscious laugh and a flicker of a glance to Alice. 'And I hope you're not suggesting any of our friends might be tempted?'

191

'God, no.' Storm smiled pleasantly. 'No, I'm sure you wouldn't let one of your servants take something that belonged to you.'

Cressida stared at her, the skin tightening at her temples. She seemed poised to speak, just as Alice pulled her jacket closed at the neck and turned to her.

'I'm sorry, but I feel the cold, I must go inside.'

'Of course.' Cressida stretched her face into a smile. 'Let's go and find that coffee.'

Storm lit a cigarette and laughed softly as she watched them walk across the lawn.

'Poor cow,' she said. 'Must be such a strain, keeping up the facade.'

From the other end of the house, Lucas approached, shoulders hunched, fists deep in his trouser pockets. He slid into his father's empty seat and didn't look at Jo.

'You OK, hun?' Storm said, bending her head to try and catch his eye under his fringe.

'Yeah.' He pushed his hair back. 'Just couldn't sit through all that happy anniversary bullshit, you know? They're such fucking hypocrites. I could do with one of those if they're going spare.'

'Help yourself.' Storm pushed the packet across the table to him. When he lifted his head to blow the smoke out, Jo saw that his face was blotchy; she wondered if he had confronted Becca, but didn't dare ask in case he disappeared again. She wished Storm had not needled Cressida, dropping such an obvious hint; Jo would rather it didn't come out that she had known about the video all along.

'Did you see that photo?' she said, after a pause.

Storm plucked a strand of tobacco from her tongue. 'What photo?'

'Arlo found a photo on the table in the hall with all the

wedding pictures. A Polaroid. It really seemed to upset him, and Leo. I wondered if you'd seen it?'

Storm leaned back and gave Jo a long, evaluating look. 'What was it of?'

'The four of them in a pub, when they were at college.' She affected to consider this.

'I was late down, I didn't stop to look at those photos. Why did it upset them?'

Jo watched her. She knew that Storm was lying, and suspected that Storm was well aware that Jo knew she was lying; her chin tilted as if she were waiting to see what Jo would do about it.

'Don't know, but Leo and Dad both went all weird about it,' Lucas said. 'Dad's been really agitated all night.'

'Memories can do strange things to people,' Storm said.

'I think something happened,' Lucas said abruptly, picking up an abandoned glass of wine and taking a large gulp. 'In their final term. Dad had a place at MIT for grad school, did you know?'

Jo shook her head.

'Yeah. He got the top computer science degree at Cambridge for, like, *ever*. He could have gone anywhere, people were throwing money at him. And then suddenly, instead of going to the US, he marries Mum, who he literally started dating three months earlier, and switches his doctorate to London instead. There must be some reason he changed his plans.'

'He fell in love,' Storm said, though her tone was heavy with sarcasm. 'It was a whirlwind romance, by all accounts.'

Lucas rolled the ash along the edge of a dessert plate. 'Yeah. That's how they tell it. Except . . .'

'What?' Storm rested her chin on her hand and fixed him with an encouraging look. He glanced guiltily at the house.

'My grandad, Hugh. Dad's father.'

'You mean Lord Connaught? He of the famous "deserving poor" speech?' Storm leaned back and blew out a plume of smoke, grinning.

Lucas grimaced. 'Yeah, OK. I know his politics were a bit—'

'Nineteenth century? Borderline fascist?'

'He was still my grandad. He was always nice to me when I was a kid. I used to go and see him at the end, when he was ill. Dad never did. But sometimes Hugh thought I was Dad. And this one time—' He broke off to take a short, impatient puff. 'One time, out of nowhere, he slapped my knee and said, "Thank God I sorted out that bloody mess for you, eh. Fixed you up nicely with the Molyneux girl." Meaning Mum,' he added, lifting his eyes to Storm. 'I asked him what mess, and he just kind of harrumphed and said he'd told me never to speak of it. Then he said, "I never did like those boys you hung about with at Cambridge. Still, they've all done very well for themselves, eh? I hope they're grateful."'

'Grateful for what?' Storm crushed out her smoke and leaned forward, intrigued.

Lucas shrugged. 'Dunno. The next time I went back, he thought I was the German ambassador. I tried to bring the conversation round to the bloody mess, but he never rose to it again.'

'Did you ever ask Arlo?' Jo said.

Lucas looked at her properly for the first time since sitting down, and she saw that he was quite drunk. 'God, no. He didn't know I was visiting Hugh, he'd have been furious. After he died, I forgot about it. I only thought of it tonight, the way Dad was about that photo. Leo too. It's like it reminded them of something. You don't know, I suppose, Jo – since you brought it?'

Jo shook her head. 'I don't know anything about that picture,' she said truthfully, glancing at Storm. There was a complicity in the girl's smile that only added to Jo's unease.

'I did wonder at first,' Lucas said carefully, spinning Storm's lighter under his finger, 'if Dad was secretly gay at college.'

Storm threw her head back and let out her deep, throaty laugh. 'You're not serious. *Arlo?*'

'Only – that's exactly the kind of thing Hugh would have wanted hushed up when he was in government. Like, I thought, maybe at uni Dad got caught with a bloke and the others helped cover it up, and Hugh gave them money to keep quiet or something.'

'I feel pretty confident your dad's not gay, Lucas,' Storm said, still chuckling. 'Right, Jo?'

'Yeah, I know that *now*,' Lucas said heavily. 'But I couldn't think what else—'

They were spared any further speculation on Arlo's sexual preferences by the sight of headlights rounding the curve of the drive.

18

'Is that Max?' Lucas said, half-rising to squint across the dark lawn.

'Could be,' Storm said, off-hand. 'He said he was on his way.'

'It *is*,' Lucas cried, pushing his chair back as the car pulled up and the driver's door opened. '*Max!*' He yelled and waved his arms as if flagging down a rescue helicopter; Jo saw a figure peer into the dark and raise a hand briefly as he pulled a case from the back seat. Storm didn't move, except to stub out her cigarette. She appeared to be gathering herself, as if preparing for a performance. As Max crossed the lawn towards them, she inhaled hard through her nose, paused, and turned to him with a dazzling smile.

Lucas was there before her, racing across the grass and flinging himself on his godfather, almost knocking him over.

Max ambled to the table with an arm around Lucas. Jo felt a little flush of warmth at the sight of him; dishevelled as ever, with a growth of stubble that always seemed halfway to becoming a proper beard but never did. Perhaps it was absurd, but she had a sudden sense of reassurance; of all

Oliver's group, Max was the one who had, as her father would have put it, his feet on the ground. Now that he was here, she dared to hope that everything would settle into its right place and all the drama would abate.

Max came around the table to greet Jo with a hug, and she realised, with some surprise, that he did not look quite his old self.

'You've lost weight,' she said.

'I'm glad you noticed,' he said, at once pleased and self-conscious. 'I've been doing the 5:2, it's agony.'

'Well, it's paying off,' Jo said, holding him at arm's length. She realised it was nearly three months since she'd last seen him. 'Please tell me you haven't bought cycling shorts.'

'No, that's next-level mid-life crisis. I've scheduled that for a couple of years' time.' He let go of Jo and turned his gaze to Storm, as if he had been saving the sight of her for last. Jo took her seat again, noticing how his eyes lit up, and felt an odd pang that she could not identify. Storm tilted her face to receive the kiss Max planted chastely on her lips, though he hesitated there, as if unsure whether he was permitted to linger in public. Lucas looked pointedly away.

Storm patted the chair beside her. Max sat with a thud of relief, clasping his hand proprietorially over her thigh. He cast an anxious glance at the house.

'I should probably go and say hello.'

'Yeah, you'd better,' Storm said, lighting another cigarette. 'Cressida's been wetting her knickers about you getting here since Thursday.'

'I don't know why – she knew I wouldn't be able to get away. You've no idea how much I'd rather have been here. Have I missed much excitement?' His gaze travelled cheerfully around the table as he took a drink.

'Oh God, *so* much drama. I'll tell you later.' Storm shivered and rubbed her upper arms; Max immediately took off his jacket and draped it around her shoulders.

'Dad's got a French government minister in there doing some kind of backroom deal,' Lucas said.

'I know. He messaged to warn me. Do you think there's any dinner left over? They'd run out of sandwiches on the plane, I'm starving.'

'There's enough to see you through till Christmas,' Storm said. 'Shall we go and ask Marcel?'

'Don't go in yet,' Lucas said suddenly. 'Can't we just hang out here? Everyone's so wound up – Mum's terrified someone will fart in front of the minister, Dad's freaking out about that photo, God knows what's going on with Leo. We're the only sane ones left. Let's get another bottle and stay out here.'

Max looked at him with concern. 'I'd love to stay out here, Lukey – this is obviously where the real party is. But you know your mother will kill me if I don't show my face. Fill me in quickly – what photo?'

Lucas explained and Max's frown deepened. He glanced at Jo.

'I haven't thought about that Polaroid in years. So Oliver kept it then?'

She stared back at him in confusion, feeling Storm's eyes on her. If he had not given it to Storm, then how had she come to have it in her notebook? Why did everyone assume Jo was the one who had brought it? There was no way to have this conversation in front of Storm.

'Leo said it was from university days,' she said, instead.

Max watched her for a moment and she could feel him weighing up how much to say. He lifted his hand from Storm's leg and picked up a stray spoon, turning it between his fingers. 'There was a pub we used to go to sometimes,

198

in our final year. Not a student bar – it was a horrible place, right on the edge of town. Proper grubby old man pub.'

'So why did you go?' Storm leaned back and let a line of smoke drift from the corner of her mouth. 'Did you all think it was a laugh to slum it with the plebs?'

'No.' Max half-turned. 'It wasn't my idea. One of the bar staff sold cheap coke and other bits and pieces, so once a week we trotted out there in Oliver's car. Not my thing, but the others . . .' He glanced up at Jo apologetically.

'Yeah, you never inhaled, right?' Lucas grinned, but Max looked irritated.

'I honestly didn't, Lukey, I never touched any of that. I'd have a pint and read the paper while they all sloped off to the loo – only ever a pint, because I was the one who had to drive home. But it was one of those pubs that liked to put pictures of the customers on the noticeboard behind the bar, rather desperately trying to prove what a great time people had there. It was a thing in the Nineties. They kept a Polaroid camera under the counter.'

'That's a terrible idea if they're dealing drugs,' Lucas said, with an air of inside knowledge.

'Or a brilliant idea,' Storm said, standing her lighter up on the table. 'Means they've got a record of everyone who's been in buying, in case anyone causes trouble.'

'I'm not sure they'd thought it through to that extent. I'd be surprised if the landlord even knew what was changing hands out the back,' Max said gloomily. 'I hated the place. Every week I decided I wasn't going to go, and then I'd get talked into it, I didn't want to let the others down. But I remember that photo, because Arlo was adamant he didn't want his picture up there. Part of the attraction of that pub was that it was well away from the student bars, no one knew us. I think he didn't want any hard proof that we'd been there, in case it came out about the drugs and his dad found out. Or, worse, the tabs got hold of it. They'd have loved that, one in the eye for Sir Hugh. I think we all worried about that a bit. I certainly didn't want to become collateral damage in any tabloid story about Arlo; my parents would have been furious. So we'd refuse every time they came round with the camera. But then one week, Oliver—'

'Oliver what?' Jo said, wary.

'Oh, it was a long time ago.' He glanced up, embarrassed. 'He was showing off for the barmaid who had the camera, the others were a bit drunk. Somehow Ollie persuaded us to pose for her. Afterwards he said he'd sneak round and take it down when no one was looking. We stopped going shortly after that. Finals,' he added, by way of explanation.

'So Dad's pissed off because that picture reminds him of when he used to like a cheeky toot? Is that all?' Lucas looked at once disappointed and triumphant.

There was a long silence. Max stared at his hands spread out on the table. Eventually he raised his head and Jo saw how tired and drawn he looked. 'Something like that. Oliver never told you anything about it, Jo?' He was looking at her with the air of a teacher waiting for a guilty pupil to confess. She glanced away and caught Storm's eye, calm and steady behind her veil of smoke.

'No, not a word.'

'But it's not like he needs to worry any more, is it?' Lucas said, scraping at spots of congealed wax with his fingernail. 'Hugh's dead and literally no one would give a shit now that Dad did a bit of blow at college; it's not like that's blackmail material these days. He's got a bloody nerve having a go at me for the odd spliff, though.'

'I think we'd all rather it didn't come out, even so,' Max

said, his tone surprisingly terse. He picked up his glass, but Jo could see he was uneasy; his eyes flitted to hers as if he needed to communicate something, but was unwilling to say it in front of the others. Jo wanted a chance to speak to Storm alone, but could see no prospect of engineering it. Before she could speak, the conversation was cut short by the sight of Cressida rushing across the lawn, the ends of her wrap flapping behind her.

'Max, darling? Is that you? I thought I heard a car – you are naughty, we've been longing to see you all weekend and you're skulking out here.'

'Just wanted to say hello to my lady,' he said, slipping an arm around Storm's waist. Cressida's smile froze into a rictus. Behind his back, Lucas made a small gagging motion.

'Is Leo OK?' Jo asked.

Her smile collapsed. 'No. God knows what's going on, but his agent says a journalist has got hold of some story about the show, he's in a terrible panic, making phone calls.'

'What story?'

'Nina says some of the actresses have come forward with claims about inappropriate behaviour. Of course, they're all girls who've either had their contracts cut short or didn't get a second audition, presumably because they weren't good enough, but they obviously want to pretend there was something else behind it so they can feel better about themselves – it's just bitterness.' She pulled her wrap tighter. 'This is what happens these days. I have every sympathy for women who are genuinely victims of assault, but it's ridiculous now. Everything from a compliment to a hand on the knee is treated as if it's the same as violent rape.'

'No, it isn't,' Storm said, with undisguised contempt. 'If those women felt pressured or unfairly treated, they have a right to speak up.'

201

'How would you feel if it was Max?' Cressida said, rounding on her. 'If a young colleague of his had misinterpreted a friendly gesture or a compliment and was accusing him of terrible things?'

'I'd want to know she *had* misinterpreted it first,' Storm said. 'Because it's on him not to make gestures that could be ambiguous in that way.'

Cressida weighed up whether to argue the point, and evidently decided it was not worth the trouble. 'Well, I feel sorry for Leo – I just hope he can shut this down before anything's published. Come on in now, you dirty smokers – you'll all get hypothermia. Max, we've kept a ton of food for you.'

She hooked an arm through Max's and began marching him away; he cast a helpless glance over his shoulder.

'Max, I'll take your case up,' Storm called after them. Jo spotted her chance and followed her into the house.

Raised voices carried down the landing from Leo and Nina's room. Storm held a finger to her lips and Jo stood motionless beside her, listening.

'It's not my responsibility if they take that out of context!' Leo was shouting.

Then Nina's voice, tighter and more measured, saying something about sending signals.

Leo's reply was cut short by the ringing of a phone. Storm twitched her eyebrow at Jo with a puckish twist of her mouth and gestured her inside the room.

'So.' She tucked Max's case into a corner by the dresser. 'What do you want to ask me?'

Jo jerked a thumb at the next-door room. 'Is this your doing? Did you talk to the press about that text?'

'Me? No. I talked to Sooz. My actress friend. She's been

getting in touch with women for the last year or so, trying to persuade them to speak to a journalist she knows from the *Huffington Post*. Actors from the show, and other shows he's worked on. Directors, assistants. There are a lot of girls with stories. This has been a long time coming.'

'But you triggered it, sharing that text,' Jo persisted.

'Maybe that was the last little nudge they needed. I didn't expect them to be on it quite so quickly,' she said. 'I thought it would take a few days and we'd all be safely away.'

'Did you plan this when you came here?' Jo asked. 'To trap Leo?'

Storm's face darkened, then she laughed unexpectedly. 'Now that is beneath you, Jo. I fully expected Leo to be smarter when his wife and kids were around. But no, he thinks he's untouchable, and he dropped that little proposition right in my lap like a gift. What was I supposed to do?' Her expression turned cynical. 'Anyway, it'll come to nothing. There'll be a couple of pieces, he'll deny it all, make a non-apology for any misunderstandings, Nina will defend him, for the next while he'll be a bit careful about what he says to young women, and eventually it'll be business as usual.'

'So why bother?'

'Because he needs to learn that women are not disposable.'

Through the wall they could hear Leo's muffled protestations and the occasional thump, which suggested he was hitting furniture.

'That Polaroid,' Jo said. 'I've never seen it before.'

Storm raised her chin and looked at her with a half-smile. 'Really? Then where did it come from?'

'You tell me.'

'It was you went through my room, wasn't it?'

'Where did you get that photo, if Max didn't know about it?'

Storm appeared to be weighing her words. 'It was passed on to me.'

'For blackmail? Was it someone who knew them at college, who wants to blackmail them about doing drugs?' Her mind raced through the possibilities; if Storm had a history of attaching herself to older men with money, it was possible that she had encountered people who had known the four at university, who might hold on to some buried resentment and see an opportunity.

Storm only laughed. 'Blackmail? That's very unimaginative of you, Jo.'

'Then what?'

'I wanted to see what reaction it would get.'

'And?'

'Well, you saw them. How did it strike you?'

'What Lucas said. It seemed disproportionate, if it was just reminding them of a place they all dabbled with a bit of coke. Besides, the photo is hardly damning evidence, it's not like they're actually snorting anything in it. It's just some guys in a pub.'

'It's not about blackmail, I told you.' Storm took off Max's jacket and laid it on the bed. 'It was more about jolting their memories.'

'But not in a good way,' Jo said. 'And you knew that.' She waited for a response; when none came, she said: 'I could just go down and tell them it wasn't Oliver's.'

'You could,' Storm said evenly.

'Give me one good reason why I shouldn't.'

Storm quirked her mouth as if she were considering how much to give away.

'Let's say Lucas is right about it reminding them of an incident they'd rather forget. You want to know what happened, don't you? Especially if it concerns Oliver.'

204

Jo folded her arms. 'So tell me.'

'No time now. We'll go out tonight, to the chapel, when they're all asleep. I'll explain everything, I promise.'

'No, I'm not doing that again, I'm tired. Besides, the nanny saw us last night, she'll tell Cressida.'

'You don't need to worry about her. Come on, Jo,' she said softly, when Jo hesitated. 'One last hurrah. I promise you, this is something you want to know. After tonight you'll never have to see me again.'

She reached up to tuck a stray lock of hair behind Jo's ear, then cupped her hand around Jo's cheek, stroking her thumb ever so gently over Jo's lips. Without warning, she leaned in and kissed Jo full on the mouth, so that the breath went out of her and she was left, half pulling away, half responding, the shock of the sudden contact scattering her thoughts, until they heard steps outside the door and Jo jumped back, flushed, heart pounding, as Max opened the door and said cheerfully,

'Ah, ladies! We were wondering where you'd got to.'

19

The clearing with the old chapel looked subtly different in the moonlight when Storm switched off the torch and Jo allowed her eyes to adjust. It seemed to her that the trees were closer together, the shadows thicker between them, though she knew this must be a trick of the light. Perhaps it was just that she was more or less sober, and not in the mood to be seduced by its strangeness any more.

'Let's make this quick,' she said, wrapping her arms around herself as Storm knelt to set the fire. 'Tell me about the photo. I'm tired and cold and I don't want to be out here half the night.'

'OK. I'll get this going first, though, or we'll freeze our arses off.'

Reluctantly, Jo sat on a lump of fallen masonry and watched as the flames caught and licked around the wood. Neither of them mentioned the kiss; she wondered if Storm would simply pretend it hadn't happened.

'What did your mother die of?' Storm said, crouched on her haunches, her back to Jo. The question was so casual and unexpected that she answered it without hesitation.

'Motor neurone disease.'

'Really? God, I'm sorry. That must have been hard. People are sick a long time with that, right?'

'Not always. With Mum it was about two years from diagnosis to – the end. I was grateful it wasn't longer. But then I ended up looking after my dad.'

Storm turned, frowning. 'Why, was he ill too?'

'No. He was just a man who expected to be looked after by women. It was my job to take her place, take care of the domestic stuff. He was that generation of working-class man who could barely boil an egg for himself and was proud of the fact. I don't think he ever forgave me for going to university and moving away.'

'Christ.' She curled her lip. 'Well, that explains a lot. Do you see her?'

'Who? My *mother*?' Jo laughed, unsure if this was a joke. She felt the skin on her neck prickle.

'Yeah. Do you ever see her now? I'm serious,' Storm added, catching Jo's expression.

'Well, no, because she died twenty-four years ago,' Jo said, aiming for sarcasm.

'I see mine,' Storm said thoughtfully, resting her chin on her knee. Jo looked for a satirical glint in her eye, but could find none. 'Not often, but – I've seen her. Sometimes she stands by my bed.'

'I used to dream about mine,' Jo conceded, more gently. 'When I was a teenager. Not for a long time.' The thought saddened her, though she had not considered it until now.

'I'm not talking about dreams – my mother is *there*. In my room. I can't explain it, but she's there. She put her hand on my head one time, I felt it.'

'Dreams can be vivid,' Jo said uncertainly. 'But you were

too young to remember her, surely? Is it an image you have from photographs, maybe?'

'You'd think. But when I see her, she looks like she'd look now. She'd be forty.' She poked the fire and shrugged. 'Listen, I know it sounds mad, I wouldn't have believed it myself. I was always the first to laugh away anything like that when my grandmother talked about it. But I've realised I can't. The women in my family see things, that's just how it is.'

'Do you mainly see things after you've been smoking?'

'Haha. Actually, no. Only ever when I have a clear head. I've had to accept that she watches me.'

Jo glanced towards the empty chapel, disliking the chill creeping up her neck. 'You don't really believe that, though? I mean, I can see it might be comforting—'

Storm made a noise that was somewhere between a laugh and a yelp. 'Christ, no. Comforting is the one thing it isn't. My grandmother saw the dead, she was quite matter of fact about it. She said they had something to tell us, if we could only learn how to listen. For a long time I didn't know what my mother wanted to tell me. She never speaks.'

'And now you know?' Jo didn't like the tenor of this conversation; anywhere else she might have laughed it off, but in the shadow of the chapel she found herself imagining cold fingers on her head. She wanted to steer things back to the Polaroid, but she had an unsettling sense that it was all connected.

'Yes,' Storm said, but she didn't elaborate. 'It's why I'm intrigued by those stories of the *dames blanches*, you know? Angry women who won't rest until payment is made.'

'How did she die?' Jo asked, though she didn't really want to know the answer.

'It was like your Oliver,' Storm said.

'Car crash?'

'I mean, in the sense that everyone knew she'd killed herself, but it was officially an accident.'

'Did your grandmother tell you it was suicide?'

'God, no. It was not to be spoken of. It had to be an accident, for everyone's sake, and then buried and sealed up in silence. After my grandmother died and I went to clear out her house, I found a locked box in the attic full of my mother's diaries and letters. Other stuff too. Photos.' She gave Jo a meaningful look and threw a twig into the fire. 'My grandmother must have meant for me to have those one day, otherwise she'd have destroyed them. Maybe if I hadn't run away she'd have told me sooner.' She rolled her shoulders. 'I don't think my mother ever really got over what happened to her. Having me, and then denying I was her daughter. Do you know why she had to do that?'

'Because it was so conservative? You said—'

'Nah. It was the Nineties, not the Fifties. My grandmother had to pretend I was hers because my mother was afraid she'd go to prison if anyone found out she'd had a baby. She'd taken money, you see.'

'Stolen, you mean?' Jo frowned, confused.

'And she was fragile to begin with, my mother,' Storm continued, as if Jo had not spoken. 'That's what everyone in the village liked to tell me. *Fragile*. I assume that was their word for depression or some other mental health issue. She was twenty-one when she died. I've almost outlived her – freaks me out to think of that sometimes. Here—' She reached into the bag again and brought out a bottle of wine with a cork stuffed in the top. 'This one's legit, it was left over from dinner. Marcel gave it to me. No word of a lie.'

'It's quite hard to believe that,' Jo said. 'Pretty much every-thing you've said since you got here has been a lie.'

Storm looked at her, and all Jo could see was the

reflection of the firelight in her eyes. 'No, not everything. I do think you need to put a higher price on yourself. You've spent ten years of your life abasing yourself for a man who was trash.'

'Just stop it,' Jo said, scrambling to stand. 'Stop talking about Oliver and my marriage like that. You didn't know him, you've just got these scraps of gossip from Max—'

'I know he was trash,' Storm said stubbornly, tugging the cork from the bottle with her teeth. 'Why did you stay with him so long?'

'Because he was the love of my life,' Jo said fiercely. 'You don't just walk away from that. We had a daughter.'

'And that was a good example for her, was it? To see you taken for granted by a man who didn't value you at all? The love of your life – did he tell you that? Did he make you believe you'd never find anyone else like him? That's a *sickness*, Jo. It's called co-dependency, and you need help. I'm saying this for your own good.' She held out the bottle.

'Fuck you. How dare you presume to know anything about my marriage or my husband? You think you can just play with people? I don't even know what I'm doing here.' Jo turned to walk away, sounding braver than she felt.

'You're going the wrong way,' Storm called after her. 'OK, I'm sorry. Sit down, Jo, and I'll tell you about the photo. If you don't want a drink, at least have some of this.' She brought out her old tobacco tin and took out a small, pre-rolled joint. Jo shook her head. 'Ah, come on. Tomorrow you'll be back home ironing school uniform or whatever you do with your evenings.'

Reluctantly, Jo sat down and accepted it. 'Just this one, and then I'm going. I want to sleep.'

'Well, this will help.' She leaned across and held her lighter flame to the tip. She took out another from the tin and lit it for herself. 'One small one each, it'll relax you, and we'll head back.' She reached out and laid her free hand over Jo's; Jo snatched it away. They smoked together in silence for a while, the familiar loosening easing through Jo's limbs, making her head heavy. Suddenly Storm jolted upright, holding up a hand in warning.

'Did you hear something?' She was staring off into the trees. Jo could see nothing beyond the circle of firelight. 'Hello?' Storm strained to listen a moment longer, before sinking back against a fallen log.

'Animals,' she said, as if to herself. 'My mother drowned. She was walking on the rocks around the bay – they said she must have fallen and been pulled under. The tide was high. She didn't fall, though. I read her diary.'

'She drowned?' A thin, high note of alarm had begun to sound through the gathering fog in Jo's head. 'Wait, where . . .' she tried again, but her tongue felt thick and clumsy. 'Where did . . .'

'Where? Galway. That's where I grew up. One of the things I regret,' she continued, kneeling up to poke the fire with a long stick, 'is not reconciling with my grandmother before she died. She might have been willing to answer questions. As it is, I've had to piece everything together from what was left. Kind of like a detective.'

'What was her name?' Jo managed. 'Your mother?'

Storm appeared lost in thought.

'Oliver had a cutting—' Jo persisted, wishing her mind would focus enough to make connections; something important was sliding just out of reach, but her vision had begun to blur and she was feeling strange. This was not the gentle, mellow buzz of the day before; belatedly it occurred to her that she was smoking something quite different, and that she was only in the foothills of its effects. 'A newspaper

211

cutting. About a woman drowning in Galway Bay. In his desk. I found it after he died. Why would he—'

'Let me ask *you* a question first,' Storm said, twisting around to face Jo, and her voice sounded far away, as if she were speaking from the depths of a cave. 'Did you follow me today, in Saint-Émilion?'

Jo tried to shake her head, but the movement caused a wave of nausea to rise in her throat.

'See, I think you're the one lying now. Because I thought it was odd, you mentioning a grey van, when the nanny had talked about seeing me with a man in a white car. And you had a picture of a grey van on your phone.'

'How do you . . .?'

'Well, I checked, while you were in the shower before dinner. I came to get those videos. Don't worry, I've deleted the photo. But I didn't like that. I felt a bit betrayed, if I'm honest. I wondered who'd put you up to it?'

'How did you get into my phone?'

'Your wedding anniversary. I told you, people are predictable.' She threw the remains of her joint into the fire.

'Who was the guy, the – with the van?'

'No one important. But you've messed things up, you see, Jo. You've created a bit of a problem. Are you all right there?' She leaned in, frowning with concern, but her face stretched and wavered in Jo's vision, the eyes monstrous. Jo shifted on to her knees and bent forward, thinking she might throw up. Her skin had grown cold and slick with sweat. 'OK, you're just having a whitey,' Storm said, in her ear. 'Breathe deep, nice and steady.'

But her breathing was coming too fast, and she couldn't rein it in. Storm rubbed her back in broad circles, and the motion felt briefly soothing, until Jo raised her head and saw, beyond Storm's shoulder, figures moving among the trees around the chapel. She tried to point to them, but Storm made a shushing sound, and beneath it Jo could hear an undercurrent of whispering voices, all speaking on top of one another in words she could not catch, but their tone was malicious and Jo was certain they were talking about her, saying things about her, in a language she was not meant to understand. The trees had moved closer still. This was a bad place, a place steeped in centuries of suffering; she could feel it soaking into her. She whimpered and cowered by the fire but she was cold to the bone now, and she saw Storm move away and pick up an object from the rubble by the chapel wall, but how could that be, since the hand went on stroking circles on her back? Jo wanted to scream, but her throat was closed; she squeezed her eyes shut against another rising wave of nausea, and when it had passed, she looked down and saw that she was holding the broken neck of a bottle, and that Storm's hand was closed around hers, with the jagged glass lined up against the tender white flesh of her wrist.

'Good girl, Jo, that's it,' Storm said, her voice calm and clear over the babble of whispers. 'It'll all be over soon, and you can sleep.'

Though blurring eyes, she watched as the point broke the skin, saw the sudden bright welling of blood, and noted her surprise that she could feel no pain. She looked up and for a moment she thought Lucas was there, looking straight at her; she tried to call his name, but no sound came, and then the face slid back into Storm's features and Jo bent all her concentration, as the glass cut deeper, to form the words,

'Who. Are. You?'

And Storm laughed, and brought her twisted face close to Jo's, and said, in a perfect, cut-glass English voice,

'*I'm your dirty little whore.*'

It took a moment, through her whirling thoughts, for the words to resonate. As their meaning solidified, deep in her core a flood tide of rage surged; she felt it rise, physically shaking her, and as it burst its banks she knew she was more powerful than anything else in the clearing; with a roar she wrested control of the broken bottle, felt the shard score along her arm with no pain as she threw off Storm's hand, and held it aloft, aimed at the girl. The noise coming from her throat split the sky, until it no longer seemed to be her voice but to emanate from the land itself, from the trees and the fallen stones and the massed figures in the depths of the chapel. Storm, caught unawares, scrambled backwards, a hand held out as if that would stop her.

'Jo – no, put it down. You're having a bad trip, you need to sit—'

'*You.*'

Jo was invincible now; she moved towards Storm with the broken glass aloft, the voices singing high and pure in her ears, the trees closer still. Storm grabbed a branch from the fire and held it towards her, the end alight, like a medieval villager fending off an ogre, but Jo kept advancing as Storm backed towards the shadows of the chapel.

And then, in a blink it seemed, there was blood covering her hands and she was running, hurling herself through the forest with hostile branches scratching at her face and tearing her hair, pushing herself faster than she'd ever run, though her breath still came in short, frantic gasps and her heart raced fit to explode. There were no voices now, just the scrape of her breathing and the sound of her feet on centuries of fallen leaves, and all she knew was that she had to keep running, to put as much distance as possible between herself and that place. The forest was silent and as she ran she glimpsed them, slipping in and out of tree trunks, the faceless women in their white dresses, holding their hands out for a dance, and she knew she must not stop for them or she would never leave. She ran until her right foot twisted against a tree root, sending her crashing headlong, teeth jarring as she hit the ground, as the trees closed overhead and the last thing she remembered was the image of Storm falling, one arm raised to defend herself, into the shadow of the chapel.

PART TWO

20

Sunday

Max is woken by the sound of screaming. It drills down through muddy layers of dreamless sleep until it triggers a response; slowly he surfaces, pushing himself on to one elbow and fumbling on the bedside cabinet for his glasses, knocking over an empty wineglass. The clock says 6.51. His head feels thick and claggy, with a dullness behind the eyes, like a hangover but more banal, which is odd because he doesn't remember drinking much, although the empty glass suggests otherwise.

He sits up and registers several things seemingly in the same moment. The other side of the bed is empty, though an indentation remains in the pillow next to him. He is wearing the same clothes he travelled in the day before, which he notes with a touch of shame; so he fell asleep in his clothes? He must have been drunk, then. He hopes Storm wasn't disappointed last night. He is disappointed in himself, regardless.

The screaming continues, overlaid with the thin, high wail

of a child. Several pairs of quick footsteps echo overhead and he hears a man's voice shouting staccato orders. Belatedly, he understands that something very bad is happening outside the door. *Fire*, is his first thought. There is a faint smell of woodsmoke in the room, he notices. Where is Storm? Has she already fled? *What, and left him sleeping?* says the voice in his head.

He casts around for his shoes, grabs up his passport, phone and wallet from the drawer in the bedside table and stuffs them into his pockets, but when he rushes out to the stairs, there's no sign of smoke; it's clear that all the noise is concentrated on the floor above, where the children sleep. The screaming voice he thinks is Cressida's, with another soft, low keening beneath it, like something from a Greek tragedy. He finds Leo on the bend of the stairs in his boxers and a T-shirt, shouting 'Ambulance!' into his phone in a bad French accent. Grace is awkwardly hoisted on his hip, though she is really too big to be held, and keeping up a determined hiccupping sob into her father's neck.

'Ambulance, *urgent*,' he says again. Max hears rapid-fire speech from the other end. 'No, *Anglais*?' Leo says, in desperation. 'It's my son.'

'Do you want me to—' Max whispers, holding his hand out. Leo looks up and thrusts the phone at him.

'Tell them to get an ambulance here now, it's an emergency.'

Max relays the information and the address to the woman on the other end. When she asks him what's wrong, he turns to Leo.

'Oscar,' he says, helplessly. 'We can't wake him. And' – he glances back up the stairs – 'they need to come *now*.'

Max conveys this and answers subsequent questions as best he can.

'How long?' Leo demands, shifting Grace's weight.

'She said it could be twenty minutes, half an hour.'

'For Christ's *sake*. Did you tell her it was a child?'

'Yes.' He spreads his hands wide. 'She says they'll do their best but it's a Sunday.'

'Fuck that, I'll drive. We need to get him to a hospital.' Leo grabs the phone back, hitches Grace up his side and sets off up the stairs, colliding with Cressida as she comes hurtling down, wild-haired and barefoot, her robe flapping open, calling Clio's name. When she reaches the downstairs hall she turns to look up at Max.

'For God's sake, *do* something,' she shouts.

'What should I—' he begins, but she has disappeared. The main door slams after her. He takes off his glasses and rubs his eyes; more than anything he would like for someone to make him a coffee and explain what chaos has descended. Where is Storm?

'Max? Is that you?'

He looks up; Arlo's face has appeared over the bannister.

'Get up here,' he says. 'I need you.'

The child safety gate at the top of the stairs is hanging open and the first door on the landing is ajar; through the gap Max can see Nina perched on a tiny chair, leaning over the lower bunk bed. Leo stands beside her, a hand on her shoulder, murmuring low and urgent; Nina shakes him off.

'We shouldn't move him,' she says, with a catch in her voice. Max backs away, remembering how he used to read Lucas bedtime stories in that room, back when he was Oscar's age. Arlo is further down the corridor, fully dressed, waiting. He appears composed, but his face is colourless and his nostrils flare when he breathes.

'Clio's missing,' he says.

'What?' Max glances to his left; the door to the nursery

stands open and he can see that the side of the cot has been lowered. 'How do you mean, *missing?*'

'I mean, she's not here. And the nanny—' Arlo stops, as if his mouth has dried. 'She's gone too.'

'Well, then' – Max shakes his head, confused – 'hasn't she just taken Clio out for an early walk? Maybe she was crying and the nanny didn't want her to wake everyone.'

'She wouldn't have done that.'

Max is baffled; in his limited experience, this seems like exactly the sort of thing a highly paid nanny would do to spare her employers the inconvenience of their own child on the morning after a party. He feels that he is missing a crucial piece of the picture. 'What's wrong with Oscar?' he asks, trying a different tack.

'No idea. Grace came down to Leo and Nina just now when she couldn't wake him, and said Becca wasn't there.' Arlo continues to stare at the empty cot as if willing it to give up answers. Max still can't make the connection between Oscar's condition, which is certainly worrying, and Cressida's full-blown hysteria.

'Well, there's an ambulance on the way, although Leo wants to drive to the hospital. Maybe Oscar had an allergic reaction to something, or – is there a medicine cabinet up here? My nephew ate a handful of Nurofen when he was little because he thought they were M&Ms – he had to go to A&E. If the nanny left something lying around—' He breaks off as Arlo's expression freezes.

'Sedatives,' Arlo says, pointing at him as if Max has made a brilliant deduction.

'Anything like that. Even a simple aspirin, if a child takes a few—'

'No – she could have given them sedatives. The twins.'

'Who? You mean the nanny? Why would she do that?'

222

'So they wouldn't wake. When she took Clio,' he adds.

'I don't understand. Are you saying you think the nanny's, what, *abducted* her?'

'It's the only explanation,' Arlo says.

Max looks at him, wondering if he is ill. He can think of a dozen more likely explanations.

'Why would she want to do that?'

'She's unhinged.'

Max waits for him to elaborate, but he doesn't offer any further detail.

'In that case, shouldn't you call the police? Do you want me to do it?'

'No,' Arlo says immediately. 'Keep the police out of it until we know what's happened.'

'You just said you think the nanny's kidnapped your daughter. Surely you want to—'

'Maybe *kidnapped* is a bit strong. She can't have gone far.'

'Are any of the cars missing?'

Arlo's eyes widen. 'Good point. We need to get down there and look.'

He is already halfway along the landing when Max grabs him firmly by the upper arm and forces him face to face. 'Arlo, what's going on? Why is Cress in such a state? I want to help, but I'm in the dark here.'

Arlo seems to sag under his hand. 'I don't think she'd hurt Clio,' he says, although he sounds as if he is reassuring himself. 'She wants to frighten us, that's all. I hope that's all.'

'Why?'

His eyes slide away. 'Because we've sacked her. Becca, I mean.'

'I see.' Max lets go of Arlo's arm, takes off his glasses and

223

rubs a hand over his face. This is the kind of conspiracy theory he might expect to hear from Cressida, not his ultra-rational friend. 'Well, let's go and look. If she's taken a car, you should probably call the police straight away.'

Arlo nods, distracted, his gaze roaming around the room as if looking for something. 'You go. Give me a minute.'

Max replaces his glasses. His head feels as if it's stuffed full of wet wool. He would like to believe that there is a logical explanation for all this. 'Maybe you shouldn't touch anything in here,' he says, 'just in case,' but Arlo is already opening drawers. He decides to leave him to it.

In the entrance hall, the front door stands open, letting in a gust of cool morning air. As Max passes the console table under the stairs, he notices that the receiver of the landline is off the hook, which strikes him as odd. He replaces it, thinking that perhaps Leo tried calling the ambulance from here and left it like that in his panic. There is still no sign of Storm. Did she go out early, before all the madness kicked off? He wonders if she is angry with him for ruining their weekend, first with the constant work delays and then by falling asleep like a dead weight the minute he arrived, but it seems unlikely; she has not, in the short time he has known her, shown any sign of being the kind of woman who demands to be the sole focus of his attention and reacts with sulks when she is not. It is one of the things he likes about her. Even so, he wishes he had managed to have sex with her before blacking out completely the night before, and hopes she won't blame it on the age difference; he is insecure enough already on that score.

From the garden he can hear Cressida's increasingly shrill cries, calling her daughter's name. He wanders into the court-yard and traces the sound to the swimming pool, where he finds Cressida with her arms wrapped around her narrow ribs, sobbing and hyperventilating; for a heartbeat he fears the worst, but there is nothing in the water. When she sees him, she hurls herself against his chest, clutching at fistfuls of his shirt.

'I told him this would happen! He let it go too far and now – my *baby*, Max.' She stares up at him. 'She's taken my baby.'

'We'll find her,' he says, prising her fingers loose and guiding her as you might an elderly dementia patient. Her feet are still bare, he notices, and she is shivering violently. 'Come on back to the house and get warm, then we can work out what to do.'

'What we need to *do* is look for that *fucking bitch*,' she spits, with surprising force, but she allows herself to be led to the kitchen. He settles her on a bench at the table, fills the kettle and casts around for something to wrap around her. He looks in the utility room by the kitchen door – surely there will be some kind of picnic rug or throw – but the best he can come up with is a pile of the striped outdoor towels. A breath of warm air touches his face as he passes the open mouth of the industrial-sized tumble dryer. He reaches out and feels the residual heat on the glass window. Violette must have been in early to do the laundry, perhaps she will have seen something? Although presumably she would have no reason to remark on the nanny taking Clio out for a walk.

He drapes a towel around Cressida's shoulders like a shawl.

'Where is everyone?' he asks, casting around the vast kitchen.

'Marcel has the day off and Violette's not coming in until lunch, because they were here so late last night,' Cressida

225

says mechanically. 'I said we could fend for ourselves this morning.'

He doesn't contradict her; evidently Violette's commitment to the household goes above and beyond, though he wonders where she is now. The kettle whistles on the hob and he occupies himself making a pot of tea, his mother's universal salve for all situations involving extreme emotion. He is desperate for a coffee himself, a filthy strong espresso that will blast a hole through the fog in his head, but one glance at the gleaming silver machine in the corner and he knows that its array of gauges and dials is outside his skill set in his present state.

He presses a mug of strong tea into Cressida's hands as Arlo appears in the doorway, holding his phone. He is still pale, but the fear in his eyes has receded.

'None of the cars are missing,' he says, 'but the outside security lights have been switched off.'

Cressida turns slowly to look at him. 'I thought they were automatic. On a motion sensor?'

'They are. You have to disable them with the main fuse box in the cellar. Which someone evidently did.'

Cressida levers herself up from the bench, sloshing tea over the table. 'She planned this! Oh my God, Arlo – she must have taken her in the night and made sure the lights didn't wake us. I'm calling the police.'

'Not yet. Sit down. Let me at least think about this logically.'

'If she doesn't have a car, she can't be far away,' Max points out.

'Exactly. It's what I said – she wants to scare us. She'll be hiding somewhere on the property with Clio, you'll see.'

'Have you tried calling her?' Max asks.

Arlo looks at him as if he is an idiot. 'Obviously. Goes

226

straight to voicemail. We need to get out there and search. All hands on deck. I'll wake Lucas – Max, can you find Jo?' He turns to his wife. 'If you want to do something useful, call Violette and Paul, tell them we need them out looking. And for God's sake get yourself dressed in case we do have to get the police in,' he adds, with a curl of contempt.

Perhaps it's his tone that does it; Cressida launches herself at him, raging that this is his doing and raining blows on his chest with her small fists until he grabs her by the wrists.

Max looks out of the window, embarrassed. He can guess at the underlying story; the only thing that surprises him is that Arlo would be so careless as to allow this situation to arise in the first place. He wishes again that Storm would come back.

'*Calm down*,' Arlo is saying, still holding her wrists, as if emphasis alone will de-escalate her fury.

'Mum? What's going on?'

Lucas has sloped into the kitchen unnoticed, bed-headed and bleary, in a Ramones T-shirt and sweatpants. He stares at his parents, rubbing his eyes like a child abruptly woken. 'What's all the noise?'

'Your sister is missing,' Cressida shrieks, wresting one arm from Arlo's grip. 'Get out there and look for her.'

'What?' Lucas turns to Max, bewildered.

'Nothing to worry about,' Arlo says sternly. 'We're just not quite sure where Becca and Clio have gone. If you could put some shoes on and have a look around the gardens, that would be a big help.'

'I don't understand. *Clio*—'

'Just do as you're told,' Arlo snaps. Something chases across Lucas's face, too quick to catch, though not his usual mutinous teenage response. *He knows what this is about*, Max thinks. *Or at least he suspects.*

227

Lucas shuffles away, followed after a moment by Cressida.

Arlo turns to him after she has left, and again Max sees it: the tremor of fear under the contained exterior. From the moment he arrived the night before, he has had the sense of walking into an atmosphere of imminent catastrophe; the shock of that Polaroid, then Leo and Nina pouncing on him over this news story, and now the baby vanishing.

'Are you going to tell me what's happened here?' he asks.

Arlo drags a hand across his mouth. 'It will be fine. It's just got a little – out of hand.'

'Is Clio in danger?'

'No. At least – no, I can't believe that. Becca adores her.'

'I still think it would be wise to call the police.'

'You may be right. But I'd prefer to deal with it ourselves if we can. Let's find the others – one last hunt around the grounds before we do anything.'

He moves towards the door. Max understands his reluctance; the police would ask intrusive questions, and Arlo likes to keep his private life private. He learned that from his father.

Arlo pauses in the doorway, grasping the frame on either side.

'Max. Why did Jo bring that photo?' He is facing the dining room, but the set of his shoulders is eloquent. 'Did she say anything to you?'

'No. She clammed up when Lucas was asking about it. She seemed uncomfortable.'

Arlo turns. 'You don't think Oliver *told* her? Before he—'

'Why would he?'

'Fit of conscience?'

'She'd have said something before now, surely?'

'*Would* she, though? Or would she just keep it up her sleeve until the time was right?'

They hold each other's gaze for a long moment.

'Jo's not like that,' Max says. 'She's too – upright. If she knew about that business, she would not be spending time with us. She might not have said anything directly, but she wouldn't be here. I'd bet she has no idea. Cress said bring old photos and she grabbed that one up at the last minute. I'm surprised he kept it all this time.'

'He always did have a masochistic streak.' Arlo taps his fingers against the door jamb.

Max pushes his glasses up and pinches the bridge of his nose. 'Listen, can I just get a coffee? I can hardly see straight. I didn't think I drank much, but I don't even remember getting into bed.'

Arlo frowns. 'You didn't take a sleeping pill or something?'

'Of course not. The last thing I wanted yesterday was to knock myself out before I'd even taken my clothes off.' And yet he *was* knocked out. Arlo is right: out like a light, black dreamless sleeping-pill sleep. He recalls the empty glass on the bedside cabinet. He would never usually take a glass of wine to bed, but he has a dim recollection of Storm pulling at his arm, laughing, *Bring it with you, finish it in the room, come on, don't be boring.*

This troubling line of thought is interrupted by the sudden drilling of the buzzer at the main gate: the ambulance has arrived. Everything happens fast after this. Leo appears in the kitchen, wearing jeans now, Grace still clinging to him, maintaining her rhythmic sobbing with grim dedication; Cressida returns, pale but groomed; Violette tumbles through the back door in a flurry of distress, her husband Paul silent and stoical behind her. Then the strobing of blue lights in the drive, paramedics running up the stairs with bags of equipment, Oscar carried down shortly after on a stretcher, Nina and Leo tearfully following, Grace howling louder when she is handed to Violette and told she can't ride in the ambulance with them. Max finds himself volleying questions back and forth in French and English between Leo and Nina and the paramedics, until the facts have been established: what time Oscar was found, what he could have eaten, if he had access to any medicines; it seems they think some kind of accidental overdose the most likely explanation. Leo and Nina are adamant that this is not possible, but Arlo's comment about sleeping pills pokes at Max like a stone in his shoe.

After the ambulance has left, he tries Jo's room only to find it empty, which seems odd; he hasn't seen her downstairs during all the commotion. Storm still hasn't returned either; perhaps they are searching together. Cressida had mentioned a couple of times, in her pointed way, that they seemed to have become close over the weekend. Max crosses the courtyard, past the yoga studio and around the back of the house, scanning the ground for any sign that Becca and Clio have passed this way.

A flicker of movement catches his attention; he straightens up and removes his glasses to peer down the sloping lawn towards the trees. A figure is approaching from the brook, moving at an urgent, erratic pace; he shades his eyes with the edge of his hand.

'Lucas?'

The boy is shaking uncontrollably; his face is bone-white and as he lurches into Max's outstretched arm, Max smells vomit laced with last night's alcohol on his breath.

'You have to come,' Lucas manages, breathing so hard he struggles to form the words. Max has to hold him up. The cold bud of dread that had appeared in his gut since he awoke blooms into full-blown terror.

'Oh God. Not – Clio?' he asks, not wanting to hear the answer, but Lucas shakes his head, looking past him.

Max turns to see Arlo running towards them; he lets go of Lucas and the boy collapses on to the grass, pointing at the line of trees beyond the stream. 'The chapel,' he says, through chattering teeth.

'I know where he means,' Arlo says, setting off at a run. Max hesitates, glancing at Lucas; he doesn't like to leave a child in an obvious state of shock, and if he is honest, he would rather not see whatever has produced this effect, but after a moment he follows Arlo, struggling to keep up with his long strides.

Across the stream, through the trees, to a clearing with the ruin of a tiny chapel and the remains of a campfire. Arlo slows as he approaches the crumbling walls; Max jumps back as a couple of crows flap up from the ground, protesting at the disturbance. He comes to stand beside Arlo and they look down without speaking, as if there is a delay in processing the scene that presents itself: the stiff torso in the doorway; the head crooked at an unnatural angle, facing away; the curled white hand flung out, as if grasping at air. At the foot of the wall by the door, Max sees a splatter of fresh vomit – Lucas's, he presumes. He fights down his own rising bile and clears his throat, as a prelude to suggesting that now would be a good time to call the police, but before he can stop him, Arlo is kneeling by the body, lifting the shoulders, brushing the hair back from the face.

'Christ, Arlo – get away!' Max surprises himself with the force of his shout. 'You're not supposed to touch anything, you'll contaminate the scene.'

Arlo draws his hand back and looks up at Max; he appears stunned, as if he has received a blow to the head. Before Max can speak, there is a rustle in the trees behind them

231

and he turns to see Jo emerge on the other side of the clearing and stand, swaying on the spot, staring at them as if she doesn't know who they are. He takes in her appearance, uncomprehending: her hair is matted and spiked with dirt and leaves, her clothes filthy and stiff with what looks like dried blood. She stumbles a few paces, wild-eyed as if she is in the grip of some kind of manic episode, and he sees that she is injured; a vertical gash running down the inside of her wrist. She glances past him at the chapel and lets out a long scream that reverberates through the trees and echoes off the old stones.

Again, Max has the sense of being lost in a fever dream; he holds an arm out to Jo and staggers back under her weight as she falls into him, ranting incoherently about Oliver and white women and glass.

21

It is early afternoon, around the time their flight home should have been departing, when Jo is returned to the chateau, in the back of an unmarked car driven by an athletic-looking woman in a trouser suit who'd introduced herself in excellent English as Lieutenant Christine Lemaître. Jo watches the smudged lines of fields and vineyards stream past the window. The doctors gave her something at the hospital that appears to have stopped her mind whirling but hasn't brought any corresponding clarity; if anything, the events of the night before seem further out of reach, separated from her by a thick, muffling smog. The only thing that is fixed and certain is the image of that stiff arm in the doorway of the chapel. Max had tried to bundle her away before she could glimpse the body; she had lacked the strength to fight him, but she had seen enough: its awful whiteness, the fingers curled upwards. So that part, at least, was real.

A police car is parked across the entrance to the chateau with two uniformed officers standing sentry, though they step back with a nod and open the gates when Lemaître shows her badge. As they round the bend in the drive, Jo looks past the box hedges at the courtyard to see that it has been sealed off with blue-and-white tape. Another gendarme stands at the door to the entrance hall as a figure comes down the stairs in a white crime scene bodysuit and gloves, something Jo has only ever seen on TV shows. The person is holding a clear plastic bag with an unidentifiable item bundled inside it.

'Can I get changed?' she asks. It is the first time she has spoken since leaving the hospital. Everything hurts: her head, her throat, her arm – especially under the dressing. Three stitches, though she has only a vague sense of that happening; they did it while she was under sedation, but apparently there is nothing else wrong with her. She is still wearing a hospital nightgown and slippers with Lemaître's coat around her shoulders. Her own clothes, Lemaître explained, have gone to forensics.

'Wait here,' the detective says, and exchanges a few words with the officer outside the door. She slips on gloves and shoe covers before disappearing into the house, her long red ponytail bouncing with each quick step. Jo pulls the coat tighter around her chest and shivers. In the courtyard, two men wearing police armbands stand by the horse chestnut holding German shepherds on leashes. The sight of the dogs' quivering noses turns her stomach cold.

She is taken to the yoga studio, where the detectives are conducting interviews while the main house is processed by forensics. Jo has been in the studio a handful of times over the years, when Cressida had press-ganged the wives into early-morning well-being sessions. It's a purpose-built cabin behind the main house, all bleached wood and glass and lemongrass-scented diffusers, but today the mats are rolled away and someone has set out the trestle tables and chairs used for wedding ceremonies. A laptop is open on one of the tables, its screen facing away.

Standing by the floor-to-ceiling window with his back to her is a trim older man, hands in the trouser pockets of his suit. He remains there, unmoving, for at least a minute, though he must have heard the door. When he eventually turns, she has to mute her surprise. He is much younger than his silver hair suggested; mid-forties perhaps, dark-browed, with a smooth, tanned face, less like a detective than what her mother would have called a matinee idol.

He smiles, revealing expensive dentistry.

'Joanna. Commandant Dominic Bouvier, Bordeaux Criminal Investigations Unit.' He gestures to a chair. 'Please.'

She perches stiffly on the edge of the seat, angling it so that she doesn't have to see herself in the mirrored wall to her right. Bouvier settles himself opposite her, one ankle crossed elegantly over his knee, and takes out a sleek fountain pen and a leather-bound notebook from his inside pocket. She notices an iPad in a blue case on the table by his elbow.

'How are you feeling?' he says.

He really is very good-looking; careful with that, she tells herself. There is a quality to his gaze that has her shifting in her seat and blushing just from proximity, so that for a moment, to her own irritation, she finds herself wishing that she had been allowed to shower and tidy up. She senses that he is well aware of his powers and knows how to deploy them when it serves him. His shoes are fine black leather lace-ups; on the sole of his raised foot she can see the Ferragamo insignia. He watches Jo as if he is poised to leap up at any moment and fetch her an extra cushion or a glass of water.

'OK,' she says. 'Well – not great.'

He nods. 'If you become unwell at any time and you want to take a break, you tell me, *d'accord*?'

She mumbles agreement and he favours her with another dazzling smile.

'Are you happy with me?'

'I'm sorry?'

'With me asking questions. Because my English is not always perfect.' He produces a self-deprecating shrug, knowing that she will contradict him.

'Your English is very good,' she says obligingly.

'I have worked some years in Canada,' he says, off-hand. 'Montreal. And Lieutenant Lemaître, she also speaks good English, so between us we will try our best. But if at any time you don't fully understand a question, you must stop us and say so, OK? And we find another way to say it until everyone is clear. Because we don't want for you to look back and say you were misled or the meaning was confused. OK?'

The warning siren starts up again in her head, shrill and loud. She thinks of the famous case of the American girl in Perugia who confessed to murder, and later claimed she was bullied into it by Italian police who made her stay up all night and sign a statement without a translator.

'Do I need a lawyer?' she asks.

Bouvier leans forward, pen poised between his fingers, all concern. 'Why would you think that you need one?'

'Well, I don't know what this is.' She gestures to the studio and the space between them. 'Is it – I mean, on the record?'

'I will take notes, of course. And later I will need you to make an official statement. But let us call this a preliminary conversation. We are simply looking for information that might help our investigation.'

236

'So can you use anything I say?'

'If it becomes necessary to give an official caution, I will tell you.'

She doesn't feel reassured. On the other hand, if they had any concrete evidence, surely she would have been arrested, they would have taken her to a police station? She knows she ought to have a solicitor, but if she asks for one, will that make her look guilty? She has no idea how this works in France, or how she would go about finding the right person.

The door opens and Lemaître enters balancing a cup of coffee, a glass of water and a plate of gallettes, which she arranges next to Jo's chair.

'For your blood sugar,' she says, with a friendly twinkle, and finds herself a place by the window, leaning against one of the wooden supports. Jo looks past her to the distant tree line.

'We need to piece together a picture of what happened last night, Joanna,' Bouvier says, his voice neutral.

Jo nods; she would like this too, though she is afraid of what she might discover. Her best course, she decides, is to say as little as possible.

'I don't – my memory is shot,' she says, offering an apologetic smile.

Bouvier looks politely nonplussed.

'Uh – there are holes here,' she says, tapping her temple. 'Last night. Parts I don't remember.'

'Understandable,' he says. 'Was that the first time you have taken PCP?'

'I don't know what that is.'

'Maybe you call it Angel Dust. No?'

She shakes her head, and the movement sends a jolt of pain pinballing around her skull. She presses the flat of her palm against her brow. Bouvier regards her with concern,

237

then speaks briefly to Lemaître in French. In response she crosses the room to open a window.

'It's a psychoactive drug,' he says. 'Can be extremely dangerous. Produces auditory and visual hallucinations, distorted perception, amnesia. Sudden aggression and violence, sometimes.'

'I didn't take anything like that,' Jo says, although this would explain the mess of memories from the chapel. 'I wouldn't touch anything serious.'

'You might not have known. If you smoked marijuana that had been laced. The doctor thinks this is what happened.'

She makes a non-committal noise. The doctor had asked her a lot of questions about what she had taken; it had seemed sensible not to give any definite answer. Now she wonders if it might work in her favour; could you be held responsible for something you did under the influence of a psychoactive substance you didn't know you had taken? It is exactly this kind of detail that a lawyer would know.

'Well, we will confirm soon – we found some half-smoked joints in the remains of the fire so they will be analysed. Where did you get these drugs?' Bouvier's tone is light and pleasant and he keeps his gaze fixed on her, steady, inviting confidences. 'Listen, Joanna,' he continues, when she doesn't reply, 'I am a murder detective – your recreational use is not a priority for me, except as far as it relates to the events of last night.'

Jo reaches for the glass and takes a sip of water. The word 'murder' hangs in the air.

'Storm had it. I thought it was just a joint. I don't usually – it's the first time I've been away without my daughter since my husband died,' she adds. 'I suppose I wanted to let my hair down for once.'

He frowns at the idiom; Lemaître murmurs a translation and he nods.

'What time did you go to the forest last night?'

She looks down at her hands gripping the glass. Her nails are crusted with blood and dirt, though she'd tried to wash it off in the hospital.

'Some time after midnight. I don't know exactly.'

'Why go so far? You could have a little smoke in the garden without being seen, no? It is big enough.'

'I don't know. Storm liked that place. It felt . . .' She had been going to say *sacred*, but worried that sounded cultish. 'Secret. Lucas showed it to her.'

'Lucas?' He looks interested at that; she sees him make a note. 'He was there with you?'

'Last night? No.' Immediately she wishes she hadn't brought him into it.

Bouvier unfolds his long legs and recrosses them the opposite way. His socks are charcoal grey, discreetly pattered. 'You know it was Lucas who found the body. How did he know to look there?'

Jo presses a hand to her mouth and shakes her head. How awful for Lucas to have been the one to find her. She would never have wished that on him, or anyone.

'I suppose because he knew she liked it.' She realises that for the second time she has referred to Storm in the past tense.

Bouvier's brow creases briefly. 'And you are quite sure Lucas wasn't with you last night?'

She hesitates. Now that he says it, she is not sure at all. There was a moment, as the drug first hit her, when she thought she saw Lucas's face, but then she was sure she saw the *dames blanches* dancing in the trees and whispering to her; she was sure, for a moment, that Storm had said the exact words that Oliver's lover had spoken on the phone, in the exact same voice, but now that she knows about the PCP, she realises she can't be certain of anything that happened last night. Except that there was a body in the chapel, and Lucas found it.

'He wasn't there,' she says firmly.

'And Rebecca Ridley? Did she go with you?'

It takes Jo a moment to work out who he is talking about. '*Becca?* No, of course not.'

'Why "of course"?'

She sits up; there is something behind his question. 'Because she wasn't' – *She wasn't our friend*, she had almost said, but realised this made her sound as if she was Hannah's age. 'She wasn't invited.'

'Ah. So she followed you?'

'Not that I saw. Why would she—' But it occurs to her that Becca, with her sly little threats and intimations, Becca – who is not above filming people in compromising situations for her own advantage – might easily have been watching from the window or the landing last night, waiting for them to sneak out again, and followed in order to furnish herself with some kind of leverage. Perhaps she could tell someone had looked through her phone. In which case – Jo feels the blood draining from her face – these detectives could well have video evidence of what happened between her and Storm, and all the questions are a series of traps to see how far she is prepared to lie.

'I'm sorry,' she says, setting the glass on the floor beside her, 'I'm not feeling good. I need a break.'

Bouvier's head is bowed; all his attention is on his notebook and Jo wonders if he heard.

'I said I need—'

'Where is the child, Joanna?' he says, snapping his eyes up to meet hers, all friendliness suddenly vanished.

'What?' Jo stares at him. 'Which child?' She looks at Lemaître.

'Clio. The Connaughts' baby,' Lemaître says. 'What was your part in it, Joanna? Did you know she planned to take the child?'

Jo wonders if she is still hallucinating. She understands the words coming out of Lemaître's mouth but can't process them in any way that makes sense.

'Your friends have assured us that you would not knowingly hurt a little girl,' Bouvier says, more gently. 'So however you got mixed up in this business, Joanna, you will agree the most important thing is to find Clio and keep her safe. You want to help us do that, yes? It will be taken into account, that you have co-operated.'

'I don't know what Clio has to do with anything,' she says, when she finally manages to make her voice work. Is this why they are asking about Becca?

'What happened after you took the baby into the forest?' Lemaître asks, leaning forward, hands on her knees. 'I know there are holes in your memory, but try to think. Did you hand her to another person or take her somewhere yourself?'

'Clio wasn't in the *forest*,' Jo says, sitting back, incredulity expressing itself in a strange inadvertent half-laugh. Whatever they think they know about the night before, they have this part wrong, she can be certain of that. Perhaps Becca didn't record anything after all.

She sees them exchange a glance.

'Let me show you a picture,' Bouvier says, reaching for the iPad. He strokes it into life, swipes through various images and holds it out to her. 'Do you recognise this?'

On the screen she sees a photograph of a clear plastic evidence bag containing a forlorn-looking object stuck with

241

leaves and dirt that might once have been pink. Her mouth dries.

'That's Clio's rabbit.' She has no idea what this means.

'This toy was found in the clearing by the ruined chapel this morning,' Lemaître says. 'How did it get there, if Clio was not in the forest?'

'I don't know.' Jo can hear the panic rising in her voice. 'Maybe Becca dropped it, if she followed us?'

'OK.' Bouvier snaps his notebook closed, sets both feet flat on the floor and hitches his trouser legs up a minute fraction. 'Tell me this, Joanna, and think very carefully before you answer, because we are talking about a child's life here. I know maybe you are afraid of her, and I'm not surprised, after what she has done, but the sooner we find her and the baby, the less you will have to fear. Have you had any communication with Storm since last night?'

Jo thinks she has misheard. '*What?*'

'Texts, calls, anything at all?'

Her face is frozen. Her throat pulls tight, like the neck of a drawstring bag; briefly, she thinks she has forgotten how to breathe.

'You seem surprised that we would ask you this?' Lemaître says.

Jo nods, mute.

'Why?'

'Because—' She has the sense that she is sliding down a rock face, gathering speed, grasping at scree. 'I thought she was dead.'

His eyebrow lifts a fraction. 'Why do you say this?'

'I saw the body, in the chapel.'

That white hand, reaching. She can hear her heartbeat in her ears. She grips on to the chair to stop herself falling.

'You saw *a* body, certainly. I was hoping you would remember something about that.'

Jo allows her eyes to close and sees again the upward arc of her own arm, the glitter of the glass shards. But maybe that never happened. *Don't say a word*, says a voice of self-preservation in her head.

'Was there an argument?' Bouvier persists. 'Last night, in the clearing – something that got out of hand, a physical fight?'

If not Storm, then *who*? But she realises they have already told her.

'*Becca?*' she asks, hardly giving it credence.

'So you did see her,' Lemaître says, as if she has scored a point.

'No, but – if it's not Storm in the chapel, then—'

'Did Rebecca try to stop you and Storm taking the baby? And one or maybe both of you fought her?'

'*No*. I didn't see Becca last night. I had no idea she was there. And Clio definitely wasn't there. I smoked a joint with Storm, we talked, and then – everything went weird, I don't remember much after that. I woke up in the woods.' She sits back after this outburst, wipes her mouth with the back of her hand. The room has grown hot; she can feel beads of sweat standing out along her brow. 'Why would Storm take Clio? That's crazy.'

He taps his pen against the notebook. 'Not so crazy. Clio is the daughter of extremely rich people.'

Jo thinks of Cressida's paranoia, her cynicism about Storm's interest in Max, the way she and Storm had ridiculed Cressida for it behind her back.

'Although there is another possibility,' Lemaître adds softly. 'In cases of child abduction, the usual motives are sexual exploitation or money – or both together, if it's a question of trafficking. But there is a third motive, which we see more often than you might think. Punishment.'

Jo says nothing, waiting for the explanation.

'If you want to hurt someone,' Lemaître continues, 'there can be no more effective way than to threaten their child. But I must say, we see this most commonly with estranged partners. Usually the men, sadly. They punish the wife for leaving by taking the child. In some cases, killing them. Often themselves also.'

Jo looks past her to the grey wash of cloud through the studio windows. It begins to come back, their last conversation in the clearing: Storm's mother drowning herself, the photo with the boys' names in her diary. Lemaître is right; Storm had come after them deliberately. This is about punishment. But for what crime?

'You see, Joanna,' Bouvier says, noting her change of expression, 'if the motive was punishment, then that would change our focus.'

'Right,' she says, since some response seems to be expected.

'Did you have reason to feel angry with Mr and Mrs Connaught?' Lemaître asks. It takes Jo a moment to comprehend.

'*Me?* No, of course not. Why would you think that?'

Bouvier flicks back a couple of pages to check his notes. 'Storm told Mr Steadman that you had been complaining about them when you were alone with her. She said you resented Mr and Mrs Connaught because they hadn't done enough to help you after your husband died. You said, I quote, *They had no idea what it meant to suffer, with their perfect life.*'

'None of that is true. She's lying.'

'You never said this?'

'No. I mean, I might have said they haven't been around much, but not the rest of it.'

'Storm told Max' – he consults his book again – 'that she was worried about you, that you seemed like someone who was on the edge of a breakdown. Mrs Connaught, Ms Gregorian – they both said your behaviour has been out of character this weekend. And you said yourself, you've been using drugs, which is not typical for you.'

Jo can't think how to respond to this, so she says nothing.

'This,' Lemaître says, indicating Jo's arm. 'Do you remember why you tried to harm yourself?'

Jo touches her right fingertips to the bandage. A faint spot of blood has begun to seep through the gauze. 'Storm did it,' she says.

'Was it Storm's idea to take Clio?' Lemaître asks. 'And perhaps you thought it was a chance to teach the Connaughts a lesson?'

'You think I would help take someone's *child* because I was upset with them?' She is half out of her seat, staring at them. 'That's insane. I'd never put a child in danger, if I'd thought Storm had anything like that in mind, I'd have—' She breaks off. A quick blink of a memory: Storm in the nursery, holding Clio face to face. *Imagine being this little princess.* But that hadn't rung a warning bell; why should it? Again she feels that sick, dropping sensation that she had felt in Saint-Émilion, when she realised Storm had only invited her as a cover. All the time she had thought Storm wanted her company, she was being set up as a kind of misdirection. Unstable, bitter, grieving widow, edge of a breakdown, penchant for drugs, memory glitches, self-harm: how could they not think she must be guilty, even if they didn't know exactly how?

'One other curious thing,' Bouvier says, reaching again for

the iPad as if he has only just remembered. 'Do you recognise this?'

Jo blinks hard to focus on the screen: another photograph of an evidence bag, this one containing a twisted, blackened shape that might be charred plastic or rubber. She shakes her head.

'I can't even tell what that is.'

'It's a phone case,' he says helpfully.

Jo looks closer, until she can make out patches where the thing is still off-white, where the pink dots of the cartoon character are just about visible through the burn marks.

'It's not mine,' she says, avoiding his eye. 'I don't think it's Storm's either.'

'No, we know that. You haven't seen it before?'

'No.' Her mouth is dry; she badly wants a sip of water, but if she picks up the glass now they will see her hands shaking.

'It belonged to Rebecca Ridley. Someone had thrown it on the fire in the clearing – I doubt we can get prints from it, which I imagine was their intention. But here's the strange thing, Joanna – we haven't found the phone.'

'Don't you have ways to trace it?'

'Unfortunately not if it has been switched off and the battery removed. Which seems to be the case with Rebecca's phone. Storm's too, in fact. You see,' he goes on, leaning in, hands clasped, elbows resting on his knees as if he is about to confide privileged information, 'one theory is that Rebecca's death was an accident. There were signs of a struggle around the entrance to the chapel. It's plausible, don't you think? Rebecca was trying to stop someone taking the baby, there was a fight, the injury was unintentional. Perhaps the person didn't even realise they had killed her, they just ran away.' He lifts an eyebrow. Jo doesn't respond. 'The problem with this theory,' he says, tapping his notebook as if he is about to give the big reveal, 'is the missing phone. The fact that it has been taken out of the case and there was clearly an attempt to destroy the case. So naturally, we are interested in what might be on this phone. You can see how that would make a difference.'

She thinks of the video clip that she and Storm had giggled over like teenagers – 'my *eyes!*' – a clip that was still, presumably, on Jo's own phone waiting to be discovered. It is only now that it registers: she doesn't know where her phone is. She had it that morning when she woke in the woods, and somewhere between the hospital and her return it had disappeared. Had the police taken it? Were they allowed to do that? If they saw the video, it would bolster their theory that Jo was harbouring a grudge against Arlo and Cressida. Despite Bouvier's reassurance that they are only gathering information, the questions have begun to feel much more targeted, and tricksy, as if designed to catch her out. Storm has made sure that Jo looks implicated, even if the police aren't quite clear how.

'Sorry, I can't help you.' She pushes herself unsteadily to her feet. 'Excuse me. I need some air.'

The detectives exchange a look; they murmur a few words in French.

'What?' she says, when no one offers permission. 'Can I go out? Or am I under arrest?'

'No, Joanna,' Bouvier says, with evident weariness, standing and brushing invisible specks from his suit. 'You are not under arrest. But obviously do not leave the grounds. We will have more questions for you.'

22

Jo stumbles out, expecting to be followed. But when she glances back at the studio, she sees the two detectives standing at the tall window, shoulder to shoulder, conferring as they watch her. She pulls her sleeves over her hands and hurries along the path, around the corner of the studio, out of sight. She doesn't want them to see how badly she is trembling. All this has triggered memories she thought she had buried, of the last time she was interrogated by police officers in the days and weeks after Oliver's death. Then, as now, she was convinced that they were withholding crucial information, that they knew perfectly well that she was lying to them and were just waiting for her to trip herself up. She didn't ask Bouvier about her phone, on the slender off-chance that they didn't have it and she had dropped it somewhere in the forest; it seemed premature to alert him to its existence and cause him to take an interest in finding it.

The lawn of the main courtyard is empty, the dog handlers gone. More leaves have fallen overnight around the old horse chestnut, the chandeliers still hang from its branches like tired Christmas decorations. She walks slowly across and turns to look up at the chateau. Pale light whites out the windows in the roof, where the children's rooms are.

She can't piece it together; it still sounds so outlandish. For those few hours, between her glimpse of that cold, white hand and her interview just now, she had come to believe that she was a murderer. Even then, the idea had been so distant, so abstract – although that might have been the effect of the antipsychotic – that she couldn't begin to connect it with her real life, or come to terms with what it would mean to live with that knowledge. All she had been able to think about was how she would break it to Hannah. At least now she is spared the weight of that – she can say, with absolute certainty, that she did not see either Becca or Clio last night – and this should have brought some relief. But it is clear that the police still believe she is guilty of something; she is not safe yet. Oliver would know how to find a good lawyer in France, she thinks, and briefly – stupidly – feels irritated that she can't call him and ask. She could try asking one of his old colleagues, although she is not sure how inclined they would be to help. Oliver was regarded with admiration but not necessarily affection at his chambers. People found him arrogant, he always told her, dismissing the absurdity of this with an incredulous laugh. Because he won more cases than them, obviously, and because there was still a persistent view that human rights law was a bit touchy-feely; some people, he said, didn't want to acknowledge that these were the cases that demanded the most ruthlessness in an advocate.

Jo wanders across to the children's play area and sits heavily on a swing. She has no desire to face the others yet, wherever they are. She can only imagine what Cressida must be going through with Clio missing.

'Jo!' The word comes to her in a hiss, accompanied by

the crackle of footsteps through the leaves; she whips around to see Max, unshaven and hunted, quickening his pace towards her. Part of her wants to fling herself into his arms, but she has no idea if he too is wary of her and what she might have done. She is not even sure if she is allowed to talk to him, or if any exchange between them will be taken as proof of collaboration.

'How are you doing?' Max asks, lowering himself into the swing beside her with a creaking of ropes. She blinks at him; where to start? 'OK, stupid question,' he says. He drags his hands across his face.

'You look as if you haven't slept.'

'I know. Ironically, since I slept like the dead.' He stops, realising what he has said. 'This is all my fault,' he says, eventually. 'I let her in.'

'You couldn't have known.'

'The others won't see it that way. They'll think I, of all people, should have done some basic checks. But she was so . . .' He lets the sentence trail away, one hand half over his mouth. 'It's been lonely, since Fran left. Well, Christ, I don't need to tell you about that. But at least you have Hannah.'

'At least you can still see Fran,' she fires back.

'True.' He tilts his head, acknowledging that their situations are not comparable. 'We have a tensely amicable lunch once a month, where she tells me how great her life is now, and I pretend I'm happy for her.' He shifts position. 'Until I met Storm, I think I was still hoping Fran would change her mind. Stupid, I know. But that's why I hadn't tried meeting anyone. Plus, it's hard to join a dating app when you've been on TV. You don't know if you're going to get psychos.'

'Yes, God forbid you attract any psychos,' Jo says, rubbing her bandage meaningfully. 'I think that ship has sailed.' They catch one another's eye and let out a guilty laugh. Max's face turns suddenly serious.

'A girl is dead, Jo. I still can't get my head around it. And Clio missing, Oscar in hospital. I can't square that with what I thought I knew about Storm. None of it seems real.'

'They think I had something to do with it.'

'I know. They kept asking about your relationship with Storm. I told them as far as I knew you'd never met before she turned up here.'

'How did Becca die?' Jo asks, after a long pause.

'No idea. I suppose there'll be an autopsy.'

'You saw her, though. You don't need an autopsy to notice if someone's been stabbed.'

'Stabbed?' He frowns. 'No, I don't think so. There was blood on her head. I didn't go too close. Lucas did, unfortunately – he panicked and tried to wake her. The detectives were furious with him and Arlo for touching the body. Why did you think she'd been stabbed?'

'There was a broken bottle.' She holds out her injured arm. 'Storm had it in the clearing last night.'

His eyes widen. 'She attacked you with it?'

'Sort of. I don't really remember.'

'And she didn't say anything to you about Clio? Nothing that rang alarm bells?'

'No.' She gestures towards the yoga studio. 'I've just had all this from them. Of course not. Didn't *you* notice any alarm bells? You knew her better than me.'

Max sighs. 'Sorry. No. I mean, she seemed interested in my friends, but only in the way people are curious about anyone who's been in a Sunday supplement.' He scrapes a palm over his stubble and looks for a moment as if he might be sick. 'You just have to hope,' he says, his voice barely there, 'that she wouldn't harm a baby. I can't believe that she would. If she wants money, she'll hold out for that. Won't she?'

Jo touches her arm. 'She tried to make me cut my wrists. They think she killed Becca. I don't know what she's capable of.' She hesitates. 'The police don't think it's about money.'

This startles him. 'What, then?'

Jo fights to remember her conversation with Storm in the clearing the night before. All the pieces are floating within her grasp, she just can't make them fall into place, and she blames the murk in her head. Max might make better sense of it.

'That Polaroid,' she says, and leaves a space for him to fill in the gap. She catches a flash of something in his eyes; is it fear? 'Why are you all so antsy about it?'

'Ah. OK.' He shifts again, stretches his leg out. 'Shall we walk?'

He points towards the wildflower meadow behind the formal garden. In the still air, the sound of the dogs carries from the woods.

'Did Oliver ever say anything to you about why he'd kept it?' Max says, when they have walked a safe distance from the house.

She turns to stare at him. 'Oliver? What are you talking about?'

Max studies her face, confused, as if he can't work out where the wires are crossed.

'You obviously didn't want to get into it last night. So I wondered if you already knew the story.'

'Max, I'd never seen that photo before this weekend. It wasn't Oliver's, it was Storm's. I saw it in her notebook. But I couldn't say so last night without revealing that I'd been through her bag. Everyone assumed it had come from Oliver, I don't know why, so it seemed easier to say nothing.'

'*Storm* brought it?' He shakes his head. 'That's not possible. How? Did she say where she got it?'

'Oliver was having an affair before he died,' Jo says, trying to keep her voice matter of fact. Max takes a moment to focus; he is thinking about the photo. He nods, distracted.

'You don't seem surprised. Did you know?'

He concentrates on his shoes. 'Not specifics. I mean, he didn't confide any details or come to me pouring his heart out. But there was one occasion – it must be three or four years ago now – he called me late one night and said he'd told you he spent the evening with me and Fran, so if you ever asked, could I back him up.'

'Lie for him, you mean?'

'Yes.' He chews his lip. 'I wasn't happy about it, obviously, but you never did ask, so I didn't have to. And I told him very firmly not to use us as an alibi again. I said we cared about you and I didn't want to be in that position. But I guessed from that episode that he played away from time to time.'

'Did you ever talk to him about it?'

'No.' A silence stretches between them, spiky with accusation. 'He knew how I feel about cheating, he wouldn't have wanted a lecture. I'm sorry, Jo. I didn't feel it was my business to interfere. I had enough going on, trying to hold my own marriage together at the time.'

'Did he tell you about the phone call I intercepted, not long before he died? What the woman said?'

Max shakes his head. 'No. Like I say, he never gave any details and I didn't want to hear.'

'So you definitely didn't know about the call? The exact words? You're absolutely sure you didn't tell Storm?'

'I've no idea what you're talking about, Jo,' he says, with a trace of impatience. 'I would never discuss your marriage with anyone, especially not someone I've only been seeing a few months. I'm amazed you think I would. What does this have to do with the photo?'

'Then . . .' She squints towards the treeline on the horizon, trying to make sense of it. There is only one possible explanation, the one that struck her last night in the clearing, that lit the fuse of her rage. 'Then I was right. It was her. Oliver's lover. That's who Oliver was seeing, before he died.'

Max stares. '*Storm?* That's absurd. Why on earth would you think that?'

She takes a deep breath. This part of the story is humiliating; in any other circumstances nothing would persuade her to share these details with Max. She explains about the CarPlay, John W, the woman's voice. *Hey you, it's your dirty little whore.*

She pauses, swallows. Her throat feels raw. 'It was Oliver's thing,' she adds. Her face is burning; she can't look at him. 'You know, that he liked women to say to him in bed. So I knew it was someone he was sleeping with.'

'But Storm doesn't have a posh English voice. Why would you think it was her?'

'Because she said it to me last night. In the clearing. Those exact words, in that same accent. No one else knew about that except me, Oliver, and the woman he was fucking. I thought maybe he'd told you and you'd told Storm, but if not, then – there's only one way she could know. She wanted me to know it was her. She's had Oliver and now you.'

Max is having a hard time taking this in. 'You mean, she targeted me on purpose.' It is barely even a question; he knows the answer.

'I think so. It's all connected, somehow, with that photo.'

'Where did she get it?'

'She didn't exactly say. But I think it was her mother's.'

'Her *mother's?*' Max is staring at her as if she's gone mad.

And then, suddenly, he makes a small, shocked sound as if the air has been punched out of him, and an expression of terrible recognition slowly freezes his face. 'Oh God,' he says, and doubles over; his face is an alarming shade of grey-green. At the top of the rise there is a bench looking back towards the house. He lets Jo steer him to it like a sleepwalker and falls heavily, staring into the distance.

'What did she tell you about her mother?' He sounds dazed, as if he is mildly concussed.

'She drowned herself when Storm was two, apparently. In Galway. That was another thing. After Oliver died, I found an old newspaper cutting in his desk. It was a story about a young woman who drowned in Galway Bay nineteen years ago. It was only a couple of lines – I couldn't understand why he'd kept it. I thought it must have something to do with one of his old cases, he sometimes did hang on to news reports, except that this one was in an envelope postmarked this summer, addressed to him at his chambers.'

'What was the name? The girl who drowned – do you remember?'

'Róisín.' She wasn't sure why the name had stuck in her memory. Oliver had occasionally represented relatives of people accused or disappeared during the Troubles; she had assumed the woman had some connection with one of those cases. 'Róisín Caffrey.'

Max leaps up as if he has to be somewhere, then stands, uselessly, twisting his hands. 'I've been so stupid. I can't believe I didn't see it. But none of us knew – Arlo said it was all dealt with. All this time, we thought – and she—' He sits again, rocking forward with his head between his knees. 'Oh fuck, *Oliver*. It all makes sense.'

'What does? Oliver what?' When he doesn't answer, she hits him in the arm, but he barely notices.

'Oliver called me one night, the week before he died,' he says, peeling his fingers away from his face. 'He was drunk. I mean really out of it, incoherent, in a total mess. He was sort of crying and raging and he kept saying, "Max, it's all over. I've fucked my daughter." I thought he meant Hannah.'

'*What?*'

'Jesus, no, not like that – I thought he meant in the sense of fucked up, you know – the way you might say, oh, I've really fucked my driving test. What I *thought* he meant' – he draws in a great ragged breath, tries to steady himself – 'I thought you'd found out about his affairs and you were leaving him. And he'd got self-pityingly drunk and was berating himself for fucking up Hannah's life. That's what I assumed. But if he'd slept with Storm, and she told him about her mother, then – he meant something else entirely.' His hands are shaking. 'He thought he'd literally fucked *his own daughter.*'

'But that's insane, how could Storm be – *oh*. That pub in the photo. The barmaid. He had a thing with her.' It feels like being slammed into a wall. She remembers Storm kissing her. Hannah's sister. Oliver's— No. It couldn't be true. '*Did* he? Is that it?'

'It's more complicated than that.' Max starts walking, as if he might be able to outpace the revelations. Jo scrambles to catch up, and they follow the path that runs between the meadow and the vineyard to the west. From the forest, a dog starts up a furious volley of barks.

'Are you sure you want to hear this?' Max says, glancing sidelong.

She gives him a long look. 'How much worse could it be?'

He sets his mouth in a grim line and looks away.

23

Then

Max dropped the others at the door and found a parking space three streets away. Within seconds of switching off the engine, rain had turned the windscreen opaque. He sat and watched the water sluicing down the glass. It occurred to him that he could just drive back to college, let them get a taxi back. Later, he would remember this moment; he would wish, over and over, that he had obeyed that instinct. Instead, he reached into the footwell for his umbrella as a sheet of lightning strobed the sky. The wind was growing worse; there had been severe weather warnings for the whole of East Anglia, the kind of storm that could pose serious risk to life, they had said on the news, which made it all the more idiotic to have left the refuge of the college bar.

He buttoned his coat and opened the door; this would be absolutely the last time he drove them. Although he had told himself that the week before, and let Oliver cajole him into it again. Oliver told him he was a people-pleaser, and he supposed it was true. 'You're going to have to work on that if you want to be a journalist, mate,' he'd said, laughing, 'the whole job is screwing people over.' And yet Oliver was quite happy to take advantage of Max's people-pleasing tendencies when it suited him.

His shoes and trouser legs were soaked before he reached the end of the street; a slicing gale wrenched the umbrella inside out and when he couldn't right it or fold it, he dragged it along behind him, metal spokes scraping the pavement as he passed a shuttered off-licence and a mini-cab office whose sickly yellow light fractured in the overflowing gutter. Not much sign of dreaming spires out here; he doubted many students even knew this part of the city existed. But that was the whole point, to be anonymous. Oliver had been tipped off about the place by one of the hippie guys who worked on the punts under Silver Street Bridge. 'Do us all good to get out of the bubble once in a while,' Ollie had said, when trying to sell it to the rest of them, and it was true that, some nights, while the other three were traipsing into the toilet, bounding back each time with the exuberance of a game show host, Max had struck up conversations with some of the regulars, people whose paths he would never have crossed in the ordinary course of student life. They had been hostile at first, but he'd discovered he had a knack for listening, and that often people welcomed the chance to tell you their story if you learned how to prompt in the right way. It was good experience for a writer, he told himself.

There it was, up ahead: grimed pebble-dashed walls, the sign on its rusted bracket flaking so badly you wouldn't be able to decipher the pub's name if you didn't know it already. He pushed open the door to a blast of hot yeasty air and tried not to think about the fact that it was Friday night, tried not to picture his parents and sisters sitting down to dinner,

258

his mother lighting the candles, and how they would react if they knew what he was doing right now.

'Here he is,' she said from behind the bar, revolving a dishcloth briskly around a pint glass and flashing him a wink. 'Usual, is it? Jesus, you look like a drowned rat. Sit yourself down and warm up, I'll bring it over.'

Max smiled, feeling the heat rise to the tips of his ears. She was professionally charming to all the customers, he knew that rationally, but he could never help the jolt that ran through him when she turned her smile in his direction as if she meant it, as if she'd never been so pleased to see anyone in her life. Of course, he would never dream of – she was out of his league in many different ways, and in any case, Oliver had made quite clear that if any of them was going to have her, it would be him. There was no doubt that the presence of Rosie the barmaid was a large part of what gave these Friday excursions their frisson, and would have been even if she wasn't the one selling wraps of cheap coke behind the bins outside the kitchen. She was, Max thought, quite possibly the most beautiful girl he'd ever seen, but her appeal was more than just her exquisite face, the high cheekbones and dark brows framing wide green eyes; it was the way she looked at you, with a kind of indulgent amusement, as if you weren't fooling her with your gallant gestures, she'd seen it all before. At the same time, there was a wholesomeness about her; her lilting voice and radiant skin conjured images of soft rain and fresh butter and rolling deep-green hills, though he was well aware that this was a cliché bordering on offensive.

Max took his seat beside the others, who had already piled their damp jackets on a spare chair and nestled into their regular corner opposite the Gents (for ease of access). Oliver lifted his glass (vodka and tonic, he said beer weighed

259

him down and was therefore incompatible with the evening's pursuits) towards him in a gesture of acknowledgement, cigarette jutting between his first two fingers. Leo was midway through an anecdote that involved a party where he had inadvertently run into two girls he was seeing simultaneously, neither of whom knew about the other, and the increasingly farcical contortions required to keep them apart while he figured out which one to go home with; no one was really listening, but that was beside the point. All this was preamble. Max peeled off his sodden coat, shook the rain off his hair and settled back against the bench. The preamble was the part he enjoyed, before the real object of the evening appeared: the four of them around a pub table, talking nonsense, the way they had all the way through their first term, when they had found themselves living on the same staircase and somehow arrived at an unspoken agreement that they would look out for one another. And they had, Max reflected; through heartbreak and drunken nights and exams and anxiety and (in Leo's case) the serious illness of a parent, they had made sure between them that none of them was ever left without a shoulder to cry on, or someone to raise a glass with. That, Max supposed, looking around the table, was why he kept coming back here on Friday nights: he had been a solitary boy by nature, a situation that had not bothered him as a teen, since he had never aspired to be part of the popular crowd at school and his mother and two sisters were gregarious enough for all of them, but he had not known until he met Ollie, Arlo and Leo what it meant to belong to a solid group. He had never had *mates* before, in that sense. And he couldn't help but wonder what would happen in a few short months when they left, if the bonds forged largely by circumstance would survive outside the sixteenth-century walls of their college.

He was afraid, he realised, that they would not, and that their time together was already taking on a sepia tinge of nostalgia.

He noticed the others sit up straighter, as if on cue, and turned to see Rosie approaching with his pint. He smiled as she set it down deftly on the mat, but she was looking at Oliver, who raised an eyebrow; the girl glanced back at the landlord, absorbed in the evening paper at the end of the bar, and gave a minute shake of her head that Max took to mean *not yet*.

'Wait there, though,' she said, with a sudden flash of that smile, and ducked behind the bar to emerge again clutching the chunky red Polaroid camera that was kept under the counter.

'Come on now,' she said sternly, raising a hand against their objections. 'It's not right we don't have your portraits in the rogues' gallery, you're some of my best customers.' She caught Oliver's eye and winked.

'That's precisely why' – Oliver began, when Arlo, who usually wore an air of distraction, as if the greater part of his considerable brain was elsewhere, suddenly snapped back to the present.

'You absolutely cannot take our picture,' he said, in the kind of voice accustomed to giving orders. Arlo may have been a man of few words, but when he did speak, he sounded as if a computer had been trained by the Royal Shakespeare Company; the effect was unfortunate. 'We've told you that.'

If Rosie minded his peremptory tone, she didn't show it. 'What's the problem? Are you a Russian spy? I hear they have a few of those at this place.'

'Of course not, I—' Arlo stopped when he realised she was teasing. 'I'm a very private person,' he added.

'What if I said it was just for me?' Rosie persisted. 'Not

261

for the pinboard, just to remember you all by. You're my favourite regulars, after all.'

'Remember? Why, are you leaving?' Max said, alarmed.

She looked up from fiddling with the viewfinder and checked that the landlord wasn't listening. 'I think so. *This*' – she made a gesture that took in the pub, its peeling varnish and tobacco-stained walls, as well as the corridor beside the Gents that led to the fire exit and the small yard where she conducted her off-the-books transactions – 'is not really what I dreamed of doing with my life, you know? Time to get my shit together.' She grinned and lifted the camera.

'But where will you go?' Max asked, as if it were his responsibility.

'Home, maybe. I've got a bit of money saved and I want to go back to college to study nursing. England's not all it was cracked up to be.' She offered a rueful smile.

'I'd like to see you in a nurse's uniform,' Oliver said, predictably.

She nodded to the drink and cigarette in his hand. 'Keep all that up, you're going the right way about it. You'll be seeing someone in a nurse's uniform soon enough, anyway.'

'All right, *Mum*.'

'Your mammy would thank me for taking care of you.'

'Our vices have paid for your savings,' Oliver said, slinging an arm around Arlo's neck. 'You should be encouraging them.'

'You're not wrong there,' she said, and before they could object, she had clicked the shutter and the camera began the whirring that was the prelude to spitting out a picture. 'Gotcha.'

'Seriously,' Arlo said, half-rising with a hand outstretched, 'you can't legally' – but Oliver pulled him down as Rosie spun laughing away from them, flapping the Polaroid to dry it off.

After that, the evening unfolded according to the usual pattern. At a certain point, Rosie gave Oliver the nod and he slipped out down the corridor to the fire exit; on his return, Leo casually strolled to the toilet to meet him, and when Leo re-emerged, Arlo took his place. Max tolerated their turbo-charged chatter for a while, then drifted away to talk to the regulars at the bar, old men nursing pints and grudges who were used to him by now and enjoyed the chance to grumble to a willing stranger. If he was lucky, he would exchange a few words and smiles with Rosie as she moved efficiently between the taps and the cash register, throwing cheeky ripostes over her shoulder to any man (it was almost all men in the saloon bar) who attempted a clumsy chat-up line, but Max was not blind; it was obvious, he noted with regret, how often she glanced back at Oliver.

Shortly before last orders, he had returned to their table in the corner and was making his usual show of gathering up his coat as a hint to the others, when he noticed a disturbance on the other side of the room. A group of young men, a few years older than them and obviously townies, had arrived in the pub perhaps ten minutes earlier and commandeered a table at the far end of the bar. One of them – tall, with a studded leather jacket and a swagger – had immediately disappeared out the back with Rosie, presumably to make a purchase. But she had returned from the yard in a hurry, pale and tight-lipped; Max had observed the studied way she avoided the tall guy's eye after. Now they had formed a circle around her as she cleared the glasses, standing too close, jostling her; for the moment, it could be read as good-natured teasing, but there was an edge to it, Max could tell. Rosie was no longer laughing or participating in the back-and-forth banter, the way she did with their group; she looked cornered. The landlord was nowhere to be seen.

Max nudged Oliver and drew his attention to the unfolding drama. Ollie, his confidence artificially buoyed, took in the situation and stood up.

'Right,' he said, knocking back the remains of his drink.

'Mate.' Leo grabbed his sleeve and pulled him down. 'Don't be a dick.'

'What? They're giving her hassle, you want me to stand by and watch?'

Leo sighed. 'No offence, but you're a skinny posh boy who's never had a proper fight in your life. They'll take you apart. And I'm not getting my hands dirty for shitheads like that. There's better ways to deal with it.'

And he slid out of his seat and across to the bar, where Rosie had managed to escape and was aggressively pulling pints with her back to Leather Jacket guy and his friends. Leo leaned across and exchanged a few words with her; she glanced up sharply in their direction and nodded, relief washing over her face. Leo returned to his seat and casually informed them that they would be taking Rosie home after she had cashed up.

'What, all of us?' Oliver said, aggrieved. In his mind, he had appointed himself Rosie's white knight and clearly didn't like the idea of Leo muscling in. Max, who already had the car keys in his hand, found, to his shame, that he was also reluctant to be part of this deployment; while he had no wish to leave Rosie to the mercies of a bunch of coked-up Neanderthals, he also knew he would be worse than useless if it came to actually defending her.

'Yep.' Leo draped his arm along the back of the bench. 'That fucker in the biker jacket already tried to grope her out the back. They'll hang around till she leaves, she said they've done it before. She only lives a few streets away, so we'll drive her home, yeah? They won't mess with four of us. Plus it's pissing down out there.'

He was right; you could hear the rain drilling like gunfire on the overhang of the bay window behind them. Max was still quite certain that his presence would not be any kind of deterrent, but he could hardly drive off without the others, so he agreed. Rosie brought them a tray of drinks – 'on the house,' she whispered – and he smiled his thanks, though the thought of yet another half of orange juice made him queasy.

So they waited for Rosie beneath the leaking roof of the delivery bay out the back while she locked up, and when she appeared they surrounded her and hurried her out, coat pulled up over her head against the rain, like bodyguards ushering a celebrity (or a criminal, Max thought) through a phalanx of press. Leather Jacket and his mates, who had been hanging about at the front, followed them up the street at an intimidating distance. Willing himself not to let the keys slip through his wet fingers, Max braced for the first blow, when Leo suddenly turned 180 degrees and stopped dead, causing their pursuers almost to stumble into them.

'Leave it, mate,' Leo said, surprisingly calmly for someone who had done several lines. 'She told you she's not interested.'

Leather Jacket bunched his fists at his side, nostrils flaring, as he locked eyes with Leo, the desire not to lose face vying with the instinct for self-preservation. Leo didn't move, and Max became aware of the power of his friend's stillness; Leo's whole bearing made clear that he was not someone they wanted to fuck with. Leather Jacket seemed to realise it too; after a few moments' hesitation, he muttered something that was not quite audible but almost certainly racist and turned on his heel, followed by his friends, who cast dark threats over their shoulders about what would happen next time as soon as they were at a safe distance.

'He's such an arsehole,' Rosie said, as they bundled into the car. 'He knows my step-cousin's friend, the one I sell for. He's been trying it on since I got here. Doesn't deal well with rejection. I owe you.' She leaned through the front seats and tapped Max on the shoulder. 'Left at the end here.'

He could feel her warm breath on his neck as she directed him down narrow streets of terraced houses. Rain hammered so hard against the windscreen he could barely see ten feet ahead, even with the wipers full-pelt, and the windows grew dense with steam from five bodies and wet clothes. When he glanced in the rear mirror, he noticed that she had a hand on Oliver's thigh.

He pulled up where she indicated and left the engine running.

'You'll come up?' she said, as Oliver opened the door. 'Least I can do. Look, I liberated this from behind the bar. That fat fuck'll never notice.' From inside her coat she drew out a bottle of vodka. 'And I've got more supplies upstairs.'

'We have to get back to college before they lock the gates,' Max said, his hands still on the wheel. He was tired and sober and still shaky from the adrenalin surge of nearly being beaten up.

'Lock the—' Rosie laughed, incredulous. 'It's Friday *night*, lads. What is it, boarding school?'

'It's actually an ancient statute that says—'

'We can climb the gates if we have to,' Oliver cut in. Max caught his eye in the mirror.

'I'm not stopping you,' Max said.

'How am I supposed to get back?'

'Call a cab.'

'This is my car,' Oliver said, petulant.

'Fine. I'll call a cab, you can drive it home.'

'You know I can't.' Ollie liked to think he was daring, but he wasn't stupid; a drink-driving charge would end his legal career before it had started.

'Come on,' Rosie said, scraping her hair into a ponytail and squeezing rain from the ends, 'there's plenty of booze, you can all get dried off, it'll be fun to hang out. I need to unwind after tonight.'

'I need a piss,' Arlo said abruptly, climbing out of the car. It was hard to tell how drunk he was; enough that he was solely focused on meeting his own needs and oblivious to Max's desire to get home. Oliver stepped out to let Rosie past, and stood on the pavement, collar turned against the weather while she rummaged for her keys; the rain hit the tarmac so hard it bounced up to knee-height. Max glanced at Leo, who shrugged and opened his door.

'We don't have to stay long,' he said quietly. 'If Ollie's on a promise, we can leave then. But he'll be pissed off if we wreck it for him.'

Max sighed and cut the engine, wondering if Oliver would do the same for him if the situation were reversed. He was fairly sure he knew the answer.

After this, everything became a little blurry. Rosie cranked up the electric fire to its highest setting and arranged chairs in front of it, where they draped an array of wet clothes so that the tiny flat was soon choked with the smell of damp. Oliver cracked open the vodka while their hostess put on a disc of Nina Simone and pulled the fridge away from the wall, revealing a loose panel in the skirting board from which she withdrew a strongbox containing the supplies she had promised. Arlo took out a wad of notes from his wallet, insisting against Rosie's protestations that they pay for the goods; Leo set about cutting lines on a CD case while Max lurked uneasily by the door, car key clutched in his fist, wondering how long he would have to hang around until Oliver made his move and the rest of them could leave him to it.

Rosie appeared in high spirits; she knocked back shots of vodka as if to make up for lost time, dancing exuberantly around the cramped living room, pausing now and then to light a cigarette or drape an arm around someone's neck in a burst of breathless laughter. Whenever a sheet of lightning blanched the room, she would shriek in delight and press her face against the window to watch as if she wanted to absorb its energy, declaring that this storm was nothing compared to the ones they saw over the bay back home. She was doing her best to flirt with them all, to make sure no one felt left out; even Max found himself the object of her attention at one point, as she teasingly eased him out of his coat and led him to a threadbare armchair by the fire 'to warm up'. When she sat down close to Oliver on the sofa, Max turned pointedly away. At the edge of his sightline he could see Arlo and Leo opposite each other at a folding Formica table; Arlo determinedly putting away shots with single-minded focus, Leo's head bent in concentration over the rolled-up note in his hand. He had not seen Arlo drink like that often, and he didn't like it; he wondered briefly if he ought to intervene, or whether he would be ridiculed for trying.

In the event he did nothing, because he must have drifted off. He was not sure for how long, but when he snapped to with a jolt, as if he had missed a stair, he saw that the room had reconfigured. Oliver was still on the sofa with Rosie, now hungrily kissing her open-mouthed, one hand down the front of her open jeans. On her other side, Arlo had pulled down the left strap of her vest top and was licking her bare breast. She seemed indifferent to this, though she had her left arm slung loosely around Arlo's shoulder, her thumb moving in a gentle, metronomic movement up and down his neck. Max felt, in the same moment, arousal and disgust.

He watched for a second longer, unwilling to acknowledge that the discomfort he was experiencing was partly disappointment that Rosie had not lived up to the pure image he had constructed around her. Eventually, not wanting to seem like a pervert, he tore his eyes away and stood, adjusting himself awkwardly; this was indisputably their cue to leave. As he reached for his coat the movement must have registered with Rosie; she peeled herself off Oliver's face, pushing Arlo away, and lurched to her feet, unsteady on her long legs like a newborn giraffe, her breast still exposed. She teetered uncertainly until Oliver stood and took her firmly by the elbow. For a moment, her eyes locked with Max's and in that brief glance he saw that she was very, very drunk, and perhaps under the influence of something mind-altering – he was not familiar enough with the effects of different drugs to discern, but her expression was glazed and her mouth slack; she looked as if she had no concept of what was happening.

'We should go,' Max said, rattling the key.

Oliver looked at him and then at Rosie, who had slumped against him as if spent by the exertion of getting to her feet. Her face had taken on a greyish tinge. 'She needs to go to bed,' he said.

'Fine. Get her to bed and let's go,' Max said, choosing to ignore the ambiguity. 'Put a washing-up bowl or something beside her, in case she throws up in the night.'

Rosie pulled at Oliver's arm, leading him in the direction of a half-open door at the back of the room, through which an unmade bed could be glimpsed. Oliver winked at Max, and guided her through. Arlo stood and followed like an automaton, leaving Max so astonished that he was still staring when the door closed behind them.

A toilet flushed and Leo appeared from the bathroom that led off from the kitchenette, zipping himself up. He followed Max's gaze to the bedroom door.

'Are they all . . .?' he jerked a thumb.

Max nodded. 'We need to get them out,' he said, twisting a loose thread on his sleeve. 'She's a bit of a mess,' he added, in case Leo hadn't understood.

Leo laughed. 'She likes to party, that's all,' he said. 'You saw how she was putting it away. She was on a mission to get fucked up.'

'They're both in there,' Max said doubtfully.

Leo reached out and pinched his cheek humorously, waggling it the way you would with a young child. His eyes were very bloodshot. 'OK. I mean, she did ask all of us in, so . . .'

'I don't think she necessarily meant for . . .' She had pushed Arlo away. Or had she? 'She didn't look very with it,' he finished lamely.

'Maybe I'd better see what's going on,' Leo said, still grinning. 'But I'm telling you, that girl knows how to have fun. She's up for it. Don't stress.' He patted Max's shoulder and slipped into the bedroom.

Perhaps he was right, Max thought. He was so far out of his depth in this situation, he had no fixed point by which to steer. It was entirely possible, he told himself, that in a world far from his own conventional, somewhat sheltered upbringing, there were girls who would happily, willingly, invite four guys home for sex. It was possible that, all over the city, people without Max's collection of hang-ups and inhibitions were having orgies every night of the week. It was true that Rosie had brought them all into her home and provided the drugs and booze. Perhaps when she put her hand out to Arlo she was just levering herself up, not pushing him off her. And yet he couldn't shake the unpleasant needling in his gut, the sense that this wasn't right. He waited another five minutes for Leo, watching the door, and thought he caught the sound of a muffled female giggle. Whatever was going on in there, he was not part of it, and suddenly felt very strongly that he had no wish to be. It was gone one o'clock. He poured himself the dregs of the vodka and downed it angrily in one. Then he placed the car key on top of the pile of money Arlo had left on the table and walked out into the rain.

24

Now

'So they raped her,' Jo says flatly.

'I don't know what happened – I wasn't in the room.'

'You don't *know*?' She stops dead, turns to him with a new hardness in her tone. 'You fucking *do* know, Max. You just said, you could see the girl was out of it, you felt bad enough to run away. But you didn't try to stop them.'

Max presses his lips together and shoves his hands into his pockets. They stare at each other in silence. A skein of geese flies overhead with a melancholy chorus of honking.

'There's nothing you can say that will make me feel any worse,' he says eventually. 'Of course I should have stopped them. But I was timid at college. I was a bit in thrall to them, really – especially Ollie and Leo. They had a confidence I envied. I've told myself over and over that they wouldn't have listened to me, but you're right that I could have tried harder.'

'So you persuaded yourself that she was up for it?'

'I suppose. The next day, though – I didn't see the others

until the evening. They'd all walked home in the early hours, and got caught by the porters climbing over the college gate. They had to see the senior tutor. At dinner they were trying to josh about it, but it was clear they didn't feel good about whatever had gone on. It was coming up to the end of term. We talked about how it was time to get serious, next term we'd have finals. We sort of agreed, without ever quite mentioning what had happened, that we would draw a line under the business and just never go back to that pub. Arlo was unhappy about the fact that they had that Polaroid of the four of us behind the bar, in case she decided to say anything – Ollie said he'd get it when he went back to pick up his car, so that's why I assumed he'd had it all this time. The arrogance, now I look back, of thinking it was our decision to make.' He lets out a small, bitter laugh.

'She didn't want to draw a line? Rosie?'

'Ollie left it a couple of days before he went back for the car and when he got there, the windows had all been smashed. That was the first thing. Then, when we didn't go to the pub on our usual night, she showed up at his room in college the next day. He said – although this might just be Ollie putting a gloss on it – that she'd come expecting to sleep with him again. And he wasn't very nice to her, I'm afraid.' They turn along the far edge of the meadow. Jo wraps her arms around herself against the buffeting of the wind and wonders if there is anything he can tell her about Oliver now that will surprise her.

'He was freaked out that she'd been able to find him,' Max says. 'We'd used fake names at the pub, we paid cash. Maybe she'd looked in his wallet, or the boys had been drunk enough the night before that they'd forgotten and called each other by their real names. Anyway – she started making a bit of a scene and he told her to get out, he said he'd meet her in town for a drink later, but she wasn't to come to college again or he'd make sure the porters knew she was a dealer. She accused him of assaulting her, he told her she was a slut who should learn to keep her legs closed. Something like that – I wasn't there. She left eventually, and he never did arrange to meet her. We went home for the Easter break a few days later.'

'She didn't give up, though.'

'She went after Arlo instead. At the beginning of the next term, she hung around outside the CompSci lab until he came out, and she told him she was pregnant from that night.' Max has picked up his pace, as if there's a kind of relief in talking about it, after two decades.

'Did she want money?'

'At first she told him she was going to keep the baby, and she wanted them to agree to a DNA test when it was born, and then to child support from the father. She wanted it in writing. And if they wouldn't agree, she was going to report it to the police. She said she hadn't consented to sleep with him and Leo, so it was rape. She told Arlo she knew exactly who he was, who his father was, and she would go to the press if she had to. She'd thought it all through – she even told him she'd kept the clothes she was wearing that night for evidence. Arlo didn't know what to say – he's not good at emotional confrontation at the best of times. He called us all to his room that afternoon.'

'You must have been relieved you weren't in the frame,' Jo says drily.

'Oh, I was shitting myself, believe me. At least I knew I couldn't be the father. But I was there – I was part of the whole sorry mess, it wouldn't do me any good to claim I hadn't touched her. I was already picturing my parents and their friends reading about my drug-fuelled gang rape in the tabloids. It would have destroyed them. As for Arlo—' He breaks off and shakes his head. 'You never met Sir Hugh, did you? Arlo lived in fear of him. Hugh was a real old-school bully. So Arlo was all for doing whatever this girl was asking, if it meant keeping his father out of it.'

'What about the others?'

He closes his eyes briefly. 'Oliver wanted to play the big bad lawyer and call her bluff. He said she'd never have a case. He was probably right, too – she was a girl with no money or family who sold drugs out of a rough pub, people had seen her flirting with us, she'd invited us to her place and got in the car willingly, and then given us more booze and drugs. No one was going to believe she'd said yes to one guy but no to the others. A good defence lawyer would have taken her apart in seconds. But none of the rest of us wanted to risk it becoming public. Ollie was the one who said we couldn't just hand over money when we didn't know if she was even pregnant, or if there were half a dozen other boyfriends in the background, otherwise she'd keep coming back for more. So I suggested they might actually try talking to her.'

'What, make a deal?'

'Well. I was no expert on women then – or now, clearly – but it seemed obvious to me that she was lashing out and making threats because she was angry and upset. I thought she probably didn't even want to be saddled with a child, and maybe if they didn't insult her and talk to her like she was dirt, she might calm down and they could find a solution.'

'Treat her like a human being? Radical.'

'OK, I know.' He clenches his jaw. 'Ollie didn't like that idea – he hated to be criticised.'

'Tell me about it.'

275

He glances at her and nods. 'He said, "No, you're right, Max, I should have taken her home to meet my mother. Tell you what, why don't you invite her to dinner next time *your* parents visit." Then I got riled and said I would do, but it wasn't their grandchild, thank God, and Ollie said a few disparaging things about my virility, and it was all turning nasty when Arlo stepped in and said I was right. If we could persuade her not to have it, and to keep quiet, that would be the best solution all round.'

'So they talked to her?'

'I did.' He catches her look. 'I know – this whole story makes me sound like their useful idiot. But I don't think she'd have sat down with any of them at that point. She was even scared of me when she found me waiting outside her flat. I took her for a coffee and I realised, of course, that she wasn't this worldly, confident siren I'd supposed. She was only nineteen, a long way from home, she was ashamed of what had happened that night and fighting back with the only weapons she had. She admitted she didn't want to have a baby – she just didn't want to come out of the whole thing feeling she'd been used and discarded. I asked her what it would take to make it go away.'

'She agreed to have an abortion?'

'Essentially, yes. But she said there had to be something in it for her. She wasn't stupid.' He rubs the back of his neck. They turn up along the last boundary of the meadow, heading back towards the house. 'She hoped to study nursing. It was quite modest, what she was asking for, compared to what a more calculating person might have come up with – that was why I believed she'd keep her word. She wasn't out to bleed us dry, she just wanted a leg-up, to stop scrabbling in those shitty minimum-wage jobs and selling drugs to pay the rent. That's the impression I got, anyway.'

'Did the others go for it?'

'Arlo did. He was just relieved to think she might be willing to make it disappear. Leo didn't have that kind of money in the first place – he liked the idea of paying her off, but he was dependent on Arlo and Ollie covering his share. Ollie thought I was a fool, that she'd wrapped me around her finger and if we gave her money now we'd never be rid of her. I think that's when we realised this had to be fixed in a way that was beyond our capacity. Fixed by people who had experience in making scandals go away.'

'Sir Hugh, you mean.'

Max nods. 'Arlo was the only one who could get his hands on that kind of money up front anyway, and there was no way he could do it without his father knowing. But Hugh knew about things like non-disclosure agreements, ways to sew it up tight legally so she couldn't come back later without bringing a whole pile of trouble on her own head. Arlo and Ollie went down to London to talk to him.'

'And he agreed to pay her off?'

'I think he felt there wasn't much choice.'

They are almost back at the garden. Jo slows her pace; she would rather avoid the others for a while longer.

'So you all believed that Rosie had had an abortion?'

'There was no reason to think otherwise. We had to sign a legal agreement, the four of us, never to speak about the business publicly. I think Hugh didn't trust any of us not to try and use it against Arlo at some point in the future.'

'Storm said her mother had taken money. I thought she meant stolen it, but that makes sense now. Storm's grandparents pretended she was their daughter because her mother was afraid she would be in legal trouble if anyone found out she'd had the baby.'

'They'd have made Rosie sign something too. They gave

her twenty grand, Arlo said. We weren't supposed to know that. A couple of weeks later, Arlo went home for the weekend and when he came back, he told us it was all sorted. The relief, Jo, I can't tell you. I know that must sound awful—'

'Because the rest of it has sounded just terrific so far.'

He dips his head. 'It's far and away the most shameful, appalling thing I've done in my entire life, and we've never been able to speak about it. It affected all of us for the worse, in different ways.'

'Not as much as it affected Rosie,' Jo says, wrapping her arms around her chest again. 'She drowned herself two years later.'

'I didn't know about that.' Max speaks quietly. 'Neither did the others, I'm sure. We buried ourselves in finals, and then there were jobs to think about, and moving to London, and Arlo was getting married. Hugh hated us, of course. He despised us for dragging Arlo and therefore him into our sordid lives, he made that painfully clear at the wedding, but at the same time he knew he had to keep us close.'

'And he really didn't know Rosie had kept the baby?'

'I'm sure he didn't. His secretary dealt with it all and he trusted her.'

'Did you never try and look her up? Rosie, I mean? You're a journalist, you must have had ways, even before social media. Weren't you curious?'

'Honestly, Jo? I wanted to forget the whole thing. I tried to write it off as a stupid teenage mistake.'

'You were twenty-one.'

'A stupid undergraduate mistake, then. The truth is, I preferred not to know. I felt wretched about what happened, and I hoped some good came out of it, that the money had helped her to a better life. And yes, I do know how paternalistic that sounds. But I didn't want to google her and find that wasn't true. Years went by, I thought she'd probably married and changed her name, so I never did look her up. And all the time she was dead. Poor girl.'

'And it didn't occur to you that she might have had a child who would resurface one day, looking for payback?'

'No.' His face is grim, and Jo hears the bitterness as he remembers all over again how thoroughly he has been played. 'No, I think it's safe to say that never crossed our minds.'

They are approaching the fence nearest the house. Someone – she presumes one of the police officers – is calling across the garden; they are too far away still to hear clearly. Max swipes at a stalk of wildflowers gone to seed, tears it up and shreds it, scattering the pieces.

'You know' – Jo recalls the Thursday night when Storm stepped into the light wearing her crocheted hat – 'when she first turned up, I had this weird sense that I'd seen her before. She seemed familiar.'

'What, you think she looks like Oliver?'

Jo frowns. 'Except she doesn't though, does she? Do you think she could have done a test?'

'DNA test?' Max shakes his head. 'I don't think she could, legally, without Oliver's permission. But she must have convinced him she was telling the truth, or he wouldn't have—' He breaks off, kicks at a stray flurry of leaves. 'You didn't find any proof among his things, I suppose? A paternity test letter or something?'

'No, I think I'd have remembered that,' she says drily.

'Then maybe she didn't know for sure,' Max says. 'She could have been calling Oliver's bluff to see how he reacted.'

Jo presses her lips together. 'Well, she certainly got a reaction from him. But if she thought Oliver was her father, wouldn't it have been revenge enough, that he died? Why

279

would she need to—' An idea strikes her, so obvious she almost wants to slap her forehead. 'Wait – Lucas – of *course*.'

'Lucas what?'

She lays a hand on his sleeve. 'OK, don't let Lucas know I've told you, he'd be mortified. But the first night, he got stoned with Storm and tried to kiss her.'

'That's nice. My godson.'

'Yes, OK, leaving that aside. He said Storm leapt away from him like he had the plague. What if that was not because she was appalled at his behaviour, but because she knew he was her brother?'

Max fixes his eyes on the house and lets out a long, careful breath. 'Arlo. My God. You think she's *Arlo's* daughter? Not Oliver's.'

They walk in silence into the garden while they process this.

'I think that must be right,' he says. 'I mean, it would be obvious if she were Leo's, right? So it's fifty-fifty.'

'And the way she reacted to Lucas – it seems like there is a line she won't cross. She wouldn't have slept with Oliver if she'd really thought he could be her father. But he must have believed it.'

Max considers this. 'A rational person would have demanded proof, but Ollie wasn't acting rationally at the time, the pressure he was under. If he believed he'd slept with his own daughter, and it might come out? I can see how that could push a man over the edge.'

'She's come after all of you, one by one,' Jo says. Her voice is empty. She feels exhausted by this knowledge. She would like to sleep for a week, and wake up somewhere on the other side of this. Max looks as if his legs might go from under him at any moment.

'I wonder why it took her so long to find us,' he says.

'Oh, that's easy. She only found out the truth two years ago, when her grandmother died. Her grandmother had kept a box of her mother's diaries, and that Polaroid.'

'Ollie never said anything more about that picture, and we never asked. I assumed he'd taken it back from the pub and got rid of it, but Rosie must have been there before him and kept it. Fuck.' Max shakes his head slowly; he too has the air of a sleepwalker. 'Can you imagine it, Jo – you're nineteen, you haven't had a great life, and then you discover not just that your mother was taken advantage of and paid off, but the father you've never known is likely a multimillionaire who could have changed everything about your childhood, if he'd wanted to. It's like a fairy tale, except—'

'Except she doesn't want to be rescued by her rich daddy,' Jo says. 'If that was all she cared about, she could have contacted Arlo once she figured it out, asked for a DNA test, arranged some kind of settlement – I bet he would have agreed to pay out again, to keep her on side. Instead, she's set out to punish you. All of you.' She closes her eyes and sees Storm in the firelight. *I'd rip everything they cared about from their bleeding hands until there was nothing left.*

Max stops and leans against a fence post, weighing this. They are almost back where they started.

'I think,' he says carefully, 'we don't need to tell the detectives about all this history. There's going to be enough press attention as it is, with Arlo's profile, and the minister visiting last night, that makes it highly sensitive. That's why this Bouvier's been parachuted in to deal with it and they've got us all corralled here instead of dragging us down to the local nick – they want discretion. So it might be best to let the police believe she's after money.'

Jo looks at him in disbelief. 'Don't you get it? Clio's in real danger. Storm wants to destroy your lives. She started

281

with Oliver, she's helped feed those stories about Leo, now she's taken Arlo's other daughter. Think about it – if she thinks she was deprived of a mother because of him, she'll want him to know how that feels.'

'You don't really think she could hurt a baby? She can't want to make him suffer so badly that she would do that, and throw away the rest of her own life for it?'

He's still half in love with her, Jo realises, even now that he knows their whole relationship was a sham. He wants to believe he wasn't that easily duped. She almost pities him; she can sympathise with that.

'They think she killed Becca,' she says. 'For nothing more than being in the way.'

'Surely the police will find them soon,' Max says, biting the knuckle of his thumb. 'She can't have got far – she doesn't have a car.'

A wave of fear washes through Jo and she grasps his arm. 'She does, though. She has an accomplice.' The word sounds ridiculous even as she says it. She explains about the man in the grey van. 'That's why she wanted me out of the way. Because I'd seen her with him – she was afraid I'd identify him or the van, even though she'd deleted the picture.'

'Did you tell Bouvier?'

'I forgot about him. My head was spinning – I thought I'd killed Storm.'

'You thought you'd—' She sees him consider asking, then change his mind. 'Wait, the van – did she delete it twice?'

'How do you mean?'

'She'd have to delete it from your photos, and then from the Recently Deleted folder. Did you check?'

'No. I didn't think about it.'

'We need to look at your phone.'

'I don't have it.' She holds out her empty palms to

282

demonstrate. 'I don't know where it is. The police might have taken it away with my clothes, or else I lost it in the woods, or—'

'I took it,' Max says. 'When I was helping you back to the house this morning, after we found you in the woods. I felt it in your pocket and it seemed like a sensible precaution. I didn't know what had happened, but I thought the police might use the opportunity to take it away, and they don't have the right to do that without your permission.'

'Thank you.' She barely has time to appreciate the relief. 'Where is it?'

'In my bag. It needs charging, though. Let's go and look.'

25

While the crime scene teams search the chateau, the guests have been corralled in the Granary, a ten-berth converted barn on the far side of the pool, usually kept for overspill if house parties are too big for the main building. But when Max pushes the door, the two-storey, open-plan living room appears recently deserted; the coffee tables are littered with dirty mugs and scrunched-up tissues, but there is no sign of anyone. Max runs up to one of the rooms and returns with Jo's phone.

'Where is everyone?' she asks, looking around. The silence is uncanny.

'The police wanted to speak to Arlo again.' Max glances at the mezzanine floor. 'I think Cressida might have taken something and gone to lie down, no idea about Lucas. Violette took Grace back to her cottage. Quick, now. Let's see this picture.'

He locates a charger in one of the wall sockets and Jo plugs in her phone; they perch side by side on the arm of a chair while they wait until it has enough battery to restart. When she can open the photos, Jo scrolls down to the

Recently Deleted folder, and there – unbelievably – is the grey van driving away; a little blurry, but clear enough to read the licence plate.

'You were right – she didn't check it was deleted twice. Here.' She passes him the phone.

'Or she wanted to be traced.' He pinches the screen to enlarge the picture and holds it at arm's length, squinting. 'Can you read this?'

Jo takes the phone; he has zoomed in on the photo of the van as far as he can, to show a sticker in the rear window.

She peers at it. '*Laval Auto, Libourne.*'

He takes out his own phone and types in the name, then opens a website. Jo watches as he clicks through the menu and opens a page of thumbnail photographs.

'Here we are. Recognise any of these guys?'

She looks; the first is a white-haired man in a baseball cap bearing the garage's logo. He has a weathered face and dark eyes; below the picture a caption reads '*Benjamin Laval père, proprieteur*'. She scrolls past and underneath she finds a headshot of a man perhaps in his late thirties, with a sandy beard, identical cap and the same wary stare into the camera; *Benjamin Laval fils, mécanicien*. She taps the screen.

'I'm pretty sure that's him. I only saw him from the back, and for a second in profile, but he had a beard and that colour hair. Do you think he knows where—'

But Max already has the phone to his ear; she can hear it ringing.

'It's Sunday evening,' she whispers, 'no one's going to—'

Max holds up a finger to stop her. '*Monsieur Laval? Puis-je parler à votre fils, s'il vous plaît?*'

She can hear the murmur of the voice on the other end. '*Vous savez où?*'

More muttering; Max nods. '*Ça ne fait rien, je r'appelle.*

285

Merci.' A brief pause. '*Non, non, pas du tout.*' He hangs up and looks at her. 'So. Laval *fils* is apparently away hunting for the weekend. When I asked where, the father got suspicious – asked if I was English. Sounds like *fils* was expecting someone to come looking for him.'

'The police will be able to trace the van, won't they?'

'They can put an alert out for it, I'm sure. The question is how long she plans to keep him and his van around. Hang on, I've had a thought. Do you have Instagram on your phone?'

'Yes, but – I hardly ever use it.'

'Doesn't matter. Let me see.'

He has to lean across her because the cable won't stretch. She watches him click open the app and search for Benjamin Laval, scrolling through the multiple options until he makes a small noise of triumph and tilts the screen towards her to confirm he has found the right one. Laval doesn't post much; most of his pictures feature a lovingly tended Citroën DS at various classic car rallies. Max opens one of the few to feature human beings: a selfie, showing Laval wearing a hat with ear flaps this time, a rifle slung over one shoulder and his other arm around an almost identical bearded man, both grinning for the camera. Sunlight slants over rocky slopes in the background.

'Fuck. *Fuck.*' His face spasms and he starts jabbing at the screen.

'What have you done?'

'I was trying to make it bigger and I accidentally liked it. I've unliked it – will he know?'

'He'll probably get a notification. Shit, Max – he'll be able to see it was me.'

'Maybe he won't check. Doesn't seem like he's on there much. But look.' Max holds the phone as far away as he can and translates the caption. '"*Great day hunting with JP at*

Grand-père's cabin." Bingo.' He clicks on the location, and a map appears, showing a red marker in the middle of a vast expanse of green. Max zooms out and it becomes clear that the cabin is in the Pyrenees, close to the Spanish border. He screenshots the map. 'Doesn't that seem a likely destination? If you wanted to hide somewhere out of the way for a while, with the option to zip into Spain? What a useful friend young Benjamin is. Wonder how she persuaded him to help her.' There is a bitter twist to his mouth. 'We'd better talk to Arlo.'

'Shouldn't we tell the detectives right away?'

'We will. But Arlo should know about Storm first, why she's doing this, and I don't want to have that conversation in front of Bouvier. How much money did you say she had in that bag – about four grand?'

'Something like that.'

He nods. 'Not enough for a long-term plan. Enough to tide her over for a few weeks without using a bank card that could be traced, but she must have thought about what she would do after that.'

'Unless she didn't have a long-term plan in the first place,' Jo says. 'She's spent the last two years, since she read her mother's diaries, obsessing about the four of you. Working out how she can punish you. It must have taken over her whole life. Maybe she really didn't get as far as thinking about what she would do after she'd achieved her goal.'

'I still can't believe she meant for anyone to be hurt,' he says stubbornly.

'Oliver *died*,' Jo reminds him. 'And she still came after the rest of you. Can you really be sure she wouldn't harm Clio? Maybe she did originally plan to take her for a bit to scare them, but now that Becca's dead, the stakes are higher.'

'Let's find Arlo. I think he's the only one who can negotiate

287

with her now, but we don't even have a way to get in touch. Her phone's going straight to voicemail – I'd guess she's been smart enough to ditch it so it can't be traced. I'll see if I can get him on his own.' He fiddles with Jo's phone, sending himself the screenshot of the hunting lodge location, and stands, squeezing her shoulder briefly.

He is moving to the door when Jo's phone rings.

The screen says No Caller ID. She swipes to answer, catching Max's eye and motioning for him to stay.

'Hello?'

She hears a cavernous sound, a rushing of wind in high places, a silence that stretches out long enough for her to hear the pulsing of her own blood in her ears.

'Jo?'

It is Storm, unmistakably, though her voice sounds distant and brittle.

'Yes.'

'Where are you?'

'At the chateau. Why, were you hoping I'd bled to death in the woods somewhere?'

Storm lets out that big, throaty laugh. 'Ah, God, no, I knew you'd be grand. It was only a scratch. And look, here you are, back home, browsing through the old Instagram.'

Jo glances at Max, who is gesticulating frantically between his ear and the phone. It takes her a moment to realise he means for her to put it on speaker. Storm does not miss the difference in sound quality.

'Is someone with you?'

'No,' Jo tells her, motioning for Max to keep quiet. 'Just me.'

'You're smart, Jo,' Storm says. 'I always knew that. So you found my friend Benjamin. Did you memorise the number plate, or what?'

'Used my initiative,' Jo says. 'Where's Clio?'

'Here's what we'll do. Have you mentioned your Miss Marple discoveries to anyone else?'

'Tell me about Clio. Is she OK?'

'You tell me what I need to know first. Have you said anything to anyone about Benjamin? The police, or any of the others?'

Jo catches Max's eye. 'Not yet,' she says.

'All right. Keep it that way, and I promise you the baby will be fine. But I swear to God, Jo, if you send the police after me, you'll have that on your conscience.'

'You won't harm her,' Jo says, knowing the bluff is a gamble. 'She's your sister.'

There is another taut silence, with a rushing in the background that makes Jo think of pressing shells to her ear as a child. It lasts so long that she thinks Storm has hung up; she is turning to Max to apologise, when she hears a laugh, shorter and drier this time.

'So you've worked it all out then.'

'I understand you're angry—' she begins, but Storm cuts her off.

'No. You don't understand any of this. Listen, I'd love to stop and tell you all about my feelings and my daddy issues, Jo, but I'm under a bit of pressure here. I'll make a deal with you. You don't say anything to the police about my friend with the van, or what you think you might have found on Instagram, OK? And I guarantee the baby will be safe.'

'But you'll bring her back?' There is no reply. Jo hears her own voice rising. 'I mean, what is it you *want*? If you don't want to harm her, and I don't believe you do, then you have to let her go. You could take her to a hospital and tell us where to find her—'

'Tell me this, Jo. How much is your daughter's life worth?'

Primal fear twists her gut, sends flares of panic through her limbs, even though she knows, rationally, that Storm is nowhere near Hannah. In that instant, Jo comprehends a fraction of what Cressida and Nina must be feeling. 'Leave my daughter out of this,' she says, through her teeth.

'It's a hypothetical question – how much is Hannah's life worth to you? Come on, I'm interested.'

'I couldn't put a price—' Jo mutters, angry that she is being drawn into this game, but Storm talks over her.

'Mine was worth twenty grand. Did they tell you that part? Twenty thousand not to exist. And my poor old mammy, well, that was more money than she'd dreamed of in her life.' Storm is hamming up her accent; having declared that she has no time to talk, she appears to have settled into the conversation. 'She wasn't old, actually, she was nineteen. Maybe she thought it was a fair exchange. But that was what my potential fathers decided it was worth to be rid of me. So what I'd like to know' – she pauses; Jo hears the click of a lighter and a purposeful inhale – 'is what price Arlo puts on this daughter.'

'You do want money, then?'

'Oh, Jo.' She sounds infinitely weary and disappointed. 'You haven't understood at all, have you? Well, you're probably not at your sharpest – Angel Dust'll mess with your head. You should stay away from it in future. Listen, you can tell Arlo to think about what I said. Do you have a pen?'

Jo gestures at Max; he casts around the room and finds a discarded Biro on the coffee table.

'Yes,' she says.

'OK. Write down these numbers. It's a bank account.' Storm reels off a string of digits and Max scribbles them on the back of a magazine. 'Tell Arlo to put the money in there and we'll talk again. But if I so much as hear a fucking siren, or I look up and see a helicopter, or I hear a word about this on the news, I'll disappear for good, and so will she, and they won't find either of us, I guarantee it. Are we clear?'

'I can't stop the police looking. They'll find you eventually, even if I don't say anything. You must know that. They're probably monitoring our phones. They'll be able to trace you. And you won't be able to do a deal now, because of Becca.'

There is a pause; she can almost hear Storm sitting up straighter.

'What about Becca?'

'Because—' Jo can't quite believe she doesn't understand. 'Because you killed her.'

'*What?*' The silence this time is absolute. Jo glances at Max; he shakes his head, uncomprehending. 'Are you fucking with me?' Storm says, and then, decisively, before Jo can answer, 'No. *No*. It was only double a normal dose. It never would have killed her. She can't be dead. You're just saying that.'

Jo can't work out if this is a deliberate bluff, but the confusion in Storm's voice sounds genuine. 'She's definitely dead. There are police all over the house.'

'Fuck. Jesus. OK. Then you really, *really* need to keep your mouth shut. Understand? I'll be in touch.'

Jo hears the decisive click as the call is ended. Max snatches the phone from her hand and opens Instagram again. Benjamin Laval's account has been deleted.

Max takes out his own phone and begins typing.

'What are you doing?'

'Messaging Arlo. We need to give him everything we know, let him decide whether to share it with the police. But we have to talk to him without the police knowing, or we could end up being charged with obstructing the investigation.'

'Don't you think she sounded surprised to hear Becca was dead?' Jo says. 'What did she mean about a double dose?'

'Maybe she meant – they think Oscar was given a sedative. Grace said he took a bottle of fizzy drink from Becca's bedside table, it must have been in there. That's all I know – the police are testing it, I guess.'

'Orangina,' Jo says, remembering. 'Storm said last night that we wouldn't need to worry about Becca. Maybe that's what she meant – she put something in the Orangina to knock her out. I saw a medicine bottle in her make-up bag.'

Max fetches up a grim smile. 'Well, that might explain why I fell asleep with my clothes on after two glasses of wine. You think she intended to drug Becca so she wouldn't wake while Storm took Clio?'

'But Oscar drank the Orangina instead, so maybe Becca did wake and followed Storm out to the woods? They could have struggled, Becca hit her head, Storm ran off thinking she was unconscious. Perhaps she really didn't know she was dead?'

'Hm.' Max looks unpersuaded. 'If there's one thing we do know about Storm, it's that she's a convincing liar.' His phone buzzes and he scans the message. 'He's alone in his office. Come on.'

26

Arlo's office is at the end of the long side of the house on the ground floor. Max leads her around to approach it from the back, through the double doors that open directly on to the terrace; the house is still out of bounds, but Arlo must have persuaded the police to let him in. As they round the corner of the building, Jo glances towards the yoga studio to her right; the windowed wall is not visible from this path, and she wonders who is in there being questioned now, what they might be saying about her.

Arlo looks up from behind the desk as they enter, phone pressed to his ear, and raises a finger instructing them to wait. Max perches on the arm of a chair, one knee jiggling. Jo hovers by the mantelpiece, picking up a heavy glass inkwell and turning it in her hands. There is a light dusting of powder on every surface where the forensic officers have searched for prints. All the books and *objets* are subtly out of alignment, giving the room an off-kilter feel that matches her general sense of disorientation.

'Call as soon as you land,' Arlo says crisply to his phone.

'I've sent a car.' A pause. 'No, I'm not risking email. We'll discuss it in person.' A tinny voice comes from the phone, evidently the person on the other end raising an objection. Arlo hangs up and looks at them expectantly. 'Stuart,' he says, nodding to the phone. 'Head of legal. He's flying out now with the company PR. You said you had news?'

Max explains, as briefly as he can, about Jo following Storm in Saint-Émilion, Benjamin Laval, the hunting cabin, the call just now, leaning in to show the pictures on his phone as he sends them to Arlo.

'Police took my fucking laptop,' Arlo says, turning to the screen on his left. 'Like I'm the criminal. At least they left the desktop for now. Give me those map references.' He types the numbers and zooms in on the search area. 'Did she say how much she wants?' He sounds almost relieved; if it's a question of money, that is within his control.

Jo glances at Max, who draws a deep breath.

'She mentioned a sum. Twenty grand. To be paid here.' He passes Arlo the torn-off magazine cover with the scrawled bank account number.

Arlo swivels away from the computer and stares at it. 'Twenty *grand*? Are you serious? That's chicken feed. Why go through all this—'

'It's symbolic,' Max says, pulling at a thread in his cuff, not looking at Arlo.

'Of what?'

'It's the amount your father paid to Róisín Caffrey.'

'*Who?*'

'Rosie. The barmaid in Cambridge. You remember.'

A kaleidoscope of reactions chases across Arlo's face; impressively, Jo thinks, for a man accustomed to showing little emotion. His eyes flick to her.

'It's all right, Jo knows the whole story,' Max says. Arlo

looks back to the satellite image on his screen, the muscles in his jaw working minutely.

'How the fuck does Storm know about Rosie?' he says.

'She says she's Rosie's daughter.' Max waits to see if the penny will drop. Arlo continues to study the map, but he is very still. 'Arlo, she – she says she's *your* daughter.'

'Impossible,' Arlo says immediately. 'Rosie signed an agreement. Peggy Talbot took her to the clinic. Hugh's PA, you remember? She told Dad it was dealt with.'

'Well, she lied. Rosie didn't go through with it. That's why Storm had the Polaroid.'

Arlo's gaze shoots to Jo. 'I thought you brought that? Ollie had it, didn't he?'

She shakes her head. 'It was in Storm's bag, I saw it there.'

'Rosie obviously kept it,' Max says. He's speaking slowly and clearly, as if to a child, though it's not clear whether this is to soothe Arlo or himself. 'She wrote all our names on the back – you saw. She kept a diary of everything that happened. *Everything*, Arlo.'

'So why has it taken Storm this long?'

'She was raised by her grandmother,' Jo offers. 'She says she only found her mother's diary in the attic after her grandmother died a couple of years ago. That's how she knew one of you was her father.'

'Why does she assume it's me?'

'Process of elimination,' Max says. 'She's yours, Arlo, you only have to look at her eyes.' Max swipes through his phone; there's a flinch of shame as he pulls up a picture of Storm laughing. Jo feels briefly sorry for him; he would have been happy, the day he took that, hardly able to believe his luck. 'Jo, that photo of Lucas on the mantelpiece, bring it here.'

Jo does as she is told, and watches over Max's shoulder

as Arlo compares the two headshots side by side. Once you know, you can't unsee it: the similarity in the lines of their jaw, the shape of the nose and mouth, the bright blue eyes. It seems astonishing to Jo now that she didn't recognise it immediately, that Max didn't realise the first time he set eyes on Storm. She recalls Storm saying that none of them could see what was literally in front of them.

Arlo scans the pictures without speaking, his face scrubbed blank of any expression. 'Well, there's one way to clear this up,' he says, eventually. He picks up his phone, scrolls through his contacts and dials a number. 'Can you put me through to Peggy Talbot, please? It's Mr Connaught.' He glances at Jo and Max and lowers his voice. 'She's seventy-eight now, in a residential home. A very nice one. I should know, I pay for it.'

'Is she . . .?' Max taps his temple.

'No. Sharp as a knife. Can't get about so well though. Arthritis or something. Thank you,' he says, into the phone, and puts it on speaker.

'Arlo? Is that you?' says a voice that sounds like a Fifties BBC announcer.

'Peggy. I need to ask you—'

'Happy anniversary, dear.'

'Thank you. I need – how are you?' he adds, as an afterthought.

'Oh, you know. Can't complain. Well, I could, but it wouldn't do any good, would it?' Peggy lets out a bark of a laugh. Jo can picture her: tweedy, stern, impeccably groomed. 'How's your lovely—'

'Peggy, I'm sorry, I don't have much time. I need to ask you something, and I need to know the truth. You remember, my last term at Cambridge, I had a bit of trouble with a girl? I came down to see Hugh about it?'

The pause that follows stretches for so long that Jo wonders if the old lady has even heard.

'Peggy?'

'You know,' she says, 'I rather thought we'd have this conversation before now. I'm surprised it's taken so long.'

Arlo takes a deep breath.

'You know what I'm talking about, then?'

'Your father entrusted that business to me, yes.'

'And – what? You betrayed his trust?'

'I acted according to my conscience in the matter.' Peggy has adopted a lofty tone.

'That's not what Dad asked of you.'

'There is a higher authority than Lord Connaught. Even he respected that.'

Arlo drags a hand across his face and mutters something under his breath.

'I worked for your father for over thirty years, Arlo,' Peggy says, 'and one of the reasons he valued me was because I shared his principles. Not just politically, but his Catholic faith too.'

Arlo snorts. 'My father's faith was highly selective, Peggy. He tended to gloss over the bits about helping the poor and not judging others. And he had no problem paying someone to get an abortion if it would protect the family name. So – what happened?'

'I would like to make clear,' Peggy says firmly, 'that I in no way attempted to influence the girl. I took her to the appointment expecting to do as I had been instructed, with no intention of letting my personal feelings interfere. But when it was clear she had changed her mind and wanted to keep the baby, I could hardly force her to go through with it. She was extremely distressed. I acted in what I thought was everyone's best interests. Including the child's.'

'So you lied to Dad?'

'I told Hugh the matter was settled and I believed that was the case. I made very clear to the girl that I would say nothing on condition that she did the same, and she would still get the money. She was to leave the country and never contact your family again. I had every reason to think she would keep her word.'

'And you never thought to mention to me that I might have a daughter out there somewhere?'

'So it was a daughter,' Peggy says serenely. 'God brought her into the world for a reason, Arlo. We can't always know His ways.'

'Well, she's abducted my baby to pay me back. So you'd better start lighting some bloody candles for Clio's safe return, Peggy, while you're figuring out the divine rationale.' There is a sharp intake of breath; Peggy starts to speak but Arlo cuts off the call and looks up at Max.

'You haven't told Bouvier and what's-her-name about any of this?'

'No. We wanted to let you know first.'

'She said she would harm Clio if the police came after her,' Jo blurts.

Arlo looks past her, apparently at the door, though his gaze is turned inward. Jo can see him filing it away to deal with later: the magnitude of Peggy's deception, the secret that has been kept from him all these years, and its repercussions.

'Thank God I insisted we keep this quiet,' he says eventually. 'Bouvier's been telling us we need to get word out as quickly as possible, bulletins on every news channel, pictures of Clio circulating. Cress was all fired up to call in TV crews and the British embassy, but I persuaded them to hold off until Stuart gets here.' He picks up the framed picture of

Lucas and angles it so that the lamplight slides over the glass. 'I suppose we should give all this to Bouvier. Now that we know about Laval and his van, that will give the police a bit more to work with, save us having to lay everything out for the press. Not that that will last – Becca's mother is flying out, we can't expect her to keep quiet for long. At the moment all she knows is that Becca was found dead. She's assumed it was an asthma attack, and we don't need her thinking any different until she has to. But Becca was our employee and it happened in our house so we'll have to put the mother up here to control it, we can't have her in a B&B in the village saying God knows what to any journalists that turn up.'

He swivels his chair to look out of the window, where the light has almost faded over the garden. Jo watches him with a mixture of fascination and revulsion; she had expected sangfroid from Arlo, but this level of detachment about a murdered girl in his care would be breathtaking even if he hadn't been sleeping with her.

'But what if Storm sees something on the news and thinks—'

'Bluffing.' Arlo sets the photograph of Lucas down and adjusts the frame. 'She's not a fool – she must realise the police are going to be looking for her, there's nothing I can do to stop that. Bouvier seems smart, the minister asked him to take the case personally. We'll stand a better chance of finding them if he's working with us. They can trace this Laval's phone, find out where his hunting lodge is. If he hunts, we have to assume there'll be guns around.' He shifts position and looks at Max. 'How does she know this Laval guy?'

'Don't ask me.' The muscle at the side of his mouth twitches again.

'She must have been planning this for a while. When did she fly out?'

Max shakes his head unhappily. 'I last saw her the Saturday before. She said she was going to spend a few days in Paris and join us for the weekend. I didn't know she was planning to come here without me, obviously.'

'So she could have been in France for the best part of a week, setting it all up. The police haven't found any record of her on passenger lists so far, but—' He breaks off, staring at them as if he has had an epiphany. 'Of course – they'll have been looking under the wrong name. You don't know what her real name was? Something Caffrey, I suppose?'

'Not necessarily,' Jo says. 'She said her grandmother remarried. If she was raised as their daughter, she'd have the step-grandfather's surname.'

Arlo mutters something under his breath and turns back to the screen, his hand hovering over the keyboard. After a moment he lets it fall again to the desk, apparently thinking better of whatever he had been going to search. 'Listen, both of you. I don't see that the police need to know about Rosie, and Storm being her daughter. It doesn't change the demand for money and the urgency of finding Clio – that's what they need to focus on.'

'Although if all that does come out later, and it's hard to imagine it won't, just from the forensics,' Max says, 'we could be accused of withholding relevant information from an investigation.'

'It's not relevant to finding them,' Arlo says, a snap in his voice. He pushes his chair back. 'Let's get these photos to Bouvier so they can start looking for that van. What did she say about what happens when the money's been paid?'

'She didn't. She said she'd be in touch.'

'With who?'

'I don't know.' Max nods at Jo. 'She called Jo's phone last time because she saw that Jo had been looking at Laval's Instagram. But I suppose it could be any of us, or the landline.'

'Right.' He pockets his phone, brisk now, and picks up the scrap of magazine with the numbers. 'Max, come with me to Bouvier, I'll need your French. You can tell them you've remembered her mother's name was Caffrey so they can search under that – no need to say any more for now. We'd better find out who this bank account belongs to before I do anything about that. Jo, keep your phone on. If you get a call, keep her talking and come to us, we'll be in the studio. And none of this Rosie business to the police or to Cress, understood?'

Jo nods, but a deep sense of unease tugs at her, behind her breastbone; she feels that Arlo's desire to protect himself is all part of the problem, and that his failure to understand what Storm wants from him will only make things worse.

27

She wanders down to the pool to wait for the next instalment of this increasingly surreal drama. The water lies glassy and undisturbed, stray leaves floating on its surface over reflections of an overcast sky. Perching on the edge of a lounger, she looks at her phone. She would like to call Hannah, but she doesn't want to spoil her holiday, and in any case, how will she explain to Hannah that a girl has been murdered, that baby Clio is missing, that she, Jo, can't come home until the police are certain she had nothing to do with either? Max is right, though; with Arlo's profile, it's only a matter of time before this is front-page news, and if the press find out the story behind the story, of Róisín and the pay-off, Oliver will be part of the headlines, all the speculation about his death dredged up again to be picked over. His parents should have some warning too. She stares stupidly at the screen, thinking maybe she shouldn't make a call in case Storm tries to get through again, and in any case, there is only a sliver of battery life. Her chest feels constricted; her longing to hold Hannah swells into a physical ache, and she tries to imagine the terror Cressida must be enduring. Clio is no more than a baby, still in nappies; will Storm know how to feed her, change her, comfort her when she cries? Will she care to do any of those things? Despite everything, Jo wants to believe, with Max, that Storm wouldn't harm a child, but her optimism slams into the immovable facts of Becca's death, and Oliver's.

At the edge of her vision she catches a flicker of movement and jolts guiltily, but it is only Max, standing at the top of the steps between the hedges. He looks harried.

'Bouvier wants to talk to you about tracing that call.'

'How long are they going to keep us here? Should we have lawyers?'

'If they decide to interview us under caution, then, yes. Let's wait and see what happens. Arlo's got some insane idea—' He stops, rubs his chin. 'You'd better go and speak to them. But listen, talking of rights – you don't have to hand over your phone, even if they imply that you do. Not unless you're arrested, anyway.'

This does not inspire confidence. She slips the phone into her back pocket. 'Do you think it will come to that?'

He grimaces. 'I think we're all persons of interest for now.'

Jo finds Arlo alone with Bouvier in the yoga studio. The detective appears tight-lipped and irritated; Arlo, by contrast, exudes an air of control. They look like a couple who have had an argument.

'Joanna, we need to trace the call that was made to your phone,' Bouvier says, making an effort to recover his earlier professional charm.

'It said No Caller ID.'

'Don't worry. Our guys can check with the network. But we need your permission to access your phone records. Are you happy for us to do this?'

She doesn't see that she can reasonably refuse; it would look as if she has something to hide. Storm assured her that there would be no trace of the video clip being AirDropped to her phone, but Jo's own tech knowledge is sketchy enough that she can't be sure. She nods and begins to recite her number, but he holds up a hand; apparently he has this already, and her phone provider, which makes her think her permission was merely cosmetic.

'Now,' Arlo says, as if addressing a meeting. 'I'm driving down there. I need you to come, Jo, in case she decides to call you.'

She stares at him. 'To the Pyrenees?'

'I must repeat that I think this is a very bad idea,' Bouvier says. 'We have no trace on Benjamin Laval's phone since this morning – there's no confirmation that the girl is there at all. It may be her intention that we divert resources to the mountains while she takes the child out of the country by another route.'

'Well, it's your job to secure the ports and the airports,' Arlo says, impatient, 'and while you do that, I'm going to find this lodge, since it's the best lead we have. If you want to provide me with police back-up, that would obviously be useful, but either way, I'm going to find my daughter.'

'As I told you – we put up roadblocks for a radius of sixty kilometres this morning as soon as the child was declared missing,' Bouvier says, 'but if they left last night they could have covered that distance in any direction before those were in place. We are investigating Benjamin Laval – Lieutenant Lemaître has gone to Libourne to speak to his father. For now the important thing is that nobody makes any moves that might cause the abductor to react unpredictably. And since you have transferred the money, it might be better to wait—'

'You paid?' Jo asks, surprised.

'That bank account belongs to a rape crisis centre in Dublin,' Arlo says, with a meaningful look that tells her to say nothing about the symbolism of this. 'I've transferred twenty thousand, as she asked. But I can't just sit around waiting for her to call. Tell me' – he turns to Bouvier – 'is there any legal reason why we shouldn't make this trip? As long as you know where we are?'

'Legal, no, not strictly. But we cannot allow you to endanger yourselves or the child by confronting the suspect. I will liaise with the local police, ask them to look into this lodge, and then—'

'No.' Arlo takes a step towards him, squares his shoulders. 'If the police turn up there, she could harm Clio – she's already threatened as much.'

'Precisely why, *if* she is there, you need to leave it to trained officers—' Bouvier says, but Arlo cuts across him again.

'It's precisely why I need to go there in person. It's me she wants.'

Bouvier narrows his eyes. 'What makes you say that? I thought you had decided she wanted money.' When Arlo doesn't reply, he shifts his weight, folds his arms. 'Mr Connaught, if you know something that would help us find your daughter more quickly—'

'I can't just do nothing,' Arlo says, his voice winding tighter.

'I assure you, we have alerted all regional forces, we are monitoring transport hubs – it is time to make a public appeal for information. Then we can—'

'Didn't you hear me? If Storm sees this on the news, she'll disappear. I can't let that happen.'

'We will stand a better chance of finding them if people are looking out,' Bouvier says calmly.

'Not necessarily. I know how these things go – you make a public appeal and suddenly you've got a thousand sightings of a blonde baby, you have to follow them all up, and the trail is drowned out in white noise. We've got a lead right here' – he jabs at his phone. 'We have to at least try.'

'Speculation.' Bouvier shakes his head. 'We don't know where they are until we are able to trace the phone that called Joanna.'

'He's right, Arlo,' Jo says, laying a hand on his arm. 'The best thing we can do for Clio is to let them do their jobs.'

Arlo turns on her, eyes blazing. 'She's *my daughter*,' he says; not quite a shout, but as near as Jo has ever heard Arlo come to one. She stares at him. He blinks, aware of the ambiguity of his words, and passes a hand across his mouth. 'Are any of us here actually under arrest?' he asks Bouvier.

The detective sighs. 'Mr Connaught, you will be the first to know if you are under arrest.'

'Right. Pack a bag, Jo, and get yourself a warm jacket, it can be cold in the mountains. And grab whatever food you can from the Granary, enough for all of us. Violette will help. Make some coffee while you're at it, we don't know how long we'll be driving. I want to get on the road before the press get hold of any of this. Manisha can deal with all that when she arrives.' He spins back to Bouvier. 'That's my PR – she's on her way, with my lawyer. Don't do anything with the media until you've spoken to them.'

'With respect, Mr Connaught,' Bouvier says, his tone conveying the opposite, 'I will take whatever steps I feel are necessary to progress my investigation and secure the safe return of your child.'

Arlo takes a step closer. 'Look, the minister assured me you were the man to handle this with discretion.'

Bouvier inclines his head. 'I appreciate his faith. I think

we would all like to resolve this without unnecessary scandal. But' – he directs his attention to his phone, to make clear that he is the one dismissing Arlo – 'I am not your employee, Mr Connaught. Please remember that.'

Arlo sets his shoulders back, trying to reassert his status. 'Right. Well, as soon as you have the exact location of this lodge, you can call me. For now we'll head towards Pau. I can assure you we won't leave the country.'

'Does your wife support this plan?' Bouvier asks, glancing up from his messages. 'Because the last time I spoke to her, she wanted to go ahead with the press conference as soon as it could be arranged.'

'My *wife*,' Arlo says, rounding on him, 'has been given a sedative because she punched a wall. She's not in any state to be making decisions – in any case, she doesn't know about this call from Storm. She wouldn't want to do anything that might endanger Clio.'

'Then perhaps you should wait and discuss with her—'

'Let me manage my wife, Commandant.' His nostrils flare with impatience; Jo suspects he wants to set off before Cressida finds out, in case she tries either to stop him or come with him. Bouvier turns away, shaking his head, but he doesn't argue. Jo stares helplessly at Arlo, resenting the order to take care of provisions as if she has become a substitute for Violette, at the same time as something quickens in her; she realises she wants this drive, she wants to see Storm, to confront her about Oliver. If Storm is arrested, there will never be a chance to hear the truth from her.

Arlo pats Jo on the shoulder as he sweeps past to the door. She is left looking at Bouvier, whose expression conveys a weary disappointment. She is not sure if she needs his permission to leave.

'Why did you not mention Benjamin Laval, Joanna?'

'I didn't remember until just now,' she says. 'My memory is still patchy. And I didn't know where my phone was.'

'Mm.' He looks sceptical. 'Did you recognise this man? You must have taken that photograph for a reason.'

'She seemed upset when she was talking to him, that's why. I was concerned.'

'Concerned enough to ask her about him?'

'No. I didn't want her to know I'd followed her.' She drops her gaze to the floor. 'But she must have suspected. She looked through my phone and deleted the picture.'

At this he straightens, like a dog that has caught a scent. 'Why would she go through your phone? What was she hoping to find?'

She thinks of the video, Becca's glance at the camera, and feels the colour rising in her face. She had resolved not to answer any more of his questions, though he has a way of making it seem like a casual chat. He is not my friend, she reminds herself.

'I don't know,' she says. 'Maybe she saw me following her. I should go.'

Bouvier makes a grinding movement with his jaw that conveys disapproval. 'Tell me one more thing, Joanna. Why is Mr Connaught so convinced that Storm wants to see him in person? Did she say this on the telephone?'

'No, but—'

'Then why? Help me to understand his thinking. Is Lieutenant Lemaître's theory correct – that this is not about money, it's something personal? That payment – a significant amount of money, not for Mr Connaught, perhaps, but for a young woman – it went to a charity for rape victims. Is she making a point? What am I not seeing?'

For a fleeting moment, she is tempted to confide in him: who Storm is, what she wants. God knows it's not a secret that deserves to be kept, after what they all did to Rosie, and she recalls what Max said about withholding information from the police. But she knows what will happen if the story comes out; the things that would be written about Oliver. She can't bear to think of those headlines existing for Hannah to see, for other kids at school or their parents to read, or for Hannah to unearth at some later stage when she decides to search up her father. She worshipped Oliver; she is too young to have that ripped away from her. Jo's instinct to protect her daughter flares hot and fierce. She looks Bouvier in the eye and says, 'No idea. You'd have to ask him.'

He regards her with the expression of a disappointed teacher. 'You see, I think you do have an idea. There is something you are not telling me, all of you. And so I have to ask myself, what could be more important than finding Clio as quickly as possible?'

He leaves a silence for her to fill, a questioning tilt to his brow. Jo shakes her head.

'Is it safe, what Arlo wants to do? Driving down there, looking for her? I mean, if Storm killed Becca?'

'We do not know yet what happened to Rebecca,' he reminds her. 'I suppose it depends what Mr Connaught thinks Storm wants from him. I have already suggested the most useful thing he can do is to make a public statement and let us do our jobs. But he is a man who is not used to being told "no", I think? So . . .' he spreads his hands wide in a gesture of resignation. 'I will alert the police in the region and ask them to be standing by. If we believe the abductor to be in the mountains, they can make sure he keeps a safe distance while we recover the child. I have stressed to him that he must not attempt to confront Storm himself, even – *especially* – if this is what she demands.'

309

Jo nods and turns to leave.

'Joanna,' he says, as she reaches the door. 'You are still recovering from last night, you have your daughter at home to think of. Why do you want to go with them on what could be a' – he plucks at the air for the right word – 'we would say *une fausse piste?*'

'I just want to help.'

Bouvier gives her a long look. 'Then the best thing you can do is tell me everything you know. Everything.'

'I have,' she says, and she is certain that he knows she is lying.

28

The road is almost empty of traffic, theirs the only lights for miles. Jo watches the vast dark unspool past the window, her cheek pressed against the cold glass. She checks the car clock over Max's shoulder; only five past nine, though it feels like the middle of the night. She has dozed on and off in the back seat, her phone silent in her hand, while Arlo takes one call after another: from his lawyer, from his press spokeswoman, from Bouvier, from his son.

'Leo's back,' Arlo says, ending a call from Lucas. 'Oscar's out of danger. Confirmed overdose of temazepam. They're keeping him in for observation, Nina's staying at the hospital.'

'That's good,' Jo says, for something to say. The expedition has taken on a dreamlike quality that is partly to do with the fact that the landscape is nothing but shadow, the map on the satnav bare of landmarks since they passed the town of Pau, so that there is no measurable sense of progress. Curled up in the backseat, she is thrown back to childhood journeys with her parents. Max's rental car, some kind of Peugeot, is uncomfortable and smells of chemical cleaning

311

products, but Arlo thought it would be more anonymous than his Range Rover. Jo shifts to ease the numbness in her legs, leans her head against the window, thinking of how she could probably have stretched out fully across the back of the Range Rover like a first-class bed in a plane.

'Look, I really need to pee,' Max says abruptly. He has hardly spoken for the last hour, since Arlo told him to turn off the radio, which Max had insisted on tuning to a local news station to see if there was anything about Clio. 'And I wouldn't mind some of that coffee, if it's still hot.'

'We're not far now,' Arlo says, looking at the screen.

Bouvier has been in contact with them for most of the journey. Benjamin Laval's father has been questioned: his son had announced, with no warning, that he was taking a few days off; Monsieur Laval had seen Benjamin packing his rifle into the van so had assumed he was heading for the family hunting lodge, he was not aware that anyone was with him. Laval's phone had been switched off since the early morning, so the police had no way of knowing whether he had in fact travelled south, though all units had an alert out for the van. The phone from which Storm had called Jo that afternoon was unregistered and they had not yet been able to trace the location of the call.

Bouvier had refused to give Arlo exact directions to the hunting lodge and told him to wait in Pau until they had further information; local police would check the place and under no circumstances should Arlo attempt to approach until the officers had reported back. Arlo had agreed, but it was obvious to Jo that he had no intention of obeying. He had scrutinised satellite maps, checked co-ordinates against the map location of Laval's Instagram post and, when they reached the town of Pau, he had instructed Max to keep driving towards the mountains. Max had put up a show of

312

protest, argued in favour of following Bouvier's advice, but in the end he capitulated; perhaps feeling partly responsible for the situation, for allowing Storm in.

The road they are following, though tarmacked, is little more than a track running along the bottom of a valley, flanked by stands of pine trees. Beyond these, where the ground rises either side, the vast hulking shoulders of the mountains, solid against the night sky. A narrow stream runs alongside on the left, the headlights catching its white tumbling water as they round a curve. After another half-hour the track ends in a deserted car park. This is literally the end of the road; to one side is a wooden chalet-style building with toilet signs and a shuttered hatch at the front next to a poster displaying ice creams. Hiking trails lead off into the woods like spokes from a hub. Max pulls to a halt. At the far end, beyond the chalet, an unpaved track just wide enough for a car winds up into the trees, a large yellow sign at its entrance announcing '*Route Privée Sans Issue*'.

'No sign of the local police,' Max says after a few minutes. 'But then we don't even know if we're in the right place. Should we call Bouvier?'

'We're here now.' Arlo rests his forearms on the dashboard and peers out as if expecting something to happen. Moths collide in the beam of the headlamps. 'I think we should take the chance before they arrive. If Storm thinks there are police with us, she may do something stupid. I don't want to risk any harm to Clio. If I can just talk to her—'

'She said she'd be in touch,' Jo says. 'We should wait – she'll want to do this on her terms.'

'Ten minutes,' Arlo says. 'Then I'm going up that mountain. You're welcome to stay here.' His phone buzzes and he

313

fumbles inside his jacket for it. 'Bouvier,' he mouths, putting it on speaker as they all gather round. 'Where are you?' he barks, as if the detective is his underling.

'Outside Pau,' Bouvier says. He sounds harried, raising his voice to speak over the low growl of traffic. Arlo catches Max's eye and frowns.

'That's miles away. How long are you going to be?'

'We had an accident. Asshole on a motorbike pulled out of a side road without looking, my colleague tried to avoid him but we were going too fast, we clipped him, he came off. Everyone's OK, but the car is damaged – I'm waiting for the station at Pau to bring me another. Sunday night, it's taking longer than I would like. Where are you?'

'We're still on the road,' Arlo says. He has a good poker face, Jo thinks.

'Pull over and stay where you are,' Bouvier says. 'There has been a development. Benjamin Laval's friends confirmed that he met a girl who matches the description of Storm in a bar near the station in Libourne six days ago, so we know she has been in France almost a week. This has made it easier to trace her movements. We have her on CCTV arriving at Gare du Nord, travelling on a passport under the name Theresa Boyle. So now we have another complication.' He pauses; they hear a muffled conversation in French, as if he has a hand over the microphone. 'Theresa Boyle's bank card was used an hour ago in Limoges.'

'So? She could have given it to someone, dropped it somewhere—'

'She could,' Bouvier agrees, as if humouring him. 'We're checking CCTV from Limoges to see if we can locate her in the area. It could also be that this Laval business and the mountain cabin is a deliberate distraction, to send us all chasing for the border. I'm inclined to think the Limoges lead is more promising.' He breaks off and barks an instruction in French to someone.

'But you are going to check out this cabin?' Arlo says. 'Because we're on the way—'

'Of course. The local gendarmes should be there soon. It is essential for your safety and your daughter's that you wait for them and let armed officers conduct the search. Are we clear? And, Mr Connaught – I would like to ask you some further questions about—'

'Fine. Ask me when you get here.'

Bouvier begins to say something, but Arlo hangs up and raises his head to look across the car park at the Route Privée sign and the track beyond it. His phone buzzes again; he glances down at the screen.

'Cressida. Shit. I'd better take it.' He slams the car door as he strides off to answer.

Max switches off the engine.

'Theresa Boyle,' he says to the empty air. 'Do you think that's her real name?'

'She said Storm was the name her mother gave her,' Jo says, gazing out at the black peaks on either side. An owl cries, far off in the trees.

Max makes a snorting sound through his nose that conveys his contempt for himself, Storm, her name, her mother, the whole situation.

'I'm going for a pee,' he announces, turning to unclip his seatbelt. As he does so, his attention is caught by an object on the passenger seat. 'What's this?' He holds it up: a gold foil condom packet. Max peers out of the window at Arlo, who is pacing up and down by the edge of the trees.

'Did that fall out of his pocket?' Jo asks.

'Well, it's not mine,' Max says. 'I suppose it is his anniversary weekend.'

But Jo recognises it as the same brand she saw in Becca's washbag. Did Arlo remove the condoms so that there would be no questions about why the nanny had brought them? If so, *when* – before he knew she was dead or after?

'Max, wait.' She leans forward between the seats, lowering her voice even though Arlo is fifty yards away. 'What if Storm was telling the truth about Becca? Not knowing she was dead, I mean.'

Max swivels to look at her. 'Does it matter? She may not have intended to kill her, but the end result is the same. I suppose she could try pleading manslaughter, but with the abduction as well—'

'No. I keep thinking about it – what she said about the temazepam. You heard her. She said the dose couldn't have killed her.'

Max looks blank. 'So?'

'So' – she clicks her tongue, impatient – 'Storm put temazepam in the Orangina to make Becca sleep, right? But now we know Becca didn't drink the Orangina, Oscar did. And if Becca was injured trying to stop Storm taking Clio, then Storm would have known that, wouldn't she? But she assumed it was because of the dose. Which means she didn't know Becca was in the woods. And she honestly sounded shocked, didn't you think?'

'What are you saying, Jo? That someone *else* killed Becca, the same night Storm ran off with Clio?' He shakes his head. 'Who? Why?'

He follows her gaze to where Arlo stands in the shadows with his back to them, phone pressed to his ear, gesticulating with his left hand as he speaks.

'No. That's absurd. Why on earth—'

'He was sleeping with her. Those condoms were Becca's.' She sees Max's eyes widen. 'And she had a video of them

316

together on her phone, she'd filmed it secretly. I think something happened between them this weekend – I saw Becca outside his room crying. Maybe she threatened to show the video to Cressida or make it public, I don't know. But Becca's phone is missing. Storm would have no reason to take that, would she?'

Max considers this. 'Come on, Jo, this is crazy,' he says, leaning back against the headrest and closing his eyes. 'Arlo's not a murderer. I could believe he'd hide a phone to stop the police seeing it, to save himself any further complications, but not that he'd kill the girl to keep her quiet.'

'Really? When you've just told me what happened to the last woman who threatened to embarrass him publicly, twenty years ago? Which is why we're in this mess,' she adds, waving a hand vaguely at the car park.

'Well, exactly. Arlo's way is to pay people off, not take them out, he's not Tony Soprano. And Storm lies, remember? *Theresa*, I should say.' His mouth twists. 'She's an expert at deceiving people, as you and I have learned. Of course she's going to pretend she didn't kill Becca. Look, I really do have to go.' He slams the door behind him and disappears into the trees.

Jo sits back and watches her breath cloud the window, jumping wildly as the driver's door opens again and Arlo slides into the seat, rubbing his hands to warm them.

'Cress is furious with me for leaving without her,' he says, plugging his phone in. 'That's why I wanted to get away before she realised – she'd only have been a hindrance. She's threatening to get in the Range Rover and follow us, but the police won't let her, she's in no state to drive. Apparently there's already a couple of reporters sniffing around the gate. Stuart and Manisha are on their way from the airport, they can handle it.'

'That was fast. How did the press find out?'

'No idea. The police often let this stuff slip. I can't see Bouvier leaking, he's too proper, but I suppose he can't monitor everyone on his team. And Cress has called her bloody brother, even though I asked her not to worry the families yet. I wouldn't put it past Raf to have tipped off the media, he's dim enough. It'll only get worse now.'

He starts the engine and puts the car into gear.

'What are you doing?' Jo launches forward, clutching the headrest in front. She had seen this coming the moment he hung up on Bouvier.

'Going to find my daughter. *Daughters,* I should say,' he corrects, with a short, hard laugh. 'Get out, Jo.'

'Arlo, no. Bouvier told us to stay put until the gendarmes arrive. You heard him. The police know how to negotiate these situations—'

'Bouvier can't even negotiate his car down the street without hitting a motorbike,' Arlo says, releasing the handbrake. 'And now he's fucking about waiting for CCTV instead of getting his arse down here – I'm losing patience with him.'

She hears the sound of running footsteps outside, before Max flings himself into the passenger seat and clamps his hand over Arlo's on the brake. 'Don't be insane. This Laval has a gun. If they're up there – *if* – and you blunder in and Storm panics and hurts Clio – how would you live with that?'

Arlo keeps his eyes fixed straight ahead. 'And if I sit here doing nothing, while she's up there hurting her right now – do you think I can live with that? She wants to talk to me – fine, I'll give her that. I'm not asking either of you to come with me, so get out.'

Max withdraws his hand. There is a moment of held breath, before he slumps down in his seat like a sulky teenager.

318

'The only thing crazier than going up there would be letting you go alone.'

Arlo meets Jo's look in the mirror.

'Jo, you've got Hannah to think about. You should stay and wait for the police—'

Jo moves to open the door. But then she thinks about Oliver: about Max's account of that last, distraught call; how Oliver had died believing he could not live with himself. She wants to look Storm in the eye. She needs to know exactly what happened.

'I'm coming too,' she says.

29

The track curves upwards between stands of pine trees, growing steeper with every twist. As the incline increases, Jo hears the engine straining and, on one bend, gravel crunches as the wheels spin, failing to find traction. Arlo swears under his breath and accelerates. Max has his fingers curled tight around the seat edge.

'Should have brought the four-wheel drive,' he mutters. No one replies. The mood between them has shifted; there's a grim sense of resolution now, an unspoken agreement that, whatever lies ahead, they are in it together.

After a mile or so they reach a fork; to the left, the way is blocked by a barrier with an *Accès Interdit* sign. To the right, a narrower track rises at a forty-five-degree angle, barely wide enough for a vehicle. A hand-painted notice declares '*Propriété Privée*'.

'We'll leave the car here.' Arlo pulls up in front of the barrier. 'They'll see us coming a mile off if we try and drive up there. We can walk the rest of the way – it's not far, is it?'

Max looks at his phone. 'I can't get the map to load, the signal's terrible.'

Arlo switches off the engine, and in the silence the sound of running water reaches them from somewhere close by. 'OK,' he says, slapping his legs hard as if pep-talking himself, and opens the door. Jo climbs out and the cold slices through her jacket in an instant; a sharp-edged mountain wind that leaves her face chilled and the taste of ice on her lips. She watches as Arlo opens the boot and takes out a black rucksack, which he sets carefully on the ground and unzips. When he stands, there is a gun in his hands, a long-snouted pistol with a silver scope fixed to the barrel. Max yelps.

'What the *fuck*, Arlo? Where did you get that?'

'It's Paul's. Violette's husband. It's a fairly standard hunting pistol, I think – don't ask me what kind, I'm not an expert.'

'Well, that's reassuring. Are you licensed for it?'

'Not personally.' Arlo seems untroubled by this detail as he checks the chamber. 'Paul has a licence, I'm sure.'

'Do you even know how to use it?'

'Well, I've fired a shotgun before, if that's what you're asking. These are trickier than a rifle for accuracy, but I couldn't fit a rifle in the bag.'

'What, since your stag do? When was the last time you fired a gun?'

'I don't know, a year ago, maybe?'

'Ah, God.' Max raises his arms to the heavens and whirls around, as if seeking sympathy from an imaginary audience on the slopes. 'Leave it in the car, Arlo, please. This is just asking to make things a thousand times worse.'

'What, and walk in there like sitting ducks?'

Jo lets out an involuntary snort of laughter at the image, despite the pulse pounding in her throat; fear is making her light-headed.

'Don't you think we'll be more of a target if you go

321

swaggering in brandishing a shotgun you don't know how to use?' Max persists.

'I can use it fine.' Arlo snaps the gun closed. 'Like I said, stay in the car if you prefer.' He starts towards the steep path.

'At least put it in the bag for now,' Max says, scrambling to catch up. 'And promise me the safety thing's on.'

After a moment's hesitation, Arlo nods and puts the gun away, hefts the rucksack on to his back and turns to them.

'Do you want to wait here, Jo?'

She shakes her head. 'She might call me,' she says, tapping her pocket.

'She's not going to call now,' Max says. 'Have you even got signal up here?'

Jo checks. A couple of bars flicker bravely. 'Enough. She still might.'

'Phones on silent,' Arlo whispers, switching on his torch function. High above them, an animal cry, sharp and feral, carries through the trees, and Jo remembers reading somewhere that there are wolves in these mountains.

The track ends in a gravelled area facing a building nestled in the lee of a ridge, with trees above and to one side. The word 'lodge' had conjured something grander; this is a modest two-storey cottage of weathered stone that looks as if it might have stood in that spot for a couple of centuries or more. There are no lights in the small windows, but as they edge closer through the trees, footsteps crunching on dry needles, Arlo points to a new-built carport beside the house, where a grey Renault van is parked.

He makes a thumbs-up sign; Max tries to say something but Arlo cuts him off and motions for them to follow.

The carport stands at an angle to the cottage, so that it

can't be seen from any windows. Arlo crouches beside the van, hidden from the house, and sets his bag down. He takes a packet of tissues from his pocket, removes one and, with it wrapped around his hand, tries the rear door to find it unlocked. He sweeps his torch quickly around the interior, but the van is empty apart from a crumpled blanket in one corner.

'Fuck.'

'Wait.' Jo grabs his arm, directing the beam back to the blanket. 'There's something—' She is about to climb in when Arlo hauls her back.

'Don't touch anything,' he hisses. 'Pull your sleeves over your hands.'

She does as she is told, crawling on hands and knees as she reaches for the object that caught her eye and retreats, holding out to him a baby's pink spotted dummy. He stares at it for a moment, breathing hard through his nose.

'Come on.' He nods towards the house; before they can move, a sudden scuffle of dry leaves from the trees at their back startles them into freezing. Some unseen creature runs fleet-footed into the dark and the night falls silent again.

'For God's sake turn that torch off,' Max says urgently. His voice is tight with fear and his eyes shine in the dark. 'What are you going to do – walk up and knock on the door?'

'Have a look in the window, anyway,' Arlo says. 'At least we know they brought her here. They've got to be in there.' He slides the gun out of the bag. Max starts to protest, but Arlo is already up and loping across the space between the carport and the wall of the cottage, the pistol held by his right leg. Jo tucks the dummy into her pocket and peers out from behind the van as he cautiously edges towards the corner of the house. He moves slowly, but no security lights are triggered, and when Arlo disappears from view, Max shakes his head and says, 'Fuck's sake. He can't go in there on his own.'

Behind the cottage is a scrubby yard; in the moonlight Jo can make out the shape of a picnic table and behind it, a low wall. There are no trees on the far side; the house has been built on a ledge. In daylight, she guesses the view from this garden down the mountainside would be spectacular. All the windows here are dark too. Arlo inches his nose over the sill of the nearest one, turns to them with a shrug and shakes his head.

'Kitchen in there,' he whispers. 'No sign of life.'

'That's because they're waiting inside to put a cartridge through your head,' Max hisses back.

The entrance is a stable-style wooden door, both halves closed. Arlo tries the latch, but it is locked. He steps back, stares up at the facade. Then, before anyone can intercept him, he smashes the butt of the gun through a pane in the narrow window beside the door, pulls his sleeve down and reaches in to draw the bolt. Max swears under his breath and yanks Jo back around the side of the house as the crash of breaking glass echoes in the clear air and a couple of crows take off indignantly from a nearby tree. Arlo presses himself against the outside wall with the pistol cocked; Jo braces for the sound of gunfire, but it never comes. There is no noise from inside the house. After a brief pause, Max sticks his head around the corner. Arlo leans in to open the door and beckons them with his head. Jo's stomach is churning, her legs feel weak, she desperately needs to pee and her heart is pounding in her throat, but her blood is up now; she wants to see this through. She follows Max through the door into a small kitchen, glass snapping under her boots.

As soon as they enter, she knows that something is wrong. The place feels cold, uninhabited; the silence that hangs heavy in the room is the silence of empty spaces, she is certain. No house with a baby in could be this quiet.

Arlo gestures to Max to bring his phone with the torch; he needs both hands to steady the gun as he edges forward.

The main room is compact, low-ceilinged, with stone walls and a floor of scuffed boards covered by one frayed rug in the centre. A mounted stag's head looks out above a fireplace with two battered armchairs either side. Opposite, under the window, is a rustic square table with four wooden chairs. At the far end, a staircase ascends to the upper floor; beneath it, a glass-fronted cabinet housing several bottles of whisky. The place has a functional, male feel; no soft touches, no cushions or ornaments to make it cosy. The only picture is a framed photograph on the mantelpiece, of the two Benjamin Lavals, father and son, celebrating a dead animal. It seems safe to assume that Laval does not use this regularly as a love-nest; this is for guy trips, for shooting and poker and drinking.

Max sweeps the light around one half of the room while Jo does the other, Arlo keeping the pistol trained on the staircase. In front of the hearth a long gun case stands open and empty.

Arlo stares at it for a moment, his jaw tight; he glances uneasily to the upper floor. Max lays a hand on his arm and points towards the kitchen and the open door, their escape route. He is suggesting retreat. They could still get out, hide in the trees, wait for Bouvier and his trained officers. Jo turns to look back, to make sure no one has come in behind them. But Arlo is not to be deterred now; he shakes Max off and climbs the stairs.

The landing at the top is empty. Three doors lead off it,

two of them standing open. One is a bathroom. The second, to its right, is a small bedroom; Arlo kicks the door fully open and stands on the threshold with the gun raised, but there is no movement. Jo glances in as they pass and sees that it contains only a single bed with no bedding and a chair. This leaves the room at the end of the landing, with the closed door. Arlo holds up a hand and they pause, listening. There is no sound anywhere in the house, but this means nothing; Laval is apparently an experienced hunter, he would be more than capable of waiting for hours in perfect stillness, his rifle trained on that door for the moment someone was foolish enough to open it.

There is an iron key in the lock of this door; Arlo turns it as smoothly as he can and sets his hand to the latch. Max motions for Jo to stand back; she ducks inside the doorway of the second bedroom. Arlo draws the latch down as quietly as possible and pushes the door; it gives an inch or so and jams.

'There's something against it. Give me a hand.'

Max glances back. Jo can guess what he's thinking: that they have walked into a trap. If Laval is not behind this door, he could be standing in the kitchen right now.

'Get your shoulder against this with me,' Arlo says to Max. He lowers the gun; reluctantly, Max positions himself alongside with his shoulder to the door. Arlo holds up his fingers to count – one, two – and on three they shove together. Something scrapes, the door shifts a couple of feet, enough for Arlo to stick the pistol's snout into the room. When there is still no movement, he motions to Max to give it one more push, and wedges himself through the gap.

He stifles a cry; Max barges in after him and says, 'What the— Ah, *shit*.'

The light of a phone flashes on, illuminating what looks

like a bare foot in the doorway. Jo hears Arlo say, 'Is he dead?'

She squeezes her way in, shining her torch on the body of a man lying prone behind the door. She recognises Benjamin Laval from his picture on the website. He is wearing a denim shirt unbuttoned over a white T-shirt and boxer shorts; his head is cricked to one side and there is blood on his face. His naked legs look pale and vulnerable in the stark light. Max crouches beside him, fingers to his neck.

'No. But he's got a pretty nasty head injury. We need to call an ambulance.' He starts to dial; Arlo grabs his wrist.

'Not until we've found Clio.'

'For God's sake, Arlo – he needs medical attention.'

'And how's Storm going to react if she sees sirens and flashing lights haring up here? I'm not going to risk her panicking and doing something stupid.'

Max jerks his head at Laval. 'So we should just leave him?'

'He's not my top priority right now.'

'Why's he half-undressed?' Jo asks.

Max looks up at her, and flicks his gaze across to the corner of the room, where there is a double bed with rumpled sheets. 'Probably thought he was about to get his reward for helping her,' he says. 'Instead she knocked him out and locked him in. I said he'd outlive his usefulness sooner or later.' There is a grim satisfaction in his voice.

'Where the fuck is she?' Arlo says, kicking the foot of the bed. 'There's no gun in here, anyway. She must have taken it. Would she know how to use a rifle? Max?'

'Funnily enough, it never came up on our dates,' Max says, as he rolls Laval into the recovery position.

'I suppose any idiot can fire at close range,' Arlo muses. A sudden noise from downstairs makes them jump. He jerks the pistol up and aims it at the door, pulling back the safety

327

catch. They freeze, hardly daring to breathe, until the noise comes again, a short hard slam.

'It's the back door banging. Put that thing down, for God's sake,' Max says, exhaling.

'She's here somewhere, with Clio.' Arlo lowers the gun slowly, without taking his eyes off the door. 'I'm going out to look.'

Max checks his watch. 'That's what she wants you to do. Bouvier will be here any minute. She could be waiting for you to walk out there.'

Before anyone can speak, a flashing light washes up the wall, on and off, on and off. Caught by surprise, they wheel around looking for the source, until Max says, 'Jo – your phone.'

She has almost forgotten she is holding it. The screen flashes *No Caller ID*. There is only one bar of signal.

'Hello?'

A hiss and crackle of static on the other end. Then:

'Jo? You made it!' Storm sounds as if she's greeting guests at a party. Jo puts the call on speaker.

'Where are you?' she says.

'Are you still in the cottage?'

'Why, are you?'

'I'll tell you where I am when you tell me. Have you got police with you?'

Jo glances at the men for approval; Arlo nods, urging her to hurry up.

'No. Just Arlo and Max. We found the lodge.'

'I know you did, I was just testing. You were like a herd of fecking elephants coming through the trees there.'

'So you *are* here?'

She laughs. 'Put Arlo on before we lose the signal. How're you doing, Daddy?'

'Where's Clio?' Arlo shouts, into the phone. 'I paid the money like you asked. Now tell me where to find her. You promised.'

'Sure, that's how it works, isn't it? You've paid your cash, you expect your goods. All right, I'll tell you.' Her voice stutters and cuts out; the signal is shaky. Arlo grabs the phone from Jo's hand and moves closer to the window.

'Say that again, I can't hear you.'

'. . . a track through the woods behind the house. Keep going along there, till you come out of the trees. A bit further up, there's a small lake, a tarn, I don't know what you'd call it. I'll be waiting. You'd better hurry, though.'

'Why?'

'Because the clock is ticking. And come alone. I want you to guarantee I walk away from here unhindered when we're done. Is that clear? Because if there's a single fucking cop with you—'

'There's no police,' Arlo says. 'Just let me hear her, so I know she's OK.'

'I can't do that, I'm afraid, she's sleeping. See you soon.'

He stares at the phone for a second, then thrusts it back at Jo. 'All right. You two stay here.'

'No,' Max says, putting out a hand to stop him. 'It's obviously a trap. We don't even know if Clio's there with her. I mean, are you sure that was even Clio's dummy? Storm could be trying to—'

'Jesus, I don't know – she doesn't have them *monogrammed*. Why else would a baby's dummy be here? Clio's got to be wherever Storm is.'

Max looks at the window; he doesn't need to spell out the alternative. 'All we know is that Storm wants to get you up on that mountainside alone,' he says quietly. 'I don't think it's for a heart-warming family reunion.'

'I need to see for myself. If you want to help, stay here and make sure the police don't come crashing after me,' Arlo says, over his shoulder. Max follows him down the stairs and Jo hurries behind them.

In the kitchen, Arlo sets the gun on the counter and begins pulling out drawers, rummaging through one by one. Max toggles the light switch, without success.

'I'm coming with you,' he says abruptly.

'Me too,' Jo says.

Arlo straightens up fast, a flashlight in his hand. 'Absolutely not. Especially you, Jo – you've got Hannah to think of. I'll take care of this. It's my mess.'

'Don't be ridiculous,' Max says. 'I'm not letting you go alone.'

'And what are you going to do? There's only one pistol.' Arlo clicks the flashlight on, blinking away from its powerful beam.

'Well,' Max holds out his empty hands in acknowledgement. 'I could hold the light for you? You'll need both hands for the gun. I won't let you walk out there on your own like a sitting duck, you bloody idiot.' They watch one another for a moment; Jo sees something complicated pass between them. Arlo gives a short laugh and claps him on the shoulder.

'OK. But you're staying, Jo.'

'What if she phones me again?'

'You could give me your phone,' Max says.

'Then I can't contact you. I'm coming.'

'All right, Jesus,' Arlo snaps, 'we don't have time for this. But listen – you stay hidden in the trees, OK? She doesn't need to see that you're with us. And if anything happens, you run. Understand? Don't even think about intervening. Get yourself somewhere safe and call Bouvier. Promise?'

Jo nods. Arlo takes the gun and Max leads the way with the light.

The beam picks out a narrow track among the trees at the end of the yard, climbing sharply between the pines through a thick carpet of needles underfoot. The air smells clean; small branches whip their faces as they pass. There is no sound except the crunch of footsteps and their breathing, huffing out faster in the cold. Every few paces Arlo makes them stand still, straining to listen for any other steps carrying through the silence, but they hear nothing.

'There are bears in these mountains, you know,' he whispers as they climb.

'Fuck off,' Max says, with a lack of conviction, but he swings the torch around into the trees to either side. 'Really, bears?'

'And wolves. Don't worry, I've got this.' He lifts the pistol.

'I hope you've got the safety on that thing.'

'It's fine,' Arlo says. 'You have to pull the catch back to shoot. I'm not going to put a bullet through your foot.'

'Do you honestly think you could fire it accurately, in the dark?'

Arlo throws a glance back. 'God knows, Max. You're supposed to use a stand, it's too unwieldy to aim without, but I couldn't fit that in the bag. With any luck we won't have to find out.'

They fall silent as they reach the end of the treeline. Arlo turns back to Jo. 'This is where you stop. If you hear anything, run.'

'You mean, shots?'

'Anything at all that sounds wrong. Get into the trees, stay hidden, call Bouvier.'

Max turns to her. His face is white in the shadows. He

gives her a quick, brusque hug and aims the torch at the path for Arlo. It strikes Jo that they might not come back, and the thought is so absurd that it almost makes her want to laugh. She could believe she is still hallucinating, it all seems so improbable; only the dull pain in her arm persuades her that she is really here, halfway up a mountain, that Storm is waiting for them out there in the dark with a rifle, capable of anything.

She steps out from the trees to watch their backs as they walk away. The sky is suddenly vast, crammed with stars, the moon casting enough light to see that beyond the forest, the landscape is nothing but bare rock. The path continues upwards over a low ridge. As Arlo and Max reach the top, Jo catches a noise among the branches behind her; a rustling, as if something large is moving clumsily through the dark. She whips around but the dense black between the trunks is impenetrable. Bear? Wolf? Or Storm, ambushing them from behind? Her heart drills under her ribs; her hands and feet turn numb. Before her thoughts can catch up, she finds herself scrambling after the men.

From the ridge she can see the tarn, splinters of moonlight gleaming on black water. It's set in a shallow bowl, high jagged crests rising on either side, with the path running to the right. Arlo and Max have come to stand at its edge, panning the torch around, each partial glimpse of their surroundings only serving to show how much is outside the reach of the light. Arlo has the pistol raised, steadying it with both hands. Before the beam can find her, Jo ducks behind a cluster of boulders at the top of the rise, out of sight.

'Hello?' Arlo's voice echoes around the hollow and disappears into silence. He mutters something to Max; she can't catch their words. She presses her fingers around the outline of the dummy in her jacket pocket.

'Storm?' Arlo shouts again.

In answer, a loud crack splits the air. Jo slumps behind her rocks; for an instant it had felt as if her heart might burst from shock and the panic makes it hard to snatch a breath. One of the men had cried out at the gunshot, though whether from being hit or merely startled she can't know without raising her head over the boulder.

'You can put that gun down now, Arlo.' Storm's voice carries clear across the water, though the way the sound ricochets off the rocks, she could be anywhere. 'You won't be needing it. Just so you know, I've got mine trained on Max. If you don't, I'll put a cartridge through his gut. Sorry, Max,' she adds cheerfully.

Still Arlo hesitates. The torch beam moves shakily around the edge of the lake again – Max trying to keep his hands steady – but there's no sign of anyone. More significantly, Jo thinks, there is no sound that would suggest the presence of a baby.

'Do you think I'm not able for it?' Storm calls out. She sounds quite calm, almost amused. 'You don't grow up where I did without learning to use a hunting rifle. My grandad taught me. Or am I bluffing? Do you want to take the gamble? Course you don't,' she says, after a pause. 'Throw it away now, Daddy, like right away from you, and I'll set mine down, and we'll talk.'

Jo darts her head above the boulder. She can see Arlo with his hands in the air, his pistol pointed at the sky. He nods to Max, who holds the torch beam on him as he turns slowly and skims the gun away behind him across the path. It lands ten feet or so from her, though she has no chance of reaching it without being seen – and in any case, what would she do with it?

In response, a light appears on the far side of the tarn;

some kind of camping lantern. It reveals Storm in shadow, standing on a rock with her legs planted apart, her hair blowing loose behind her, rifle held by her side. There is no sign of Clio.

'Where's my daughter?' Arlo says.

'I'm right here, Daddy.' Storm lays her gun carefully at her feet.

'Don't call me that. I know who you are.'

'What would you prefer? Da? Father? What did you call your dad – *Pater*? That was quite the shock, I can tell you,' she says, straightening up and folding her arms, 'finding out that my own grandfather was a bloody *Tory*. Quite anti-Irish, as I recall. God, I wish I'd learned in time to introduce myself – wouldn't he have loved that?'

'Where's Clio?' Arlo says, his voice strained. 'I'm here. I've done as you asked. What is it you *want*, Theresa? Because I'll do it. If you want more money, you can have it. If you want me not to press charges for taking her, I'll agree to it. Just for God's sake give her back to us.' Jo hears the quaver in his voice and registers her surprise; she has rarely seen Arlo express ordinary human feeling.

Storm laughs. '*Theresa*, is it? That's what my grandmother called me. She felt it was more respectable than Storm, which my mother chose. It's a strange thing, I can tell you, Da. At the age of twelve you find out your parents aren't your parents, your dead sister was actually your mother, and everything you thought was true about your family was a lie, and if that wasn't enough of a head-fuck, at nineteen you learn you've been living with the wrong name your whole life, and you're the product of a gang rape. It does kind of mess with your sense of self.'

'Tell me what to do,' Arlo says weakly.

'I'll tell you what I want from you,' she says, raising her

voice. 'I want you to imagine my mother's death for a moment. She drowned herself.' She lets out a bark of laughter. 'I know – it's Victorian, isn't it?'

'I'm sorry,' Arlo says. 'Really, I am. But you can't blame me for that – how could I have known? We gave her what she asked for. In fact, she took the money, signed a contract and then had the baby anyway.'

Stop, Jo thinks. *Don't defend yourself.* She wills him to shut up, and in the torchlight sees Max hit him in the arm, evidently with the same motive.

'*The baby* was me,' Storm says, enunciating her words with precision. 'She wanted me. She only agreed to the abortion because she felt pressured into it. She was lucky, I suppose, that the woman who took her there was kind, the one who was cleaning up your mess for your father. Maybe she wasn't kind, just Catholic. Anyway, lucky for me, eh? But afterwards my mother lived in fear of being found out. That's what shame does, Arlo – it wrecks your head so you can't think straight, about what's best for you or what you deserve, it just lays this burden of guilt on every choice you make. It's what *men* do to women – leave us to carry their shame.'

'We never meant—' Arlo begins, but Storm cuts him off.

'She had postnatal depression, you know, but she couldn't get any help for it, because she wasn't meant to admit that it was her baby. She thought if your father discovered she'd taken his money under false pretences, she would go to prison. And she couldn't give the money back, because her stepfather had used it to save his business. She put it all in her diary. Every detail of what happened. Of course, you and I know he couldn't have done a fucking thing about it legally, that contract was meaningless, but when you don't have money, you live in fear of people who do, and what they can force on you. That's on top of the self-loathing of

335

what you'd done to her, all of you – yeah, you too, Max, you're just as guilty. You walked away.'

Max tries to speak, but Arlo interrupts.

'I've said I'm sorry.' He spreads his hands wide. 'I don't know what else I can say. If I'd known you existed—'

'*Horseshit.*' Storm's voice is pure flint. 'You'd have done nothing, except try to silence me with legal threats as well. You never gave her a second thought after that, did you? She meant so little in the grand scheme of your life that you didn't even recognise me when I looked you in the face. But the four of you took over the whole of her life, until she couldn't stand the weight of it. Doesn't seem fair, does it?'

'I can make it up to you,' Arlo says, without conviction.

'Can you, Arlo? Can you really make up to me the loss of my mother, the absence of my father, the childhood I could have had? How will you do that? Pop a cheque in a birthday card?'

'Whatever you want. We can talk about it. If we can reach an agreement before the police get here, I can speak for you. Please, just tell me Clio's safe.'

'*Reach an agreement?*' She laughs. 'No, I don't want an agreement. I want you to understand what she suffered. Don't move.' She jumps down off her rock and disappears. Jo shifts to see better; Arlo and Max are murmuring urgently between themselves. Max glances back in her direction and frowns; she can't tell if he has seen her.

Storm reappears at the edge of the water holding something in her arms. It takes Jo a moment to realise what she is seeing, and her heart catches in her throat. Storm is carrying a bundle about the size of a sixteen-month-old child, held upright against her shoulder. In the lamplight it's hard to see clearly, but the bundle is zipped into a little red coat with white fur trim around the hood.

Arlo lets out a strangled cry of recognition. He tenses as if to run, then stalls; perhaps he can't work out the surest way around the tarn, perhaps he fears the consequence of any sudden move. Storm jiggles the shape against her shoulder, the way you would soothe a crying infant. But there is no crying.

'I dream about her a lot, my mother,' Storm calls across the water. 'Róisín Bridget Caffrey. Say her name.'

'Róisín Bridget Caffrey,' Arlo says. He sounds desperate. 'Let me come and get her. Please.'

'I dream about what it must have been like for her,' Storm continues, unhurried, 'to leave her child sleeping in a warm house, and walk out into a spring dawn, step off those rocks into the sea as the sun came up, and feel that freezing water closing black over her head. Can you imagine what that would feel like, *Dad*?'

All at once, Jo understands what is going to happen. It is obvious to anyone – it must be obvious to Arlo – that the bundle isn't moving. If it's really Clio, then she is either heavily drugged, or already dead. While their attention is on Storm, Jo slides out from behind her rock and hooks Arlo's pistol towards her with one foot. She darts back to shelter with it clutched in her lap, hearing the speed of her heart. No one appears to have noticed. It's heavier than she expected; she remembers Arlo saying it needed to rest on something. She has no idea how to take off the safety catch. She eases herself slowly above the rim of the boulder and finds a place to settle the gun. She squints to look through the scope and finds she can line Storm up in the cross hairs, except that Arlo and Max are standing in the way. Her hands are shaking; the fine lines in the viewfinder shudder as she tries to hold it still.

'*Please*,' Arlo says again. His voice breaks. It must be the first time he has begged for anything, at least in his adult life.

'If you want this child, go get her. What's left of her.' Storm raises the bundle over her head and hurls it with all the force she can muster. As it hits the water, a cry rips from Arlo and he throws himself blindly into the tarn while Max runs along the shoreline helplessly shouting, '*No!*' Storm turns and Jo sees her, as if in slow motion, as she bends to pick up the rifle. A single shot cracks through the dark, followed by a scream.

30

Jo is flung back and in the moments of absolute silence that follow she understands that she was the one who pulled the trigger.

Max calls her name, shouts for her to stay down, his voice high and panicked. She looks into her lap and sees her hands trembling wildly. She shoves the gun away from her, appalled by it, the way it had bucked and kicked upwards in her hands as it discharged. She pulls herself up to see over the rock and there is only Max, frantically twisting his head between the darkness behind him and the glassy surface of the pool. Across the water, the lantern is still shining, but Storm is no longer standing in its light; Jo can't see where she could have gone. From that side of the lake comes a drawn-out cry, like a wounded animal. Jo scrambles to her feet, adrenaline spiking through her, sending her lurching over loose stones with only the light of her phone to show the way. Max spins round as he sees her.

'Jo! For God's sake, stay back.'

'I hit her,' Jo gasps, pulling herself over the rough rocks at the end of the tarn.

Max shouts something else, but it's drowned out by a furious splashing as Arlo breaks the surface, flailing and gasping for breath. Max yells at him to come out, but Arlo either ignores him or can't hear; he gathers his breath and plunges again. Max swears, pulls off his coat and wades into the water after him. Jo hesitates for a moment to watch them before pushing on, shingle slipping under her feet, the skin of her hands tearing as she grabs at outcrops to steady herself, until she reaches the shore where Storm was standing and sees by the light of the lantern that she is prone on the ground, shivering, a hand clutched to her chest. Jo snatches the lamp and crouches beside her, holding it aloft. Storm stares at her with wild eyes, her right hand clawing the air until it connects with Jo's sleeve. The front of her jacket is a mess of dark blood. Jo can't identify the source of it, so she presses both hands in the general area of Storm's heart. The girl's eyes are fixed on her, though they seem not to focus.

'Don't die, for God's sake,' she mutters, pressing harder.

Behind her, more frenzied splashing; she twists her head to see Max dragging Arlo out of the water.

'I've got to get him to the house, he's freezing,' Max shouts, though his teeth are chattering so hard he can barely speak. He wraps his coat around Arlo, who can hardly stand. 'Come on.'

'I've hit her,' Jo calls back. She doesn't really believe it, even when she hears herself say it aloud. 'I can't leave her.'

Max says something else, but Jo doesn't catch it. 'I'll follow,' she shouts. 'Call Bouvier, get an ambulance.'

The fingers tighten around her sleeve. 'Did *you* do this, Jo?' Storm draws a breath and lets out a rattling laugh. 'Didn't know you had it in you.'

'I thought you were going to shoot them,' Jo says. Her

thoughts are careering like a bird trapped in a room, smashing into every surface. If Storm dies, that will make Jo a murderer, and this time she acted consciously.

'I'd have gladly watched him drown.' Storm struggles to sit up and cries out; Jo eases her down. The girl's breath is coming quicker and shallower. 'Like she did. I wanted him to know in his bones what she suffered. I thought she would come to me again, if I could do that for her. I thought she would be – what's the word—'

Jo makes shushing noises, but Storm drags on her arm, her eyes flickering all around, unable to focus.

'*Appeased*. That's it. She doesn't come so much now. When I was a teenager I saw her all the time, but then she stopped. After I read her diary I understood why. Because he'd got away with it. I thought she would come if he was punished. But she didn't. Why can't I see her?' Her eyes lock on to Jo's as if demanding an explanation.

'He didn't drown,' Jo says. 'Max got him out.'

Storm nods, and winces. 'So he wins again.'

'They didn't get Clio though.'

A harsh laugh rips out of her. 'Clio's not there.'

'I didn't think so. Where is she?'

Storm heaves in another breath and her eyes close. Her body has started shaking violently; Jo can still feel the blood running hot over her hands. She pushes down harder with a brisk shove.

'Storm – where is Clio?'

Storm's eyes snap open. 'I'm not a monster, Jo. I wasn't going to hurt a baby. She didn't need punishing.' Even in the lamplight Jo can see how pale her face has grown. Her mouth curves into an effortful smile. 'I used to pretend I had a little sister when I was a kid.'

'Where is she?'

341

'Near Lourdes. With Benjamin's grandmother.'

'And she's OK?'

'Last time I saw her.'

Jo keeps one hand pressed on the area between Storm's left breast and her shoulder, which seems to be where most of the blood is coming from, and with her free hand reaches for her phone. Her fingers are slippery, the phone almost falls from her grasp, but somehow she manages to text Max, one-handed, a garbled variant of this information, hoping to God his phone was in his coat and not his jeans. For all she knows, Max and Arlo are lying among the trees dying of hypothermia, but someone might find the message. She should forward it to Cressida too, but Storm jerks suddenly and Jo drops the phone.

'Do you know where you're hit?' she asks. She tries to think back to the basic first aid training course she'd had to take when she started working in student welfare, not that it had covered anything like this situation. She has no idea how serious the wound might be.

'Shoulder, I think. But I can't really feel much on that side, it all hurts,' Storm says, leaning her head to the left. 'I'm very cold,' she adds, after a pause.

Jo tears off her jacket and covers Storm with it. The mountain air cuts through her jumper; she feels it like a dousing with iced water, jolting her alert.

'What did you do to Laval?' she says. She has a vague sense that if Storm slips into unconsciousness, she will lose her, and therefore as long as she keeps her talking, there is a chance someone might arrive in time. 'We found him in the house,' she continues, when Storm doesn't reply. 'He looked in a bad way.'

'He'll be grand. I didn't hit him that hard. Just had to shut him up.' She is no longer trying to look at Jo; instead she has let her head fall back, but her eyes are open, shining up at the stars. 'He kept on about calling the police. See, I told him Clio was my daughter, and my abusive ex-husband had taken her.' She manages a dry laugh. 'Laval was the type who likes a damsel in distress. He lapped it up. Couldn't have been more helpful. But I think he realised he'd got in too deep. He started getting cold feet about luring Arlo up to the mountains. He liked me better when he thought I was a tearful victim. Plus he wanted his reward. He got quite insistent about that.' She curls her mouth in disgust.

'Did he force—'

'Ah, no, I let him have it. Best way to get him off guard. Just gave him a bit of a knock with the rifle, took his phone off him.' She swallows painfully. 'I couldn't have him messing things up, when I was so close to getting Arlo here. I thought I could do it without anyone else getting hurt.'

'You killed Becca,' Jo says, uncertainly.

Storm tries to raise her head. 'No! That's – I never meant to. There wasn't enough in that bottle to kill anyone. Just make her sleep through.'

'She didn't drink the Orangina. You know that. She died in the woods, by the chapel. Did you give her a bit of a knock as well?'

'What? I never saw her.' Her eyes are opaque. 'After you attacked me and ran off – I went back for the baby. Didn't look in the nanny's room, the door was closed. Benjamin was waiting out on the old logging road in the woods. I grabbed Clio and got out as fast as I could, I was panicking you'd find your way back to the house and wake everyone. But when I got near the clearing again I could see a light moving in the trees. I thought it must be you, so I had to find another way through.'

'Did you take Becca's phone?'

Storm's face contorts in pain or confusion; she shakes her head and her eyes close.

There is no reason to believe her; she has deceived them all from the beginning. And yet Jo feels, instinctively, that she is telling the truth. Others were out there in the forest last night: Becca, and whoever killed her.

'What about Oliver, then?' she says. 'My Oliver. Was he collateral damage as well?'

Storm doesn't answer for so long that Jo starts to wonder if she even heard the question. She jolts her by the shoulder and Storm's eyes snap open in a blaze of fury.

'I *hated* Oliver. You have no idea. It was him and Arlo between them who killed my mother. The others too, but – those two, they were the ones who treated her like shit afterwards. She didn't know which of them was my father. So I decided to find out.' She is breathing hard, but her gaze is locked to Jo's and her teeth bared; the anger has galvanised her. 'Your Oliver was the one who brought the others to her flat that night. She liked him. She thought he liked her. But he was the one who encouraged them to treat her like a piece of meat. He should have been destroyed with guilt over what happened to her, and instead I found him living his nice life with his pretty wife and daughter, and everyone thinking what a fine good man he was, what a champion of the oppressed. He didn't even remember her name. You know, I didn't mean for him to die, though.' She struggles up so that her face is inches from Jo's. 'I wanted him to live, and suffer every day with the weight of his guilt. And if he didn't feel guilty about my mother, I'd give him something he could feel guilty about.' She falls back, panting. 'I didn't realise he'd be such a fucking coward.'

'What did you think would happen?' Jo is raising her

voice now, but she doesn't care. 'You let him believe he was your father, *after* you'd slept with him.'

Storm closes her eyes and a small smile curves her lips. 'You're good, Jo. Did you and Max figure all this out? He could have been my father, that's the point. *I* was pretty sure he wasn't – I studied them all, endless photos, before I tried to find them, anyone could see I look like Arlo. Except all of you, apparently.' She sucks in a ragged breath and lets it out in a hiccupping laugh. 'I told Oliver I'd taken his DNA and had a test in secret. I didn't expect him to believe me, I thought at the very least he'd demand confirmation. I wasn't expecting him to drive off a hill, that was never my intention. But the thing was—' She grasps at Jo's arm and her voice softens. 'After I found out he was dead, she came to me. My mother. Several times. And I hadn't seen her in so long. She put her hand on my face and she was smiling. So I reasoned it had made her happy. I'd done what she wanted. Then she stopped coming, so I knew I had to do it again.'

Jo turns away. She has lost patience with this mystical bullshit, can hardly believe she indulged it for so long. She wonders if Storm even believes it herself.

'What, were you going to pick them off one by one, for revenge?'

'Not revenge,' Storm says, in that same faraway, dreamy lilt. 'Justice.'

'So you targeted Max next?'

'It was Arlo I wanted . . .' she pauses to snatch a breath, 'but I needed a way in. Oliver kept me separate from his friends, for obvious reasons, and Leo would have done the same. I needed to be a girlfriend to get close.'

'Were you planning to take Clio all along?'

Storm tries to shake her head; the movement makes her gasp through her teeth. 'I didn't have a plan really, except to figure out their weak spots, work something out. It was a risk – I didn't know if Oliver would have told any of the others about me, but I reckoned they'd have tried to look for me if he had. Max wasn't suspicious at all. I kept saying I wanted to meet his friends, but it took him a while – he was wary of what you'd all think. Then when he invited me this weekend with all the families, I realised I wouldn't get a better chance. I was never going to hurt her, I just said that to keep the police away. I wanted Arlo.'

'To kill him?'

Storm swallows and breaks into a fit of coughing; Jo tries to help her lift her head but she cries out, a short sharp mewl of pain.

'I wanted to watch him make a choice,' she says, when she can speak again. Her voice sounds weaker. 'To see if this daughter was worth something to him, more than the one he threw away. I wasn't counting on any of you having a gun.'

Her eyes flicker to Jo and she manages a faint smile. Jo looks down at her. She doesn't feel pity, or anger; there is only an absence of feeling, a hollowness. It is as if they are suspended in this moment, her and Storm, under the cold stars, with everything stripped away.

'You tried to make me cut my wrist.'

'No, no.' Storm's fingers scrabble at her sleeve. 'See, I was going to take the baby to Benjamin in the night and go back so I'd be there in the morning, so no one would figure it was me. But then you followed me in Saint-Émilion, and I couldn't have you telling anyone about him and the van, I needed to get safely down here without the police looking for us. Then I realised I could solve two problems at once. If I could get you out of the way, they'd find Clio and you gone and put two and two together. I thought you'd be off

346

your head on Angel Dust, you'd likely collapse in the woods and by the time they found you, you'd be in such a state you wouldn't be making any sense, they'd think you were delusional. Grieving widow, coming unhinged, trying to hurt herself. I even took the main phone off the hook so that, if someone found you before morning, they couldn't call the house. I didn't know you had your mobile on you.' She stops and lets her head sink to the side, exhausted with the effort of explaining. Her eyes have a dull glaze and she struggles to focus on Jo's face. 'I didn't cut deep enough to do real damage. I didn't want to do it. I like you, Jo, but I couldn't let you stop me when I was so close.'

'Why didn't you just . . .' Jo hears her voice fall away; she is not sure now if any answers will help. 'Confront them? You could have told Arlo who you were, he might have wanted to make amends. You could have had some kind of relationship with him.'

Storm lets out a long exhalation and her eyelids flutter closed. 'You haven't been listening. What, reconcile with him? Forgive him? How would that be what my mother wanted?'

'Your mother is gone,' Jo says quietly. 'What about *your* life? What happens to you now?'

'You think he'd have welcomed me?' Storm whispers, as if she has not heard. 'If I'd turned up and politely asked for a paternity test? He'd have had all the power. I had to find a way to have a hold on him.' She runs her tongue around dry lips. Even in the faint light, Jo can see that her skin is sickly pale. 'I need water.'

Jo glances around; there is an entire tarn beside her, and nothing to carry it in.

'I can try,' she says, cautiously letting go of Storm's shoulder. The flow seems to have slowed; she can't tell if this is good or bad. She crouches at the shore and watches the surface part in black ripples as she dips her fingers in, sluicing off the blood, aware of its metallic tang. As best she can, she scoops up icy water in her cupped hands and carries it the few yards back to trickle the little that's left into Storm's mouth, watching as the girl fights to lift her head and swallow. Jo wipes her hands on her jeans and presses back on Storm's wound, where the patch of blood has grown cold and sticky.

'Was that what it was about with Oliver?' Jo asks. 'Power?'

Storm's eyes are closed.

'He was obsessed with me,' she says eventually. Jo has to lean right next to her mouth to catch the words. 'He was going to blow his whole life up for me. Did you know that? Couple of months I was seeing him, and already he was talking about leaving you and Hannah, asking would I live with him. He's no loss to you.'

'Ask Hannah about that,' Jo says. 'He was her father, and you took him from her. He died hating himself.'

'Well, he took my mother from me, so I guess we're quits.' Storm's fingers loosen on Jo's sleeve and her hand falls across her stomach. 'He should have spent twenty years hating himself for what he did to her. I'm not going to say I'm sorry.'

Jo understands that she will never know whether or not Storm is telling the truth about Oliver leaving. She thinks of his last hours and the despair that propelled him off the road. She pictures all the life he should have had: Hannah's graduation, her wedding, the grandchildren he will never see. The years she, Jo, might have had to grow old with him, if they had been given the chance to work things out. She wants to be angry with Storm, but there is no rage left in her to spend.

'I should leave you here,' she says, without moving.

'Jo. Am I dying?' Storm's voice comes out small and child-like, all the defiance ebbed away.

'I don't know,' Jo says. 'The police will be here any minute.'

'I'm tired now. Let me sleep. Don't leave.' Storm tilts her head to the side until her forehead is touching Jo's wrist. Storm's skin is freezing and sheened with sweat, her breath barely misting the air. Jo shifts off her knees to sit beside her. She strokes Storm's hair back from her face with her free hand. The only thing that comes into her mind, absurdly, is the Kenny Rogers song 'The Gambler', which Oliver used to sing to Hannah in an exaggerated country accent when she was a colicky baby; it had been the one thing guaranteed to quiet her. Jo starts singing it softly, one hand still pressed to Storm's shoulder, surprised to find she remembers all the words. Her voice echoes around the bare rocks and across the surface of the tarn, where a child's red coat with a fur hood is floating, empty. She is still singing when she feels the deep basso throb of a helicopter reverberate through the ground beneath her, and sees the beams of torches swinging towards her over the ridge.

PART THREE

31

December

The Christmas tree is so imposing it looks as if it is there by royal appointment. All white and silver among the glossy needles, with an occasional flash of magenta, scattered with dozens of tiny lights on filigree wires so fine that they appear to be floating, it dominates the two-storey entrance by the staircase. Oscar and Grace slide perilously close to it, skidding in their socks down the long polished hall, pulling at each other's jumpers to try and win the race; giddy with sugar and the lateness of the hour, they shriek and giggle at Jo as she passes. She smiles and lifts her glass of mulled wine out of harm's way as they barrel on towards the front door.

Swing-time music floats from the living room; through the door she glimpses Cressida standing by the French windows talking to Nina, Clio settled on her hip, pulling at strands of her hair. The little girl seems surprisingly alert, considering it's half an hour before midnight; she is dressed in a blue cord pinafore, white tights and tiny suede desert boots, pink-cheeked and smiley with everyone who pays her court. Jo hesitates in the doorway, watching. She wonders if Clio remembers anything about the strange hours she spent in the house near Lourdes full of plaster saints, with the ninety-year-old woman who had unquestioningly taken the child in at her grandson's request. A medical examination had established that Clio had not been physically harmed in any way by her adventure; whether any deeper damage has been done will be revealed in time, or perhaps not. She was away from her family for less than twenty-four hours; the old lady had given her bread and honey, and wooden animals to play with. Children are resilient, Jo thinks. They bounce back. Their forgiveness comes so readily. For now, it is Clio's mother who clings to her and can't let go.

Cressida turns and catches sight of Jo. They look at one another for a long moment, before Cressida flashes her a tight smile that doesn't reach her eyes and returns to her conversation. She doesn't invite Jo to join them. Leo is not here this evening; allegedly he has the flu, but Jo has noticed Cressida's support for him has become markedly less vocal over the past weeks, as more women and girls have come forward to tell their stories.

The Connaughts' Richmond party is a subdued affair this year; understandably, they have drawn their close circle tighter, wary of anyone whose loyalty isn't wholly beyond reproach. There have been enough former friends and acquaintances talking to the press lately. On the steps to the front door they have stationed two large men in tailored black overcoats and leather gloves, wires coiling from their ears into their collars; Cressida's security dream come true at last.

Jo has a taxi booked for 12.30, the earliest she felt she could reasonably leave. She had doubts about whether to come at all, but it was expected, a show of solidarity that feels necessary for the moment. Arlo and Max have lied for Jo, and for that she owes them – that's before you even start to add up the billable hours of the Parisian lawyer Arlo dispatched for her the morning after their night in the Pyrenees.

She had been led down from the mountainside by police, wrapped in a space blanket, taken to hospital for a check-up and kept in for observation under police guard. Early the next day she was driven to the local gendarmerie and ushered into a strip-lit room, dazed and dishevelled, her clothes stiff with blood, where a sharp-suited, expensive-smelling young man introduced himself as Francis Gaillard and announced that he was representing her. He was Anglo-French (Oxford and Sorbonne Law School) and experienced in defending Brits accused of crimes in France, he explained, in the half-American accent particular to those who grew up in international schools. She had not been clear, at first, where he had appeared from; she had simply clung, child-like, to the idea that he was some kind of *deus ex machina*, descended to enact justice on her behalf. It was only gradually that she began to understand that she must have been in shock the night before, after she had watched Storm strapped on to the stretcher. No one had made any allowances for that, but it had worked in her favour; she had been incapable of answering questions. As a result, she had not said anything that might have been used against her or jarred with the testimony the others gave.

Self-defence in French law, Gaillard told her, depends on the use of proportionate force in response to a clear and immediate threat. Arlo and Max told the police that Jo was standing at the edge of the water when she fired the pistol, and that Storm had shot her rifle at them a moment before.

'But that's not—' she tried to say, and he held up a hand to stop her.

'Think very carefully about what you remember, Mrs Lawless,' he said, as she caught on to the warning in his eyes. For her to have been hidden behind the rock and to have fired first would count as a premeditated attack; Arlo and Max had lied to save her from criminal charges. Gaillard had talked her through her defence, and how she needed to present it. But what if Storm contradicts that, she had asked, and he had given her a strange look, until it dawned on him that no one had told her.

The bullet had entered Storm's chest between her heart and her shoulder, missing vital organs, but the blood loss had been severe, combined with exposure. The medics had done their best, but she had lost consciousness in the ambulance and died in hospital during the night without waking. So there was only one story, Gaillard said, the story Jo and Max and Arlo were telling, and if they told it right she would avoid a murder or manslaughter charge and walk free.

Gaillard had successfully applied for bail to allow Jo to return home until a trial date was set. These things could drag, he told her; he knew of one case where the inquiry took three years to acquit a man who shot someone in self-defence, but he was confident that this would be wrapped up much quicker, given the circumstances and Arlo's profile. The way he said this, with an air of insinuation, hinted that Arlo's ministerial contacts had weighed in over her bail application; Jo had not asked, and preferred not to know. All that had mattered to her at the time was that she was allowed to come home.

She checks her phone for any updates from the cab company – she doesn't entirely trust their New Year's Eve booking system. Instead she discovers, to her horror, that she is on 3 per cent battery. She could swear that she had plugged the phone in at home while she showered and dressed, but she must have forgotten to switch the socket on at the wall. This is not unusual; she blunders through the days now, forgetting basic things, losing or misplacing objects, missing appointments and failing to return calls, as if she is clinging to the last vestiges of control with her fingernails, the way she did in the weeks after Oliver died. Her GP has told her this is a common symptom of stress, this feeling that everything is slipping from her grasp; she often wonders if things will improve after the trial, or if this is her life now.

But she can't afford to miss an alert from the taxi driver. She would never find another cab after midnight, and at all costs she would like to avoid having to ask Cressida for one of the many spare rooms; she does not want to be any deeper in their debt. Somewhere in this house there will be an iPhone charger. She slips past the kitchen – a bustle of waiting staff in crisp white shirts filling silver trays with champagne flutes, hurrying to line up ice buckets with bottles ready to be popped as the New Year chimes – and climbs the back staircase to the first floor.

The landing is lushly carpeted, the walls lined with contemporary artworks. Halfway along, Jo catches a movement from the corner of her eye and jumps, before she realises it is her own reflection in the tall arched window over the central staircase. Sounds of the party carry up from the hallway below. She pauses to take in her unfamiliar appearance. She has lost weight since they returned from France; almost a stone without trying, and the planes of her face have acquired a new clarity, stripped of their former softness. But there are shadows under her eyes, and a stubborn vertical line has appeared between her brows. She touches a hand

to her hair; she has still not got around to having the highlights redone. Perhaps she will leave it darker now; it was
Oliver who liked the blonde. As she lifts her arm, her sleeve
rides up and she glimpses the pink edge of the scar on the
inside of her wrist; she tugs her dress down quickly over it.

At the far end of the landing she sees a closed door with
a battered yellow Nuclear Waste Hazard sign nailed to it.
Lucas's room. She quickens her pace; if there is one place
guaranteed to provide charging cables of every variety, it is
a teenage boy's bedroom. She doesn't think Lucas would
mind; besides, he's not around this evening. When she had
asked after him earlier, Cressida had said only, 'He won't be
joining us,' and the brusqueness of her reply had deterred
Jo from any further questions; she presumed he had chosen
to spend the night with friends and Cressida was put out
by the lack of family loyalty.

Jo pushes the door open and slips inside the dim room,
closing it softly behind her; it is only as she turns that she
sees the prone figure on the bed, face lit by the blue glow
of his laptop. But it's too late; he sees her at the same time
and lets out a yelp, pulling off his headphones.

'*Fuck*, Jo. Scared the life out of me.'

Jo's apologies are so profuse they trip over one another.
'I didn't realise you were here.'

'Er – not sure that makes it better,' he says. 'Lucky I wasn't
having a wank, eh.'

'Very lucky for both of us,' she agrees, trying to banish
the image. 'I really need a phone charger, I thought you'd
be bound to have one. I'm so sorry – I wouldn't normally
barge in like this.'

'Don't sweat it. I've got spares, hang on.' He swings his
legs off the bed. 'I actually thought you were going to be
Ma telling me I have to come down at midnight, for the

sake of Auld Lang Syne or whatever. I could do without that.'

He pulls open a drawer under the bed and brings out a tangled mass of leads.

'You're not out with your friends?' Jo says, turning her phone awkwardly between her hands.

'Not really feeling it tonight,' he says, unravelling the skein of wires.

'Is everything OK?'

He gives a dry laugh. 'Oh yeah,' he says, without looking up. 'Everything's just tickety-boo.'

'Sorry.' She could kick herself for her clumsiness. He doesn't look well. He was always skinny, but now there is a hollowness to his face; his eyes, like her own, are sunken and drawn, all the sleepless nights plainly written there. No wonder, after everything his family has been through. Jo can sympathise; she wakes every night slick with sweat, tangled in nightmares where white figures flit in and out of trees, hot blood runs between her fingers, Storm's face sinks through black water, mouthing words she can't hear. Even with the anti-anxiety pills, sudden loud noises make her adrenalin roar into overdrive and her whole body shake, to the point where she has been signed off work on sick leave, although she thinks the university were secretly glad of that as an excuse; it's not the best publicity to have their student welfare in the hands of someone who has been all over the papers under headlines screaming 'KIDNAPPED!' and 'MURDER IN THE MOUNTAINS'. Poor Lucas. She realises she hasn't seen him since France; his life can't have been easy over the past couple of months. She perches on the end of the bed; he glances up, catches her eye and fetches up an effortful smile.

'Here.' He has managed to extract a cable from the cat's

359

cradle. 'Just need to find you a plug now.' He reaches into the back of the drawer and brings out a box. Jo leans forward as he lifts things out and there, underneath a microphone and a pair of VR glasses, is a red iPhone with a fan-shaped crack across the bottom half of the screen.

32

Jo dives for the phone and grabs it before Lucas can react. She watches his face as he tries to formulate an explanation.

'That's my old one,' he manages eventually. 'It doesn't work.'

She shakes her head. 'Lucas, I know whose phone this is. I've seen the video.'

His eyes widen. 'How?'

'Storm went through Becca's stuff looking for that bracelet. The Saturday night, before everything happened. She found the video and sent it to me.'

'No, that's impossible. There were no outgoing messages, I checked.'

'She AirDropped it.'

'Fuck.' Lucas presses a hand to his mouth and breathes in hard through his nose. 'You mean, you have a copy?'

'Not any more. I deleted it. But I have no way of knowing if Storm sent it to herself.'

'So it could be out there?'

'I suppose. Depends if she forwarded it to anyone.'

A silence stretches between them.

'Where did you get the phone, Lucas?' she asks carefully.

'It was on her,' he says, looking away. 'In her pocket. When I found her in the chapel that morning. So I – before I told anyone, I just took it. I know I shouldn't have, but I knew the police would come and I didn't want them to see that film.'

'How did you know about the video?' she says.

He sits back cross-legged on the floor and pulls at a loose thread in the rug.

'She was threatening Dad. I heard her. That night, before the anniversary dinner, Mum sent me to hurry him up. And I was outside their bedroom when I heard Becca's voice in there. They were arguing.' He breaks off, shakes his head.

'Go on,' she says gently.

'She was yelling that if he sacked her, she was going to put the video on YouTube and Pornhub and send it to the tabloids, so everyone would know what he was.'

'How did he respond?'

'You know Dad. He can't deal with emotion. He offered her money.' He lets out a mirthless laugh. 'That went down as well as you'd imagine. She was screaming, "Your bitch wife has already tried to pay me off, I'm not a prostitute, Arlo, you can't just throw me out when you're bored." He told her she was being unreasonable. Then he said they could talk about it later, in private, but he had to go down to dinner because the minister was coming. She said maybe she should come down in the middle of dinner and tell everyone, including the minister, what kind of man he was.' He stops suddenly, pulling his knees up to his chest. Jo notices the raw skin around his nails.

'What did Arlo say to that?'

Lucas takes a deep breath and lets it go. 'He said, "If you do that, I'll kill you."'

They sit in silence for a moment, letting this hang. If there is a correct response, Jo can't find it. She thinks of the suspicions that had needled her from the moment Storm had expressed her surprise at the news of Becca's death. So Arlo had asked Becca to talk with him somewhere private later that night. The chapel in the woods? It didn't seem like Arlo's style, but perhaps he wanted to be far from the house.

'Did you know about them before you overheard that?' she asks. 'Your dad and Becca?'

'I suspected. Something about the way she behaved around him. And one evening when Mum was away on some spa thing, I went to talk to Dad and I found Becca in his office. I didn't see anything, but they both acted really weird and jumpy when I knocked.' He shrugs. 'When Mum said Becca was moving on at Christmas, I figured Mum had got wise to it and kicked her out. Then that weekend at the chateau, I thought that by taking the bracelet she was looking for another way to make trouble. So I went up to have it out with her during the dinner, when Dad was doing all his bullshit anniversary speeches. I told her I knew about the bracelet and if she deleted the video I wouldn't tell Mum and Dad that she was a thief.'

'And?'

He looks down. 'She just laughed. Said she didn't know anything about any bracelet, but if I didn't fuck off out of her room, she'd accuse me of trying to assault her. Then she . . .' He pulls at the rug until the thread snaps in his hand. 'She played a bit of the video, so I could see it was real. Like, I *really* did not need to see that.'

Jo looks down at the phone in her hand. 'So – when you found her in the chapel the next morning, you took the phone to protect your dad?'

He nods. 'I know it's a criminal offence – I just, I wasn't

363

thinking straight. I didn't want anyone seeing what she had on there.'

'Lucas' – Jo shifts position, clasps her hands around the phone. She knows how sensitively she needs to tread. 'What did you think had happened to Becca, when you found her? What was your first, gut reaction?'

'I don't know,' he says, aggressively picking balls of fluff from his socks. 'It was crazy that morning – you weren't there. No one knew what was going on – Clio was missing, Mum thought Becca had taken her. We didn't know where you or Storm were. At first, when I saw Becca, I thought maybe she'd had an accident. I tried to turn her over and wake her up, and that's when I saw—'

'That she was dead?'

He nods again. He still won't meet her eye. 'Yeah. I couldn't move her, she was sort of stiff. Later, when we knew Storm had Clio, I realised Becca must have followed her out to the woods and tried to stop her, and Storm killed her.'

The way he says this, it sounds rehearsed, as if he is making sure to repeat the words in exactly the right order.

'I went over and over this with the police,' he adds, as if he knows what she is thinking.

'How did you know to look in the clearing?' she asks.

'It's the quickest way out to the road if you don't want to go down the main drive,' he says. 'Over the stream, past the chapel and on to the old forestry track. Listen, are you going to tell anyone?'

He means about the phone; his eyes dart to it.

'Who else knows you have it?'

'No one.'

'Not even your parents?'

'No. I thought, if Dad knew about it, he could be in serious trouble. Knowingly hiding evidence or something. Whereas

I'm a minor, it wouldn't be so bad. Every time I thought about getting rid of it, I got paranoid about it being found and traced back to me. In the end I figured it was safer here.'

'So now I'm knowingly hiding evidence.'

He stops picking his socks and fleetingly makes eye contact.

'But they're not looking for it any more. We won't be interviewed about it again, so it's not as if you'll have to lie to the police.'

The blithe confidence of youth, Jo thinks, though what difference would one more lie make at this stage? What was it Storm had said at the tarn, when she learned that Arlo had survived? *He's won again.* It certainly looked that way.

'Jo? What good would it do to say anything now?'

But something doesn't add up here; it nags at her as she traces her thumbnail along the edge of the phone, weighing up her moral dilemma.

'What did you do with the case?' she asks, as it begins to dawn.

He glances at her and for the first time she sees real alarm.

'I took it off. It was too recognisable.'

'And?'

'And I threw it in the fire. That was dumb, I realise now, but I panicked. I wanted to get rid of it.'

'No,' she says slowly. 'The fire would have been out by the time you found Becca, it had rained in the morning. Bouvier showed me the case, it was almost completely burned. It had to have gone into the fire the night before, around the time Becca was killed.'

The understanding comes as she speaks. Arlo would never have made that mistake. Even if she could picture Arlo losing control to the extent that he could smack a young woman's head into a stone wall, which was already a stretch, he would not have left evidence to draw attention to the missing phone. But Lucas, who, only hours earlier, had overheard his father's mistress threaten their whole family with public humiliation? Who might easily have acted on impulse and panicked afterwards?

'Lucas? Were you there that night?'

The boy has turned bone-white. 'Jo. Don't. The police said Storm did it.'

'But she didn't, did she?'

She sees the pressure building behind his eyes, the weight he has been carrying alone; she sees his longing to unburden himself, and his mighty effort to fight it.

'I never thought,' she says quietly, without looking at him, 'that I would ever take a life. I never imagined that being part of who I am. And I didn't mean for it to happen, but it did, and I think about it every day. I'm not the same person, and I have to learn how to live with that. But if I had to try and cope without ever being able to talk about it' – she stops and shakes her head. She is offering him a space to fill with words.

'I knew you and Storm went out to the chapel for a smoke,' he says, after a long pause. 'I watched you from my window, both times. And then on the Saturday night, I saw someone following you. I realised it was Becca. God knows why.'

'She probably just wanted bargaining power,' Jo says. 'I think she knew Storm suspected her of having something going on with your dad. Maybe she was hoping to catch us with a spliff – she knew I'd rather your mum didn't know about that.'

Lucas coils a tassel of the rug around his finger until the tip turns white. 'I didn't think of that. I went up to Becca's room, I thought I could get her phone while she was out. But I realised pretty quickly she must have taken it with her.

So I followed you all. I knew where you'd be. I just wanted the phone. I was going to take it off her – by force if I had to – and delete the video. That was all, I swear.'

'But that's not how it played out?'

He takes a deep breath. He is about to say something when the bedroom door opens, and Cressida appears in the doorway, light shimmering from the folds of her silver-gold dress. Her eyes move instantly to the phone Jo is holding with the precision of a smart missile.

'Ah, Jo. I was just looking for you. Ten minutes to midnight, you don't want to miss all the fun.' She taps the sleek watch on her left wrist. The serpent bangle is coiled around the right as she reaches out her hand for the phone.

Jo glances at Lucas, who is looking at his mother. Something unspoken passes between them, that telepathic shorthand that exists in families. Whatever he had been about to confess, she knows she will never hear it now. She wonders how long Cressida was listening outside the door, how long she has been keeping this knowledge.

'Quick word, Jo?' Cressida gestures to the landing. Jo stands, still holding the phone.

Lucas watches them both, biting the skin at the side of his thumbnail. 'Do I have to come down for the toasts?' he asks.

'Best not, I think,' Cressida says in a clipped tone, shutting him in. She motions Jo along to the master bedroom.

'The things we do to protect our families,' she says, when the door is safely closed behind them. 'I know you have, Jo. You've kept things out of the public eye for Hannah's sake, haven't you, so you understand.'

Jo waits.

'I saw you come up here,' Cressida says. 'I was afraid you might talk to Lukey.'

'I remember when you wanted him to confide in me,' Jo says.

'Not this time. I need you to give me that.' Cressida holds her hand out for the phone.

'How long have you known?'

'Which part?'

Jo almost laughs. 'Any of it. Lucas said no one knew about the phone.'

'I didn't tell him I'd found it.' Cressida wraps her arms around her narrow shoulders. 'I went through his room about a month ago. You only have to look at him, Jo – he's been like this since we came back. He doesn't eat, he won't see his friends. And he's having a year out before he starts the sixth form again, so there isn't even school to take his mind off things. I thought it was drugs – he's been so reclusive and strange. That's what I was looking for. But instead I found *that*.' She nods at the phone.

'You didn't ask him about it?'

'No. I didn't see what good it would do. The business is closed, we all need to move on with our lives.'

'Lucas needs professional help,' Jo says.

'I don't think talking about this will help Lucas in any way,' Cressida says, in a voice distilled from generations of giving orders. 'The best thing he can do is put it all behind him.'

'You know why he took it?'

Cressida gives a curt nod. 'I assume he was trying to protect his father.'

'So you knew about the videos too?'

'Not until after she died and they couldn't find the phone. Arlo told me Becca had shown him before the anniversary dinner. She'd tried to blackmail him with those clips and he was terrified the police would see them if the phone turned up.' She frowns. 'How did *you* know about the videos?'

'Storm went through Becca's room looking for that bracelet,' Jo says, pointing to Cressida's wrist. 'It disappeared from Arlo's drawer and Lucas thought Storm had stolen it, so we tried to find it. Storm had a look at Becca's phone while we were there.'

'This bloody bracelet,' Cressida says, holding her arm up to the light. 'Well, that backfired, didn't it?'

Jo stares at her. 'It was you? You put it in Becca's case?'

You need to deal with her, or I will, Cressida had said. Jo had assumed they'd been talking about Storm.

Cressida runs her fingers along the serpent's jewelled head. 'Look, you've seen these videos, I presume, so there's no point pretending. I'd been more than generous with Becca, considering she'd been fucking my husband for months. She was getting a handsome severance bonus and I found her a place with friends near Oxford who were expecting their first baby in the new year. But she was determined to make things difficult.'

'Wait, so you *knew* about her and Arlo all along?'

Cressida flutters her eyes closed. 'Jo,' she says, with a patient smile. 'Don't look so shocked. Nobody can understand someone else's marriage from the outside, can they? You should know all about that. It's really none of anyone's business, how Arlo and I conduct ours. We've found an arrangement that has worked just fine for both of us for twenty-one years, and sex isn't part of it. Not with each other, at least. But we're a good team, and Mummy always told me you have to regard marriage as a business partnership, it's the only sensible way. It was laughable, that that girl thought she would be the one to come between us.' Her expression hardens. 'I could have told him she was a mistake, if I'd known before it started. I mean, the *nanny*? Please. We'd always said discretion was what mattered most. But like all men, he doesn't think to look a gift horse in the mouth, and she did rather throw herself at him.'

'To get money?'

'God, no – she thought she was in love with him.' Cressida laughs drily. 'And quite obsessed with Clio as well. I think she'd honestly convinced herself that Lucas and I would conveniently retire somewhere out of sight and she would become the next Mrs Connaught, poor child.' She stretches her arms above her head and executes an elegant little backbend. 'Anyway' – she crosses to the window and draws back the blinds on the balcony doors to look out over the garden – 'by the time I found out, it was obvious she was becoming a problem. So I explained to her, very nicely, that Clio had different needs now she was a toddler and we would be terminating her contract before Christmas. Becca was furious, naturally. This all happened the week before we went to France. I really didn't want to bring her with us at that stage, but we wouldn't have found anyone else at short notice, and Arlo said she would be less trouble where we could keep an eye on her. Then, when he was stupid enough to leave that bracelet in a drawer where anyone could find it, I thought it might work as insurance. If Becca was seen to be stealing from us in front of multiple witnesses, we'd be the magnanimous ones, declining to press charges as long as she went quietly. Imagine my surprise when Arlo handed it to me at dinner. I thought she must have worked it out.'

'You definitely looked surprised,' Jo says, meeting the eyes of Cressida's reflection in the dark window. 'But Becca had her own insurance plan.'

'Apparently so.' She pulls distractedly at her earring. 'The next morning, I thought she'd taken Clio to pay us back. But when Lucas found her – Becca, I mean. I couldn't make sense of it.'

'Couldn't you?' Jo says. There is a silence, freighted with meaning.

Cressida turns to meet her eye. 'Not at first. When they speculated that she had tried to stop Storm and hit her head in a fight, I assumed that was what must have happened. And in fact, that's what the police concluded, so . . .' She spreads her hands, palms up, as if to say, *case closed*. She is doing her best to appear in control, but her voice is strained and the tendons in her neck are standing out like guy ropes.

It was true that the French police were not looking for anyone else in connection with the death of Rebecca Ridley, though Bouvier had been reluctant to let that go, convinced that there was a story beyond the obvious explanation. The autopsy showed that she had died of traumatic brain injury consistent with hitting her head against the fallen masonry outside the chapel, where they found traces of her blood on the stones. There was no sign of temazepam or any sedative in her blood. The forensics could not prove conclusively that Storm was guilty; the only physical evidence linking them was a few strands of her hair caught in the zip of Becca's cardigan. But the circumstantial evidence supported the theory that Becca had woken shortly after Storm took Clio and followed her to the woods, where a struggle had ensued. The presence of two separate head injuries eliminated any possibility that her death was accidental; she could have received the initial blow as the result of a fall, the pathologist said, but her head had been smashed with considerable force against the stone a second time while she was on the ground. Given how many people had left traces in the forest clearing over the weekend, and the fact that Lucas and Arlo had touched Becca's body in an attempt to revive her, there was no definitive lead that could point to anyone else.

'Storm didn't kill Becca. You know that.'

371

'I know what the police said.' Cressida crosses the room, her face set; Jo flinches away, but Cressida lays a hand on her arm. 'Look, Jo. We've all been through so much these past couple of months – not just everything that happened in France, but all the press intrusion, it was monstrous. It's natural that we're all a bit overwrought – we've probably got PTSD, my therapist says.'

Jo almost laughs at her earnest expression; after their return from France, the Connaughts had decamped to Cressida's brother's estate in the Cotswolds to avoid the press. It was Jo who had been trapped at home with the blinds drawn, dragging Hannah through a shrieking mob of photographers and reporters twice a day on their way to and from school, until Emily's family had once again stepped in and taken Hannah to stay with them.

'You saved Arlo's life in the mountains,' Cressida continues, giving Jo's arm a little encouraging shake, her blue eyes wide and blameless. 'She might have shot him if not for you. We'll never forget that. Loyalty is very important to us, and so is showing our gratitude. As Sir Hugh did for Ollie.' She catches Jo's expression. 'Oh, surely you knew? Oliver's chambers – notoriously impossible to get pupillage there, the competition's so tight, and of course Ollie didn't get the best degree in the end, what with everything, but fortunately Hugh was able to pull strings. Same with Max – he's always rather coy about how he started out on a Tory paper, but that was where Hugh had his connections. Leo's first short film, that was nominated for a BAFTA – who do you think financed that? I'm simply saying, Jo, that the Connaughts have always known how to value our friends.'

Absurdly, Jo finds herself smiling. None of this comes as a surprise now. All the years she had wondered what bound Oliver so tightly to the others, and it was this: old-fashioned

372

shame and obligation. And yet they did care for each other: she remembers Leo, Max and Arlo in step, carrying Oliver's coffin along with his father, the pain on their faces; Arlo's toast to Oliver at the chateau; Max at Laval's cabin, telling Arlo he wouldn't let him face Storm alone.

'My son did something very stupid,' Cressida says, seeming disconcerted by Jo's smile. 'Criminal, even – taking that phone from Becca's body. But he did it for Arlo. And if Hannah had done the same for Oliver, you'd want to protect her, I know you would. And I would support you.'

Jo has no idea if this last part is true, and hopes she never has to find out. Cressida is right that she would abandon every last scruple to keep her daughter safe. But is it a kindness, she wonders, to let your child suffer with their conscience the way Lucas is clearly suffering? She doesn't have the answer to that either, but she is fairly certain that, sooner rather than later, Lucas will buckle under the weight of it, and that when he does, she will have reason to be glad that she didn't hear his full confession.

'But *Storm* was the one who killed Becca.' Cressida doesn't blink. 'That's what the police said, and no one can prove otherwise. Just as they can't prove that Storm didn't actually fire at you before you shot her.'

She holds her hand out for the phone once again. After a moment, Jo drops it into her waiting palm. Cressida has made her point; they are bound together by the lies they have told, the knowledge they have buried. Jo would like to cut the knot and free herself from the whole tangle, but they are still paying for her lawyer.

'Thank you.' Cressida closes her fingers around the phone and squeezes Jo's wrist tight with the other hand. A sudden burst of premature fireworks rips through the night from beyond the garden; Jo leaps back, heart skidding, snatching shallow breaths, the familiar dart of cortisol flooding her body. For a fraction of a second she sees Storm falling from the rock, and reaches out for the cool surface of the wall to steady herself.

'Come on,' Cressida says, glancing at the clock by the bed, 'it's nearly midnight – they'll be wondering where we are. Let's go down and put this fucking awful year behind us.' She crosses to the closet and tucks the phone under a pile of clothes. 'Anything you need, Jo – you just have to ask. We take care of each other, right? That's what friends do. It's what Oliver would have wanted.'

She holds the bedroom door open so that Jo can leave first, and locks it behind her. As Jo follows her down the grand staircase to the living room, braced for the kisses and forced optimism of the year's turning, it occurs to her that she no longer has to care what Oliver would have wanted. What matters now is what she wants.

33

April

Max snaps the collar of his coat against the thin drizzle as he paces in front of the Emmeline Pankhurst statue. He glances at his watch; fifteen minutes late already, but he knows how these committees can go on, and he is not sorry to delay this conversation. He takes out his phone, considers leaving a message, when he glances up to see Arlo hurrying towards him through the gates of Victoria Gardens. He is wearing, incongruously, a tweed flat cap pulled low over his face.

'Couldn't get away,' he says, by way of apology. 'It's been full-on the past few days.'

Max nods. The government's new Centre for Data Ethics and Innovation launched with great fanfare at the beginning of the week and as its Chair, Arlo has been on every current affairs programme to explain the importance of its role in establishing a framework of principles for ethical technology. There has been a heavy emphasis on the importance of public trust and transparency, which is unfortunate, in the light of what Max has to share.

'How's it going?' he says.

Arlo grimaces. 'It's reminded me why I don't get involved with government bodies. They've recruited the top people from across the industry, but it'll be a miracle if anything actually gets done.'

'Is the bishop giving you trouble?'

'The bishop's fine. The philosopher's going to be a pain in the arse though. Doesn't have the first idea about anything to do with machine learning but by God, he likes the sound of his own voice.' He tucks his hands into his armpits. 'So what are we doing out here in the rain? Why couldn't we have a civilised coffee in the atrium café?'

Max looks back at the familiar spires etched against the grey sky. 'Because this is not a conversation to have inside the Palace of Westminster. The place is crawling with journalists,' he says, trying to make a joke of it, but he sees the expression on Arlo's face.

They follow the path across the gardens and find a bench facing the river.

'Cut to the chase, then,' Arlo says.

Max takes a deep breath. 'I had a call from Alex Webber.'

'Who?'

'She's at *The Sunday Times*. We used to work together. Her uncle was deputy editor of the *Telegraph* for years.'

'Lionel Webber?' Arlo nods. 'I remember him. He was Hugh's tame journo when he wanted to leak stuff.'

'I know. He gave me my first job, at Hugh's request.'

'And this Alex?'

'She wanted to give me a heads-up, as a favour. They're running an exclusive this weekend.'

'An exclusive on what?'

'Peggy Talbot.'

'*What?*' Arlo twists to face him. 'She's talked? About – that business?'

'Rosie. Storm. Everything.'

'Why would they believe her?'

'Why wouldn't they? She's a model of probity. She worked for your father for thirty years.'

'Exactly. Whatever happened to loyalty?' He scrapes a hand across his mouth. 'Do we know what she's said? Surely it's libellous. She can't have any evidence beyond hearsay.'

'She's got the diaries. Alex has seen them. *Rosie's* diaries,' he clarifies, because Arlo is staring at him as if he doesn't understand the word.

'*How?*'

'Apparently Storm sent them to Peggy in October. Before France. She wrote a letter saying she owed her life to Peggy's kindness, and she felt Peggy should know the full story of what she had been asked to cover up. And if anything happened to Storm, she would leave it to Peggy to decide what to do with the material.'

'So Peggy's been sitting on this since *October*?' Arlo shakes his head. 'Why now?'

Max hesitates. 'She's got cancer. Only diagnosed last month. She's chosen not to have treatment.' He watches Arlo take this in.

'She never said a word to me. So now she wants to launder her conscience in public at our expense.' He curls his lip.

'Peggy told Alex she felt she had a moral duty. She said, in the light of the diaries, she doesn't think you're a fit person to hold a government appointment.'

'But I'm a fit person to pay her care home fees.' Arlo leans forward and presses his hands together between his knees. 'What about the videos?'

'What videos?' Max frowns. Arlo looks at him.

'This Alex didn't mention any videos?'

'No. What are you talking about?'

'Never mind. Can we stop them publishing?'

'Injunction, you mean? I doubt it. Public interest. You could try, but that might make it look worse. I don't have the means for that kind of lawsuit in the first place, so . . .' Max turns away, watches a barge inching its way towards Lambeth Bridge.

'We're fucked,' Arlo says after a while.

'In a nutshell.'

'You can't talk to this Alex?'

'You won't persuade them out of a scoop like this. She only warned me because she thought we might want to leave town before it breaks. Especially the families. It'll be a feeding frenzy. We're all people who've taken the moral high ground, one way or another, all four of us. When this story comes out—' He breaks off; there is no need to elaborate.

'Have you told the others?'

'Not yet. Jo's going to take it hard. She's only just been acquitted of murder.'

'And you have no idea how hard I had to lean on the French minister to make sure that verdict went the right way. Christ, Max.' Arlo stands and adjusts his cap. 'I thought this business was over for good.'

Max looks up at him. Through the trees, over Arlo's shoulder, he glimpses the Houses of Parliament; twenty years of his professional life has revolved around that building. He wonders, briefly, if he will have a career after this weekend. 'I guess Storm was determined to have the last word,' he says.

Epilogue

August

A cool breeze gusts in off the sea and Jo pulls the zip of her hoodie all the way up. The precociously hot spring has given way to a sullen, overcast summer, but the beach is still busy with family groups huddling inside bright windbreakers, children shrieking and splashing at the water's edge. Jo watches Hannah and Dennis prancing in the white foam and smiles; Hannah's feet kick up sand as she trots backwards, teasing him, holding the ball out of reach before pitching it into the shallows and laughing as he flings himself in its wake, stubby tail ticking like a frenzied metronome. These are the moments that convince her she has made the right choice; only three weeks here, and already Hannah is losing the numb, pinched look she took on after Oliver's death. She laughs like a child again, and there is a light in her eyes that Jo has not seen for a long time. She credits Dennis, her father's surprisingly sprightly Norfolk terrier, with restoring that, and wishes she had thought of it before, though it hadn't seemed practical to have a dog in London. The hours

Hannah spends rolling around on the floor of the new cottage with him, among the still-unpacked boxes, have done her more good than all the specialist counselling Jo had paid for over the past two years.

Her father, too, though he hasn't let up on the grumbling about Jo's multiple shortcomings, is clearly pleased to have them so much closer, particularly Hannah, who accompanies him to the allotment twice a week and comes home tired and dirty and full of important facts about how to grow carrots in a bath. Jo shades her eyes against the bright glare of the water and sees Hannah stop still, looking up at the path that leads down from the hotel car park. She turns to follow her daughter's gaze, just as Hannah shouts, 'Max?' and hurls herself across the beach to meet him.

It is indeed Max, in person, dressed inappropriately for the Cornish seaside in a linen suit and brogues. He sets his bag down and swoops Hannah up, swinging her round, the way he used to when she was little; when he puts her down he pretends to stagger and clutch his back. She grabs his sleeve and drags him across to Jo, who stands, brushing sand off her denim shorts.

'Max – what—'

'Surprise!' he says, holding his arms wide but looking uncertain of his welcome. She allows him an awkward hug. 'Not a good surprise?' he says anxiously.

'You could have given me some warning,' she says, not wishing to be unkind, but not altogether pleased. 'We're not really set up for guests. Hannah and I are still sleeping on a mattress on the floor till we sort out furniture.'

'Oh, that's OK, I booked an Airbnb,' he says, sounding more cheerful. 'And I did try to get in touch. I texted last week to say I was thinking of coming down, but you didn't reply. So I figured I'd just chance it. I went to your house, but your neighbour said you were down here.'

She has forgotten this about small towns, the way your business is everyone else's. She remembers the message now, with a flash of guilt; she had read it briefly and then ignored it. She has been avoiding her phone as much as possible.

'Sorry – I'm being ungracious. You've come all this way. Did you walk from the station? Sit down – let me at least get you an ice cream.' She fishes a handful of coins out of her pocket and dispatches Hannah to the kiosk in the car park with the dog at her heels.

'She seems happy,' Max says, settling himself on the rug beside her.

'All down to Dennis,' Jo says. The wind whips a strand of hair into her mouth and she tastes salt.

'And you, I think. I'm the one who should be sorry – it's unforgivable to turn up unannounced. But you've been below the radar. I wanted to check you were OK.'

'I had to get out of London.'

He nods.

'Is it still bad?' She asks. The fallout from Peggy Talbot's interview has been relentless.

He lifts one shoulder, and Jo sees a weariness in the gesture. 'Well, the photographers have stopped camping outside the door, so that's something. I'm still on sabbatical, though – not by choice. I don't know when, or if, they'll let me have my column back. The editor's not happy about me being the story. She feels – no doubt correctly – that readers will look with some scepticism on a columnist who presumes to take shots at politicians when his own moral compass is so self-evidently shonky.'

'Never stopped the prime minister when he was a journalist.'

'True. I've been working on a book, actually.' He hitches up his trouser legs and hooks his arms around his knees, squinting out to sea.

'What about?' She has a sudden awful fear that it will be a memoir, his side of the story.

'Oh – political thriller,' he says, half-embarrassed. 'You know, corrupt ministers, heroic investigative journalist with slightly receding hairline but ruggedly handsome nonetheless.' He raises a hand and touches his hair in self-parody. 'How about you? Was it the right thing, coming here?'

'I think so.' There has been no great sense of home-coming, no stirring of her Cornish blood, but when she walks along the beach in the mornings, she feels the begin-nings of a lightness she has not known in a long time. 'It's early days.'

'I didn't realise it was a permanent move,' he says, and she hears a hint of reproach. 'When you said you were going down to your dad's. I didn't even know you'd put your house on the market.'

'I wasn't being deliberately secretive. It just sold so fast, I didn't have time to organise any kind of leaving do. And then the cottage came up, so it made sense to get down here and have part of the summer, at least, before Hannah starts her new school.'

She had been lucky with the cottage; the vendor was the childless widow of an old colleague of her father's. Houses like this – a three-storey, whitewashed, stone-walled fisher-man's cottage in the heart of St Ives – came on the market so rarely, they were usually snapped up by cash buyers for way over the asking price, but the old woman had been so pleased by the idea of selling to a local girl who actually wanted to live in it, rather than some Down From London weekenders sucking the life out of the community, etc, etc, that she had accepted Jo's comparatively modest offer to spite the blow-ins.

Before the events of last autumn, it would never have occurred to Jo that she could simply uproot her entire life so dramatically; mired in the inertia of grief, even the thought of it would have been beyond her, and she had been fixated on the idea of preserving continuity for Hannah's sake, as if they could just go on edging their way around the enormous void Oliver had left, pretending nothing had changed. But when the university gently suggested that Jo might like to consider voluntary redundancy, she had realised how little there was to keep her in London.

After she was acquitted of Storm's murder, something shifted. The French trial, in March, had been surprisingly straightforward. Francis Gaillard had earned his fee; he told a persuasive story, and the case against Jo – that she, Arlo and Max had set out armed in pursuit of Storm, with the intention of taking revenge – had relied too much on speculation. Benjamin Laval had testified to Storm's duplicity and ruthlessness. Jo was found to have acted in self-defence and cleared of all charges, and she had returned home feeling that she could finally exhale, after holding her breath for months.

'Have you seen Lucas lately?' she asks, digging her fingers into the sand.

'He's in Costa Rica,' Max says. He leans back on his elbows and stretches out his legs.

'Why? How?'

'Some volunteering thing. Wildlife conservation, I think. Cress thought it would do him good. He's out there for six months and then he's starting at a very flash boarding school in Princeton in September.'

'So they're keeping him as far away as possible.'

383

'Well, I think that's the idea,' Max says. 'This whole business has been horrific for him. I mean, he was obviously suffering from depression, I mentioned it to Cress, but apparently he's adamant that he won't see a therapist and Cress doesn't want to force it. Hence saving the turtles or whatever he's doing.'

'I bet she doesn't,' Jo says.

He gives her a sharp look. 'What does that mean?'

'Storm didn't kill Becca. I told you that in France.'

'Yes, I remember. You said Arlo did it. But it turned out he was in a Zoom meeting with San Francisco for two hours at the time she was killed.'

'I was wrong. It wasn't Arlo either.'

He takes a moment. '*Lucas?*'

'He nearly told me at New Year's. Cressida stopped him. I think that's why he made sure he was the one to find her that morning. He's not an idiot – he'd have realised his DNA would be on her.'

Max nods slowly. 'Someone had put a wash on that morning. When I went down to the kitchen, the dryer was still warm. I assumed Violette had come in early to take care of the laundry and I didn't think any more about it. Maybe he'd washed the clothes he was wearing that night. But, Jo—' there is a warning note in his voice – 'even if it's true about Lucas—'

She starts to speak; he holds up a hand.

'*If* it's true. He's seventeen. He has the chance to try again. I mean, I don't think he's a danger to the public, if that's what you're worried about.'

This has not been Jo's main concern. When she lies awake at night, she finds herself turning over the almost certain knowledge that a rich, white boy has killed a young woman, even if he didn't intend to, and got away with it. She cares about Lucas, she wants to believe that he is a good-hearted kid, but his whole life has been a series of second chances, of deferred consequences, and she is ashamed to collude in that. She feels, obscurely, that she has wronged Storm, and Becca, with her silence.

'I mean, do you have any proof?' Max says.

She shakes her head. There was only the phone, and that in itself was not enough. Besides, Cressida will have destroyed it by now.

'Well, then. You're going to have to let it go.'

He's right. The time to say something has passed, the case is closed, and Becca's death has been eclipsed by Peggy Talbot's revelations. Becca had barely featured in the recent coverage, except for an occasional mention as a tragic subplot to the main story of entitled men and beautiful, vengeful women. Unlike Storm or Róisín, Becca was evidently not even considered pretty enough to warrant a picture. So far, no copies of the video proving Arlo's affair with Becca have surfaced. Perhaps they never will.

'I so nearly didn't respond to her email, you know.' Max sits up and begins to unlace his shoes. 'Storm's, I mean. I get a dozen of those a week – please come and talk to our student group for free, tell us how to get your job. But there was something about the way she wrote, even before I'd seen what she looked like. She knew how to flatter. She was quoting columns I'd written three years ago. That's like horse-whispering to a writer – they'll follow you anywhere. Pathetic. My stupid ego. If I'd just said I was too busy, maybe all this wouldn't—'

'She'd have found another way. She was determined, Max. She'd already got to Oliver. In any case, you wouldn't have made a difference to Becca.'

'We'll never know. None of you would have been in the

forest that night if it wasn't for Storm.' He shivers. 'I suppose there's no point thinking like that, but I can't help it.'

Jo looks out at the white breakers and shakes her head. 'It's never about one moment,' she says.

'You know Leo and Nina are having a leaving party?' Max says, after a while. 'Close friends only, obviously. Beginning of September. Will you come?'

'I don't think so. Do you think they'll stay out there?'

'LA? I don't see why not. Nina's family are there, and Leo keeps saying there's nothing for him here since the show got cancelled. I can't help feeling a bit sorry for him.'

Jo gives him a look, tilts an eyebrow.

'I mean it – I know Leo's no saint, but not one of those allegations has resulted in a charge that would stand up in court.'

'You know that's not how it works. *Fifteen* women, Max. Harassment, inappropriate advances, going back ten years or more. That's not a series of misunderstandings, that's a culture. That's someone who thinks he's untouchable.'

'Nina's stuck by him. I just can't imagine she'd be doing that if she thought there was anything in these claims, not knowing Nina.'

Jo considers pointing out that this is because he can't imagine what it's like to be a woman approaching fifty, to have to choose the lesser evil and live with it, but then she remembers how much Max suffered with his divorce and decides she can't presume to tell anyone else what they know about loneliness.

'Anyway,' she says, 'September will be busy. Hannah has a new school and I'm starting my course.'

'Really?' He turns to her, impressed. 'What course?'

She tells him, almost bashfully; she hasn't mentioned it to anyone yet, not even her father, because she wasn't sure if her application would be successful. A two-year, part-time graduate diploma in Psychology at Plymouth that would allow her to go on and undertake professional training as a therapist.

'That's amazing, Jo.' He looks genuinely pleased for her. 'When did you decide on that?'

'I've wanted to do it for ages, only Hannah was too little for me to take on anything that demanding, and Oliver wasn't encouraging. Plus there was always the money.' But now, with her redundancy payout, and what's left from Oliver's life insurance and the sale of the London house, she can afford a couple of years of part-time study, and she has no fear of living cheaply. Their needs are simple. 'It means that when I eventually go back to working with students, I can be the person who actually helps them, rather than referring them on to someone else. So next time Cressida tells people I'm a shrink, it will be true. Or a step closer, anyway.'

He smiles to hear her enthusiasm, but there is a touch of melancholy in his expression. 'You'll be good at it. So you really are staying. Are you sure you won't be lonely down here?'

'We'll be fine.' On good days, she dares to hope that they might be better than fine. To Jo's amazement, her father has acquired someone he refers to, with endearing coyness, as a 'special friend': a widow named Edna who lives in the next village. They have been 'stepping out' for almost a year. Edna has a daughter, Meg, a couple of years older than Jo, an artist who works as a curator at the Tate in St Ives and sells her own paintings in a boutique gallery on the seafront. Meg is a single parent whose daughter, Willa, will be in Hannah's year at school. They have hung out a few times over the summer, initially with the awkwardness that comes from

387

being set up by your parents, but Jo liked Meg straight away; she has short pink hair and a raucous laugh that makes Jo think of Storm. Hannah has been for a couple of sleepovers with Willa and no longer asks to FaceTime her friend Emily every day. Already, Jo feels that Meg is someone she could absolutely call on in a crisis, in a way she had never truly felt with Nina or Cressida in ten years. Although she hopes that there won't be any significant crises, not for a while. She feels Fate owes her a break.

'Well, you're missed in London,' Max says, peeling off his socks and coughing to hide his embarrassment, despite his careful use of the passive tense.

She understands what he is trying to say. He has started doing this more often lately, which is partly why she puts off responding to his messages. It's not that she isn't fond of Max; quite the opposite. He is kind and steady; the one person who has been there for her and Hannah without asking anything in return, simply because he cares about them. Hannah adores him, of course; from that point of view it would be the easiest thing in the world to turn to him, fold him into their family. Max would be a safe harbour, but there is so much history between them, and she is not sure if that would be a good thing for either of them.

Since the return from France, she feels as if she is on the cusp of emerging from a long shadow, and her eyes need time to adjust to the light; she can't see yet how anyone else would fit into this picture. So for now she affects not to see his little overtures, in the hope that they will never amount to an outright declaration; she would not hurt him for the world. She knows, too, that she is the safe option for him, even if he wouldn't admit it to himself. Max likes the comfort of what's familiar; he has tried venturing out into the big bad world of dating, and look at the price. But there is also the fact that what happened on the mountainside has changed her in ways that she has not even begun to process, and that is something she could not hope to explain to him.

She looks up and sees Hannah picking her way across the sand towards them, balancing three tall cones and pursued by a mob of squalling gulls.

'Do you believe in ghosts?' Jo asks suddenly. She expects Max to laugh – he is, after all, a patron of Humanists UK – but he leans back, digs his bare feet into the sand and considers the question.

'My grandmother saw the dead,' he says, his face serious. 'She never used the word ghosts, but she saw them. Hardly surprising, really – her generation had so many to remember.'

Jo nods. 'I longed to see my mother,' she says, half to herself. 'When I was a teenager, I used to lie in bed and beg her to come to me, but no. Not a whisper. So I refused to believe in ghosts, because if there was any way she could communicate with me, surely she would have. But then Storm told me she saw hers. She said she thought if she punished Arlo, her mother would appear to her.'

She sees the way his face closes up. 'I think we've established,' he says curtly, 'that Storm said whatever suited her purposes at the time.'

'Ugh, sorry, the queue was *massive*,' Hannah says, handing out the cones before flinging herself down dramatically beside Jo and licking melted ice cream from both wrists. 'Bloody tourists everywhere.'

'Hannah!'

Max laughs and rubs Dennis between his ears. 'Spoken like a true local. She'll be marching for Cornish independence before you know it.'

Hannah slips off her flip-flops and jumps up. 'Can you skim stones, Max?'

389

'I'm a bit out of practice,' he says, biting into his ice cream. 'You might have to teach me?'

'Sure. Daddy was really good at it, I'm getting better. I'll challenge you to a competition, come on,' she says, grabbing his hand and pulling him towards the water, Dennis running delirious circles around their feet. 'And if you lose you have to buy us fish and chips for tea.'

'Deal. Excuse me, please,' Max says to Jo, with a mock bow, and Jo has the sense that he is glad to leave that conversation behind. Hannah is doing this more often, she has noticed – talking openly about Oliver in the past tense, as if something has shifted in her too. She watches them playing in the shallows and smiles. Perhaps she could suggest to Max that he rents somewhere down here while he finishes his book. Even as she considers it, she knows he wouldn't really want to leave London, and she is not sure she wants him to. But she is glad he is here to have supper with them. For now, that is enough.

Jo thinks about Storm all the time, and the future she might have had if she had lived. She thinks about what she remembers of those three days in France, and what she has pieced together from the press stories. It adds up to an incomplete picture of a fierce, angry girl, smart beyond her years, who always wanted more than she was told was permitted to someone like her. A girl who was deceived for her whole childhood, who struck out on her own, who learned that her face and body could get her anything she wanted, but always at a cost. A girl who discovered that everything she had believed about her family and herself had been a lie, and set a course for revenge. A girl who will never get to become an eccentric old woman who wears a cloak, because of Jo. Sometimes she comes back to that moment when

Storm kissed her, and wonders why she did it: to disconcert her? To apologise? To complete the circuit between the three of them – her, and Jo and Oliver? She will never know.

She knows only that, like childbirth, taking a life creates a rupture between the before and after. You can't cross back to your former self. There was a moment, before she pulled the trigger, when everything hung in the balance; if she had made a different choice, or hesitated a few seconds longer, Max might be dead now, or Arlo, or Jo herself. And the fact that she made that choice, and they are all still here, has brought home to her a sense of her own significance; not in some vague, inspirational-meme way, about making the most of every moment, but in the knowledge that she can act when it is required of her. For ten years, Oliver had turned her into someone who accepted the choices other people made. Even his death had been his choice, imposed on her before she could choose to leave him. She sees, now, that she does not have to be this person, that she has been passive for too long.

There are no ghosts, whatever Storm or Max's grand-mother believed. Jo is sure of that. There is only guilt, and memory, and what we choose to carry into the future. Except that, once, a few weeks back, she was in a card shop in Penzance when 'The Gambler' by Kenny Rogers came on the radio and Jo thought – no, she was stone-cold certain – that she felt the touch of a hand stroking her hair. She had whipped around and, of course, there was no one behind her, the shop was empty. For the space of a heartbeat, what she had felt then was disappointment.